Hunt Quest

Hunt Quest

Book 8 in the Quest Series

Lisa Wright DeGroodt

iUniverse, Inc.
New York   Bloomington

Hunt Quest
Book 8 in the Quest Series

iUniverse books may be ordered through booksellers or by contacting:

iUniverse
1663 Liberty Drive
Bloomington, IN 47403
www.iuniverse.com
1-800-Authors (1-800-288-4677)

Because of the dynamic nature of the Internet, any Web addresses or links contained in this book may have changed since publication and may no longer be valid. The views expressed in this work are solely those of the author and do not necessarily reflect the views of the publisher, and the publisher hereby disclaims any responsibility for them.

ISBN: 978-1-4401-2803-5 (pbk)
ISBN: 978-1-4401-2804-2 (ebk)

Printed in the United States of America

iUniverse rev. date: 3/26/2009

Acknowledgement

To Zachary U.
Cuz he rocks. Even though he's far away,
he is always a part of me and this book.

I'd also like to say a huge thank you to everyone who participates on the Quest Ning, the You Tube Channel and website, keeping both me and the characters on their toes with your questions and insights into the series. I love the interactive process these books have developed, and honestly? You guys amaze me daily. Thanks for coming out to play.

All Things Bright and Beautiful

Tracy Rain wearily rolled out of bed, wincing as her feet hit the chilled tile floor. She'd not slept well the night before, as the crumpled and messy blankets proved. Remnants of vivid dreams crashed in around her mind from all angles, accounting for the restless slumber. Since the early hours of the morning, Tracy had lain awake, wallowing under the sheets, feeling vaguely "off". She'd known there was no way she was going to be able to go on her usual morning run with Liz. When her friend knocked at her door a few hours ago, instead of being up and ready to run, Tracy had told Liz to go without her. Her stomach was churning, her head swimming. It was altogether an unpleasant feeling, especially since she rarely, if ever, got sick. Not since her time in the Land. The worry that realization brought had bile rising, forcing Tracy to breathe slowly and steadily until the moment passed.

Sitting on the edge of the bed, Tracy fingered the wide gold mesh band that adorned her left ring finger. She was anxious to go back to the Land and visit her husband, Orli, whom she could only see for a week out of each month.

A week out of every month. Tracy shook her head. She knew she was lucky to have that much time with her beloved. There had been a long period of time when she was unable to go to the Land at all. Remembering that torturous time apart, she and Orli certainly made the best of their time together.

Tracy rubbed a trembling hand over her forehead. She wondered if she was coming down with a cold or the flu. She hoped not, given that the next few weeks were going to be full of activities and fun. A fellow Protector of the Land, the prickly yet loving Sasha, was finally getting married. That meant parties and a house full of all the Protectors and, when applicable, their significant others, fondly called the Sigots by those in the group.

There was their leader, Katie, an Oracle in the Land and a sunny, happy person who possessed a strong will and an even stronger power. She was married to Steven, and rounding out their family unit was their adorable and precocious son, Scotty. Ben Harm was here, the man who originally hailed from the Sea Dimension. His wife, Anja, lived in the Land so Tracy and Ben had decided they'd be each other's "date" for Sasha's wedding, a situation that was becoming a habitual state for the two of them while in the World Dimension. She didn't mind, though, since she could always laugh with Ben. He also understood the rigors of being apart from his spouse for extended periods of time, which was an unspoken relief.

The bride, Sasha, was also at the beach house, awaiting her fiancé's return from New York City, where he was attending a medical conference. Sarat, once of the Land and now dwelling in the World Dimension, was present as was her husband, the children's author Owen Montclaire. Liz, who had just completed her quest in the Land, was also living in the house. As the newest member of the Protectors, she was still adorably shy around the rest of the group. Or it could be the trauma that had rained down upon her during her quest that was the cause of her quiet introspection. Regardless, Tracy was hoping that the wedding would give Liz time to come out of her shell.

Along with everyone else in their protective little group, Tracy had taken it upon herself to make the tall, beautiful Seer Apparent as welcome as possible. The last member at the house was Amber, the Protector's personal Interdimensional Fairy, or IDF as they were known. Tracy shook her head, bemused. She still could not believe that Amber was anything other than a feisty, raunchy human being. Yet it was also comforting to know they had a direct path to speak with the Grid Manager if they needed it. Not that Daniel would necessarily reply, as he was a stickler for protocol and the rules, but still, Amber often circumvented normal protocols to get Daniel the information he needed about the ongoing war between Good and Evil in the Land.

Her stomach gave a lurch and Tracy groaned, running a shaking hand over her forehead.

Tracy wondered if Liz had returned from her run yet. She was debating whether she should have Liz try and read her dreams. Her friend's talent at deciphering such things was handy. After all, it wasn't everyone who lived with an honest-to-goodness Seer. Of course, Liz was scrupulous with her abilities, and made sure to keep herself shielded so she would avoid learning things from her friends. When she did glean something, her ability to keep the information private was commendable. Tracy was honest enough to know she'd have a hard time keeping her mouth shut given some of the juicy gossip Liz was bound to have psychically divined.

Standing with slow and deliberate movements designed to help her burbling innards, Tracy headed for the downstairs, intent on getting something to drink. Maybe that would settle her restless stomach.

With each step she became more confident as the queasiness subsided. As she came into the kitchen area, Tracy spied Sarat and Amber standing by the wall of floor to ceiling windows that stretched across the front of the beach house's main living space. The petite brunette was wrapping a single lock of dark hair around her finger while the red-headed Amber had one hand on a nearby chair as if to steady herself. They were staring out at the landscape with an intent look, periodically lifting up mugs of hot coffee to take an absent sip.

Tracy poured herself a mug of coffee and strolled over to join them. The smell of the coffee did wonders for her stomach and she breathed in the scent, enjoying the reprieve.

"Whatcha watching?" she asked idly, rolling her neck from one side to the other to work out the kinks left from her restless night.

"Him," Amber pointed with her mug, her voice unusually breathless.

Tracy followed her finger and gaped. The houses in this area all had long docks that reached out towards the ocean. Most of them ended in a deck of sorts overlooking the beach area. Their neighbor's dock was currently occupied, and Tracy could see immediately why Sarat and Amber were mesmerized.

He was *gorgeous*.

The kind of drop dead gorgeous that made women swoon and men jealous. And that was from the back. He was wearing a pair of baggy workout pants, riding low over lean hips. His skin was tan and stretched over muscles that were, to say the least, amazing; sweaty, but perfect, each line and striation delineated with masculine grace. He was wearing a loose white tank top that contrasted with the expanse of sun-kissed skin stretching across his upper back. Trailing out from beneath the edges of the tank was ink, so clearly he had some sort of tattoo, or possibly two. His tush looked as hard as granite, and Tracy's palm actually itched in anticipation of testing that theory out.

Defined and detailed arms were moving in intricate, deliberate motions, curving and scooping as he went through an obviously choreographed routine. A mop of unruly dark hair curled and swayed as he continued his morning program. The sunlight displayed burnished coppery highlights in the dark curling mass. Periodically, a hint of his profile would come into view as he moved through the different steps of his routine, his eyes wrapped in sunglasses that reflected the morning sun.

"You gotta love T'ai Chi," Amber murmured.

"You betcha," Sarat added fervently.

"Who is he?" Tracy asked, feeling slightly breathless, absently wondering if it was her stomach or that man that caused her voice to sound so weak. Her left hand reached up to toy with the necklace she always wore, the cool metal of her Protector pendant brushing against her fingers.

"Dunno, don't care," Amber declared emphatically.

"He's just...just...wow," said Tracy.

Amber and Sarat nodded, Sarat absently hanging her coffee cup in midair while she used both her hands to scoop back her long, fine hair. Tracy shook her head. Seeing Sarat using her mind-bending techniques was becoming commonplace, however, Sarat had to learn to be more discreet in flashing her unique powers.

"What are you guys ogling?" Katie asked from behind them, having just sauntered into the room, Sasha stumbling behind her in search of a jolt of caffeine.

"Neighbor," Sarat said with awe.

After filling their mugs, Katie and Sasha strolled over to take a gander, the latter bleary eyed. Sasha never did well before her first cup of coffee.

"Oh, my," Katie said as she took in the view, adding in a weak voice, "Hubba hubba."

"Huh? What? Holy shit, who the hell is that?" exclaimed Sasha, her mind finally catching up to what was before her eyes.

"Neighbor," Sarat, Tracy and Amber recited at the same time.

"Can I be on the welcome wagon?" Katie asked in a low voice.

"You're a married woman," Sasha reminded her, nudging her with an elbow.

"Darlin', I'm married, not blind," Katie clarified.

"I second that," Tracy said, raising her arm.

"Me too," Sarat chimed in. "That, ladies, is prime, just prime."

"Prime what?" yawned Ben Harm from behind them, his deep male voice startling a jump out of the women. "What are you ladies doing this fine morning?"

"Bird watching," Tracy said, her eyebrows winging up as the muscles under the tank top moved in very interesting ways.

"Bird?" Ben muttered, peering out the window as he pushed his black-framed glasses up onto his nose more firmly. "Where? What kind?"

"Clueless," Sasha mouthed to Katie, who nodded, rolling her eyes in agreement.

"Oh, are you staring at the guy?" Ben said, finally comprehending. "Geesh, you guys are nuts, you know that?" He left the group by the back slider and went to grab a drink of water before heading out for his morning swim.

The women pushed him out of the way, their eyes glued to the man on the neighboring deck.

"Do you think he'll do this every day?" Katie asked, her voice dreamy.

"He better," Amber replied, shaking her head as his muscles contorted in yet another intriguing and fascinating way.

"I know I'll be checking it out tomorrow," Tracy commented.

"Same bat time, same bat channel," agreed Sasha.

In the relative safety of the kitchen, Ben rolled his eyes at Steven, who had just ambled down the stairs, dressed casually in shorts and a t-shirt emblazoned with the logo for Sasha's graphics art studio.

"The girls are drooling over the new neighbor," Ben informed Katie's husband.

"Bully for them," Steven replied in a nonchalant voice, rummaging in the refrigerator for the orange juice. "From what I saw when he was moving in, he's what would be termed a hunk. I think he's somebody famous. At least, that's what I heard at the last home owner's association meeting." He pulled out the juice container and shook it. "I didn't get a good look at him, though. Seems to be a private kind of guy, you know?"

"Doesn't it bother you that your wife is staring at another man with lust in her eyes?" Ben asked, curious. He couldn't imagine being so casual if it were Anja fogging up the back window with the other women.

Steven looked up at Ben and waggled his eyebrows. "Hey, as long as I'm the end recipient of all that pent up lust, who the hell cares?"

"Lust?" this came from Sarat's husband, Owen Montclaire, who was rubbing his stubbled chin as he entered the kitchen. "Who's lusting?"

Ben and Steven nodded towards the gang of women around the window, speaking in unison. "Them."

Owen looked over at the women clustered around the window wall. They were staring out with the same kind of intent look he recalled seeing on the faces of a pride of lionesses before they moved in for a kill. "Oh," he said, pouring a cup of coffee. "I suppose the man in question is bronzed and muscular," he guessed, gesturing with his mug.

"Definitely," Ben replied.

"So, do we hate him?" Owen asked amicably, peeling a banana from a display on the counter.

"Nah," Steven replied, snagging an apple from the same bowl and polishing it on his t-shirt. "I figure if they get all randy, we reap the benefits."

"Good plan," Owen agreed with a slow smile, then raised his voice. "Hey Sasha, when's William flying in?" He was curious to see if the woman would be able to tear herself away from the view at the mention of her fiancé's name. Apparently, she was not going to be distracted.

"Today," Sasha said absently, as the women continued to watch the play of muscles and tanned skin.

"Good," Owen replied, his smile almost completely hidden by his mustache.

"I'm actually getting the vapors," Amber said, fanning herself rapidly.

"I didn't know fairies were capable of experiencing lust," Owen commented, causing Ben and Steven to burst out laughing.

"Dude, that's Amber," Ben said. "She lusts after everything pretty."

"I heard that, Harmerwocky," Amber warned, not moving from her prime first row seat.

"I shudder with fear," he replied with a grin, knowing that when the ladies started making nicknames out of his last name, he was still in friendly territory. Steven shook his head at his friend. He had a feeling that Amber was going to definitely be taking her revenge for that comment.

"Hey, here comes Liz," Tracy said, pointing.

Sure enough, their fellow Protector could just be seen jogging towards them on the beach. She was ignoring everything around her, intent on her path. She was wearing a tank top and bike shorts, her long, light brown hair bouncing in a ponytail, topaz eyes were shaded by a baseball cap. She had a pair of headphones hooked up and was intent on finishing her run, her stride lengthening as she sped over the loose sand.

On the end of the dock overlooking a ten foot drop to the beach, their neighbor was finishing up his routine, holding his arms over his head, stretching. He turned towards his house in a slow pivot, taking a deep breath that made his chest swell.

The women in the neighboring house all sighed as his face came fully into view. Chiseled jaw, arching eyebrows, Roman nose. It was a face of precise angles and proportions, the upper half obscured by the reflective wrap around shades. But to be honest, the women didn't really care about the color of his eyes as they were more interested in the rippled abs peeking out from under the tank top's edge, as well as the man's defined pecs. What wasn't covered up by the expensive sunglasses did look really, really familiar. And spectacular. On a mega-watt scale.

"Ohhhhh," came the collective female sigh.

The sigh turned into a scream, causing the men in the kitchen to set down their drinks and food and bolt towards the noise. Tracy had already flung open the door to the deck and was pelting down the dock.

"What happened?" Steven shouted as they piled out of the house.

"Neighbor dude did a back flip off his dock—" Katie started.

"Amazing form!" chirped Amber.

"—and plowed right into Liz," Katie finished.

"At least we think he did, can't tell for sure from this angle," Sarat said, as they headed down their wooden dock at a full run.

Tracy was already at the base of the dock, heading across the sand towards Liz and their neighbor when a wave of dizziness hit her like a ton of bricks. She staggered a moment, her hand going to her head.

"What the hell?" she whispered as stars formed in front of her eyes.

Amber immediately swerved when Tracy stumbled, at her side in an instant. "What is it? What is it?" Her arm was already going around the taller woman's waist. "Hey!" she called out. "Something's wrong with Tracy."

The Protectors froze, torn between wanting to make sure Liz was all right and helping Tracy. Finally, Ben and Sarat continued on their way towards Liz, Owen in tow. The rest surrounded Tracy, who was sitting on the sand, her head hanging between her knees.

"I'm fine," Tracy was protesting from her position sitting on the fine sand. "Just a little dizzy, that's all. I didn't have any breakfast."

"Are you sure?" Katie asked catching the concerned look Steven was shooting her over Tracy's bowed head. Sasha and Amber hovered nearby, waiting.

"Yes," Tracy managed to laugh as her stomach righted and her head cleared. "I'll be fine. Honest."

"Well, to be on the safe side, let's get you back to the house," Steven said, helping Tracy to her feet. He kept one arm firmly anchored around her slim waist. "I don't like your color, not one bit."

"What about Liz?" Tracy asked, trying to turn in the direction of their friend.

"It looks like she's fine," Steven said, using his superior height to see over the heads of the other Protectors. It appeared that the Seering Heir was sitting on the sand, but seemed unhurt. Their new neighbor was in the group as well, a shaken expression on his handsome face. Steven frowned. The guy really did look familiar.

"All right," Tracy said, still sounding slightly shaky. "Just help get me inside, ok?"

Her easy acceptance of their assistance was more troubling than the identity of their new neighbor. Katie motioned for Amber to help Steven get Tracy back to the beach house. She pulled on Sasha's arm, keeping the young woman from following.

"When William gets here, can you have him check Tracy?" Katie asked her in a low voice. "This is the second time this week she's gotten weak and shaky."

"What are you thinking?" Sasha asked her pale green eyes worried. "Oh, crap. Could it be a resurgence of the Too'ki virus?"

Katie blew out her breath as the two headed back to the house. "Honestly, I don't think that's what it is," she started then stopped as footsteps pounded behind them on the dock. Katie turned to see Sarat racing towards them.

"Guess what," she said, clearly excited. "Our new neighbor is none other than the hubbalicious, delectable, amazingly handsome and charismatic Zachary Neol!"

-2-

A Work in Progress

The last thing Zachary Neol expected to do that morning was land on a pretty girl.

Granted, he didn't technically land on her, more like crashed into her. Thankfully, he was able to roll away so that his more considerable weight didn't grind the poor chick into the beach.

"Oh, damn," he said as he rolled to his feet in a smooth, lithe move. He knelt in the sand by the woman, who was flat on her back... laughing. "You're not hurt?"

"No, no, I'm fine," she said, gasping for air, then shrieked, "Don't touch me!" when he reached out to help her up. Immediately she colored prettily, the flush highlighting the clear topaz eyes and finely drawn facial features liberally drenched with freckles. Those small imperfections kept her from being neo-classically gorgeous; made her more approachable. Her long hair was pulled back into a ponytail and her clothing was drenched in sweat from her run. Thanks to his intervention, she was also covered in sand. Despite the grit, she maintained a graceful beauty that was instantly appealing. From her dangling iPod headphones a rocking beat flowed.

Zach heard what seemed like a thundering herd of people coming down the beach. Fearing some sort of attack, Zach wheeled on the balls of his feet. It turned out that it was just some people he recognized as living next door to him. The tall blond man who regularly swam in the ocean, a rugged looking cowboy type, and a petite girl with flowing

11

dark hair. More of the group gathered at the base of their beach stairs, but Zach couldn't see what was capturing their attention.

"Are you all right?" the girl said, dropping to her knees by the woman Zach had nearly plowed over. She reached out and pulled the woman to her feet—no reluctance about touching there, Zach noticed—and soon the woman was towering over her petite companion. Yet they were oddly well matched, and it was obvious some sort of connection existed between them.

"I'm fine, Sarat," the woman said, dusting off sand from various parts of her body. "Honestly," she laughed, pushing Sarat's hands away as the small woman tried to help.

Zach, his hands on his hips, turned to the two men, who were eying him with equal looks of distrust and anger. "Sorry about that," he said, flashing the winning smile that had gotten him out of many a jam. Smoothly, he held his hand out, the polite gesture seeming appropriate given he'd nearly clocked their friend.

"I'm your new neighbor. It's a hell of a way to meet, but it seems that all's well."

"Ben Harm," the tall blond said in a surprisingly deep voice as he shook Zach's hand.

"Owen Montclaire," said the cowboy, also completing the ritual. "This is my wife Sarat, and the woman you so neatly clocked is Liz Keeper."

Wife. A bone deep relief spread through Zach, who had wondered for a split second if the women might be companions of a romantic sort. Taking off his sunglasses, he hooked them to the front of the tank top he was wearing as he turned to the taller woman, his apology shining from his blue eyes. "I'm really sorry, Ms. Keeper," he said, but, respecting her earlier request, refrained from putting his hand out for her to shake. "It's nice to meet you. I'm Zachary Neol."

"You are?" Sarat breathed, deep brown eyes widening appreciatively. "Yes, you are!" She launched herself at him, hugging him fiercely. A little shocked by the exuberant yet oddly sincere reaction, Zach merely stood still, carefully eying Owen, who was looking on with amused indulgence. Yet instinctively, the actor knew this was totally different than the women who normally threw themselves in his direction.

Coming from this woman, the gesture was genuine and oddly sweet. "I am so glad to meet you!"

"All right then," Zach said, clearing his throat. He was used to fan reactions, but at times he just wished people would treat him normally.

"I loved you in *The Phoenix!*" Sarat said brightly, linking her arm through Zach's as if they were old friends. "Tell me all about how it was filming for so many months. And I want to know all the delicious details."

Owen laughed and pulled Sarat away from Zach. "Darlin', Mr. Neol doesn't want to talk about his movie role at the moment. Perhaps some other time?" he asked with his craggy eyebrows raised.

"My pleasure," Zach lied with a wide smile.

Truth be told, he detested talking about making movies. He'd been an actor since he was a child, so people assumed he loved his field. Actually, he was dead tired of discussing the ins and outs of acting; disgusted with the whole acting thing, period. Yet he'd starred in the biggest summer blockbuster in a decade, and he couldn't deny that people knew him. And knowing of him equated to knowing him, in many a fan's eyes. It was just an acting fact. Nothing could change the planes of his face or the flash of his smile. It was what it was.

Because of the notoriety associated with being Zachary Neol "the product," he'd purposely purchased a home in an isolated section of the Outer Banks on North Carolina. But, with a mental sigh, Zach acknowledged that to most people who didn't know the God-awful truth of the business, his life must seem glamorous. With effort, he managed a smile for the lovely Sarat, who was fairly dancing on the sand in anticipation. She really was an engaging little sprite of a woman. He couldn't help but be attracted to her bubbly personality.

"I look forward to it." His eyes sought out Liz, who was looking at him with intense speculation in her eyes, but it was more of a searching look rather than the usual gleam of lust he was used to receiving. Almost like she knew he was lying through his blinding white teeth. "I'll make sure I look before I leap next time, Ms. Keeper."

She gave him a smile, which enhanced the graceful planes of her face, enhancing that sun-kissed Grace Kelly aura. "You do that. And I'll certainly watch for falling Phoenixes."

"We don't fall, we land gracefully," he corrected with a playful tone. Waving to the group, he headed for his deck stairs, jogging up to the house at a fast pace. A quick glance showed that the group he had met was now joined by other people on the beach.

It was a weird thing, those people who lived in the next-door house. They were roughly the same age, yet did not seem to be related in any way. He would think they were vacationers, renting the house, but the realtor he bought his own ocean-side home from had assured him that houses in the area were not rented. It was part of the appeal of the area, which was located in a gated community; all essential for a man who needed Zach's level of privacy.

Privacy. Zach sighed as he let himself into the house. Privacy was a fallacy, one he was used to circumventing whenever possible. Moving to a beach-side community might not seem appropriate for a man seeking solitude, but he couldn't deny the pull that insisted he come to the area. One chance visit to the resort-oriented town and suddenly no place in the entire world would do for his home. And damn, he did love this house.

The bottom level was covered with a huge room, chock full of video games, a pool and a foosball table, wet bar, entertainment system and all the necessary fun toys Zach deemed essential to life. Even more so now that he had unlimited time in which to simply play, play, play.

The second level comprised the guest bedrooms, four in all, each with their own connected bathroom. Zach doubted he'd ever have people over to fill those rooms, but for the kind of house he wanted, the empty, extra rooms were worth it. The third floor was the main living space, consisting of the living room, kitchen and dining area. Light, open and airy, as befitted a beach house, the rooms were decorated in cool blues and sand colors.

Zach paused in the kitchen to pour himself a glass of orange juice. After downing the drink, he rinsed the glass and put it in the dishwasher. He was growing increasingly meticulous about his space, and was going to do everything he could to avoid having live in help. He craved solitude at the moment. If that meant fighting his tendency to be slightly messy, so be it. In the end, it would be worth it. The last thing he wanted was his boxers to show up on E-bay due to an overambitious plant-watering technician.

Zach continued up to the fourth level of his house, his favorite space in the beach haven. He'd gutted two large bedrooms to make one huge master suite area, including a sitting area, small kitchenette and sweet bathroom complete with a walk in shower he could park a small car in. His bed was massive, set squarely in the middle of a windowed section of the room that jutted out from the back of the house slightly. When lying on his bed, glass walls were on either side as well as in front of him, giving him the illusion he was hovering above the bright blue ocean. His love of wide open spaces was definitely nurtured by the room.

Zach turned on the shower and kicked off his pants and shorts, tossing them with deadly accuracy into the hamper. Stepping into the multiple sprays in the black granite space, he gave a sigh of sheer bliss.

As the hot water beat down on his skin, Zach's mind wandered. He had to check in with his agent later. The man was insistent and relentless in his attempts to get Zach to read scripts and take meetings. The man could not seem to understand that Zach was not interested in making another movie or returning to television, where Zach had gotten his start. Leaning his hands against the smooth wall of the shower, Zach lowered his head and allowed his early years to play out like so many dailies from a movie filming. If he had to title it, he'd probably call his life "Fall into Grace" or some such schlock. It had certainly started out bright and shiny.

At the tender age of five, after four years of commercials and modeling gigs, Zachy Neol had landed spot as a secondary player in a successful sitcom. He played the adorable yet geeky younger brother in a family of cookie cutter perfect people. The sitcom had run eight glorious years, fueled in great part by the growing comedic flare displayed by the young Zach Neol. He became known as the one that could close a scene with a witty one liner. He also had the opposite end of the spectrum down cold as well, showing a depth of emotion that had most critics sitting up and taking notice. In fact, he was one of the youngest actors in America to receive a best supporting actor in a comedy Emmy. It was sitting on the mantel in his game room, currently being decorated with a ratty Yankee baseball cap.

God, how Zach had loved acting back then, loved going to the set, being with the people in the cast, enjoyed the school environment with the other children on the cast. It had been an idyllic period in his life. Mostly because it had kept him away from his parents.

His parents.

Zach rolled his head from one side to the other. His mom and dad had been typical stage parents, and not in a good way. Pushing their son's agenda, or rather what they wanted his agenda to be, encouraging him to continue with the acting, to grow and become better at the craft. Zach had vivid memories of being woken up on the weekend in the pre-dawn hours just so he could work on a scene his mother or father considered to be bogging down. Rarely did they give him affection for affection's sake, and never, ever did they treat him as something other than a commodity that was going to fund the family's lifestyle. Their drive for power and control over Hollywood was the only absolute in his young life. They were his parents, sure, but more than that they were his handlers. In that regard, he was not so much raised as he was cultivated, like an exotic plant, to maximize his potential. Unlike other child stars who had parents who were perceived as friends, Zach's were task masters, and not known for their cuddly behavior, either. The elder Neol's penchants for tantrums were legendary in Tinsel Town. Often Zach was in the unenviable position of having to apologize for his mother or father's behavior, and that was all before the age of ten.

Having grown up in the business, in the beginning Zach hadn't known that his life was all that different from other kids. Earlier on, he assumed everyone had a limo driver, a masseuse and a Ferrari in the garage, just waiting for him to turn sixteen. It wasn't until the end of the run of his first television show that Zach gleaned just how radically different his life was when compared to other pre-teens. Then, he emerged from the cocoon of the studio lifestyle and entered the world as just another kid.

When the sitcom had come to an end, as most sitcoms do, Zach had been secretly relieved. Now, he'd thought, I can live my life normally. He'd actually gone to regular school for two glorious years, made friends, had some fun. But he learned very quickly that most of those friends were only hanging out with him because of his fame. True friends were not to be found.

Not to mention the fact that his parents had other ideas.

During his two-year hiatus from the small screen, Zach had his first impressive growth spurt. He'd broadened in the shoulders, his voice deepened, his facial features had evened out into the kind of physical beauty that made Hollywood sit up and notice while cameramen panted with glee.

Of course, it helped when your parents were pandering said face to every director in town. And then they reeled in what they wanted for their son's next turn behind the camera.

In the next Zachary Neol vehicle, he had been the major star. Again it was a sitcom, a light piece of fluff that lacked the kind of emotional depth or trueness that so appealed to Zach in his first experience. The show was just a way to showcase Zach and his increasing Q-factor. Soon his face was gracing almost every teen-age girl's bedroom wall and he was a driving force in the teen magazine market, not to mention the butt of many a late night talk show host's joke.

Zach had not been given a choice as to the character or the show. That would have been as foreign to his parents as allowing Zach to go to the local high school, or, God forbid, trying out for the football team. He was allowed to work out, to cultivate the kind of body that girls could pin up in their bedrooms, but to risk breaking a bone or, worse still, his nose? No way.

His contract with the studio called for three years, and Zach had gritted through those three years month by painful month. There was nothing like an adverse situation to make a guy grow up, and grow up fast. Hating every second of the sitcom's run, but knowing that he needed to give his all for the sake of the many people who were associated with the show and dependent on its success for a paycheck, Zach had manned up and given the mediocre material his best effort. Yet he made it clear to anyone who would ask, from his parents to his agent to his fans to the hated talk show hosts that he would not be renewing his contract. No way, no how. Of course, no one believed him. To those listening to his denials, it was all just a big game as Hollywood assumed that this was just a bargaining chip to get a bigger renewal contract. And his parents hadn't listened to Zach for his entire life, why should now be any different?

However, Zach remained true to this word. Since his contract expired after his eighteenth birthday, it was up to Zach and Zach alone if he was going to renew. Despite the very generous offer given him by the studio, Zach had indeed walked away, apologizing to the cast and crew but determined to make his own career decisions.

A year earlier, blessedly unknown to his parents, Zach had been approached by a highly reclusive, yet incredibly respected, director/producer/writer. The man was a genius when it came to action movies, and had the rare talent to transcend the usual grisly fare, making movies that were every actor's dream job. The director wanted Zach to star in his movie version of *The Phoenix*, based on the wildly popular comic book. At first, Zach had scoffed, but the man's passion for the material, the solid screenplay he presented, as well as his enthusiasm for the craft of acting had changed Zach's mind.

The only catch was that the director wanted Zach to keep quiet about his involvement in the picture until principal photography began in the depths of the jungles in Taiwan. Zach had agreed, and shortly after the sitcom stopped filming, he retreated into solitude to begin a rigorous training regime to bulk up for the role. He didn't even tell his parents, who had quietly and not so quietly fumed at his refusal to take another role. A role of their choosing, of course. There had been many a battle in the Neol home over his lack of gratitude. Zach had ignored it all, choosing to focus on his new project. He'd moved out of his parent's house—the house Zach had paid for through his work over the years—and hid from everyone, turning his not inconsiderable mind to the matter of the film role he'd accepted.

He'd been meticulous in his research on the Phoenix and had grown to closely identify with the superhero. The Phoenix was a loner, a man of high morals, and conflicted about his place in the world. The comic character's life and experiences so closely mirrored his it would have been impossible not to find things in common with the man. A man forced to do others' bidding during his childhood and a painful break from his past, followed by a fight for his own freedom that spilled over to the world around him. The parallels in the fiction and nonfiction made Zach even hungrier to play the role and to do it justice.

Of course, Zach couldn't make flames come from the tips of his fingers or fly, nor could he regenerate out of a pile of ash, but he'd take what he could.

When principal filming started, the critics and fandoms avid watchers on the Internet had gone crazy. Having the American boy next door, the one who graced every teenybopper's walls, playing the conflicted and tortured Phoenix? The fans went ballistic, with the Internet practically igniting with a fury not seen since the Lord of the Rings frenzy.

Zach had expected it, actually. When he had left his last show at eighteen, he'd been a gangly, attractive teenager, just coming into his own body. In the two years of preproduction, he had fleshed out and bulked up, putting on muscles and definition in a calculated way to maximize his appearance. The costume called for tights and Zach was vain enough to want to look his very best in the role. He'd also grown another two inches, a late growth spurt that evened him out at six foot, four inches. Since he'd done most of that in private, literally moving out of the country to escape the paparazzi and his parents, the public didn't really know what he looked like or what he'd done to get into the part. So he took it in stride, shrugging off the hate mail and emails full of venom.

The filming process had been a revelation as well. For the first time, his parents were not expected on the set, nor were they encouraged to attend filming. In fact, after a few torturous sessions with them present and with the producer's full support, Zach had decreed that they were to be barred, much to their vocal dismay and the director's everlasting gratitude. Zach quickly discovered that the way a film was crafted was different than television. There was a lot more down time, much more boredom, but it was infinitely more rewarding in the end. He'd grown into manhood during that grueling shoot oversees, and he wasn't ashamed to admit it. The work had been hard, physically and mentally. It had been difficult, technically and personally. The experience had given him his highest acting highs and his lowest acting lows. Zach had loved every moment of the journey, realizing early on that this movie was going to be a significant part of his life. A turning point, so to speak.

He had gone on to wow the public in the movie. It leapt immediately to the top of the charts, and stayed there. Not only was it an incredible piece of fantasy film, complete with state of the art and innovative special effects, it was backed up by a story with incredible insight, depth and emotion. Zach played the character with a sense of bravado and vulnerability that had the male fans cheering and the females swooning.

Zach was enough of an egotist to enjoy the accolades and took a great deal of pride in the accomplishment. He was damn proud of what he'd brought to the instantly iconic role.

Zach supposed you could call his transition from a child actor to an adult an unqualified success. The offers flooded in to his agent were enough to prove it. Yet none of the roles appealed to Zach. He'd had an epiphany while filming *The Phoenix*; so much so that he had asked a tattoo artist to recreate the character's legendary tattoo across his back, with a few notable changes that were all his own.

It was a symbol of Zachary Neol's rebirth.

It was also a symbol that he would not be acting in another role anytime soon.

But no one seemed to believe him when Zach stated that sentiment with conviction and pride to whatever media outlet he was dealing with. He was sick of being a commodity, a piece of ass to be posed and photographed and directed by outside forces. Zach wanted more out of life. Acting no longer gave him satisfaction; in fact it had never really felt comfortable. He was confident that there was some sort of illusive goal out there in the world, a dream he was waiting to find, a purpose to his life. Exactly what that was, he had no idea. But he was sure he would not get that kind of fulfillment from an acting role. He just needed to find that illusive something in which to focus his not inconsiderable talent and strength on. Simple enough.

Not.

Sighing, he finished his shower and toweled off, stepping commando into a pair of old faded beach shorts. He rubbed the towel over his hair, staring out at the bright blue ocean below. Knowing you wanted something more out of your life and finding it were two totally different things. Zach wasn't kidding himself; he was lucky to have the funds to wait and figure it all out. Yet there was no denying he felt adrift, floating, separate from the world around him. Yet Zach had the most bizarre feeling that what he was seeking was nearby. It was almost like he was on the cusp of something huge, yet exactly what that something was eluded him. So he relied on his instinct, which was the only thing he'd ever fully trusted in his life. So when his instincts told him this place was where he needed to be, Zach had listened.

He wasn't sure what had drawn him to this part of the world. But something had compelled him to come here. Zach was a big believer in fate and intuition. He supposed he had been drawn into the mysticism of the Phoenix, the belief that there was more out there to life than what met the eye. Some might find such flights of fantasy foolish, but to Zach, believing in magic was intrinsic to his soul. That concept had been his sole, constant companion during his childhood, the knowledge that magic was alive and well and just beyond his reach in this mundane world. Zach would always clap for fairies, root for the scarred boy-wizard, marvel at the power of a ring. He wasn't about to let anyone take that away from him.

If that made him a weirdo, so be it.

Zach's eyes were drawn to the second story deck jutting from his neighbor's house. The group he'd seen earlier was now sitting on the deck, eating breakfast and laughing.

Zach put his hand on the glass wall, an unfamiliar craving welling up inside him. He'd never had that kind of close bond with other people his own age, not even on the first show where he'd been the youngest cast member. He envied those people on the deck below their easy familiarity, the total lack of sexual innuendo he was inundated with whenever he tried to socialize. His neighbors truly seemed to care about one another. He also knew that he was spending more and more time watching them from his ocean aerie than could be considered healthy. He already knew their gestures, their quirks, and their manner. It was the actor in him that had him dissecting the different dynamics.

A few seemed to be intimately involved, but the overall gist of the group was that of platonic friendship. But it was a deep friendship, full of easy touches and laughing jokes. He couldn't count the number of times he'd seen them simply overcome with mirth to the point of tears.

His eyes were drawn to the tall woman with the light brown hair, those Raphael tresses that glinted with blond in the sun; the one whom he now knew was called Liz. Zach had watched her often over the week, sensing a fellow loner. She was cool but not aloof, friendly but not overly interactive with the rest of the group. She had the grace of an old time movie star, and the flare of a deep seeded something...if Zach had to label it, he'd call it power.

Zach shook his head at his foolish thoughts. He was reading

too much into the situation. She was just a woman. Sure, she was an attractive woman, but no more so than other women he'd met. She wasn't even really his type. He tended to be attracted to petite brunettes, not tall willowy women hiding secrets behind topaz eyes. She just wasn't for him, not at all. Yet his blue eyes were again pulled to the cool dark blond on the deck porch one story below him. For an instant, he could have sworn that her eyes met his, locking onto him with unerring precision. That topaz gaze pierced through him like a dagger. He put one hand out on the cool glass, as if to steady himself, then his finger grazed downward, as if stroking her cheek through space. Her eyes, seemingly still glued to his, widened, her neck arching as if she was experiencing his touch, leaning into it.

Fantasy was a wonderful thing, Neol, he told himself as he dropped his hand, feeling oddly bereft.

Zach withdrew from the window as his phone began to peal. His agent, or perhaps one of his parental units, was about to make their daily pitch for him to get back into the game. Zach picked up the phone, determined to put a stop to their shenanigans once and for all. Through the window, he watched as Liz tilted her head to one side and brought her hand up to her cheek, as if holding where he'd stroked it through the glass and air. Zach barely managed to turn his attention to his agent, who was shrilly berating Zach for not returning his call from the previous day.

With a deep breath, Zach launched into what, he hoped, would be his final battle regarding his life and decisions.

-3-
Protectors of the Land

He was watching her.

Liz knew it. She'd raised her eyes to the mirrored window walls that lined the top floor of his house and experienced the heady sensation of Zach Neol's eyes boring into her. Those famous blue irises, tinged with flecks of amber that made them sparkle from the screen. How many times had she sat in the theater over the previous summer, watching the exploits of the Phoenix on the twenty-foot tall screen? It was one of the joys of being friends with people who enjoyed going to the movies as much as she did.

Certainly Neol had played the part with old fashioned flare, which appealed to Liz's die-hard romantic streak. She loved the old black and white movies, the Fred Astaire, Gene Kelly and other classic shows. Zach Neol had given her a greater appreciation for Technicolor action.

When Neol had come flying off the dock, Liz had been completely unaware of his presence, which was unusual. She'd barely had time to jump out of his way. Neol seemed to think he had knocked her down but the truth was that Liz had tripped over her own feet in her haste to not make contact with the man. She was prone to having psychic flashes when she touched people she'd never met before, an occurrence the Seer had warned her about when she had been back in the Land. As of yet, she was still unable to fully control premonitions when it came to strangers and preferred to not touch them. With her friends, it was an easier task to set up the necessary roadblocks to avoid breaching their privacy. Liz was zealous about making sure she did not violate their trust.

Which was precisely why she was having such a hard time not telling Tracy the secret she harbored. She'd known for weeks, ever since Tracy had come back from her last Land visit. She was surprised that Katie had not clued into the change, but perhaps the Oracle was being as diligent about privacy as she was, and not looking at the other's auras on a regular basis.

Hmmm. She'd have to find out. All manner of illnesses or emotional upheaval could be detected in an aura. Katie should at least monitor the Protectors to make sure they were all well and physically fit.

A tingling along her cheek had her putting her hand to her face. It was as if a man's fingers were lightly running down the skin, sending goose bumps scattering over her body despite the warmth of the sun. She shivered with delicious anticipation. Damn, she could feel his eyes on her, and wondered what he could possibly be thinking at the moment. She could tell he was experiencing deep emotion, one that he kept close to his soul so that it was more difficult for anyone to read.

Liz relaxed visibly as Zach's presence retreated from the window wall, his focus no longer on her or her friends. Her fingers came up to rub the Protector pendant that hung around her neck as she pondered the curious connection that seemed to be forming between her and the man next door. His mood shifted dramatically within that glass and steel house by the sea. She shivered with reaction to his emotional state. Now Zach Neol was feeling a deep frustration that flowed from him like heat waves from a hot sandy beach. She wondered what in the life of a pampered movie star could be cause for such intense frustration. Perhaps his masseuse was unable to come to the house on time.

Immediately a flood of self recrimination had Liz berating herself for such a petty assumption. She had no idea what transpired in the life of someone rich and famous. For all she knew, he could have very real, very serious problems. In the end, what difference did it make to her? She doubted they'd ever speak again, really. More likely just pass with neighborly waves from time to time. The poor man deserved some peace.

Liz turned her attention back to the Protectors. Katie and Amber were gaily discussing the bridal festivities that would occupy their next few days; going over timetables and tasks that had to be done. Sasha was watching with the giddy amusement that only one deeply in love can generate. Ben, Steven and Owen were busy discussing some manly issue by the edge of the dock; the three of them tossing a ball back and forth with Scott, Katie and Steven's young son. Tracy was sitting in her chair, trying her best to look interested in the conversation, but her face reflected concern.

Again Liz wondered if she should tell Tracy the truth. She couldn't stand the thought of the woman worrying about a Too'ki relapse. That made her sit up, a decision made. Allowing someone to wallow in such negative emotions was not healthy. She would tell her friend the truth.

"Hey Tracy," she said, standing up, settling her filmy sundress around her legs. "Come inside and help me with something, would you?"

Tracy stood up slowly, as if expecting to be hit by the strange dizziness at any moment. She followed Liz inside, then, flopped onto the sofa staring at her friend with apprehensive chocolate eyes.

"So what is it?" she said bluntly as the Seer closed the glass door behind them. "I know you know, Liz. So just tell me the truth. Is it the Too'ki virus? Am I reverting? Decompensating? I have to know."

Liz perched on the arm of a chair across from Tracy, folding her hands in her lap. "You aren't having any sort of relapse," she assured her friend, who relaxed visibly.

"Then what is this? I've never felt this way before. Ever," Tracy said, clearly confused.

Liz laughed. "My goodness, Tracy. Didn't you ever take high school health class?" When the other woman continued to look at her blankly, Liz crossed her arms with mock dismay. "Come now. Don't you know what happens to a man and a woman, who love each other very much, and often indulge in the more physical aspects of said love? The consequences of those actions, so to speak?"

It was almost comical to see the look of comprehension that passed over Tracy's face like a tidal wave. She pressed her hand to her stomach in wonderment. "A baby?" she breathed. "But we never thought…"

"Well, have you or Orli used precautions?" Liz asked frankly.

"No," Tracy replied, still holding her belly. "We just assumed…I mean, Ben and Anja have been trying for years with no success. And I guess we figured that cross dimensional pregnancies just don't happen."

"Looks like you thought wrong," Liz said with great amusement. "And remember, Ben's from the Sea Dimension, Anja from the Land. Then there's the added issue that Anja is a mermaid. That might be what keeps them from getting pregnant. They're from completely different species. Anja told us that there was no evidence of any children born of a Lander and mermaid."

"Somebody better warn Sarat," Tracy murmured with a shake of her head. "I don't think she and Owen are planning on starting a family just yet."

"Sound idea," Liz agreed wholeheartedly. There was just so much they did not understand about the Interdimensional relationships they were forming. Then Liz stood up and held out her arms. "Now, don't I get to hug the new mommy?"

"Mommy," Tracy breathed, her face glowing as she stood up and hugged Liz tightly. "I'm really going to be a mommy!"

"She finally figured it out?" Katie asked from by the doorway, a huge grin on her sun kissed face.

"You knew?" Tracy whirled on the Oracle, who held up her hands in mock defense.

"I kinda, sorta knew," hedged Katie. "There was a subtle shift in your energy that showed up shortly after you came back from the Land. I watch all the Travelers when they return for any signs of illness or such."

"I wondered about that," Liz said. "It's a good idea, actually. You never know if Evil is going to try and slip a fake Protector into the mix. I need to up my aura watching."

"Exactly," said Katie with a firm nod, then turned to Tracy. "I wasn't sure what the change entailed, but I knew it wasn't something negative. Then you started showing other symptoms. If you hadn't figured it out, I would've told you after the wedding. Honest!" She crossed her heart then gave a pretty pout. "Now, am I forgiven?" she asked, holding out her arms.

Pulling Katie into her embrace, Tracy laughed. "I can't stay mad at you, I'm pregnant!" she shrieked. "Oh, I can't wait to tell Orli. To see the look on his face…"

Katie sobered slightly. Not wanting to put a damper on her friend's happiness, but wanting to be realistic, she was compelled to point out the other issue that plagued her. "Wait a second, honey. We don't know how Traveling will affect a pregnancy. I think we'll need to ask Amber if there are dangers associated with going back and forth through the Interdimensional Void while carrying a baby."

"Oh," Tracy said, taken aback. "Oh, that's right. Wow. There's so much we don't know about this."

"We'll muddle through," Liz said staunchly, wrapping her arm around Tracy's waist.

"Muddle through what?" Ben asked as he and the rest of the group headed inside.

Tracy hesitated, clearly torn. On the one hand, she wanted nothing more than to run to Ben and tell him her news. On the other, she knew how desperately he and Anja craved having a child, and how elusive the fulfillment of that wish had been for them. She did not want to cause pain to one of her dearest friends. And she knew her joyous news would do just that, which made her uncharacteristically apprehensive.

"He's going to find out eventually," Amber said from behind Owen.

"Did everyone know but me?" Tracy exploded, throwing up her hands.

"Know what?" intoned Ben, Owen, Sarat and Sasha. Steven just looked sheepishly at the floor, scratching the side of his nose.

Tracy took a deep breath. Staring at Ben, whose reaction she feared the most, she opted for the honest, rather blunt truth.

"I'm pregnant."

Ben blanched as if hit with a wall of cold water, actually staggering back a few steps. Sasha and Sarat quickly raced over and hugged Tracy, exclaiming over the good news. Owen gave her arm a squeeze, his craggy face shining with happiness. Steven dropped a kiss on her cheek. Then, all that was left was Ben.

To his credit, he recovered quickly. Following the rest, he enfolded Tracy in his arms, hugging her tightly. "I'm so happy for you," he said, his voice thick with emotion. "So very happy for you and Orli."

"Oh, Ben," she said helplessly against his shoulder.

After giving her a squeeze, he stepped back, a smile on his face. "Honestly, Tracy. Be happy. This is your time, your joy. Don't waste it on worrying for me. Or Anja." He tweaked her nose with a finger. "I do, however, expect to be the godfather."

"Absolutely," Tracy vowed.

It was no surprise when, about an hour later, Ben slipped from the house to head for the beach. Everyone noticed it but none remarked on his passage, respectful of his need for privacy in the wake of the rather startling news.

Liz watched him dive into the waves, striking out to sea. She kept an eye on the ocean, while listening with interest to the continuing discussion regarding Tracy's blessed event, and its not so blessed repercussions.

"So you're saying that there's no evidence that Traveling is dangerous to a fetus," Tracy was trying to clarify with Amber, who shook her head.

"I'm saying there's no evidence of what happens to a pregnant Traveler, period," she clarified, raising her hands. "It just isn't something we have statistics on."

"What does Daniel say?" Katie asked, leaning forward with her elbows on her knees, not liking the way that Tracy's eyes were narrowing at Amber.

"He says that he doesn't think Tracy should Travel," Amber admitted reluctantly. The group groaned, bracing themselves for the new mother's response. They didn't have to wait long.

"I can't believe this!" Tracy said with heat. Pacing in front of the windows, her face was set in mutinous lines. "This is the most special time of my life, and I can't share any of it with the baby's father?"

"Well, we don't know what will happen, what could happen," Katie tried to reason with her, but Tracy was beyond listening to reason.

"I don't care. I want to visit Orli. I need to. He has to be a part of this. To feel the baby move, to plan and prepare, for God's sake I need someone to scream at during labor!" Tracy was in a full rant now as she stalked about like a wild animal in a cage swinging her arms in agitation.

"There's more," Amber said, her discomfort growing but obviously resolved to get it all out in the open. "You do realize you can't have traditional prenatal screenings and monitoring, don't you, Tracy?"

Tracy paused mid-step, hanging her head. "Too'ki," she said on a sigh. Turning tortured eyes to the fairy she pleaded, "Please tell me that the infection won't be passed along to the baby." All of the blood work William had done on her led to the conclusion that the Too'ki within her acted much like a virus, although it had properties that could not be fully understood due to its other-dimensional origin.

Again, Amber shrugged, her hands held out in front of her. "We don't know," she said simply. "There are so many new variables. But Daniel feels that, given we've no idea what happens to the body when you Travel, and given the Too'ki blood that flows in your body, to try and go through the Tree might have very serious consequences to the baby."

"You do want a healthy baby," Katie said softly. "And as difficult as it'll be, all of us will be there. Be with you. Support you. And Ben will keep Orli apprised of everything. You won't be alone. I promise."

"What can you promise that could possibly make up for the fact that I don't get to share the most important thing in my marriage with my own husband?" Tracy spat, eyes narrowed.

"I'm sure that once he knows of the situation, William will do everything he can to monitor the pregnancy," Katie maintained, her voice calm in the face of Tracy's vehemence. "But when it comes to Traveling, we have to listen to Daniel. He wouldn't deny you access to the Tree out of spite. He must have a good reason."

Tracy sat down on the edge of a sofa, her hands clenched. "It won't be the same," she said softly.

"I know that," Katie said with real sympathy, closing her hand over Tracy's. "But you need to do what's best for your health, and that of the baby's."

"When do you think I'm due?" Tracy asked.

"You're five weeks along," Liz answered absently, her eyes still fixated on the beach, one long finger curling a lock of hair. Realizing that everyone was staring at her, she blushed. "I'm sorry. It just came to me."

"But I've only been back from the Land for two weeks, and

I only spent a week there," Tracy said, confused. "That would be impossible."

"Perhaps," Sarat said slowly, "your pregnancy, since it was conceived in the Land, will be slightly accelerated. Time in the Land tends to go faster than the time here. Or it could be Too'ki pregnancies don't last that long."

"Shortest pregnancy on record," Sasha chimed in. "Cool. You know that William will be glad to be your doctor and help you through this. He understands all about the different…variables."

Liz stood up, having seen Ben's blond hair coming in from his swim. She excused herself from the group and moved to the beach. Waiting while Ben stood just above the shoreline and dried off with his towel, she watched the soul weary sorrow the man carried. Making another decision, she stepped forward.

"Ben."

He turned, carefully schooling his face into impassive lines, as if he knew she was worried about him and didn't want her to know how deeply Tracy's news affected him. Then he visibly gave up, and all the emotion radiated from those remarkable aqua eyes.

"I didn't want to be a drag on the festivities," Ben admitted, toweling off his hair, his Protector pendant a silver gleam against his chest. Gesturing, he led them to the bottom stair of the house dock where they settled, looking out over the expanse of the white beach, the smell of salt saturating the breeze.

Leaning his elbows on the step behind him, Ben looked out at the sea with a frown. "I didn't enjoy myself out there today. That's a first. Usually the ocean gives me peace, even when I'm troubled."

Liz put her hand on his arm and squeezed, then let her hand fall into her lap, sitting with him in the quiet, listening to the sea gulls rant at one another overhead. After a long silence, he finally admitted, "It's the not knowing that's beginning to get to us. We just don't know if it will ever happen. And the uncertainty is just…wearing."

"If you could know, once and for all know, would that make things better?"

Ben's ocean hued eyes turned to meet hers. There was a trueness to his answer that left no doubt in her mind. "Yes, it'd be better. Then we wouldn't torture ourselves with the what ifs and the maybes and the false alarms…"

Liz sighed and looked out to the sea that gave her friend a great deal of his strength, mystery and depth. He'd grown to be such an important person in her life, a dear friend who was suffering. And she could help him. Unwrapping her arms from around her legs, her back straight, Liz picked up his large, sun warmed hand and held it between both of hers. Then, she cast her mental gaze forward. Her topaz eyes unfocused; her breath became shallow and even.

The sense of her leaving her body and reaching out, reaching forward, was clear. And powerful. God, so powerful. It was so damned good to stretch out with her senses, to use her gift, to do what she had been ordained to do in this lifetime. As her unique chemistry kicked in, and brought all her extraordinary powers to full bear, the flush of power and certainty was intoxicating. This was so the right thing to do.

Ben sat extremely still. Liz had never willingly done a future search on any of them, not to his knowledge. It was a testament to her growing skill and growing bond with the Protectors that she did so now. Did it for him. It touched him deeply, in a way that had him closing his eyes with thankfulness that he'd found these wonderful people.

Concentrating on his palm, he could feel the power from Liz radiating through his skin and up his arm. It was disconcerting, but not in a bad way. Comforting and scary, all rolled into one big ball. Although, if Ben were to be fair, the scariness was from his own anxiety over what she was trying to ascertain.

As the ocean continued its eternal ebb and flow, the seagulls crying out indignities to the sun, Liz probed through the future of her friend. Seeking one specific bit of information while judiciously ignoring other insights that could affect his future, she burrowed through the murky tomorrows, hoping to see the little face her friend so craved to see. It was perhaps the most delicate and far-reaching reading Liz had done since returning from the Land, and although it strained her abilities, it was also exhilarating. Her toes curled into the sand as she found the thread she sought and followed it through the twists and turns of the possible futures.

Ben watched the emotions play on his friend's face. As she read him, her inner beauty grew to a level of fierceness that was breathtaking. He couldn't look away from her if he'd tried. All the hairs on the back of his neck were standing straight up from the electricity vibing off of the woman. He was used to Katie's underlying sense of power—as an Oracle she carried it with her like a shawl at all times. But Liz was good at hiding her special abilities and at times it was easy to forget she, too, was a Primary Power of the Land. After this reading, Ben knew, he would not easily forget that little fact.

Finally Liz opened her eyes again and turned to him. The regret in her eyes told Ben more than he wanted to hear, but Ben steeled his heart. He needed to know this. Anja needed to know. Then they would deal with the fall out together, as it should be.

"I don't see biological children for you and Anja," Liz's statement did not come as a complete surprise to Ben, but her next words did, "but I do see children in your lives. Children who bring you both joy and fulfillment. A sense of completion far beyond what either of you could imagine or want or desire. Yes, you will have children, and they will be beloved and cherished and…special. So very, very special."

Ben pondered her words. One part of him was slowly dying; the thought of never holding a child of his genes in his arms a dream that he was loath to give up. He really was the last of his kind, then. After he died, all that was unique to his dimension would be gone. Forever. With his death, his race would truly be extinct, and that a wrench he couldn't ignore. The other part of him was buoyed by the knowledge that all was not lost.

"Adoption?" he guessed.

Liz shrugged. "I don't know," she said honestly. "Ben, please understand. I'm new at this. I may be wrong. You may still have children with Anja. I just don't know. The future fluctuates. We could suddenly find ourselves on a path far different than what I saw today. You just never know for sure. But…the strongest feeling I had was that you would not have children biologically with Anja. I'm sorry."

Ben pulled her up against his side, dropping a kiss to her temple. "You did just fine," he assured her. "Seriously. I'd rather know than wonder and worry. And knowing that children are in our future, well, that's a gift. A gift I thank you for with all my heart. Now, I better go up and see Tracy, join the fun. Are you coming?"

She demurred, saying she needed a little time alone after the reading.

A bit of solitary recharging before returning to the larger group was necessary, or else she might inadvertently do a reading on someone. As Ben left her on the steps, Liz sighed, feeling lighter, more "right" with the world around her. Being a Seer had its benefits, after all. She'd actually helped her friend and it was good, despite the fact that she'd given him some unwelcome news in most respects.

She sat still, listening to the ebb and flow of the waves, listening to the seagulls screech on the winds. From far away came the sound of a child's laughter, while nearby someone was barbecuing hamburgers. It was peaceful here at the end of the dock. Quiet and peaceful and… home.

Out of the corner of her eye, Liz saw Zach Neol step off his dock. The actor ambled towards the ocean, dabbling his toes in the surf. He looked incredibly tired, incredibly alone. The set of those broad shoulders was slumped, his aura dark with memories and fraught with tension. On impulse, Liz stood up and walked over towards the man. She had no idea why, but she was compelled to go and speak with him.

-4-
Beach Combing

Zach knew Liz Keeper was coming towards him, even though his back was to her. He'd seen her talking with the blond man—Ben was his name, wasn't it? He wasn't sure why he was compelled to go to the beach at the same exact moment that her companion left her behind. It was odd, that feeling of needing to be out there with his feet in the water at that particular moment.

He wasn't sure what he expected, but to have her walk up to him was quite surprising. She didn't seem the type to make the first move. Zach shook his head. He knew nothing about her, he thought with derision. Assigning her qualities that he had no idea if she really possessed. Like a director casting for a new film, he was moving her into a character that he sought for her to be, rather than the woman she was. Silly of him, really. She was probably star struck and wanted an autograph or something frivolous like that.

"Hello there," Liz said to him, feeling extremely foolish with her schoolmarm greeting.

"Hello yourself," he replied with a flash of smile. "This is a better way to meet than a smack down, isn't it?"

She blushed prettily, pushing a long curl out of her face with one slim hand. "That's what I wanted to tell you, Mr. Neol–"

"Zach," he interrupted.

Liz nodded graciously. "Zach," she repeated, "I wanted you to know that you didn't really knock me over. I saw you coming and was able to move back before we made contact." She was holding her hands in front of her almost primly.

Zach appraised her, running a bare toe in the wet sand. A pair of joggers ran by and didn't give them a glance. Zach was glad that he had donned a white tank top to cover his conspicuous tattoo. More often than not going without a shirt was like waving a banner proclaiming his presence. Some days he really regretted the decision to get the tattoo.

"The way I see it," Zach drawled slowly, oozing as he spoke, "if I hadn't done that stupid trick off the back deck, you wouldn't have ended up flat on your back in the sand. I'd say that still makes me guilty of a smack down."

Liz laughed. "Why did you do the back flip?" she asked, wrapping her arms around her waist. She and Zach started to stroll down the beach, not even realizing they were wandering along together. "It's not the standard ending for a T'ai Chi routine."

Zach hung his head in mock shame. "I was showing off," he admitted, casting a glance her way out of the corner of his eye.

"Showing off?"

Now Zach was the one blushing. "I could see the ladies in your house watching me. So I figured, what the hell, give a little flourish at the end of the routine. And, well, I guess I got carried away…"

Liz burst out laughing, the sound like a thousand musical birds. "That's priceless," she gasped. "I can just see them all gathered around, watching you."

Zach scratched his nose. "Well, your windows aren't mirrored like mine. It was flattering. In a nice way, not a meat locker kind of way. Which is weird. I'm not making any sense."

"It's ok. I rarely make sense myself."

The two continued down the beach for several feet, silent.

"Why were you watching me earlier, from your bedroom window?"

Busted. Zach mentally winced, but wondered how she knew he'd been watching her, of all the people on the deck.

"I'm curious about you and your friends," he admitted, scooping up a piece of sea glass and tossing it into the tide. "How you all interact, the different dynamics of the group. It must be the actor in me. I'm always trying to figure out how relationships formed, what makes them tick. How did you all meet?"

"We belong to a group…it's difficult to explain."

"Group?" he asked.

"It's not a cult or anything," she assured him quickly. "It's more that we work for something. It's nothing illegal, but we don't discuss it with strangers. Oh, I'm not doing this right at all," she cried, covering her mouth with her hand. "You must think we're a bunch of kooks."

"I lived in Hollywood," Zach said with a laugh, "it doesn't get much more kooky than that."

"True, I guess," Liz said. They fell into a comfortable silence as they walked along. Almost in sync, they turned around and headed back down the beach toward their houses.

"So, Liz Keeper, when you aren't working for this group thing, what do you do?"

She shrugged. "Nothing much. I'm a trained librarian. Research mostly, but I gave up that job about six months ago. Now, I work for the group, doing research and reading."

He stopped in his tracks, astonished. "You? A librarian? No way."

"Way," came the laconic reply.

"Wow, the librarians in my town were never as good looking as you," Zach observed, eyeing her out of the corner of those amazing eyes.

Liz stopped in her tracks and stared. "You *are* smooth," she said with a startled little laugh as she resumed walking again. "I almost believed you for a moment."

Zach stooped and picked up another glass piece worn slick by the ocean's waves. Flinging it out to sea, he gave her another sideways glance. "You can't be so oblivious to the way you look."

Shrugging, she shaded her eyes with her hands, watching the stone's path. "Nice throw," she commented, adding, "I just don't think much about my looks. One way or the other. What is, is. I'll always have curly hair and freckles. You can't change it so why worry?"

"I like your curly hair and freckles."

She slanted him a look that was pure librarian. "Slick again. I was just stating fact, not trying to fish for compliments."

Zach quirked his lips. "I'm not used to that way of thinking," he admitted, knowing that with every other woman he could have been strolling down the beach with, their looks would be a top priority.

"But I like it. Believe me you don't have anything to worry about in the looks department. Trust me on this."

"I guess I will."

They waited to pass by a family taking advantage of the almost empty beach, setting up for their day in the sun with towels, chairs, and a boom box blaring music. Once out of range, Zach jerked a thumb back in the direction of the family.

"That reminded me. What music were you listening to when I almost knocked you over earlier? I can usually figure it out, but it was unfamiliar. Catchy, though."

Liz wrinkled her nose. "I was listening to Wizard Wrock."

"What the hell is that? Wait...you mean those indie bands who write songs about Harry Potter? You?"

"Why is that so strange?" asked Liz, indignant.

"You just don't seem like the type," admitted Zach.

"I'm a librarian. Of course I'll listen to bands who write songs about books."

"Ah. Yes. That makes sense, then." Zach made a mental note to check out the book rock movement when he got home.

Again the silence stretched, but it was not uncomfortable in any way, shape or form. Then Liz sighed, and asked, as if she couldn't help herself, "Can I ask a really personal question?"

Zach gave a mental sigh. This was going to be it, he reckoned. The questions about the parties, the nightlife, the tabloid rumors. The 'what's it like to be a celebrity?' questions that were uncomfortable and prying. Irritation rose in his throat like bile. He'd never escape it, and it was honestly partially his own fault. Best to just get over it.

"Sure," he said, forcing his tone into one of jovial lightness, but a muscle in his cheek started to twitch.

"Why are you so lonely?"

She might as well have hit him with a two by four. Zach halted, the foamy sea rushing around his ankles and stared at her. "What makes you think I'm lonely?" he said finally. One dim part of his mind recognized that they were back at the base of the dock that led to the house she lived in.

Liz was holding her hair loosely bundled at the nape of her neck so that the wind did not whip it about her face, her head tilted slightly to one side. "Well, you're supposed to be some huge movie star, but you're living alone in that large house, without any kind of posse or hangers on. Your parents aren't here, and I do know enough about you to know that you are estranged from them." *Plus I can see your face,* she added silently. The quiet withdrawal of self from the world. The loneliness that oozed from him like lava, making it easy for her receptors to pick it up even if she wasn't focusing on a Seer reading. "I mean, let's face it, the Outer Banks isn't the usual choice for a Hollywood star."

"Maybe I'm not the usual Hollywood star."

She gave him another inscrutable glance with those whiskey colored eyes. "No, I don't think you are."

Zach laughed. "How did we get so serious?" he asked. "It's a beautiful day, the sun is shining, I'm walking on the beach with a gorgeous woman."

"There's that smoothness again. I have a feeling you're used to hiding behind that suave exterior." She was waggling her finger at him. "That won't work with me, Zachary Neol. I won't stand for it."

Without thinking, he playfully reached out and grabbed her finger.

It was like grabbing a live wire. The shock raced through his system like a shot, and he literally saw golden sparks flying from where their flesh met.

Liz gave a wordless gasp, then wrenched her finger from his grasp. Taking several steps backward, she tripped over a piece of driftwood and, for the second time that day, ended up on her butt in the sand.

"Don't!" She threw out a hand in warning as Zach instinctually moved forward, obviously intent on helping her to her feet. Untangling herself from the long dress, Liz struggled to stand. When she finally looked back at him, Zach was standing still, looking down at the hand that had met hers.

"What the hell was that?" he asked softly, without any real anger but more with a sense of wonderment.

"I don't touch people," Liz whispered helplessly.

"I can see why," he said with a shaky laugh. "Hell of a static charge you build up, Liz Keeper." Seeing her look of true self-recrimination, he hastened to add, "I'm fine, really. Don't worry about it. I've had worse shocks on set. Honest."

"I should be going," she said quietly, easing away from him. "It was really nice talking with you, Zachary. Enjoy the OBX experience."

"I hope to see you again," he called after her as Liz hustled up the stairs. She gave him a noncommittal thumb's up as she disappeared over the beach walk.

Just my luck, Zach thought as he turned towards his own house. The first girl in a long time that interests me, and she runs like a scared deer at the first touch. He looked down at his hand, which was still throbbing slightly from the contact. Frowning, he amended his thoughts, ok, so it was more than a touch. More like a bolt of lightening.

Liz let herself back into the house with a sense of great relief. Shaking her hand to rid it of the residue of touching Zach, she scanned the room quickly. Almost immediately, Sarat met her gaze, and her eyes widened. Liz nodded, and Sarat gestured towards the kitchen.

Once in the deserted kitchen, Sarat rounded on Liz. "What's happened?" she demanded.

"I touched him," Liz stammered, rubbing her hand on her side. "I touched him, and I saw something."

Sarat frowned. "Touched who?"

"Zachary Neol."

"Goodness gracious, girl, when you decide to go big, you go real big," Sarat said with great appreciation. "What part did you touch? His hiney?"

"It wasn't like that," Liz waved her hand at Sarat irritably, although in truth it was difficult to stay angry with the young woman, who was just a bundle of energy and wit.

"No? So where did you touch him?"

"Sarat!" Now Liz had to laugh. "I swear your mind is in the gutter. He grabbed me, if you must know."

Now Sarat's eyes narrowed dangerously. "Grabbed you?" she repeated ominously. "Let me get the guys and Tracy. We'll go set him straight. Maybe not Tracy now that she's preggers, but…"

Liz grabbed Sarat's sleeve as she started to leave the room. "Oh for heaven's sake, Sarat. He grabbed my finger, which I was waving in his face like an idiot."

Sarat leaned back against the counter, somewhat mollified. "And then what happened?"

"When we touched, I felt something tug, deep inside me. And then, I saw." Liz raised her fingers to her lips in remembrance.

"What did you see?" Sarat asked quietly.

"Death. Death and destruction, hovering all over that poor man like a glove, waiting to be slipped on. Waiting. Waiting to devour."

Sarat chewed on her lip. "Maybe it was just a flash of some of the movie work he's done," she suggested. "Merely a memory of a character."

"No," Liz whispered. "No. It wasn't a movie role. I'm sure of it."

"Then what was it?" Sarat was curious.

"He was in the Land," Liz said with absolute conviction.

"I'm getting the others," Sarat said immediately.

"Wait, Sarat, wait!" Liz pleaded with her friend. "Sasha's getting married soon. We can't let anything interfere with her magical day. She's had so much heartache and pain in her life, I don't want what I just saw to bring back her time in the Land. Not now. Just get Katie. Tell her to meet me in my room. I'll tell her everything. But I don't want the other Protectors to know. Not yet."

Sarat nodded and swept from the room.

Within a few minutes, Katie, Sarat and Liz were enclosed in the room Liz was using. While the petite Oracle perched on the side of her bed, Liz paced back and forth, telling her everything that happened on the beach. When it came time to talk about the vision, Liz faltered only slightly.

"I could see walls, like an old fort or something. They were reddish brown…what's the word…oh yes, terra cotta. Old, very old it seemed to me, but with an odd sense of newness as well. There was greenish brown moss growing out of the cracks. Zach was walking down the corridor, holding a torch in one hand, a golden sword in the other."

"What was he doing, besides walking?" Sarat asked, encouraging Liz to look beyond the obvious walls of her vision.

Liz paused and closed her eyes, her body swaying slightly as the vision took over. When she spoke, her voice was lowered almost an octave. Sarat and Katie exchanged a startled look. They doubted that Liz was even aware of the change in her stance and voice, but there was no denying it was real. It made the recitation of the vision that much more vivid.

"He's searching for something. Something he needs desperately. He's been hurt, hurt badly, but he still keeps moving forward. The fate of the Land is in his hands. And he fears he's failing. Failing the Land, failing…me."

Liz's eyes flew open and she stared at the two women, fingers raised to her lips in shock. "Why would he fear failing *me*? He hardly knows me."

"Maybe you're meant to know him better," suggested Katie. "Let me ask you a question. How many times in your life have you willingly gone up to a man and started a conversation like that. Out of the blue?"

Liz gave a wry grin. "Never," she admitted. "I can't help it, I'm shy."

"So the first time you do approach a man, take that initiative, it's with a movie star of Zachary Neol's standing?" Katie raised her eyebrows. "You didn't just go big, you went universal."

"So you are saying that I could've been pushed into talking with him?" Liz did not like the sound of that. She'd had enough manipulation in her time in the Land.

"No, not necessarily," Katie said, well aware of Liz's concerns regarding outside influences shepherding her down a rosy path. "Look at it this way, I met Steven for a reason. Sasha met William for a reason. Sarat met Owen for a reason. People are placed in our lives to help us through whatever it is we're experiencing. You think it's manipulation. I prefer to call it fate."

"She's right," said Sarat. "There was a reason for your meeting Zach today. I'll bet that you were meant to get some sort of premonition from him. That way, we know we need to prepare him for a visit to the Land."

"Premonition…" Liz reflected on it, remembering a time back in the Land when she'd cast her future and seen herself at a party. A party where Sasha and William were talking about their wedding. Where she'd seen a woman on the balcony with a tuxedoed man the woman wearing a sea foam green dress. *Crap*. Hadn't Katie just given Liz a dress that was-big surprise-sea foam to wear to William and Sasha's engagement party.

Liz groaned and put her head in her hands. "No. It's not him. It can't be. That would be…horrible. No, it isn't him."

"What isn't?" asked Sarat. "Who isn't? Are you still talking about Zach Neol?"

"Nothing."

"He's a potential Protector," said Katie, steering back to the main topic at hand.

"He probably won't believe it," Liz warned them. "He's from a world where make believe is broken down into finite, easy to understand collaborations of writing and filming and special effects."

"That doesn't matter," Katie waved the idea away. "We have to at least try."

"There's another issue," Liz insisted. "This isn't some normal guy we're going to pluck up and set onto the path of the Land. This is a major movie star. He can't just disappear like many of us could, without repercussions."

"All the more reason for us to prepare him, get a story in place," Katie said stubbornly, her blue eyes resolute. "So that when he does disappear off the face of the earth–"

"Literally," put in Sarat.

"—there is a valid reason in place. For his sake. And ours," finished Katie.

Giving up, Liz threw up her hands. "Ok," she said, "I don't think he'll believe us for an instant. But I'm willing to try. What do we do first?"

"I say you get to know the esteemed Mr. Neol a lot better," Sarat said, winking and bumping shoulders with Liz.

Liz paled. "No, I can't do that," she squeaked. "I mean, now that I know what's going to happen, I'll just feel so self conscious about the whole thing."

"Well, lucky for you, we have a whole bunch of excuses to invite him over during the next few weeks," Katie reminded her. "The cocktail party/fundraiser, the wedding…we'll just be neighborly. If it would make you feel better, one of us could invite him."

"Thanks." Immediate relief flooded through Liz. Accidentally running into Zach was one thing, but purposely setting out to corner him was completely against her character. Not to mention it was awfully close to lying, and she had issues in that regard.

"There is always the possibility that this is a false vision," Sarat was compelled to point out.

Liz knew it wasn't but didn't say a word.

"That will show with time, right?" Katie clarified. "If it's false, then other signs won't be there. We'll just keep an eye on Zachary Neol and see what happens. If he's meant to Travel, we'll be able to tell. And we'll do what's needed to prepare him for his adventure."

The brush of gloom and doom from her vision washed over Liz like a misty fog. It made her shiver. "Somehow, I doubt he'd be so keen to go if he'd seen what I've seen."

"We'll cross that bridge when we get to it," Katie asserted firmly, wrapping her arm around Liz. She was one of the few in the group who felt no compunction about touching the Seer. As a Primary Power she was somewhat insulated from an accidental reading. "We'll make sure he's as prepared as he can be before he Travels."

Liz looked out the window of her room, which faced the ocean. Zach was gone, probably inside his house. She had a sudden wish that she had never met Zach Neol. Because she was suddenly terrified she was leading him to his death.

-5-
Practice Makes Perfect

The next morning, Zach was walking down towards his house, having just finished his morning T'ai-Chi routine at the end of the deck. No women had been watching him today from the neighboring beach house. At least, none he'd been able to detect. Certainly not the tall, cool blond with golden eyes that he was aching to see again. Pity, that, but it could not be helped. But his attention to the intricate martial arts movements had been compromised by his lack of concentration. He'd have to work extra hard the next day to make up for his inattentiveness.

As he neared the house, the sound of Euro-tech music came from the bottom level of his neighbor's. Zach picked up a towel and wiped his face and torso, listening. Not really his style, but it certainly had a good beat. Then he began to hear an unusual noise beneath the pulsing rhythm. He cocked his head to one side, listening intently. Then a huge grin spread over his face as he placed the sound.

Making a quick decision to get a closer look, Zach jumped the balustrade lining the walkway to the beach. Pushing his way through the sea grass and standing on his tiptoes, he peered over the fence that separated his property from the group next door.

He could see a small sliver through an open door. There was an impression of moving bodies, lunging and retreating, twisting and twirling. The clash of metal was even more unmistakable from here. They were sword fighting in their basement, Zach thought with astonishment and a sense of happiness.

"Excellent," he breathed, hoisting himself up and over the wooden fence with great care. No need to get any splinters, especially with the fun that was waiting. Light as a cat, he landed on the opposite side of the fence, heading towards the basement door. As he pushed it wide open, all activity in the room stopped cold.

Ben was standing with his sword extended, crossing blades with one of the women Zach had not yet met. On the sidelines, two women were sitting; both attired in workout gear, swords resting nearby. One was the tall girl who had fainted on the beach the day before. The other was shorter, with bright blue eyes and short blond hair. She gave him a dazzling smile that warmed him to the soles of his feet. They were all staring at him.

"Hi!" Zach said brightly, raising one hand in an abbreviated wave. "Heard you guys and wondered if anyone needed a sparring partner."

"What?" Ben said rather dumbly. Then he lowered the sword. "Oh, you mean…" he held up the sword.

"Well, yeah, that was the thought. That's a great sword you've got there," Zach said, appreciating the clean lines of the silver sword that was set with aqua and green gemstones. Then he quirked his head to one side as they continued to look at him as if he were from another planet. "What? It's not like you're doing anything illegal. Sure, I admit it's odd to find people using broadswords in the basement, but hell, I'll take the practice any way I can. Do you do re-enactments or something? Got any spares? I left my sword back in California. Never thought I'd have an opportunity to use it outside of a movie set."

The woman on the floor with Ben gestured towards a cabinet, which was always locked unless they were practicing. "I'm Sasha," she said to Zach as he came up to her side.

"Nice to meet you, Sasha," he gave a low, appreciative whistle as the cabinet door swung open. "Quite a nice collection you have here," he complimented, taking in the arsenal that was on display. Swords, arrows, quivers, and an excellent set of throwing knives were all on display, nestled in black velvet and spotlighted as if they were precious jewels.

Selecting a long sword, he sighted down its length, testing the sprung steel blade with the palm of his hand. Finally, he took a few cautious swipes through the air. "Nice. Bloody nice," he said in obvious appreciation. "I don't recognize the work, but whoever did this was a freaking master of the craft, that's for damn sure."

He looked Ben up and down with an appraising eye. The blond would have a long reach, but those really big feet of his might trip him up. He moved to the center of the floor, facing Ben.

Sasha settled next to Tracy and Katie. "This oughta be good," she whispered with excitement. "I read that Zachary Neol was considered to be one of the best. The swords master who trained him for *The Phoenix* said he'd never met anyone who picked up the sport more quickly, and with more finesse. Better than Viggo Mortensen from Lord of the Rings." The women all looked highly impressed at that comparison.

"Oh, why do I have to feel morning sickness today?" Tracy moaned with disgust, rubbing her belly lightly. "I wanna piece of him, I do. In a purely weapons to the mat kind of way," she hastened to add as Katie and Sasha gave identical snorts.

Then the women fell silent as the men faced each other on the exercise mat. They spent a moment sizing one another up. Then with a sudden, vicious movement, they were engaged. The women sat up straighter as a raging battle ensued, full of intricate footwork and brute strength. It was a glorious display of swords. The blades moving so fast that they blurred; the ringing sound of metal hissing and purring in the gym.

"That bastard has been holding back on me," Tracy muttered as she watched Ben go on the defense, working Zach back into a corner. "He's never that aggressive when we spar."

"I think this is a case of good old fashioned testosterone coming to the forefront," Katie replied. "Male marking his territory and all that macho crap." Tracy sniffed, obviously not mollified.

With a gleeful shout, Zach pushed past Ben, rolled in a somersault and came up behind him. Ben whirled, his blade cracking against Zach's sword in just the nick of time. Ben gave a yell and pressed forward. All the noise had the rest of the group from upstairs filing into the room. Soon everyone was watching the match of wills and strength that was being demonstrated on the gym mat.

Ben did have the greater reach and more practice with the blade, but Zach moved through the exercise like he was dancing, weaving and bobbing while not relenting with fierce parries. Light on his feet and with considerable strength, again and again he was able to beat off Ben's attack. Sweat poured from the men, their grunts filled the room.

"Wow," Sarat said. "They're really good."

"How long should we let this go on?" Katie asked.

"As long as they wanna go," Amber said, eyeing the phoenix as it rippled on Zach's back. "I'm having fun." She settled down next to Tracy with a grin, plopping her chin on her hand.

"Yeah, well, it's all fun and games until someone puts an eye out," Katie muttered as a particularly close swing from Zach had Ben leaping back, just barely missing his midsection. "This isn't a stunt team, you know. Those are real swords that can do real damage."

"Yes, mother Oracle," Tracy said, then hissed under her breath, "Get him, Ben. Get him!"

"Yeah, well I'd rather not loose a potential Protector because Ben's got a hard on to be Alpha dog," Katie said, wincing at another near miss.

Liz was frozen on the stairwell, staring at the match. A part of her had to appreciate the fact that she was watching two experts, two men at the peak of their physical fitness and prowess with the sword. The other part of her realized that Zach being so familiar with the sword could actually play into her vision about him, wandering in a ruin, carrying a sword in one hand.

She moved into the room fully, leaning against the wall. Her motion caught Zach's attention. He watched her entrance out of the corner of his eye, and that small distraction was enough for Ben to gain the upper hand.

With a vicious thrust and swirl of the blade, Zach's sword went flying through the air, scattering the Protectors as they scrambled to get out of the way of the soaring blade. Then they broke into spontaneous applause.

"Damn," Zach said, putting his hands on his thighs and hanging his head. He glanced over at Ben with a smile. "Thanks, man. That was fun."

"Yeah, it sure was," Ben replied, leaning on his sword and holding out his hand. "You can be my sparring partner anytime. I miss having a guy to go against. No offense, Tracy," he added over his shoulder as the growl from the woman reached him. He rolled his eyes at Zach, leaning close. "She's good, really good. Watch it when you go against Tracy. Don't give her any slack for being a chick. She's got the upper body strength of a gorilla. Trust me, I know."

Zach shook his hand with gusto. "You're on, and thanks for the advice. How often do you practice?"

"Pretty much every day."

Zach's eyebrows rose. "Really? Wow. That's dedication. I know my muscles are going to be sore as hell tomorrow," he said, twisting his neck one way then the other.

"I can help with that!" Amber exclaimed, raising her hand, then lowered it when Katie gave her a sharp look of reprimand and muttered something that sounded suspiciously like "Daniel," under her breath.

"Well, maybe not," the woman amended meekly.

The rest of the group came up to speak with Zach or Ben, congratulating them on the match. Liz hung back, unsure of what to do.

Zach eyed her over the crowd of people. She was wearing a long dress again, one that outlined her slim form to perfection. Today, her hair was up in a loose bun, tendrils flowing down from the concoction. Her wide topaz eyes were smiling, but the movement didn't reach her lips. Zach started to move towards her, slowly and cautiously circling to get closer to her. It was a technique he utilized at parties when he wanted to get as close to the door as possible before ducking out.

Soon, he was standing next to her, leaning against the wall. "Sorry I distracted you," she said, looking out at the group. Tracy was showing Sasha a new grip on the sword and Sarat was discussing weapons with Ben and Owen by the cabinet.

The rest of the Protector group had disbursed, some heading outside or upstairs after congratulating Zach and Ben. Liz was left quite alone with Zach, despite the presence of her friends.

"You didn't distract me," Zach protested, then laughed and rubbed the back of his neck. "Yeah, you distracted me," he admitted. "But honestly? Ben would have taken me out within a few minutes. He's got more stamina in this kind of sparring. I haven't practiced like that in almost a year."

"You learned swords for *The Phoenix*, right?" Liz asked, angling towards him.

"Yep," he replied, the amber flecked blue eyes scanning the crowd.

"Watching interactions and dissecting relationships again?" Liz could not believe she was actually teasing him. Teasing Zachary Neol. And it was easy!

"Caught me," he replied with a grin.

"So what do you see?"

"Ben and Owen are amused by Sarat. She's so enthusiastic in her knowledge of weaponry that you can't help but find her enchanting, I guess. And Owen wants to sweep her off her feet and have his way with her," Zach paused and waggled his eyebrows at Liz, who hid a smile as she ducked her head. "Ben, although he's giving a pretty good front of talking with them, is actually keeping a hell of a close watch over you. He's very protective of you, and the other girls…er women," he corrected as Liz gave him an arch look. "Sasha is just humoring the tall girl."

"Tracy," Liz supplied the name and Zach nodded.

"Tracy. Sasha's just pretending to be interested in the grip. She really wants to leave, you can tell by the number of times she's looked at the door. As for Tracy, well, she's hard to read her at the moment. She looks half sick, half thrilled and majorly confused by her own body at the moment. Typical pregnant woman reaction."

"You knew she was pregnant? Just by looking at her?" Liz was astonished at the insight.

"Well, to be honest, it was more the sum of the whole. No way would Tracy be sitting out on the swords match without a sweat on, which would mean she'd already had her turn. She wouldn't abstain without a reason. She's a true warrior, you can tell it, plus Ben admitted she's the one to watch for in a match. I didn't miss that fainting spell yesterday on the beach, either. But the big question is: Who's the father? Is it one of the guys here? Somehow I don't think so. But she's wearing a wedding band. So who is he?" Zach was completely into the game now.

Liz's smile faded completely. This was a quandary. How was she supposed to explain who Orli was to Zach?

"Well, it's complicated," she finally admitted. "He doesn't live near here, and they don't get to see each other often. But they have a love, a true and abiding love. He's going to be thrilled when he finds out about the baby."

"Going to be?" he was a little taken aback. "I would've thought Tracy would have told him already. I know I would want to get that kind of information immediately."

"As I said, it's complicated," Liz hedged, then lapsed into silence.

"Well, I should go take a shower," Zach said finally, pushing away from the wall. "It was good seeing you again, Liz. Do you practice down here as well?" Somehow he doubted it. She did not look the type to be wielding a sword.

"Liz's better at archery than swords, and no one can beat her at knives," Tracy's voice came from across the room. Zach laughed, knowing his entire conversation with Liz had been eavesdropped on from the beginning.

Mistaking his laugher for scorn, Liz's eyes narrowed and a light flush appeared over her cheeks. "Don't laugh," she warned. "I didn't come by my skills without a lot of hard training." A flash came through her mind, the memory of standing on the long, empty beach on the Isle of Silence, tossing knife after knife at the target, Valdeen watching from under the palm trees, encouraging her...

Liz shut the memory off with a snap. No use going down that path. One hand came up to touch her upper arm, feeling the scar left there by treachery. It was a pretty damn good reminder of what she'd been through.

"I wasn't belittling your skills," Zach said slowly, unsure of how to respond to her sudden prickliness. "I would like to see you in action."

"Maybe."

The frost was still there, he noted with a frown.

Ben ambled over, his face open and cheerful, but those ocean eyes of his were watching closely. "Great match, Zach," he said again. "I meant what I said about coming over and sparring. Any time. Just give us a holler, ok?"

Knowing he was being dismissed, Zach forced a grin on his face. "That's really good of you, Ben. I can't say how much I enjoyed this, although I'm sure there'll be hell to pay tomorrow."

"Well if you aren't too sore, stop by around the same time," Ben suggested as he untwisted a silvery necklace from under his shirt. "Maybe Tracy will be feeling up to taking you on," he added with a grin over his shoulder at the woman, who stuck her tongue out at him.

"I'll do that," Zach promised, and then turned towards Liz. "I look forward to seeing that demonstration with knives, Liz. I have a feeling it'll be one of the many things about you that will be amazing."

"Stop flirting with me," Liz demanded with frustration. It was impossible to stay angry with him for very long. "I much prefer you being honest and open than hiding behind that fake Zachary Neol exterior." She bracketed the air with her fingers as she said his name, like he was a brand name.

He put a hand over his heart as if wounded. "But I am Zachary Neol."

She shook her head slightly. "No you're not," she assured him. "You're so much more than that."

Zach's smile faded as he stared at her. "But I'm not joking about the amazing part," he said softly before moving off, saying goodbye to the others in the basement room.

As he let himself into the house, he was not surprised to find the phone ringing. Zach was tempted to ignore the incessant noise. His discussion with his agent yesterday had not gone well at all. Obviously, the man was bringing in the bigger guns; then he looked at the caller ID. It was his parents. Zach rubbed the phone against his forehead. Did he really want to deal with Harvey and Adele just now?

Deciding against it, he tossed the phone onto the sofa and headed for the shower. His muscles were already beginning to tighten up, and, if he didn't get them loose, he'd miss his chance to go back next door tomorrow. He was intrigued by the group of people inhabiting the house and was going to try and figure out what was making them tick. He also wanted to speak with the elusive and pretty Liz again.

The day seemed to creep by with excruciating slowness. Zach tried to entertain himself, playing some video games, surfing the Internet, reading a book. But nothing grabbed his attention more than keeping an eye on the house next door.

Tantalizing glimpses of Liz greeted him throughout the day as she and the others moved in and out of the house. They spent a lot of time on the deck, it seemed.

Seeing her playing with the small child—who did the child belong to, he wondered. He was amazed at the openness in her face. She allowed the little boy to hug her and climb on her, but Zach noticed that few of the others in the group touched her very often. Other than the petite brunette, Sarat, that was. She had no problem being near Liz, touching her often, and looking up at her friend with such impishness that it made Zach smile. But the rest gave her, if not a wide berth, at the very least, distance.

That, in and of itself, was odd because the group seemed to be very touchy-feely by nature. Hugs and kisses on the cheek seemed par for the course, as were arm and face touches. It was all very sweet, Zach thought. It certainly made him wistful for that kind of companionship. Sure, he could pick up the phone and with one or two calls have a house full of people. But would they be close friends? Zach had to admit, that would not be the case.

It was partly the fault of his lifestyle. Hollywood did not garner the kind of close friendships that ordinary Americans were used to experiencing. But if he were to be honest, it was partly his fault as well. He never wanted to find friends in that glitzy world. It never seemed worth it, although the logical part of him acknowledged that not all people in Hollywood were base and shallow.

It was best for him to stick to his current course of action. Stay out of the limelight, ignore the call of the press, his parents, his agent, and all the others. Let Zachary Neol fade into the woodwork. Then perhaps he could live a normal life. The residuals from his television shows were gone, thanks to his parents, but they couldn't touch the money he'd earned from *The Phoenix*. That income was enough to keep him in comfort for the rest of his life. He didn't need to work. Right now, he didn't want to work. Not as an actor, anyway.

Hell, he thought with a laugh. *I just don't know what I want to be when I grow up.*

-6-
Wooing the Protector

Zach could barely wait to get back to the basement. He came early intentionally, hoping to catch some of the people in the house alone. He wanted to find out more about Liz, and was hoping that he could glean some information from the others. Or, if he was going to be incredibly lucky, maybe he'd find the former librarian alone.

When he poked his head around the door, Zach gave a slow smile. Obviously, he was incredibly lucky. Liz was in the basement. Her back was to him. Today, she was clad in sweatpants and a clingy tank top that did wonders for her slim, yet delicately curved figure. At the opposite end of the basement was a large target.

As he watched, she sighted along her arm, her hand clenched around a knife blade. With a sudden movement, she drew her arm back and fluidly let loose.

Thud. It was a bull's eye, naturally. Zach let out a slow whistle and clapped, coming into the room.

Liz whirled at him, her next knife already back and ready to throw in his direction. Zach ducked to the side, throwing up his hands in self-defense.

"Wait, wait, wait!" he cried out, laughing. "I come in peace, I swear it!"

"Don't ever sneak up on me like that," Liz demanded, stamping her foot as she lowered her arm. "I could've hurt you."

"Judging by that target, I'd have to agree with you on that one," he said ruefully. "I won't make the same mistake again, I promise."

Liz crossed to the target and pulled out the knife. "You're early," she accused him. "Ben doesn't come down for another fifteen minutes or so. You can set your clock to that man when it comes to his morning workout. Swim first, then swords."

"Actually, I was kind of hoping I'd get a chance to see you," Zach admitted, hopping up on a table, his legs swinging. Liz gave him a sour look over her shoulder. "Seriously, I was, honest."

"I don't think you're being serious about this," Liz said irritably. "I think you're seeing me as an easy mark for your flirting. I fluster easier than the others would. Does that amuse you?"

"Hey, what the hell is this?" Zach said, jumping down and crossing over to where she was standing. Mindful of the personal space issue, he stopped several feet back. "I don't think you're an easy mark, as you say. I find that I like being around you. Why is that so far fetched?"

"Look at it from my point of view," she suggested, keeping her eyes on the cabinet in front of her, not daring to look back at him for fear of losing her nerve. "I'm a research librarian, you're a movie star. Not just any movie star, but the star of the biggest grossing picture of all time. Honestly, what would someone like you want with someone like me?"

"I don't know," he said with absolute honesty. "All I know is that I'm compelled to get to know you better. Do you have so little self worth that you feel you can't be interesting to a man like me?"

"Of course I'm worthy," Liz snapped, putting the knives in their holders with a harder push than was necessary. "It's just unexpected, that's all. I can't help but wonder if it's only the boredom of being stuck out on the isolated coast."

"This isn't the outer reaches, it's the outer banks," Zach chided her. "I've met all kinds of women, from all over the world. None of them, I promise, have made me want to come into a stinky, smelly basement gym and kiss them senseless."

She stiffened and Zach cursed. *Way to put step over the boundaries, Neol,* he told himself.

"It's too fast," she whispered. "It can't be real."

"It's too fast," he agreed, daring to reach out and finger one silky lock of her hair. It curled around his finger like a living thing.

Zach couldn't fathom why this attraction was so strong. It pulled at his body like an emotional tug of war. "But who is to say it isn't real. We won't know unless we try and find out. Who knows? It could just mean we are meant to be close friends. It could mean more. We'll never find out if you don't let me near you."

"Don't touch me," she whispered helplessly, turning towards him. The longing and terror in her face had him moving very slowly towards her, as if approaching a wild animal. "Don't," she repeated softly as he leaned near.

A hairsbreadth from her lips, he stopped. "Ok," he whispered. This close he could see every adorable freckle. "But I don't know how long I can hold off." He moved back smoothly.

Liz stared at him, a cascade of emotions crossing her face in a split second. Her brows creased slightly. "Sasha's getting married," she finally blurted.

Zach crossed his arms, because he was itching to touch her hair, her arms, her hands. "Really?" he said, not entirely sure he knew which one in the group was Sasha.

"We're having a party tomorrow night, a cocktail party," Liz rushed ahead. "It's actually a fund raiser for the Wrightstone Foundation, but we're also having it double as a kind of kick off to the wedding festivities."

"Ah, the Wrightstone Foundation. They do a lot of charity work."

"Yes. Anyway...would you like to go?" she asked breathlessly.

Zach gave a long, slow smile. "Yes," he said simply. "But only if I can call you my date."

"I think I can handle that," Liz managed as she turned and locked her knives away. Brushing her hands on either side of her hips, she gave him a little nod. "Tomorrow night, then. It's a black tie event, sorry about that. Seven o'clock?"

"I'll be there," he assured her, then frowned when she moved past him. "Wait! Aren't you staying?"

Ben came thundering down the stairs, pulling up short as he saw the two of them in the basement.

"No, I'm not staying," Liz was replying easily. "I have a dress fitting for the wedding to go to." She gave Ben a smile as he moved towards the weapon cabinet. "He's all yours, Harmertime."

"Hang on a second, Liz."

She paused on the steps, looking at Zach expectantly.

"What happened to your shoulder?" His voice was even, but she could sense an ocean of emotion just beneath the smooth surface.

"My shoulder?"

"I think he means your scar," said Ben, trying to be helpful.

Liz colored delicately, one hand reaching up to cover the jagged cut. "I was hurt."

"Car accident?"

"No. Blade. Knife."

Her curt words told Zach more than she knew. This was no accident. Someone had hurt her. The sensation of wanting to rip someone apart limb by limb sprang foremost into his mind. But before he could say anything, Liz moved lithely up the stairs and out of sight.

"It's just you and me, buddy," Ben said, clapping his hand on Zach's shoulder. "All the chicks are heading out for the bridal store." He rolled his eyes expressively.

"Good," Zach said with a real gleam in his eye. "I need to work off some tension."

"Live near this house long and you'll only survive by having these sparring sessions," Ben assured him, unlocking the sword cabinet. "I swear these women will make me gray before my time."

"You're close with them, huh?"

"Yeah," came the simply and steady reply.

"How did you guys meet?"

"I met Katie and Tracy several years ago. Then we found Sasha, then Sarat and finally Liz. Glad to see someone else male, let me tell you," Ben decided it prudent to skip the other male Protector, Jay, seeing as he was still living in the Land. It was all confusing enough without adding that to the mix.

"Veritable harem you've got here," Zach observed, taking up the sword he had used the previous day and thinking it was weird that Ben wasn't including any of the men he'd met in the dissertation of the relationships.

"Don't let them hear you say that," Ben advised. "They start thinking up horrible names for me when I start acting too male-ish for their likes. Besides, they know that I'm deeply involved with my wife. I have no time for anyone else in my life romantically. It actually makes it all easier on us, without there being sexual tension between us. We're all just friends. But sometimes it's difficult with them all being females."

"What about Katie's husband and Owen? And that doctor guy I keep hearing about? Don't they count?" Zach asked, watching Ben carefully. If he hadn't been looking so closely, he would have missed the slight hesitation in the man's swinging arm. But he did see it, and filed it away for later consideration.

"They definitely matter," Ben said finally, "but the girls and I, well, we're the core of the group. I know that sounds self righteous and corny, but I really can't explain it any better."

"Can't or won't?" Zach challenged, raising his sword.

"You figure it out," Ben said back, doing the same. Within seconds the battle had begun, as fierce and thick as the one the day before.

It was a long bout, with several rest periods where Ben and Zach prowled opposite ends of the gym like large jungle cats stalking their prey. Zach was in his element. His blood was singing in his veins, he was more alive than he had been in months. It was wonderful, this feeling. Damn, he loved sword work. It had been his favorite part about working on *The Phoenix,* and he was kicking himself mentally that he'd let it slide after the movie's wrap. He should have found someone to spar with long ago.

A couple hours later, bruised, and in Zach's case bleeding, they finally ground to a halt. Ben was lying on the mat, his arms outstretched as he gasped for breath. Zach was sitting with his back against the wall, his head hanging, an empty bottle of water in one hand.

"We cannot do that every day," Ben declared.

"No way. We'd kill each other," Zach said, agreeing wholeheartedly.

"Every other day?"

"Done."

"All righty then," Ben sat up, groaning and twisting his head first one way, then the other with a resounding crack.

"Ouch," Zach said absently, examining the shallow cut on the inside of his forearm.

"Sorry about that," Ben commented, honest regret in his voice as he eyed the nasty scratch.

"I was referring to that God-awful sound your neck made, not my arm. Don't even worry about that, it was my own fault. I'll consider it a war wound."

Ben shook his head. "You do that," he advised, lying back down on the mat. "Hope it doesn't scar, though. That'd be hard to explain to your agent, I'm sure."

"That is the least of my worries, mate," Zach said flippantly, then he turned serious. "So you're a painter, right?"

Ben rolled on his side. "Right," he said only, keeping his gaze steady on the actor.

"Owen Montclaire is the famous children's author," Zach continued, "and Katie and her husband are the executors of the vast Wrightstone Estate."

"You've been doing some homework," Ben observed slowly.

"Well, I'd already figured out that it's you, Katie, Tracy, Sarat, Sasha and Liz that are in this little group Liz was talking about. You confirmed it for me when I came in earlier. You all wear the same necklace. Like a talisman or a badge of honor." Zach smiled as Ben rubbed his pendant self-consciously. "See? You guys are always touching them, fiddling with the chain. It's some sort of tangible reminder, but of what, I haven't a clue."

"You're damned observant," Ben said slowly, feeling he was in unchartered waters.

"I'd be a fool not to be," Zach replied. "Tell me about Liz."

"Well that's pretty blunt," Ben said tartly, giving Zach another searching look. "If you want to know about Liz, I suggest you ask her yourself."

"I plan on it," Zach promised, "I was just wondering if you'd care to give me any insight, that's all."

Ben sighed, running a thumb over the edge of his sword. "Liz is...complex. Just walk carefully, Zach. She was involved with a guy about six months ago. He hurt her badly. Not just physically hurt," he hurried on as he noticed Zach stiffen in outrage. "It was more a mental thing, with the exception of well...you saw the scar. I think it's pretty insignificant compared to what happened to her mentally. Liz is going to be leery, and understandably so, when it comes to men. I can't blame her. And I will protect her if I think she's being played. That's a promise, Zach."

For several seconds Zach simply couldn't think through the fog of anger that crowded his cerebrum, demanding vengeance and retribution and all manner of dark things. With effort, he shoved them aside. This was not going to be about his outrage at Liz's hurt or Ben's insinuation that he would ever harm her…it was about Liz.

There was a thundering sound overheard. "The girls must be back," Ben said. "Owen, Steven and William hightailed it out to sea for some deep sea fishing first thing. They won't be home yet. And they don't make near as much noise."

Sure enough, Katie, Amber, Tracy, Sarat, Sasha and Liz came tumbling down the stairs, a chatty mass of laughter, bouncing hair and perfume. They stopped short when they spied Ben and Zach, taking in their exhaustion.

"Battle to the end, eh?" Amber said, wandering over and eying them appreciatively.

"The bitter end," Ben agreed with an easy smile.

"Zach, you're hurt," Katie exclaimed, rushing over to examine his arm, Amber and Sarat close behind.

Zach let them tut over his wound, a minor scratch to his way of thinking. There was something comforting about the way the women were worrying about him. Katie gave Ben a scathing look. "Shame on you, Benjamin Harm! He's out of practice and you went and hurt him."

"I'm not that out of practice," Zach said, while Ben chimed in, "He said it as his own fault."

Liz silently handed Amber some gauze she had retrieved from the first aid kit on the shelf. "That's going to scar unless you get it bandaged up and keep slathering it with antibiotic cream."

"I can do it," Zach said, trying to take the kit from Amber, who waved him off and started to care for the wound, sprinkling a little fairy healing on the skin when Zach wasn't paying attention. He was just too pretty, in her estimation, to allow that cut to scar.

"This is pretty deep," muttered Amber.

"So how was shopping?" Ben asked desperately, seeing that Katie's eyes were narrowing, a sure sign that the Oracle was getting ready to slam him again for putting their neighbor, and possible Traveler, at risk. Any diversion would do.

"We found the best CDs!" Sarat exclaimed. "For the reception. Listen to this."

She slapped a CD in the portable boom box. A swing band tune blared forth, ricocheting off the walls and filling the basement. Sarat snapped her fingers. "I love this stuff."

Ben exchanged wry glances with Sasha. "Sarat has discovered swing music," Sasha pointed out unnecessarily. "God help us all."

His wound medicated and bandaged, Zach stood up, bouncing on the balls of his feet. "Excellent," he said, then swooped Sarat onto the middle of the dance floor. With a series of exuberant steps, he guided Sarat into an impromptu swing dance lesson, shouting out words of encouragement and instruction as they went.

The rest of the Protectors watched, laughing. Ben stepped out with Amber, who proved she was no slouch in the dance department either. Zach wheeled off Sarat and grabbed Sasha's hand, pulling her out for a spin, then moved on to Katie, who actually squealed when Zach tossed her high in the air.

Zach approached Tracy with a gleam in his eyes. "Not going to flip me or anything, are ya?" he asked with such good humor that Tracy had to laugh and shake her head, joining him on the mat. Zach was careful not to spin the tall woman too much, cognizant of her probably still uneasy stomach.

Finally, Liz was the only one left. Zach was out of breath, and curious to see if she would actually take the hand he outstretched to her. She hesitated visibly, and then seemed to steel herself and put her hand in his. Little did he know that in that hesitation, she had bolstered her internal defenses against penetrating his mind or seeing his future. As she took his hand, the music changed to a tango beat.

"Ah, the dance," he whispered, pulling her close to him. "You've got the height and build for it, Liz. Go with the flow, darlin'."

With Zach whispering instructions and pulling long ago ballet lessons from the dim recesses of her mind, Zach and Liz moved across the floor. "It's like being in a movie," she said to him at one point, then blushed at his laugh.

"Then lets give it a movie finish," Zach vowed, twirling around tightly then dipping her deeply. As she looked up at him, his blue eyes so close to hers, Liz's defenses slipped slightly and her agile Seering mind reached out almost instinctively for Zach.

Instantly, images assaulted both of their minds, a mutual corridor of thought flowing freely between them, unstoppable. Terra cotta blocks, slightly damp and decrepit looking, a corridor of stone lit by the torch behind held aloft. Desperation and dismay at not finding what is being sought. The sense that danger was just around the corner, and behind, and above, permeating the space like fog. The images and sensations slammed into them full force with wrenching emotional fervor. They could smell the moldy dampness, feel the grainy texture of the air pressing against them like wet gauze.

Zach's hold on Liz slipped, and she fell to the floor cracking her elbow against the mats. Zach landed next to her, barely catching himself in time to keep his famous nose from crashing into the mat. He rolled to one side, sitting up in a lithe motion.

"What the hell was that?" Zach cried out, clutching at his head. Liz looked equally stunned.

Katie moved forward, the glow in her palms almost nonexistent. She'd become very good at disguising the outward show of power when she used it. Passing a hand over the back of Zach's head in the guise of helping him up with Ben and Tracy's help, she eased his headache greatly.

"Sorry," Liz gasped, crabbing backwards on the mat, tripping over herself in her haste to get away from him. "I'm so sorry."

"Was that the future I just saw?" Zach asked into the dead silence that descended over the room, making the room throb with suppressed tension. "Because that was unlike anything I've ever seen in my life."

"I don't know what it was," Liz said, miserable, swiping under her eyes.

"It's ok, Liz. I don't think you did it on purpose. What are you, psychic or something?" pressed Zach.

Tracy moved forward, chin thrust forward aggressively, "She doesn't have to answer that."

"Yes, I do," Liz said with great dignity. Standing up she looked down at Zach still on the floor. "I'm not a psychic dabbling with crystal balls or tarot cards. I don't predict that people will meet someone tall, dark and handsome. I never mess with the black arts. I am what is known as a Seer."

"A seer…" he mulled the word over, worrying it in his mouth as his mind slowly cranked back into gear. "Ok, just what is that?"

"I am a Seer, and whether or not you come to understand what that means will be up to you and how you deal with the future we just saw together, Zachary," she said before she turned on her heel and stalked off.

"Huh," Zach said as he stared at her going up the steps. "Guess she told me," he said in a wry aside to Katie, who was glaring at him with her wide blue eyes. "Seer, huh? What does that make you? I did see that pink glow of yours…"

"You don't want to even go there," Katie warned him softly.

Zach's smile faded in the face of her vehemence, as well as in response to the welling of power that was emanating from the petite woman.

"All right, then," Zach said slowly, rising from the mat. He looked around the room, taking in all the serious faces. "Look, I know I just stepped my foot into something bigger than I understand. I'll just go home now, and leave things be. Thanks for the work out, Ben," he said as he left the gymnasium, closing the door behind him.

Moonlit Flora

Zach was decidedly nervous about how he was going to be received at the cocktail party/fundraiser. He wasn't sure if he was even still invited after the debacle in the gym, but decided to take a chance. He'd dressed in his custom fitted tuxedo, carefully setting the studs and cufflinks he'd given himself after completing *The Phoenix*. It was hard to do by himself, but finally he had the ruby and gold cufflinks in place. They were a favorite of his, the gold shaped into a flame with a single round ruby at the end. Although truth be told, most people thought the gold looked like a leaf. He checked himself in the mirror to make sure everything was ready to go. He smirked slightly when he realized that the last time he had donned the tux, it had been for the Oscars a mere month earlier. My, how times had changed.

Zach picked up the two bouquets of flowers he'd gotten at the florist that afternoon. He glanced out the window of his bedroom overlooking the party in progress next door. People were floating in and out of the house, onto the back deck, the pool area. The whole house was lit up with lanterns and Christmas lights, and the sound of music was wafting over the surf's rumble. Zach could see waiters circling, handing out appetizers. Although he looked closely, and could see many of the other housemates, he did not see Liz roaming about in the mix.

Taking a deep breath, Zach walked to the bottom of the house, tossing his cell phone to one side. No way was he taking that thing with him. He didn't want, need, or desire to speak with anyone. Not anyone who had his cell number, anyway.

He'd given a great deal of thought to the weird vision he'd had the day before and to Liz's words.

So she was a Seer. He knew the term and had actually looked it up on the Internet to make sure he was giving it the right definition. He'd been right that the word meant someone who has the gift of prophecy.

Zach had lived long enough in the make believe world of television and movies to have met a large number of people who believed in different ideologies and concepts. He liked to think he was open to such individuals and open to learning more about their different viewpoints. He wasn't ready to rule out the possibility of someone being able to foresee the future. He wasn't ready to embrace it, but he wasn't ready to completely deny the possibility.

Because that vision had seemed so…real. He had been able to smell the musty dampness, feel the mist on his skin. The large terra cotta bricks were vaguely familiar to him, as well. He'd literally felt the metal of the sword in his hand, the weight of the steel familiar. But it had not been his sword, the one he had used in *The Phoenix*. It had been different, the golden hilt more elaborately carved and set with various stones. Odd, how he could remember the way the hilt had looked with surprising clarity given he'd only been in the vision for mere seconds.

Zach decided it was time to stop stalling. Letting himself out of the house, he walked up his long driveway and then down the walkway of his neighbor's house. A tuxedoed butler was at the door taking names and invitations. Zach gave his name, although the rather stunned look on the man's face indicated he had recognized Zach. After consulting the list, he nodded and moved to the side.

"Welcome, Mr. Neol. The bar is off the main living area, and a secondary bar is by the pool. We hope you enjoy the evening, and be sure to visit the silent auction on the upstairs terrace. Mr. Harm has rounded up some very nice artwork to be auctioned off tonight."

"What's the cause?" Zach asked, suddenly realizing he had no clue what the fundraiser was for and feeling rather foolish about that fact.

"The Alicia Wrightstone Foundation. They research various medical conditions, but tonight's event is for the branch that deals with those who are suffering irreversible comas." The butler intoned, as if reading from a script.

"Ah," Zach said and moved into the room. Spying Sasha standing next to a tall man he'd never seen before, Zach walked over.

"Good evening," he said, handing one of the bouquets of flowers to Sasha. "May I take the chance to formally congratulate you on your upcoming wedding?"

Sasha dimpled prettily. "Oh, how sweet of you to bring me flowers," she exclaimed, breathing in the scent of the white roses. "Zachary Neol, I'd like you to meet my fiancé, Dr. William Luke."

The man at her side also smiled, extending his hand for a firm shake. "Nice to meet you, Mr. Neol. I must say, I thoroughly enjoyed your movie." His crystal blue eyes were sincere in his praise, his sunburned, aristocratic face glowing as he looked back down at Sasha.

"It's Zach, and thanks for the compliment," said Zach, glancing around. "Um, have you seen Liz?"

Sasha eyed the peach roses in his hands. Quirking up an eyebrow, she grinned. "Nice touch," she chuckled. "Liz is a sucker for roses."

"She's a romantic, not a sucker," Zach protested lightly, earning him an appreciative look from the pair.

"She's up on the terrace, I think," William said, sliding an arm around his beloved. "Watching over the artwork and the auction. Liz… doesn't like crowds. Tonight's going to be very difficult for her."

"Because she's a Seer?"

"I still can't believe she told you that," said Sasha sharply. "And I'd thank you to keep your voice down when discussing the issue."

William's hand squeezed his fiancé's waist as he leaned over to whisper in her ear just loud enough for Zach to hear, "Trust Liz's judgment, Sasha." To her credit, Sasha refrained from further comment.

Zach gave them a wave and headed in the direction Sasha had pointed. As he passed, he nodded at Amber, Katie, and Tracy, grouped by the front window looking delectable in their formal wear. Sarat and Owen passed by him as well, the former giving him a kiss on the check as she sauntered by in a red dress designed for sin. He gave an appreciative wolf whistle as she passed causing the woman to giggle with delight. To his relief, no one seemed bent on tossing his sorry ass out into the cool OBX night, so whatever his transgression in the gym, it appeared to be forgiven. Of course, other party goers recognized him, and he was forced to stop and shake hands and sign the occasional autograph as he worked his way across the room.

Zach climbed the stairs to the next level, passing by several interesting paintings hung on the walls. He examined them, not surprised to find that they had been painted by Ben. He found he liked the quiet strength of the works. As he rounded the corner, he found Ben himself sipping a drink as he perched on the short wall that lined the top of the stairwell. The man was dressed in a tux with a black shirt, making his blond hair and blue green eyes much more pronounced. Zach noticed with amusement that Ben's shoes were kicked off, his long toes beating time to the music floating up from the poolside DJ.

Noticing where Zach was looking, Ben gave a chuckle. "Hate shoes. They never fit me right," he complained, sliding them back on. "For little ole' me?" he asked, tilting his head to one side as he took in the roses.

"No, they aren't your style. You're more a carnation guy, I would think," said Zach, grateful that the man also seemed to take his appearance in stride.

Ben laughed. "Sorry for the scene in the gym," he said, reading Zach's mind. "We're a little touchy about some things."

"No worries."

"Want to see the artwork?" Ben stood up and gestured towards the first easel. "We've gathered several originals from local artists to auction off. The proceeds will benefit research into those in long-term comas. It's a special project of ours."

"Because of Alicia Wrightstone," Zach murmured, looking at the paintings. Most were the usual insipid nautical themes, but a few had the bright colors and sharp angles of modern art. There was one that was clearly a Harm, since it was similar in style to the ones in the stairway. Zach walked back and forth in front of it, enjoying the different views of the oceanscape and how the light reacted against the canvas. Yeah, he did like the man's artistic style. Making a snap decision, Zach picked up the pen beneath the painting and made a bid on the clipboard, knowing the sum he put down would guarantee him the Harm for his house.

"You didn't have to do that," Ben said quietly from behind him.

Zach met his gaze steadily. "I know," was all he said before turning to look at the next piece. As he did, a movement out on the terrace caught his attention.

It was Liz.

Wearing a filmy long dress in sea foam green, gathered on one shoulder in a Grecian way, panels of flowing chiffon blowing in the breeze, she was staring at him. Her hair was in an intricate bun, the kind that Zach knew took forever to pull off but still managed to appear delicate.

Without another word to Ben, Zach moved out onto the terrace. Liz was watching him, her topaz eyes clear. "You look amazing," Zach breathed, then handed her the roses. Out of the corner of his eye he saw Ben heading down the stairs and took a moment to silently thank the man for leaving him some privacy with Liz.

"Thank you, and might I add, you don't look to bad yourself," Liz admitted as she took a deep sniff of the fragrant flowers. "You clean up nicely, Mr. Neol."

"I do," he agreed, putting his elbows on the terrace wall and looking out to the sea. "I'm sorry if I offended you yesterday," he said sincerely. "It just surprised me. You have to admit, it's not every day one meets someone who can foresee the future."

"Don't laugh about it," she warned him, her voice low and harsh.

"I'm not," Zach assured her quickly, "just seeking a little more information. Have you always been able to see the future?"

"No. Yes. Sort of," she said hesitantly, then plowed forward. "When I was young, I had flashes about people and events, but it was uncontrolled and I was able to suppress it after my parents died. Then, about six months ago, I had an…event. You could say my inner eye was revealed and couldn't be covered, no matter what. Since then, I've been learning the craft of Seering. I can't always keep from seeing flashes of someone's future when I touch them, so I tend to avoid that kind of contact."

"Ah, that's why you don't want me to touch you," Zach said knowingly.

"Doesn't matter now," she admitted wryly. "I can read you loud and clear whether we're touching or not. You have a very insistent subconscious, Zachary."

"Really?" he was intrigued despite himself. "I must say, I'm kind of surprised you're telling me all this. I get the feeling that you guys don't go around proclaiming your abilities to the world."

"You guys?" she parroted, tilting her head to one side.

"Well, Katie's got something going, that much I know. And I'm beginning to wonder if that group Ben talked about has something to do with the necklaces…" He trailed one finger under the delicate silver chain around her neck, but Liz pulled back slightly and he didn't press.

"We don't talk about it much," she said enigmatically.

"Then why are you telling me?"

"Because you need to know," she said calmly, despite the pulse beating wildly at the base of her throat. "You are going to be Traveling, Zachary. I'm sure of it. I need to give you as much information as possible before you do."

"Where am I going on this great trip?" Zach asked, trying to interject a joking tone to the conversation, which was getting far too serious for his liking.

"You aren't ready for that information," Liz said in a slightly chiding voice.

"Ah, mystery. I love a good mystery. Here's one I'm working on right now," Zach said, pulling Liz's drink from her hands and setting it on the railing along with his own. "I'm wondering what will happen if I kiss you. Will I see my future again?"

"I don't know," Liz said truthfully. Her mind was busy turning over the interesting angle of kissing and how that might affect her inner sight, when suddenly his lips were on hers.

He'd leaned over so just their lips were touching. Liz barely had time to register the fact that she was kissing Zachary Neol when, just as suddenly, his lips withdrew. Liz raised her fingers to her suddenly tingling lips, her forehead creasing into a frown.

"Now, that solves that mystery. If just our lips touch, no visions," Zach said with approval. "But it's not a very satisfactory way to kiss, is it? So let's take this experiment a step further and go for the gusto, shall we?"

Liz realized he was really asking her permission to kiss her again.

Her head was nodding before her mind could catch up with common sense.

"Excellent," Zach said and pulled her into his arms, this time kissing her with, as he put it, gusto.

Liz grabbed at his shoulders, the only solid thing in her existence at the moment. His arms came around her waist, firmly holding her against him as his mouth, that glorious mouth she had seen on the huge movie screen, worked magic.

The sound of people laughing as they came up the stairs had them breaking apart like children being caught by their parents on the living room sofa. Zach melted into the shadows as a group came up ooh and aah over the paintings. Liz, despite her pounding pulse, managed to pull it together enough to go inside and explain the auction. When the last one had clattered down the stairs again, Liz returned to the terrace, warily holding up her hand as Zach moved forward.

"Stay back," she warned, her voice still shaky.

"Why?" he pressed, smiling. "You were enjoying that as much as me."

"I know I did," Liz said, then blushed hotly at his laugh. "Stop it, I'm serious, stay over there!"

"Ok, no more kisses. For now," Zach said, realizing she was truly frazzled. He enjoyed knowing he had gotten her that way. He leaned against the balcony, picking up his glass again, taking a bolstering sip. "Honest," he said when she continued to eye him, her fingers running up and down the silver chain she wore around her neck.

"All right," Liz said reluctantly, leaning her hip against the wall.

"So tell me about this trip," Zach suggested, reaching for her hand.

"Can you come over tomorrow?" Liz asked in way of reply. "I'd like you to read something. You'll find it easier to understand if you have some background."

"Yes, teacher," he said, making her laugh.

A shout came from below. Liz pulled her hand from Zach's and leaned over the balcony. One floor below, Tracy, Sasha and Ben were looking up at her.

"How's the auction going?" Ben called up, amusement in his voice.

"Fine," she called back down, itching to throw an ice cube at the man.

Zach came up behind her, slipping his arms around her waist. "Is this ok?" he asked into her ear. Liz shivered and nodded, easing into his chest infinitesimally. Zach relished the sensation.

As they watched the sea, the scene before them shifted slightly. Liz instinctively started to pull away from Zach, but he whispered into her ear, "Be still. Let's see where this takes us, Seer of mine."

The ocean became more blue and calmer. The smell of the sea was tangy and close, the breeze was balmy and soft to their skin. Instead of standing on the balcony of the beach house, Liz and Zach were standing on the stone terrace of a tall tower overlooking a pristine, white beach bordered on one side by the ocean, the other side by swaying green palm trees.

"The Isle of Silence," Liz whispered, recognizing it from her time in exile. "I stayed there when I was learning to become a Seer. I actually think I hate that place...is this the past I'm seeing?"

As if in answer to the question, the two of them soared off the terrace, over the sea. It should have been a disconcerting sensation, but seemed so normal, so natural that Zach didn't have a chance to panic as he flew on unseen wings. Zach had no knowledge of what he was seeing, but Liz knew. Oh, she knew. Ahead, the Beaches of the Land loomed, the Mountain Region rising behind them. Quickly they passed over the rocky heights until they came to the Meadows Region. The grasslands stretched on, farmland dotting the countryside like a patchwork quilt.

Then they saw it. The terra cotta brick was familiar to them from the previous vision, but, clearly, this was the outside of the structure. It was built like an old Aztec temple, a step stone pyramid, squat and dense. It was overgrown with vines and appeared completely windowless. The structure looked completely out of place in the Meadows Region, an anomaly that was alien to the delicate plants and flowers growing around it.

"I've never seen that before," Liz said, bewildered. "Surely someone would have said something about a huge pyramid structure in the middle of the Meadows Region, or I would have seen it when I astral projected before..."

"Shhh," Zach admonished into her ear, watching the scene as if it were a giant movie he was immersed into. "You're talking too much. Just…take it in." He was still close behind her and she leaned back into him, enjoying his solid weight from shoulder to hips, knowing he was there, and she was…safe.

They circled over the temple-like pyramid, dropping closer to it. The vines, they could see, were adorned with spikes easily a foot long. In addition, animals with large teeth seemed to be crawling all over the bricks snarling up at them; their black fur bristling. Finally, they could discern a doorway, nestled in one of the sides of the pyramid. It could be seen from overhead, but not, they noticed, when their viewpoint dropped down to see the structure from ground level.

"What's being kept in there?" Zach wondered.

"Why do you say that?" Liz asked.

"It's obviously a fortress of some sort," Zach replied. "Hidden doorway, no windows, defenses along the outer walls. Someone has gone to a lot of trouble to keep something or someone safe inside that structure."

His words seemed to trigger a response as they pulled back rapidly, zooming straight up until the Land was but a pinprick before their eyes. Then it simply blinked out, leaving them looking out over the Atlantic Ocean.

"Well, that was different," Liz said, passing a hand over her eyes, swaying slightly. She swallowed, disoriented, a little nauseous from the vision, her head aching.

"I'll say," Zach agreed, keeping a grip on her as he experienced the aftereffects of the projection himself. "You recognized part of it, obviously. Where is that place?"

"We call it the Land," Liz said, emphasizing the 'L' so that Zach knew it was said with a capital letter.

"Is that where I'm going to visit?" Zach asked, feeling the whole night had taken on a surreal aspect.

Liz slanted him a look over her shoulder. "You seem to be taking this rather calmly," she said, remembering her own rather hysterical response to learning about the Land.

"Believe me, I'm a sea of turmoil," he said with a chuckle. The beads of sweat on his forehead seemed to emphasize this fact.

"We'll talk about it tomorrow," she promised, leaning back into him. For several moments they rested against one another, both painfully aware that this kind of easy intimacy was alien to both of them, yet it was so damn good and right that indulging in the sensation was essential. Finally, Zach stirred.

"Fair enough. Listen, I have another silly question. What's up with that little tree in the corner? I noticed it when you were inside with that last group of people."

In his arms, Liz stiffened noticeably. "What tree?" she asked carefully and slowly.

Zach released her and turned her by the shoulders pointing into the shadows. "The one over there. Is it some sort of prop or something? Because if it is, you shouldn't have it in the shadows. You can barely see the colors from here."

"What colors do you see?" she asked faintly, her hand running up and down the silver chain rapidly, pulling the necklace out from her skin. Zach could see her pulse beating frantically at the base of her neck.

"Golden leaves. Dark red trunk. And fruit on it, but that fruit is a different color red than the trunk," Zach recited, squinting slightly as he studied the tree. "Hey, they kind of look like my cuff links, now that I think about it. Damn, maybe the gold is leaves instead of a flame." He held up his wrists so that Liz could see them. Her topaz eyes widened as she looked at the cuffs, then at the tree, then back to Zach.

Liz leaned over the balcony. Seeing Ben was still on the next level, now standing with Katie and Tracy, she yelled down at them.

"*Guys!*"

They looked up, startled. Liz never bellowed. Liz gestured at them to come upstairs. She turned around and told Zach, "Don't touch that Tree, do you understand me? Wait right here and don't move."

That's the funny thing, Zach thought as she raced inside. When someone tells you not to do something, it becomes the only thing you want to do. He wandered over to the tree, trying to get a better look at it without touching it. It was hidden in a planter with some potted flowers clustered around its base.

Liz was waiting at the top of the stairs as the Protectors ascended. "He can see the Tree. Land colors and all," she said breathlessly. "We saw the Land, a vision of some sort of fortress in the Meadows and he kissed me and he saw the Isle of Silence."

"He kissed you?" Tracy said, delighted, then fell silent. "Ok, that was obviously the wrong thing to focus on," she muttered as they raced across the room. As she came onto the terrace, Liz gasped at what she saw.

Zach was kneeling next to the Tree, having pushed the flowerpots surrounding it out of the way. He was reaching for the pot holding the Tree, but he didn't realize that one of the branches was dangerously close to his skin.

Ben dove past Liz, pushing her to one side with a barely muttered apology. He grabbed onto Zach's jacket with one hand just as the actor's wrist brushed the Tree branch. With a snick and a click, they were both gone.

-8-
Wayside

Zach fell face first into dirt, Ben landing heavily on his back.

"Ge' off!" the actor yelled into the ground, spitting out dirt. He gave a sigh of relief when the man rolled off him. Damn, that guy was big. It was dark, but a full moon overhead shone down on them.

"What the hell just happened?" Zach asked as he stood up, brushing off his tux pants. Peering down, he frowned at a grass stain on the knees that was barely visible by the light of the moon. He turned to see Ben standing near him, scanning the night sky. His mind recalled a fuzzy vision of melding colors, a sense of up being down, and the strange belief that he was, finally, coming home.

"We Traveled," Ben replied, turning and looking in the opposite direction. "Ok, so we're in Meadows Region. But where? *Where*, damn it?" he muttered, spinning in another circle, trying to get his bearings.

"Traveled? Through a tree?"

That was a bizarre enough statement, yet Zach could not deny what had happened. He remembered a folding sensation, the vision of a kaleidoscope of colors cascading around him, the feeling of Ben's hand as it grasped his tuxedo jacket, nearly dragging it from his body. And now, Zach knew he was definitely someplace different. Beneath his feet was a carpet of grass, and there was not a hint of salt in the air, nor the sound of the ocean. Instead there was the gentle ripple of a breeze over grass. He could smell flowers, and the soft earth. Also a suggestion of wood smoke, as if someone had lit a fire nearby. The air was incredibly fresh and clean, a clear shot of energy that was singing through his veins with every breath. Involuntarily, he sucked in a deep lungful, savoring it like a fine wine on his tongue, sifting through the nuances of the sensation with delight.

Ben pointed. "Aha! I think there's some sort of town over the next hill. See how the night sky is lighter? Not Convergence, it's far too small, but we're near the mountains." His voice was musing, as if confused.

Zach looked to one side and sure enough a dark mass appeared to be rising along the horizon. Those must be the mountains Ben had referenced. Lord knew, he was absolutely lost. None of the stars above looked familiar to him, and the feeling of distance, travel, time…it was all indelibly marked on him.

A wary voice came out of the darkness. "Who are you? Where did you come from?"

Ben held out his hands in the universal sign of peace. "I am Ben Harm, Protector of the Land, from the World Dimension," he replied loudly. "We just arrived here, but I have to confess, I don't know where we are."

A flare of light and a torch was lit. It showed a trio of men, all holding some sort of weapon. The two not holding the torch were training arrows on Ben and Zach, while the one with the torch was holding a short sword in his other hand.

"Ben Harm?" the man with the sword said dubiously. "And how do I know this assertion is true?" He was tall and thin, with a long fall of dark hair that fell past his shoulders.

"Hang on," Ben tugged at his bowtie. "Damn these things," he muttered, then pulled apart his shirt, tugging out the necklace around his neck, the pendant twisting and turning in the meager light thrown from the torches.

Zach stared at it, dumbfounded. At the beach house, the pendant had been dull pewter, with a barely perceived tree etched in it. Now, it was a circle of bright gold, with a ruby tree and gold leaves. The glint of the pendant's appearance had an immediate effect on the men. The weapons were lowered and smiles revealed.

"Welcome, Ben Harm, Protector of the Land," the man said, bowing with one hand over his heart. "I am Azi, of the village Wayside."

"Wayside?" Ben repeated, his voice puzzled. Zach was not feeling entirely confident about the whole thing.

"We are a small trading village along the border of Mountains and Meadows Region. For those who do not wish to go into Convergence," said Azi in a helpful voice.

"Ah, I remember that town now," Ben said, smacking his forehead. "I recall seeing it marked on a map at the Capital City."

"You were not expected to be here tonight, but I can take you to the Seer if you would like," Azi offered, sheathing his sword.

"The Seer's here?" Ben asked, his voice raising. Azi nodded, and gestured towards a path. Ben followed, Zach trailing behind, mulling over the fact that there was a seer, here, as well. Connections began to form in his agile mind.

"Any chance of filling me in on what is going on here?" Zach asked Ben in an undertone as they walked over a small hill. Now, ahead of them, they could see a grouping of low-lying buildings, most of them dark for the night. Smoke curled from chimneys, which explained what Zach had smelled earlier. Ben looked at him and shook his head.

"Later," he said, nodding pointedly at the other men surrounding them. "I need to figure it all out first."

The trip to the village did not take long and soon Azi was showing them to a cottage settled in the middle of the town. Ben thanked the man for his assistance then knocked on the door. Azi and his companions faded back into the village, probably going back to their stations to continue the night watch. The door of the cottage opened; the light from within casting a golden glow around the woman on the threshold.

She was tall and slender with a shaggy haircut in deep auburn. The small laugh lines around her brownish green eyes were a testament to her cheerful nature. She was barefoot, clad in a long slender dress of soft yellow. Zach was strongly reminded of Liz by the way the woman held herself, so tall and straight, but with an aura of serenity that was tangible. When she saw Ben she clapped her hands delightedly, then held out her arms.

"Ben," she exclaimed, pulling him into a massive hug. "I can't believe it's you. I had just decided to call out to you tomorrow but you show up on my doorstep. Serendipity." She chatted excitedly as she pulled him into the cottage. Ben, his face wreathed in smiles, looked back at Zach.

"Come on in," he told the actor, who followed him into the cottage.

Inside, a fire was dancing in the hearth and several lamps were assisting in casting the area in warm yellow light. There were two narrow beds against one wall and a table and chairs against the other. In front of the fireplace sat two rockers, one of which was occupied by a bear of a man. He stood as Ben and Zach entered showing that he was roughly Zach's size. He was dressed in forest green and brown with a red slash of material across his broad, muscular chest. He pulled Ben into a solid hug, thumping his back soundly. It was obvious that Ben was well known by the pair.

"Who have you brought to visit us?" the woman asked, looking at Zach curiously.

"This is Zach Neol," Ben gave the introductions, turning to the actor. "Zach, I'd like you to meet the Seer of the Land and Maxt, Captain of the Prince's Guard. They're old and dear friends."

"Who are you calling old?" the Seer said to Ben in a mockingly vicious tone. "Don't you look handsome, Benjamin Harm. Two gorgeous men in tuxedos visiting me in Wayside. Of course, I am curious to know how you knew I was in this particular town, but I'm sure that will all come out eventually." As she spoke, she pulled two chairs out from the table and set them near the fireplace. Then she turned to Zach, holding out her hands. Automatically, Zach took them. Her hands were warm to the touch and her gaze was direct.

"Welcome to the Land, Zachary Neol," she said softly. "Sit. I am sure you have a lot of questions. Perhaps we can answer them." She gave his hands a reassuring squeeze before releasing him to resume her seat in the remaining rocking chair.

Zach settled on the chair. The other man, Maxt, was assessing him with shrewd green eyes that were shot through with molten gold. Zach had a feeling that not much got by the man. He seemed to be, by his very nature, a watcher and a warrior. Not sure why, Zach gave the man a curt nod in response to the appraisal. Maxt's lips curled into a slow smile.

"You were going to call me tomorrow?" Ben said to the Seer, settling his pants crease with one hand as he reclined in the chair. "Why is that? Why aren't you in the Mountain Village?"

"Because the Village Elder has become opposed to anything connected with the Protectors," said a voice from the shadows of the room. A tall man came forward, the firelight bringing the angled planes of his face and piercing brown eyes into sharp relief. He, like Maxt, was dressed in browns and greens, an ivory shirt underneath the short jerkin he wore over his surprisingly broad shoulders. Yet his outfit didn't remind Zach of a uniform the way Maxt's did.

"Orli!" Ben exclaimed, leaping from his seat and embracing the man firmly. "Damn, but it's good to see you." Orli's face creased into a smile as he hugged Ben back.

"It is good to see you as well. How is Tracy? Is she, by chance, with you?" he asked, looking around to see if she was with him, his face expectant.

Ben shook his head, casting Zach one inscrutably searching look. "Nope. We Traveled rather, well, unexpectedly. She's back in the World Dimension, probably having a fit about not being here."

"Well, perhaps she will come along later," Orli said philosophically.

"What's this about Hardin?" Ben asked, sitting back down, eager to divert the man's attention from his wife. Beside him, he could sense Zach's growing impatience. He couldn't blame the man, he'd hate listening to all of this and not understanding much of what was going on. Yet, now was not the time or place for the man's first discussion about the Land. He needed time to adjust to being here before he learned exactly what 'here' entailed. Ben kept his eyes on Orli, who went to lean against the mantel, his arms crossed.

"Hardin has grown, shall we say, disenchanted with the Protectors," Orli said wryly, his face set in lines of disgust. "Since the last debacle with Liz, he has been working on the village council to decree the Mountain Village a no-Protector zone."

"I knew that he was unhappy," Ben said with a frown. "But each time I have Traveled lately, I've gone to the Capital City. Tracy never said a word."

"We were hoping that cooler heads would prevail, and why create animosity if it is not warranted?" Orli said philosophically. "However,

Hardin has laid down the law. Protectors are no longer welcome in the Mountain Village."

"What? Why?"

"He feels that the Worlder…influence brought death to our village and therefore…he has banned them. It took quite a while of constant badgering and discussion, but he finally swayed enough of the village council. Fools."

Ben looked over at the Seer. "Can Hardin do that? Simply outlaw Worlders?" He'd always thought Hardin was a rather dense man, but a harmless one. This was a rather overt and harsh response given all that the Protectors had done for the Land.

The Seer's face was set in hard lines, her anger clear in her eyes. "I'm afraid he can," she muttered viciously. "I cannot leave, because of the Cave of Souls. If not for that, I would be out of there so quick his head would spin."

Zach's ears had perked up with the mention of Liz. He was also intensely interested in the Seer, since she was a clairvoyant of some sort. Like Liz. Zach also had a good idea how Orli fit into the whole mix of things. The look Ben had shot him was obviously intended to forestall him from saying anything about Tracy's pregnancy. Orli had to be the father. The one that was "away" and didn't yet know about his wife's state.

"What about when Tracy visits you?" Ben asked Orli, confirming Zach's assumption. "Where will the two of you stay when she visits if your home is off limits to Protectors?" He could not imagine anyone telling Orli or Tracy they could not live where they wished.

"I am staying in the village of my birth," Orli said stubbornly. "And Tracy, as my wife, is welcome to be with me. I would like to see Hardin try and keep her away from the home we have in the Mountain Village." He was obviously looking forward to the confrontation.

"All in due time," the Seer said soothingly. "We will handle Hardin and his possible reaction to Tracy when it comes. For now, I would like to know how Zach came to be our guest." She smiled warmly at the man. Zach, whose mind had been wandering during the last conversation, turned his attention back to the woman, having heard his name mentioned. He returned the Seer's smile automatically.

"We were at a party for Sasha and William's wedding when Zach here saw the Tree," Ben was saying to the group, his hands clasped between his knees, elbows resting on his thighs. "He accidentally touched the Tree when he was trying to get a closer look at it." Zach resisted the urge to squirm in his chair, knowing full well his arrival in this place was his own bloody fault. "I grabbed his suit jacket at the last second. So here we are."

"Good timing," the Seer told him. "As I said earlier, I was going to communicate with you through the crystals tomorrow. Something is happening. We aren't sure what. But there is a great disturbance in the Meadows. No one can figure out what it is, actually." The Seer frowned slightly. "I was just trying to convince Maxt and Orli to take me to the place where I sense the disturbance, but they are reluctant to risk me for something that could, in all fairness, simply be a trap. So we had compromised on calling you over to get your take on things."

"My take?" Ben said slowly.

"Well, has Amber told you anything? Has Daniel communicated with her about any of Evil's plans?" the Seer pressed, leaning forward eagerly.

Ben shook his head. "Nope. Nothing," he admitted with great regret.

"Who is Daniel?" asked Zach.

All eyes turned to him. "You do not know who Daniel is?" Maxt asked, his voice a deep rumble of confusion.

It was Ben's turn to keep from squirming. "We didn't have time to debrief Zach," he told the others finally. "He knows nothing about the Land. He has some understanding of what a Seer is, though. He and Liz seem to have made some sort of, well, connection."

Orli raised his eyebrows at Zach. "A connection? Really?" he said dubiously, raking his gaze up and down the man. Zach narrowed his own blue eyes back at him. "He does not seem the type she would be interested in."

Zach arched an eyebrow at the man. Orli simply quirked up one side of his mouth.

But the Seer was leaning forward eagerly. "What kind of connection?"

"Yesterday, she touched me and we both saw a flash of my future," Zach said, feeling the need to speak for himself. Then he hesitated, because what they had shared on the balcony had seemed rather, well, private. "Then tonight, we saw what I'm assuming is the Land. Together. She said the first place was the Isle of Silence, and then we went over the sea, the mountains and the meadows. At least, she called it the meadows. There, we saw a fortress-like structure, heavily guarded and patrolled. Then it all faded away." He raised his hands to mimic the idea of something flying away suddenly.

Maxt looked sharply at Ben, who raised two hands in defense. "Hey, that's the first I've heard about that vision."

"It just happened, right before Liz went to get you," Zach said evenly. No way was he going to tell this group about the kiss, he decided. Some things deserved to be held in confidence, although Ben was slanting him a look that indicated the blond might know there was more Zach was leaving unsaid.

"There is no such fortress in the Meadows," Maxt said with certainty, leaning back in his chair, his craggy face resolute.

Zach swiveled his head towards the man. "I don't know squat about this place," he said calmly. "But I do know what I saw when I was with Liz. It was a stepped pyramid, made of terra cotta colored brick, covered in vines and crawling with creatures. It looked windowless, and the door was hidden from view. As we flew overhead, we could see giant ferrets combing over the outside. Huge suckers. Big teeth."

"Ferrets?" asked Ben, frowning.

"Astral projection. Dual astral projection," the Seer breathed, shaking her head, holding a trembling hand to her neck. "Amazing strength that girl has, let me tell you, to pull that off."

"I think she was being shown the fortress for a reason," continued Zach. "It was a deliberate orientation of the place so that the position of the pyramid was easy to ascertain."

"So that is the disturbance that is calling to me," said the Seer. "But...why? What is it about this fortress that haunts my dreams without showing any substance?"

"Have these kinds of dreams happened before?" asked Zach.

"My Lady does not disclose her dreams," said Maxt with overtones of steel.

"Well excuse me for not knowing anything about anyone or

anything about this place," shot back Zach. "I'm just tryin' to figure out what is going on here, thank you very much."

The Seer held up a slender hand. "My usual dreams, my Seering ones, all fall within a particular, familiar pattern. This dream does not."

"She wakes screaming from them," muttered Maxt. "Screaming until she is hoarse from exertion and exudes tears of blood."

Ben looked startled—and worse in Zach's eyes—scared. "Do you think Evil is trying to hurt you through these dreams?"

The Seer looked thoughtful and then shook her head as memories of her dreams clouded her eyes. "No. This is something here, in this dimension. Something from the Land is calling out…"

"Something. Not necessarily someone," said Ben slowly. "So, the structure that Zach saw, it could be that the Meadows Region is sending out some sort of distress signal?"

Maxt nodded. "Could be. But none of us have seen this anomaly. We have scoured the region time and again, and nothing."

"Who's looking?" asked Zach sharply.

"Guardsmen," replied Maxt in a similar tone.

"Think Army or Marines," suggested Ben.

"These are all men familiar with the region. They have reported nothing like the building you describe."

"We cannot be sure that what he saw was in the Meadows at all," said Orli. "It could have been a Seering dream, a manifestation of something abstract."

"It was real," grit out Zach. "I could see it, feel it, sense it in a way I've never experienced in a dream."

"But there is no fortress in the Meadows Region," said Maxt stubbornly. "Someone would have seen it. Someone would have reported it."

"Unless they couldn't see it," put in Ben, feeling he needed to stick up for his fellow Worlder.

"They cannot see it because there is nothing there. I think Orli is right. It is her gift, her mind showing her that there is danger in the Meadows Region."

"It wasn't a dream," said Zach, equally stubborn. "Is anyone listening to me?"

"You claim it is not a dream. But no one has seen the actual structure, and we live here. That means we do not have a way of proving your assertion, do we?" said Maxt.

"Well, then, I guess it's significant that I was shown the way to get to the damn thing, then, isn't it?" said Zach easily, although his temper, slow to boil, was beginning to rise.

"Guess who gets to be the voice of reason in a sea of Alpha males?" muttered the Seer holding up her hand to halt Maxt's further words.

"I believe in Liz. I believe Zach. I think we owe it to ourselves to seek out this fortress and see exactly what it is."

"Well of course," said Maxt with a huff. "I was not about to say we would not go look, just that I do not want this man to assume that he will find what he and Liz saw in her Seering dream."

"My name is Zach," the actor said in steely tones. "And I would appreciate it if someone would tell me, once and for all, what the hell is going on here."

-9-
The Hunt Begins

Zach did not get the answer he wanted right away. Shortly after his temper ignited, he was overcome with a weariness that literally had him keeling over mid sentence. To his supreme embarrassment, only the quick actions of Ben and Maxt saved him from the indignity of landing sprawled on the ground. Vaguely aware of Ben and the Seer telling him he was suffering from "post-Travel exhaustion" and that it "happens a lot the first time through the Void," Zach allowed himself to sink into a bed in the back room of the cottage. In fact, he had no choice but to do so, given the physical state he was in.

Luckily, he was up early the next morning, and the overwhelming state of exhaustion left as quickly as it had come. It was somewhat of a surprise when instead of having the expected long discussion, he was handed several large notebooks by Ben.

"Read these," the blond told him. "They'll explain it much better than we ever could."

Zach looked at the notebooks dubiously. "What are these?" he asked, opening the book labeled with a big '1', stretching to work the kinks out from sleeping on a mattress that could never qualify for the local motel hell, much less a five-star hotel.

"They are an accounting of everyone's quest for the Land," Ben said, tapping the cover of the book. "Luckily the Seer travels with them, just in case a Traveler comes through. I'm going to go have a chat with Orli while you read."

"Going to tell him the big news that he's gonna be a papa?" Zach said absently, setting aside all the books but one, intending to dive right into reading.

"I am going to be a *what*?" Orli's voice came from the doorway of the cottage. Neither man had noticed his arrival, much to their surprise.

Zach groaned then hit his forehead several times in a row with the closed book. "Stupid, stupid, stupid," he chanted, while Ben stood there frozen, like a deer caught in headlights. His mouth opened and closed several times like a fish landed on a pier.

Orli's smile faded as he took in the two. "What is it? That word... papa. What does it mean?"

"Well, I wasn't going to spring it on you like this," Ben said, casting a reproachful look in Zach's direction, who grimaced, accepting the rebuke. Ben gave an all-over body shake, like a Labrador just out of the lake, then stood very straight and still, meeting his Land friend's gaze head on. "Orli, Tracy is pregnant. She's going to have a baby. You're going to be a father."

Zach figured the look of stunned joy that passed over the man's face was worth all the self-recriminations. It was amazing to see the concept of impending fatherhood settle in and take root, the news snaking through the synapses of Orli's brain.

"Pregnant?" Orli echoed, weakly grabbing for the back of a chair. "Baby? Father? Me?"

"Yes, yes, yes, and yes," Ben said, smiling at his friend's reaction.

Orli let out a yell and grabbed at Ben, hugging him tightly. "This is incredible," he shouted to the rafters, bringing the Seer and Maxt running in from the outside, the later with his sword drawn.

"I am going to be a father," Orli exclaimed, his face a study of joy.

The Seer clapped her hands, then hugged Orli, kissing his cheeks fondly. "I am so happy for you," she said sincerely. Maxt clapped a hand on the younger man's shoulder, his rugged face wreathed in smiles.

"I cannot wait to see her," Orli exclaimed excitedly, pacing in a tight circle, unable to stand still. "To be able to share this with her. What an amazing time in our lives!"

Ben's face went crestfallen. "Orli..." he said hesitantly. Damn, but he hated to be the one to break the news to Orli. "I'm not sure how to tell you this, but, Tracy won't be able to Travel while pregnant."

The Seer raised a hand to her lips, then nodded as sympathetic tears coalesced in her eyes. "Yes, I can see how that might cause a problem."

Orli's eyes grew thunderous. "What do you mean, it might cause a problem?" he said, raking Ben with narrowed eyes. "Why cannot Tracy Travel?" he looked slightly alarmed. "Is there something wrong with the baby?"

"No, no, nothing is wrong," Ben hastened to assure him. "Amber checked with Daniel about the Traveling thing, but for now, the consensus is that since we don't know what exactly happens to the body during Traveling, exposing the fetus to that kind of stress might be harmful."

"You do want a healthy baby," the Seer said softly, laying a hand on Orli's sleeve, unconsciously echoing Katie's words back in the World Dimension.

"I want to be with my wife during her pregnancy," Orli gritted, turning his gaze away from the Seer. "She deserves to have my full support and comfort."

"If it's any consolation, Tracy is just as pissed off as you are," Ben said helpfully. "Maybe more."

Orli glared at him for a moment then turned and stalked out of the cottage.

"He just needs some time," the Seer predicted. "He will have to grieve the fact that he may not have the normal passage to fatherhood that he anticipated, to be able to watch Tracy grow, feel the babe move, all the things that an expectant father looks forward to."

"Well, there is something else he needs to know fairly quickly," admitted Ben, rubbing his hand on the back of his neck. "The pregnancy appears to be progressing by Land standards and timetables. She's already about five weeks along, even though she has only been back in the world for two weeks. But William is keeping an eye on her, and running a series of blood work to track the Too'ki virus and make sure that the added hormones don't cause a resurgence of Too'ki cells. Also to make sure the accelerated rate of pregnancy doesn't overtax her physically. It's one of those times when I can't help but be glad we have a doctor who understands all our particular needs and issues. William is a Godsend."

Zach was sitting at the table, listening to it all but not understanding much of what was going on. He picked up the seven books that Ben had given him, juggling them in his arms, deciding that it was time he got caught up.

"Um, I'm going to go outside and read," he told the others, desperate to get away from all the confusion. He left the cottage and wound his way through the streets to a hilltop, where he stood on the soft grass and tossed the books on the ground next to him.

Looking around, he was amazed. So this was the Land, he thought. Overhead, an impossibly blue sky stretched, complete with fluffy clouds edged with a pinkish tinge. The grass was short and smelled sweet, dotted with flowers and small bushes and trees. Insects flitted about, and, when a butterfly landed near Zach, he was startled to see that it had wings dappled with tiny jewels. On one side, the mountains loomed, lofty peaks covered in snow.

That morning, he'd put his tux pants and shirt back on, but had left the jacket back in the cottage. After looking around to make sure he was alone, he kicked off his shoes and pulled off his shirt. Taking a deep breath, he started the breathing exercises developed to calm and center him. God knew, he needed both. Balancing his weight on bare feet, toes digging into the soft loam of the Meadow's grass, he experienced what could only be described as a basic connection with the physical earth of the Land. It tingled through his toes and spread throughout his body, anchoring him at his core. Almost like a piece of him that had been floating was now firmly locked into place, making him complete for the first time in his life. Right here, right now, he was…himself.

A little disconcerted by the feeling, he ran through an abbreviated routine, not wanting to take to much time for himself but needing to ensure he was fully centered when so far out of his element. By the end of fifteen minutes, he was covered in a light sweat but was grounded enough to plow through the books that Ben had brought him.

Taking one last deep breath, he picked up his shirt and tossed it on, not bothering with the buttons. Sitting on the grass, Zach picked up the first book and began to read.

One of the tricks that Zach had learned early in his life was the art of speed reading. It made learning scripts much easier and allowed him to rush through his schoolwork quickly enough so he could have his full amount of playtime. Even with this skill, it took the better part of the morning to get through the first four books. By then, he was hooked. The stories were not written as books, per say, but they were interesting just the same. Since he was sitting in the middle of the Land, breathing the incredible scents, it was easy to believe and absorb the tales of Griffins and mermaids, Too'kis and Princes, Seers and Oracles. He went back and re-read several important passages, then set them aside.

He pulled book five to him. A few pages in, he realized it had a completely different slant. In this quest, a Land person had come to the World Dimension. "A plot twist," Zach said with satisfaction. "Excellent."

Zach breezed through the next two books, but his hands hesitated when he got to the final one, the cover marked with a large seven. This had to be Liz's story, he thought. He lightly ran his hand over the black binding, then opened the book and immersed himself into the Seer's account of her journey through the Land.

When he was done, Zach closed the book. Liz's quest had been harrowing and fraught with danger from all sides. All alone on that cursed island while her mind was manipulated and her emotions played with in a most foul way. She'd been so isolated that she hadn't realized how the man imbued by Evil had influenced her. A surge of anger welled up inside Zach at the way she'd been used by Valdeen. He was absurdly grateful that the man was dead, otherwise he'd be compelled to hunt the man down and kill him for what he'd done to Liz.

Zach stacked the books and stood up, carrying them back to the cottage. He was completely unaware of the looks he was receiving from the villagers, having long ago learned the art of ignoring being in the spotlight. Ducking into the cottage, he was surprised to find that he was alone. Carefully piling the books on the table, he snagged a piece of fruit from the bowl and bit into it, chewing while he thought and put the books into perspective.

Well, it certainly explained the dynamics of the group. Why Katie, Tracy, Ben, Sasha, Sarat and Liz were so close. The power that defined them as a group. He idly wondered if he would meet Jay, the Protector who had chosen to stay in the Land and pursue his Wizard career. God, how that guy's life must have changed. Much like Zach's own life had taken a decidedly different bent since meeting up with his neighbors.

His thoughts were interrupted as the door opened and Orli ducked through the frame. He gave Zach a curt nod and set his quiver and arrows to one side of the doorway. Like Zach, he grabbed a piece of fruit from the bowl and took a healthy bite.

"I've read all the books," Zach ventured into the uneasy silence.

Orli grunted. "No one reads that fast," he said in way of reply.

"I do," Zach arched an eyebrow. "If you would care to test me, I'd be happy to oblige."

Orli blew out his breath, rubbing the back of his neck. "I hate this."

A swell of compassion for the man had Zach leaning forward. "Orli, I saw Tracy yesterday. Is there anything I can tell you to assure you that she is fine? Well, a little nauseous, and there was the fainting thing, but other than that, she seems to be carrying the pregnancy very well."

"Fainting?" Orli's head snapped up. Zach cursed himself silently.

"Well, only once that I saw," Zach said slowly. "But she was working out the very next day and seemed to be fine. And at the cocktail party last night, she looked, well, she was glowing. Honest."

Orli seemed slightly mollified by the admission. "This is not the way I had envisioned our starting a family. In fact, we were not entirely sure we ever would start a family. To find out she can get pregnant, and then not be there for her? With her? It is unbearable."

"I can imagine that it seems that way," Zach agreed readily. "But as the Seer said, you do want a healthy baby, don't you?"

"Yes," Orli said fervently. "But it is just too hard to imagine her going through this alone."

"She has the Protectors," Zach said softly, feeling for the man. "I've never seen a more supportive, loving, caring group of people than that bunch. The way they closed ranks around Tracy when they found out about the baby…it was amazing. She's in good hands."

The door opened and the Seer, Maxt and Ben trooped into the cottage. "Good, you are both here," the Seer said, dropping a kiss on the top of Orli's head. "Is your funk over?" she asked him fondly.

He smiled up at her. "For now."

"Good," the Seer replied. Maxt was pulling out some charts from a bag, spreading them on the table.

"We were wondering if you could help us pinpoint where that fortress you saw is located," he said to Zach, who stood up eagerly.

The map before him was unusual, to say the least. A large round circle dominated the document. It was bisected down the middle by two broad sections, one labeled 'Desert' the other 'Marshes'. The large half circle to the east was neatly cut in two, the top half labeled 'Forest' and the bottom labeled 'Rivers'. The west side was similarly divided with the bottom half denoted as 'Mountain' and the top as 'Meadows'. All around the circumference of the circle was another broad band, neatly marked as 'Beaches'.

"So this is the Land?" said Zach, smoothing down the edges, running his hand over the parchment as though absorbing the nuances of the map with his skin. "It's definitely as precise as described in the books you gave me."

Maxt pointed at a spot in the sea near the Mountains Region. "This is the Isle of Silence. From what you described, your vision with Liz started there. Can you tell me where you went, where you ended up?"

Closing his eyes for a moment and orienting himself mentally, Zach opened his eyes and traced a finger over the map as he spoke. "We started at the Isle of Silence, then flew straight over the sea. We crossed the Mountains, and then over the Meadows. It ended somewhere in the middle, because I could not see the Beaches anywhere. I do recall a smudge like fog to the west, which may have been the Marshes."

"So we are looking in the middle of the Meadows," Maxt said with a heavy sigh. "That does not narrow it down much."

"I do remember seeing a lot of yellowish orange flowers," Zach said. "I haven't seen any like it around here. Perhaps there is a part of the region that has them? They were quite unique, a seven part petal with a bright green stem and light green leaves."

"Very detailed memory," Orli said slowly.

"Perhaps it is detailed because I was meant to be able to recall them vividly," Zach replied, not the least bit offended. His fingers were circling an area of the Meadows Region, a place that seemed to call to him.

"Those flowers sound like what we call 'Spring's Blossom'," Maxt said. "They grow only in this area," he pointed to a position somewhat in the middle of the Meadows, but towards the Marshes Region rather than the Beaches. Near where Zach's forefinger kept touching the parchment.

"Are there any towns in that area?" the Seer asked.

"No, but there is a barracks right here," Maxt's finger shifted slightly west. "It might be a good place to reconnoiter."

"Ben?" the Seer asked the large blond, who had been quiet until now.

"I can try," he replied evenly. "We don't have control over the Grid, you know. But it seems like I tend to go where I'm needed, so if you're at the barracks, I should end up there as well. If not, there are always Griffins."

"What's going on?" Zach asked slowly. "Why is Ben going to 'end up' at the barracks?"

"Ben is going to go back to the World Dimension for a day, which in our timeline can be a few days. He'll inform the Protectors of the situation and assure them you are safe. Then, he'll meet up with you, me, Orli and Maxt at the barracks." The Seer was staring at Zach with even eyes.

"I'm going to the barracks," Zach stated.

"We'd like you to help us find this building you have described," the Seer stated. "We know of no such place in the Land, but both you and Liz saw it, so it must exist. Will you help us find the pyramid?"

"Your eyes are the ones who will be able to find it," Orli said with confidence.

Zach looked at Ben, who was also eyeing him with interest. "The choice is always up to the Quester," Ben said gravely. "No one will force you to help."

Zach rubbed the back of his neck. It seemed pretty harmless after all, compared to some of the life and death situations others had endured. "Sure, I'll help you find the pyramid," he said to the Seer with a shrug of his broad shoulders.

She smiled at him, and then turned to Ben. "While you are gone, I will send word to Anja. Perhaps she can meet us at the barracks as well."

Ben's eyes crinkled happily at the thought. He leaned over to give the Seer a hug, and then clasped forearms with Orli and Maxt. Finally he stopped in front of Zach.

"If you don't mind, we can bring you a change of clothes or two," he told the actor. "That way you aren't running around the Land in a tuxedo. It's really the only reason I'm coming back. I hate for you to be without your gear."

Zach plucked at his white shirt, which was slowly but surely turning a grimy gray. "That would be aces," he said with a smile. "And my kit bag, if you don't mind. It's on the counter in my bathroom." He rattled off the security code for Ben. "Oh, and Ben? I had something mailed to me from the coast. If it's arrived, would you bring it back for me? I have a feeling I may need it."

"Sure. What is it?"

"The sword I used in *The Phoenix*. I asked my assistant to send it out to me."

Ben gave a slow, long smile, his eyes burning azure. "Excellent. I'll be sure to bring it with me. If not, how about the one you used in practice?"

"That'll work, but I hope my other one is there," Zach said easily.

"Any messages for people back home?" Ben asked Zach, searching his eyes. "Anyone you want to warn you may be gone for awhile? That's another real reason for me to go home. We need to make sure your situation, in particular, is taken care of."

"Yeah. If I'm out of contact for too long, my agent and parents will think I was kidnapped," Zach said with a sigh, the complications of his going missing swarming his brain as he rubbed the back of his neck. "Can I use some paper? I'll write a note, saying I'm going deep sea fishing and visiting some friends in the Caribbean. If someone could fax it to them that would be great."

The Seer gave him writing instruments, which Zach was glad to see were definitely Worlder in nature, and soon Zach was sitting at one end of the table, diligently writing a note to his parents and agent. At the other end, Orli was also writing a letter to Tracy, although he was using a quill and ink. They waited until the sun set and the time was approximately twenty-four hours from the time that Ben and Zach had entered the Land. The Seer, Maxt, Orli and Zach accompanied Ben to the Land Tree located near Wayside.

"That's not the Tree," Zach protested, pointing at the stunted tree they gathered around.

"What do you mean?"

"Maxt, it's not red and gold," Zach replied, gesturing.

"Well, that just proves that you are not ready to go home yet," Ben said with a shake of his head. "That is a Land Tree, and it is clearly in red and gold to me."

"Huh," Zach said, staring intently at the Tree. To him it was a normal looking tree, brown and green. Ben gave a wave to everyone and walked over to the Tree, placing a hand on the branch. There was snick and click and he was gone.

The Seer turned to Zach. "Well, we have a long hike in the morning. Let us go back and pack, then we should turn in early."

Zach fell behind the others as they walked back. He glanced over his shoulder at the Land Tree, but it was still a study in brown and green to him. Looks like he was here for the duration.

-10-
Rolling Meadows

Early the next morning, Maxt woke Zach by roughly shaking his shoulders. Zach rolled over, groaning as his shoulder met the unforgiving floor beneath him. He blearily glared at Maxt. "You aren't room service," he said dully, then shook his head to clear it. Maxt grunted and spun on his heel, striding from the door.

Dressing quickly, Zach stumbled out the door after Orli. Damn, he had never liked early calls. It was barely dawn, the eastern sky just beginning to lighten. The air was brisk, causing their breath to fog in front of their faces.

Maxt had given Zach a leather jerkin, which was warmer than his summer-weight tux jacket. He'd also scrounged up a pack for Zach, in which the actor had placed his tux jacket, some toiletries he'd borrowed and several pages of Liz's book, which he'd snuck out of the binder before returning the books to the Seer.

The Seer was dressed in brown leather pants and a shorter leather vest, over which she had draped a poncho in heavy woven fabric. She gave Zach a reassuring smile as they headed out into the Meadows, Maxt in front and Orli trailing, his brown eyes constantly roving over the horizon.

They hiked in silence, which suited Zach fine. He was content with his thoughts, which centered primarily on this rather bizarre turn of events. If someone had told him a few weeks ago, when he'd walked down the red carpet at the Oscars with the up-and-coming-starlet-of-the-moment on his arm, that he would be slogging through an alternate dimension on some sort of search mission, he'd have told them they were insane.

But the truth of the matter was that Zach was enjoying himself. This was an adventure of the grandest sort, and he decided he had better enjoy every waking moment of it. So he kept casting his eyes around, taking in the scenery and trying to figure out if he recognized any part of the landscape from his fly-over with Liz. He also watched his companions, who fascinated him to no end. Much like he did with the Protectors, Zach found himself analyzing the way the trio interacted, and piecing together the fabric of their personalities. He liked the resulting tapestry his observations developed. He found himself casting the group in his mind, assigning character traits like a veteran director.

Maxt's gruff exterior was no front; it was definitely a part of his make up. Yet despite his no-nonsense exterior, there was no denying the man was very much aware of the Seer. Bristling with weapons, he moved with a lithe grace that belied his height and bulk. He kept a brisk pace, but was cognizant of the Seer with every step. Zach found the man's courteous treatment of the woman charming, and it was clear how devoted the large warrior was to his lovely lady. Once, when Maxt was assisting the Seer over a small creek, Zach looked back at Orli, who was watching the pair fondly. Catching Zach's look, Orli flashed the actor a smile, shrugging one shoulder.

"They love one another," he said simply. Zach grinned back, nodding.

"I think it's cool."

Orli gave a nod and resumed his march in silence. He was an interesting man, at least to Zach. The mountain villager was as watchful of the surroundings as Maxt, casting his gaze to the horizon frequently, tracking hawks overhead. He rarely spoke, but often smiled at the group's banter. While he seemed quiet by nature, Zach had the distinct feeling the man could turn from laconic watcher to formidable fighter in a split second. It was woven into his being, in the easy way he carried himself and his weapons.

As for the Seer, she reminded him so much of Liz that he couldn't help but adore her. Like Maxt, he was quickly falling under her spell. She wasn't a complainer, which was a huge relief given the rapid pace Maxt set. She spoke to Zach often, pointing out a plant here, a formation there, all the while weaving in the story of the Land in a way to educate Zach without patronizing him. Lying underneath her gracious exterior was a hardened steel core, one charged with power and might and a will to succeed. This woman was of the Land, for the Land, and with the Land in everything she did. Even if Zach didn't know the background of Seering and what it entailed, he would not have been able to deny the fact that the Seer was a force to be reckoned with if riled.

That night, he helped Orli start the campfire, grateful for the research he did for his *Phoenix* role. He had a feeling that the villager expected him to be a complete novice, but building and tending the small fire seemed to redeem him in the man's eyes. After a dinner of meat and fruit, the companions sat around the flames.

"Tell me what you think about this fortress," Zach said finally, linking his hands behind his head and looking up at the night sky. None of the constellations looked remotely familiar. "What do you think it's for?"

From across the fire, the Seer spoke softly. "I am more interested in what you think about it, Zachary. You have read the books about the Protectors."

"The Land is fighting Evil and the Protectors are helping," recited Zach.

"Correct."

"And this new structure is unknown to those who are from the Land, such as you, the Prince, or anyone else in this region."

"Correct again."

"So we can assume that since I'm from another dimension, I'm able to see this thing; perhaps because I formed some sort of attachment to Liz."

"You already know this, Zachary. What is your real question?" asked the Seer, tilting her head to one side.

Zach sighed, rubbing the back of his neck with one hand. "Why me? What is it about me that makes me the right person for this task?"

The Seer smiled and shrugged. "I don't have an answer for that, Zachary. All I can tell you is that you were called for a reason, and I know you will do your tasks here to the best of your abilities. It is one of the most admirable traits of those whom the Land beckons to her bidding."

"I'm nothing special." His voice sounded defensive, even to his own ears, making Zach wince. How often in his life had others told him how special he was; and how wrong had that always seemed? He was a little sensitive to the label.

The Seer laughed aloud this time. "Katie and the others said the same thing. The human being is a marvelous, adaptive creature, Zachary Neol. There are unplumbed depths in each of us, just waiting to be released. You, I think, have a little something extra special. I sense it, like it's just outside my grasp to ken. It will come to me, though."

"So what is the plan, exactly? I'm going to lead the three of you to the fortress and then you'll raze it to the ground? Seems like we'd need a little more power for that kind of feat."

"We are going to the barracks closest to the area where the fortress is located," said Maxt. "There, we will wait for Ben to return from the World Dimension. We are hoping Liz has more information on the structure. She may have done more astral projection since you left the World; may have seen more and know more at this point. If not, well, we are going to have to go look for the structure. I would prefer the whole battalion accompany us."

"And I would prefer a smaller number," retorted the Seer. The bite to her voice told Zach, as much as her taut body language, that this was not the first time this particular discussion had taken place. "I saw only four on the journey, Maxt. You know this. It is what I saw."

"I didn't think Seers said what their visions were," said Zach, recalling Liz's reluctance.

"Normally, we don't," the Seer glowered, "but Maxt is being beyond stubborn. He would prefer every barrack in the Land to be with us, as well as the Prince, the Griffins, and a couple of irritated mermaids to boot."

"I would not say no to a Too'ki going with us if there were any left in the Land," muttered Maxt, shifting in his place. "I do not like the sound of this fortress, and I do not want to go marching up to it with a puny force of four!"

"Perhaps this discussion could wait," said Orli, a reclining form on the darkest side of the fire. "We have to reach the barracks, talk with Ben, perhaps get a pigeon from the Prince. Then we can make a decision about how to proceed."

"Why can't a Griffin just fly me over the region?" asked Zach after a few moments of silence.

"They are refusing to fly in this area," replied the Seer, scrubbing at her short hair with one hand. "Well, I should say that they have agreed to bring Anja to the barracks, but they won't do anything else. And there is no forcing or coercing a Griffin to change its mind," she warned as Zach opened his mouth again. "We can forget the help of our furry feathered friends."

"Seems they know something is wrong in the area," said Maxt as he poked at the fire, sending a cascade of sparks up to the indigo sky. "I trust those beasties with my life. If they refuse to fly over the area, it is because they fear it. And that makes me…cautious."

"And cautious equals massive amounts of guardsmen," concluded Zach. Maxt nodded at him, his green eyes glowing like a cat's. "I think Orli has the best plan for now. As much as I hate to wait and see, it seems the best option at the moment."

"Evil has a plan afoot. One that I am close to gleaning, and one that I know involves my station with the Land," said the Seer. "I will be a part of the group that seeks the fortress. End of discussion. Evil is messing with the Seers, and I will do all I can to protect Liz and myself."

"Well," Zach said slowly, staring at the Seer. "Evil may be trying to draw you out, luring you with the intent to cause you harm. This could be the bait, and the trap is waiting to be sprung upon you."

Maxt looked at the Seer. "He has a point," the warrior said quickly. "This is a strategy that I have been trying to tell you about for days."

"It would be a good one," Orli said quietly.

The Seer cocked her head to one side. "Then we proceed carefully, and with full knowledge that this is perhaps a trap," she said calmly and nothing Maxt could say would dissuade her. Both Orli and Zach heard them arguing about it late into the night.

The second day passed much as the first. At least the hike was over easy terrain, Zach thought with relief, recalling the harrowing desert, marshes and mountains region treks that some of the Protectors had taken.

They arrived at the barracks late that day, a grouping of single level buildings set in a horseshoe pattern. Maxt called out to the guards who poured from the main lodging to greet him. Zach and Orli were both eyed with differing levels of distrust and skepticism, but the Seer was greeted with great deference.

The guards seemed to be an insular group, keeping to themselves and excluding Zach and Orli as outsiders. That suited the men fine as they left the low building after dinner to get some fresh air, leaving Maxt inside to discuss strategy and current events.

"They don't seem to like us much," said Zach as he hooked his foot over the bottom rung of the fence surrounding the compound and staring out over the Meadows.

"I noticed that," Orli said wryly, his eyes scanning the horizon, as always. Zach couldn't imagine that the man could see very well in the growing darkness of night. "I think they feel that if you are a man and do not deign to join their ranks, then you are by nature a, what does Tracy call it? Oh, yes, a wimp."

"Dude, you aren't a wimp," Zach stated with certainty.

Orli grunted, his attention riveted to the sky.

"What is it? Do you see something?" Zach asked trying to see what was up there.

"It is a Griffin," Orli said with a smile. "Ah, the lovely Anja has been found."

"Ben's mermaid?" Zach's eyebrows rose high. He was interested in meeting the woman who had captured Ben's heart. "The Seer said she'd send word."

The Griffin landed lightly in the center of the clearing. A few guards who were on duty outside raced forward, but then shrank back as they recognized the beast. A small, slender form dismounted from the Griffin, patting the creature on the neck before it launched back up into the sky.

Orli hurried forward, a smile creasing his face. "Anja."

"Orli," she launched herself at the man, who swung her around in a circle before putting her down. "It is so good to see you." She pushed the dark cloud of hair from her face, smiling up at him, exposing a sweet face graced with large brown eyes and a dimpled cheek.

"Anja, I would like you to meet Zach. He is from the World

Dimension," Orli said, gesturing towards the actor, who moved forward.

Zach bent over her hand formally, brushing his lips over the back of her hand in a courtly manner. He looked up at her and graced her with his most wicked smile. "Charmed," he said softly.

Anja stared at him, then pulled her hand back slowly. "You are a smooth one," she observed with good humor. Then she looked around. "Is Ben back yet?"

"No," Orli informed her. "But I expect he will be showing up soon."

"So what news is there from the World Dimension?" Anja asked as she leaned her back against the fence, looking around the compound. Zach had a feeling this was an exchange that happened frequently between the two friends.

"Tracy is going to have a baby," Orli blurted, as if he could not contain the news any longer.

Zach had been watching Anja so he was the only one privy to the flash of intense pain that crossed her face before she carefully masked it, reaching out to hug Orli tightly.

"I am so happy for you," she exclaimed. If Zach hadn't seen the emotion that had flashed in her eyes, he would have sworn she was deliriously happy for the man. "I cannot wait to see Tracy fat and miserable."

Orli sobered. "Well, do not hold your breath," he muttered, kicking at the ground. "It appears that she will not be able to Travel while pregnant."

"Oh, Orli," Anja said, clearly feeling his misery. She laid a gentle hand on his arm. "I am sure it will be fine. We have to trust in that fact."

Maxt called to Orli from the barracks. The tall villager excused himself and strode over.

"That was nicely done," Zach said to Anja, who looked at him oddly. "It was very sweet of you not to take away from his happiness at the news."

"I do not know what you are talking about," she stated evenly.

"Orli's news floored you. Took you completely by surprise. And, strangely enough, it caused you pain to hear that Tracy is pregnant. But you hid it well and made sure that Orli was all right. That's the mark of a true friend," Zach said, watching her closely.

She reddened noticeably and pushed away from the fence. "You hardly know me," she said coolly, "therefore I find your assumption that I was in pain to hear that two of my dearest friends will be parents to be rather presumptuous."

Zach gave a half bow, reacting to the courtly mannerisms that seemed so appropriate for the Land. "Forgive me," he said. "I truly didn't mean to offend you. I was just trying to say that I admire your ability to put your friend's feelings first."

Anja gave him an inscrutable look. "I think I shall go find the Seer," she said finally. "I should give her my respects."

Zach watched her go, knowing that he had just pissed off the mermaid captain. That would certainly not endear him to Ben, and right now, Ben was about his only ally in the whole place.

"Great job, Neol," he told himself. "Way to win over the locals." Then he jogged towards the barracks, deciding it was time to turn in before he lodged his foot more firmly in his mouth.

Zach slept hard and long, the cot in the barracks infinitely more comfortable than a thin pallet in front of a fire. When he woke the next morning, it was to find Ben Harm had returned. His spiked blond hair was easily recognizable in the middle of the guardsman. They were clustered around the table, looking down at the object displayed on the rough wood.

Zach pushed his way towards Ben, glad to see a familiar face. Then he caught sight of the object on the table. It was a sword. To be more precise, it was *his* sword. The one he'd asked Ben to bring back from the World Dimension.

The sword boasted a silver blade and hilt; the latter carved to look like a bird's head. A Phoenix, to be exact. It had been a plain sword with no adornments, which he'd used for practice. When onscreen, the sword's smithy had made a fancy version, complete with fake ruby eyes and gold gleam on the bird's head. He'd had the practice sword made to the same calibration as the onscreen version, preferring to beat the hell out of the one that wasn't going to be viewed on a twenty-foot screen. It was not sheathed in its black leather scabbard and belt combination, which surprised Zach slightly.

Ben was smiling at Zach.

"Sorry, couldn't resist showing it off," he said with a wink, making Zach realize something.

"Hey! You aren't wearing your glasses," he said, shaking Ben's hand firmly while exchanging a thumping back slap. "I meant to ask about that when we first got here."

"I don't need them in the Land," the painter said with a shrug.

Zach reached for the sword. "Thanks for bringing it back," he said appreciatively. "Hope it wasn't too much of a bother."

"Not at all," Ben said, placing a small duffle bag on the table. "Here's the other stuff you requested. Liz tried to put everything in that you would need."

The thought of Liz going through his dresser drawers had Zach cross eyed for a moment, but he recovered when Maxt stepped up, eyeing the sword with a gleam in his eyes. "May I?" the guardsman asked, holding out his hand.

Zach flipped the sword easily, handing it to Maxt hilt first. "Be my guest."

The warrior hefted the sword in one hand, then tested the equilibrium of the hilt and blade by balancing the cross grip on his hand. Finally he swiped it through the air a few times before handing it back to Zach.

"Nice blade," he acknowledged, then gave him an assessing look. "The question is, can you use it?"

"I can."

"Really," this came from the leader of the barracks, a stocky man by the name of Tomikil. Clearly, the man did not believe Zach.

"Really," Zach replied with steely resolve.

"Perhaps a demonstration?" Maxt suggested. Ben stood with his arms crossed, trying to hide his smile behind his hand.

"Any time," the actor said, pawing through the duffle that Ben had brought back with him.

"After breakfast?"

"If we have time? Sure," said Zach, holding up a pair of silky black boxer shorts adorned with little red hearts and casting a questioning glance at Ben.

The painter held up his hands in protest, "I think Amber helped

Liz pack," he said with a laugh. Zach shook his head and pulled out his sweats and a t-shirt, along with his favorite cross trainers and Yankees baseball cap.

"Bless the girl," he said with a grin. He couldn't wait to be out of the hard-soled dress shoes. Hiking in them had not been the most comfortable thing.

Zach quickly changed and, using the shaving kit Liz had packed, completed his morning routine. Once that was done, Zach was back to normal again, more himself as he crossed through the main lodge. He sat with Ben, Anja and Orli for breakfast, finding that their easy camaraderie was as compelling as that of the Protectors back home. It was clear that Orli and Anja were friends, and it was even more evident how much Ben and Anja were in love. The mermaid even told Ben about the courtly kiss on the hand that Zach had given her the night before, earning Zach a wickedly dark look from the man.

"Don't make me hurt you, Zach," he growled, the sound mitigated by the twinkle in the man's aqua eyes. "I'm liking the fact that there may be another guy Protector, but I could still make ya cry."

Zach laughed, holding up his hands, "I'm a natural flirt, Ben. No harm intended."

"Hey, Orli, I almost forgot," Ben dug into his jeans pocket and pulled out a folded piece of paper. "William sweet-talked his way into a clinic and they let him use the ultrasound. I still can't believe they did it so fast, but I guess they figured I would be back and wanted to have this for me to bring to you."

"I have no idea what you are talking about, you know," Orli said as he accepted the paper, opening it. His face became curiously blank.

"That's your baby," Ben said with a grin. Zach shot a quick look at Anja, whose face blanched but then carefully smoothed out. She caught Zach's look and quickly turned her attention back to her food.

Zach looked over Orli's shoulder at the piece of paper, then clapped the mountain villager on the shoulder.

"Congratulations, Orli. You're having a blob."

"It is not a blob," Anja protested hotly, then looked at the paper. "Wait. Maybe it is," she took the paper from Orli and turned it around, looking at it from all angles.

"Apparently, they are supposed to look like blobs at this stage," Ben said. "Anyway, Tracy thought you'd like to have that. She wrote a letter, too."

Orli lightly traced the picture, his finger lingering on the light smudge in the center. "Our baby," he whispered, then looked at Ben with such joy in his eyes that it was impossible not to react. "Thank you, Ben."

"My pleasure," he replied, meaning it. Zach could tell that he was damned glad to bring good news to Orli.

-11-
And In This Corner...

Maxt indicated he was awaiting a pigeon from Capital City with instructions from the Prince of the Land and wouldn't consider leaving to look for the temple until he received word from his liege. The bird wasn't expected back until evening, making Zach chafe at the delay. They were going to waste another entire day at the barracks, it seemed, before they could go out and find the fortress.

Zach couldn't say why, but there was a growing itch in his sternum, a press of emotion that was urging him to find that fortress, and find it fast. He couldn't say what it was, or why it was, but he was becoming increasingly antsy to find the fortress.

After breakfast, which Zach purposely kept light in anticipation of Maxt's challenge, they left the lodge. Sure enough, when they left the barrack, Zach carrying the sheathed sword in one hand, it was to find the rest of the guardsmen busy in their practice field. Obviously, the presence of the Captain of the Guard was making the men much more alert than normal as each tried to impress Maxt, who was walking through the fields accompanied by Tomikil. The latter was gesturing and explaining things to Maxt, who walked with his hands clasped behind his back.

"Ben, may I speak with you in private for a second?" Zach asked. Ben obliged, hanging back from the rest of the group.

Anja and Orli continued, walking up to the fence, hooking their arms over the top railing to watch.

Zach spoke quickly and quietly. "Listen, Ben. This may be none of my business. But you should know that when Orli told Anja the news about the baby, she had a look of absolute pain on her face. It was clear that it was difficult for her to hear."

Ben hung his head with a sigh, then looked at Zach with a similar ache in his oceanic eyes. "Thanks, Zach. We've been trying but, well, according to Liz it's not going to happen for us. I haven't told Anja yet. It didn't seem the place or time."

"I wouldn't wait too long," Zach advised. "Women are funny about things like that, you know."

"Agreed," Ben said as they continued to walk towards the practice area. "Zach, seriously, thanks for the heads up. I appreciate it."

Ben and Zach joined their companions at the railing of the fence. Orli's eyes were on the archers. "He is dropping his front arm," he mentioned as one guardsman let loose an arrow, which fell just below the bull's eye. "And that one must restring his bow if he has any hope of hitting the broad side of a barn." He pointed at another.

"They seem to be doing well with knives and jousting poles," Ben said, nodding towards the two large areas where those combat techniques were being demonstrated. Anja tilted her head to one side.

"Yes, but the ones jousting need to work on their balance," she commented. "They are standing too flat footed. They need to be on the balls of their feet more." She demonstrated, her heels rising from the earth.

"Well, that guy over there simply sucks," Zach said, frowning at the area where the sword work was being displayed. "Must be new."

They watched in silence for a long while. Zach finally ventured, "Where's the Seer?"

"I think she is off meditating or doing whatever it is that Seers do to get prepared for a quest," Ben replied absently, his finger's playing with Anja's hair. "She mentioned to Maxt that she felt there were more pieces to this puzzle, and that she wanted to try and figure them out."

Maxt walked up to Zach, his green eyes gleaming. "Ready for our match?"

Zach ducked under the fence. "Sure," he said eagerly. "Just let me stretch out a bit and I'll be good to go."

"Can he hold his own?" Orli asked Ben, his forehead creasing slightly, arms crossed over his chest. "Maxt is formidable and will not go lightly on Zach just because he is a Worlder."

"Zach's better than Tracy and me combined," Ben said in way of reply, causing Orli to give Zach another assessing frown.

"Well, Maxt is widely recognized as the best swordsman in the Land, so we shall soon see," Anja replied as they moved through the crowd to stand on the edge of the ring.

The other guards were done with their practice and were also gathering around the large circle where swords were parried. They laughed and jostled one another as Zach went through a slow series of stretches, an abbreviated T'ai Chi exercise. He studiously ignored their jeers and whispers as he concentrated on making sure his muscles were loose and limber.

Maxt watched the man with narrowed eyes, clearly assessing his physical strengths as much he could.

Finally Zach entered the ring. Maxt handed him a heavy leather jerkin to put over his t-shirt. "For protection," he said in his gravely voice, "against the errant cut or slash. Not as effective as chain mail, but we will not be going for blood, so this should be sufficient."

Zach nodded and donned the vest, lacing it up the front. Then Zach unsheathed his sword, handing the scabbard and belt to Ben for safekeeping. The Sea Dimension man gave him a solemn nod.

"Just do your best," he said to Zach.

"I'll do better than my best," Zach said confidently, earning him a chuckle from Ben.

Zach and Maxt saluted one another with their swords and in the next instant the match was on.

Damn, the man can really move for someone so large, Zach thought as he barely parried a vicious swipe. Soon he was lost in the concentration of coordinating his feet and hands, arm and leg motions; the dance of the sword consuming his entire thought process. The two men moved as a unit back and forth across the large circle, neither giving an inch. Small clouds of dust dislodged by their feet rose, and the sound of steel rang throughout the barracks, accompanied by the occasional grunt or groan from the watching audience. The guardsmen stilled considerably when the match started, and it became evident that they were watching two highly skilled combatants.

Orli whistled appreciatively. "You are right," he said to Ben, his sharp eyes never leaving the two circling in the ring. "He is beyond good."

Anja was dancing from one foot to the other while Ben was standing stock-still. It was one thing to be in a match with a man, but quite another to watch it from afar. Zach was fluid poetry in motion with a blade, the steel seeming to be an extension of his own arm. His footwork was flawless, his concentration absolute. The blades were beginning to blur with the quickness of their parries and thrusts. Ben noticed something else as well. Zach was better, much better, in the Land than he had been back in the World Dimension. And since he was pretty kick-ass in the World, which meant that here in the Land, Zach was the master of the blade.

"I'll be damned," he whispered. "Welcome to your Land gift, Zach."

The Seer slid in to stand beside Ben, her eyes widening as she took in the spectacle.

"Oh my," she said simply. "One doesn't quite know who to root for, right?" Like the others, her eyes were glued to the men circling and parrying.

"I will root for Zach, you root for Maxt," Anja said with a laugh, having apparently forgiven Zach for his actions the night before.

"I do not think I will ever see a better match," Orli said, an appreciative grin on his face.

A water break was called, and Zach took a long swig from the skin that Anja held out to him. He was drenched in sweat but smiling happily.

"This is a blast," the actor crowed. "I can't believe how much fun it is." He was breathing rapidly but hardly in distress, which surprised them all. Obviously, he had some pretty impressive stamina. "Damn, but Maxt is bloody good."

"You're better," Ben said quietly, eying Maxt as he also downed some water and listened to words of advice from Tomikil. "He was assessing you in the beginning, just in case you were a novice. He knows your exceptional skill level now. He'll come out fighting hard. He won't want to loose face with his guardsmen. Watch it when you move into a down thrust. Your eyes betray your movement a split second before you strike. He'll have clued in to that, and may try and take a jab at your chest when you do."

"When Maxt pivots, he leaves his left flank open for a split second," Orli added, having watched the battle with the eyes of a strategist, "but you will have to time it carefully. Too hard and you may crack a rib, too soft and you will not have the speed needed to make the kill stroke."

Zach nodded, blowing out a deep breath. "Thanks, guys," he said, flashing them his million dollar smile before striding back out to the ring.

"Yowza," Anja said, borrowing a word from Ben's vocabulary. "He does just ooze with charm, does he not?"

Ben wrapped his arm around Anja and pulled her to him. "Don't be getting any ideas," he warned with mock intensity. She laughed and pushed him away.

A whistle sounded, and Maxt met Zach with a flurry of rapid fire thrusts, forcing Zach back across the ring. The actor parried every step of the way and fairly danced out of the corner with a spin and swipe that had Maxt jumping back to avoid a hit. The fight was getting down and dirty now, with the guardsmen yelling their encouragement to the leader. Yet Ben was seeing some quiet wagering going on in the circle of men and wondered with a smirk how many were betting on the newcomer to win.

Zach was watching carefully, mindful of Orli's words. He waited past the first pivot to the left to observe what the villager had indicated. Sure enough, a small window remained where Zach could strike—if he were fast enough. But he'd have to pull his swing at the last second or he could seriously hurt his opponent.

Zach waited and bided his time. The next time Maxt began to pivot to the left, Zach moved in quickly. With a roar of victory, Zach brought his blade up and around his head, halting it just before it would have struck Maxt's side. The amount of control needed to stop the blade was immense, and he gritted his teeth with effort, veins cording in his arms. A sudden silence fell over the ring.

Shocked green eyes rose to meet fiery blue ones. "Kill," Maxt said softly, then grinned. "Damn it all, you got me." He tossed down his blade and raised his hands, the signal of defeat.

Ben, Orli and Anja let out yells of approval, but most of the guardsmen began to mutter ominously. Tomikil looked particularly angry for some reason. Maxt put his hands on his hips and turned in a slow circle, taking them all in.

"What, are we going to ignore the fact that the man bettered me in a fair fight?" he challenged the guardsmen, his green eyes raking them with disgust. "Be grateful you had the chance to see such a fine display of swordsmanship in your lives. Take note of his technique. You will not find a better swordsman in the Land, I dare say." Maxt put his hand over his heart and bowed his head to Zach in tribute. All around the ring, the guardsmen copied the gesture, Ben and Orli joining them.

Zach was breathing heavily in the center of the ring, his sword held loosely at his side. He tossed it to the other hand, so that the blade curved end over end in a silvery arch. Then he held out his right to Maxt for a handshake. "The honor was all mine," he told the captain honestly, who shook his hand firmly. Then Maxt put his right forearm to Zach's, showing him the common way friends greeted one another in the Land.

After another small, courteous bow, both men walked from the ring to thunderous applause and cheers.

Zach could feel his blood singing in his veins, accepting the praise and congratulations from the men as he passed by them. He walked over to the fence, his biggest supporters following him. Stripping off the leather jerkin, he tossed it on the fence, then pulled his t-shirt off over his head, since it was plastered to his skin with sweat.

Out of the corner of his eye, Ben saw the Seer flinch and stop dead still in her tracks. He turned to her, concerned. She was staring straight ahead, her eyes wide. Ben followed her gaze and shook his head in dismay. What was it about Zach's back that caused women to swoon? Ben turned to tease the Seer about her infatuation with the man's skin.

Then he noticed that it wasn't appreciation for Zach's muscular physique that had her flummoxed. On her face was etched pure shock, and her cheeks were drained of all color. She actually swayed in place, as if in danger of keeling over.

"What's wrong?" Ben asked anxiously, putting a hand on her arm. Anja came to stand on the other side of the Seer, her brown eyes showing that she, too, was worried about the woman.

"Bird eternal," the Seer whispered. "I thought it was referring to the astral projection."

"What are you talking about?" Ben pressed gently. Zach was laughing with Orli now, the Phoenix tattoo on his back rippling as he recreated some of the moves from the sword fight. "Is this about Zach's tattoo? It's from a movie he did, called *The Phoenix*."

Her color was returning as the Seer reached up to fiddle with the long chain of crystals that were draped around her neck. She was taking a long time to answer. "When Liz was here, I read her," the Seer admitted finally. "Liz did not write about it in her accounting, because it is such a private and special thing, when one Seer reads another."

"Can you share with me the results?" Ben asked.

"I think I have to, given what I see before me. I told Liz she would be saved by the bird eternal. We both believed it referred to her ability to astral project. She has incredible skill in that arena, better than any Seer on record. She can use her mind to fly over the Land like a bird. I just assumed..." her voice trailed off, then became more steady and resolved. "We thought it meant that perhaps Liz could Seer in my stead from the World or something, thus saving her from having to live here permanently. I was wrong. It's Zach. Zach is supposed to save her."

Ben, Anja and the Seer turned to stare at Zach. He looked at them and winked, then gathered his gear and headed for the lodge to wash up for lunch.

"So his quest isn't just to find the fortress," Ben said softly.

"No," the Seer replied. "He is here to save Liz from having to take my place. But how? And will he do what's needed?" She worried her bottom lip, staring into the distance.

Ben said grimly, "All he's planning on doing is finding the pyramid. If there's more, we need to tell him."

"We start the hunt for the fortress tomorrow," the Seer replied. "I'll need to talk to him before we go, however. I can't let him go off with us and not be honest with him that I feel he is connected to Liz's future. There's more to this than just hunting down the temple. I know it in my soul."

Ben watched her for the rest of the afternoon, but the Seer did not approach Zach until after the evening meal was completed. She walked up behind Zach and placed her hands on his shoulders.

"Walk with me, Zachary."

Zach was tempted to decline, knowing that the Seer was seeking him out for a reason. He just wasn't sure if he wanted to hear what she had to say. But her presence was powerful and his manners too well entrenched. There was no way Zach could refuse her request. He pushed away from the table and followed her out the door.

"It is chilly tonight," the Seer observed as they wandered in the cleared area between the barrack buildings.

"Somehow I doubt that you asked me out to consult the weather," Zach replied easily.

The Seer laughed. "You know, I recognized your name," she confided, linking her arm through his. "I know you're aware that I lived in the World Dimension for several years. Your sitcom was a favorite of mine. But my, Zachary, how you have grown up."

"Kids tend to do that," he replied stiffly. Christ, he'd come all the way across the Interdimensional Void of space and he still had to deal with fans. Great. Perfect. Wonderful.

"Now I have made you uncomfortable," the Seer observed lightly. "No more discussion about fame, then. Let us discuss something of much greater import."

"Liz?"

"Your mama didn't raise a fool," the Seer said, the lilt of the south creeping into the common phrase. "Although I gather your mother did little to raise you. Regardless, yes, I want to talk with you about Liz."

"You want me to rescue her."

The Seer stopped and stared at him, then laughed until she had to hold her sides for the ache to subside. "Damn, Zachary," she said, wiping her eyes. "Just who is the Seer here, anyway? Yes, I want you to rescue her. Yet I find it odd you would use that word. Rescue. It implies that she is a damsel in distress waiting for you to save her. Liz would not take kindly to that terminology, you know."

Zach scuffed a toe in the dirt as a dog barked in the distance, the crickets ratcheting up their nightly song. "I know she wouldn't," he said quietly. "The word was used... I don't know. I don't care. It's just semantics. I don't view Liz as needing me to save her or anything. I think, perhaps, it might be the other way around."

The Seer tilted her head at him. "What do you need saving from, Zachary Neol?"

"You know, you and Liz are the only ones who call me Zachary."

"You're evading the question."

"I know."

The Seer continued to look at him. The kindness in her eyes, the understanding reflected in those golden green depths, was his undoing.

"I have not been very happy in my life." He held up a hand. "Wait. That sounded outrageously wretched. I've been happy. I've had bursts of absolute joy, in fact. But overall, when I look back at my life, I have an overwhelming sense of futility, like I've missed out on something vital to me. I used to think it was my childhood," he bracketed the word with his fingers in the air, "but after this last movie, I realized it was because I was missing my mission in life.

"Mission?"

"It's hard to explain." Hands raked through his hair as he struggled to express the inexpressible. "All my life, I've done what other people told me to do. Even in my last role, which was the most free I've ever been to express myself, I was under the constraints of what the director and writer wanted me to portray. I'm always the amalgam of what the writer put on the page and the director wanted to see. I've been what my parents wanted me to be when off stage, as well. I've lived my life so much in the open that I've lost who I am inside. I'm…struggling with that.

"But when I was with the Protectors…in that basement…I was alive. I was more me, if that makes any sense whatsoever. Meeting Liz was liberating. I literally felt my heart lighten. It was a miracle, ma'am, an absolute miracle. And then I came here." Zach looked around and the Seer frowned at the emotion seeping from the man.

"Why does the Land make you feel melancholy, Zachary?"

"I'm here, and I find out I might be a Protector, and you know what? It's another role. Another part. I'm not here for me. I'm here for the Land. And for Liz, although I can't figure that part out just yet. But she's tied up in it somehow. I just feel like…I fought my way to get to a place where I was in control of my destiny and boom! I'm still fulfilling a script, although I haven't been given the courtesy of a read through. I don't know what is expected of me until I turn the page, so to speak."

"And when you turn the page now?" asked the Seer. "What is your morning call, Zachary?"

"I see myself going with you to find this strange fortress. Seems the part I am to play is reluctant guide, unsure of his actions and half certain he's going to fail."

"A noble part."

Zach was silent for a long moment, then turned to the Seer, who was a dark shape in the evening's gloom. "What do you think is in that fortress?"

"The future." When Zach opened his mouth, the Seer put up her hand. "I don't know why, or how, or what, but that's what I see. The future. Not a specific one, but just…future. I can't explain it any more than you could explain your Q factor. Let's go back inside, Zachary. It's chilly out here and I think we're going to need our rest."

-12-
Fortress Tracking

That night, Zach tossed and turned on the cot in the guards' barracks. The snoring of the other men was a din to be reckoned with, and the absence of the ocean's surf was beginning to affect his sleep pattern. Not to mention the fact that he was a mass of aches from head to toe from his battle with Maxt. He'd give his eye teeth for a hot shower and a bottle of ibuprofen.

Ben and Anja had been granted one of the small, private bunkhouses, and the Seer and Maxt were given the honor of using the main lodge's guest room. Zach had not argued about sleeping with the men since he figured the couples deserved a little privacy. But damn, the men snored loudly. And the amount of gas that was being expelled from the various bodies made Zach infinitely grateful they were leaving in the morning. He'd need to air out all of his belongings.

In the wee hours of the morning, Zach rolled over on his stomach, hugging his pillow tightly as he tried to will himself to go to sleep. He was going to need his sleep given the hike that was sure to come the next day.

When he finally did slip into slumber, the dream that came was a pleasant surprise. Slender hands began to work on his knotted shoulder muscles, which were aching from the day's exertions. Zach buried his head into the pillow, grateful for the massage, even if it was only a dream. In small circular motions, the hands brought him gentle relief. He could smell a waft of heady perfume, so he knew his savior was a female. The friction of her skin against his was building all sorts of pleasant sensations and sparking all kinds of nifty responses in his body. *God bless the imagination,* he thought as he drifted along. There was only one person he hoped his subconscious had conjured for this nocturnal wandering…

"Liz?" he whispered drowsily.

"Shhhh," came the soft female voice, as she leaned over him, her hair tickling his back as she whispered into his ear. "Relax."

Zach complied; simply let himself go into the tranquil place the hands were taking him. Around and around went her palms, digging and pulling at his muscles until they relaxed completely. Zach moaned softly as they worked over a particularly tender spot along his side. Finally the hands smoothed over his entire back in smooth, long, even strokes. It was simply heaven. When a soft butterfly kiss was pressed against his tattoo, Zach smiled against the pillow.

"Nice," he murmured.

"I can be nicer," came the purred reply.

Zach turned his head to look at her, his eyes sleepy and sexy. Instead of seeing Liz's image, which was what he fully anticipated, what he saw was a head of curly dark hair spilling over a white shoulder, a woman's beautiful face that was graced with wide green eyes and red lips made for kissing. She was smiling at him with wicked intent clear in those remarkable eyes.

Zach bolted upright in the bed, his arms shaking and his body rock hard. He was alone in the barracks. Well, not alone, given the fact that about twenty men were sleeping in their cots all over the place, but there was no brunette woman crouching over him, giving him a massage, that was for sure. He rubbed his hand over his sweaty face, groaning as he realized it had in fact been a dream. A rather vivid dream, but clearly his mind had wandered while falling asleep. Yet, his muscles were decidedly looser, more flexible and the general aches were subsiding. It was very disconcerting.

It was a long time before Zach fell back asleep, and then it was morning before he knew it. The men in the barracks roused early, their banter and noise waking Zach. Quietly, he got dressed and ready to start the hike. He told no one about the dream, not even Ben or the Seer, feeling vaguely guilty for having such a vivid dream about another woman when he was clearly forming an attachment to Liz. He was left feeling rather used and, well, dirty, if truth be told.

The memory of the dream and lingering feeling of unease did not portend a good morning for Zach, causing him to be more irritable than he normally would be. Coupled with the fact that there was no such thing as coffee in the Land, he was quickly becoming a veritable bear. He was itching for a fight, and he knew it.

The first argument began bright and early, right after breakfast. Maxt had laid out a grid for them to search for the fortress and was intent on taking it one portion at a time. When shown their first excursion's path on the map, Zach protested vehemently.

"I'm telling you that the fortress doesn't lie in that direction," he found himself shouting at Maxt, pointing in the general way Maxt wanted to explore first.

Maxt stood with his arms crossed, his eyes narrowed, the map still spread on the table before him. The rest of the guardsmen were staring at the pair uneasily. It was clear that people rarely, if ever, disagreed with an action Maxt had decided upon.

"We need to go about this in a logical fashion and not run amok like a chickens," Maxt gritted, not giving an inch. "The terrain is more conducive to such a structure in these other areas. Where you want to search is very hilly. I doubt a fortress could be built there. We need to be reasonable and look in the areas that make the most sense first."

"Fine! You go about it your way, and I'll go in the direction that I *know* the place is located," Zach said, equally stubborn, his arms crossed as well. The two large men glared at one another. They had similar yellowish flares in their eyes, and the blue and green orbs were visibly clashing.

"Perhaps we should let the Seer decide," Ben suggested, hoping to ease the uncomfortable situation. All it earned him was a hard smack on the shoulder from the Seer. "Ouch, that hurt," he protested, rubbing the spot.

"Smooth move, Ben," she muttered at the Sea Dimension man. "Making me choose between my man and Zach. That is just not fair at all."

Zach and Maxt, still glaring at one another, both nodded tersely.

"I'm all right with the Seer deciding which way to go first," Zach agreed.

"I would agree with that decision as well," Maxt said with gruff approval.

The Seer tossed Ben a look that clearly said he would pay for his actions, then stepped up to face the two men. She took one deep breath, then another. Closing her eyes she was quiet for a long while as she searched her mind for an answer.

Finally, she opened her eyes, smiling up at Maxt. He gave her a grin, as if confident that she was going to bend to the wisdom of his plan. She placed a gentle hand on his arm.

"I love you more than anything in this Land, Maxt. You are my heart and soul. But my conscience tells me that in this matter, we need to listen to Zach. He is the one on the quest, and his instincts in this matter are paramount."

Maxt slowly lowered his arms, staring at the Seer, the smile fading from his face at her words. He opened his mouth as if to say something, then closed it abruptly again. He gave a swift nod then turned on his heel, ostensibly to go and speak with Tomikil before they left.

Zach flinched as the Seer put her hand on his arm. She frowned when she noted the muscles under his skin were tightly clenched as if he were ready to start a battle. "Zachary," the Seer said quietly, "I think you know where we are to go. But that doesn't mean it is going to be an easy journey for anyone involved. Maxt is used to being in charge. It will be an adjustment for him to turn those reins over to you. Be mindful of that fact, would you? For me?"

Zach closed his eyes, the tension draining from his body at her honest words. "All right," he said slowly, turning to the Seer. "But I know what I'm doing in this. You have to trust me on that fact."

"I do trust you, Zachary," the Seer said quietly as the man walked over to where Ben was saying his goodbyes with Anja. "I trust you with more than you will ever know."

Ben looked up as Zach approached. "I have to leave you here," he said slowly. "Experience has shown us that when a new Worlder is questing, it is best for all the other Protectors to be out of the Land. Something about the different dimension presence detracting from the one who was called or some such nonsense. Amber can explain it better, but oh, well. I do know that I'm leaving you in excellent hands."

Zach nodded. "I had a feeling you'd be leaving, actually," he told Ben agreeably, handing him a small folded piece of parchment. "Give that to Liz, would you?"

Ben nodded, putting the paper in his shirt pocket and patting it to indicate he would guard it well.

"Good luck, Zach," he said, giving the man a firm handshake. Zach returned it with relish, knowing he was going to really miss Ben's easygoing presence, especially since he and Maxt seemed to be constantly at loggerheads and Orli was not entirely enamored of him either.

Zach watched as Ben and Anja walked towards a small tree. Ben kissed his wife passionately, ignoring the catcalls from the men in the barracks. After a final caress of her cheek, he turned away from her. Then he walked over to the tree without a backward glance and wrapped his hand around it. Right before he disappeared, Ben's eyes pierced the distance to bore into Anja's.

When he was gone, Anja's shoulders slumped suddenly, as if some of her natural spark had left with her husband. Orli hurried over to wrap his arm around her shoulders, speaking to her urgently as they walked away together. The Seer spoke from behind Zach's shoulder.

"It is always difficult when their loved one leaves," she said, nodding towards Orli and Anja. "I am grateful that they have formed a strong friendship. They give one another strength, and that is a good thing. Especially since Anja has been told of Liz's vision for her parenting future."

"I was wondering if Ben had told her. I guess that Anja and Orli are sort of like how Tracy and Ben are in the World Dimension, the odd ones out but relying on one another to help get through the tough separations." Zach observed, nodding. He'd never thought about it from the Land point of view but it made sense that Orli and Anja would develop a bond just as Ben and Tracy had back in the World Dimension.

Maxt, Orli, Zach and the Seer headed out after Anja left on the Griffin, starting in the direction that Zach had indicated. Maxt had tried to convince the beasts to assist in their search, but the Griffins had flat out refused to help, leaving the group to hike to the temple.

Their path was leading them to the heart of the Meadows Region. The plan was to travel where Zach led, with a maximum of five days out of the barracks before heading back in for more supplies. The fewer items they took with them, the faster they could travel, that was the consensus. Zach agreed out of form, because he was convinced that their current path would lead them to the fortress well within the five-day limit. Zach was infinitely aware of the passing of time and feeling an increasing sense of urgency to get to the temple as soon as possible.

They kept a swift pace, Zach ranging ahead of the group periodically. It was strange. His every nerve was heightened, putting all his sense on alert. It was as if he could perceive what was over the next rise before he saw the vista.

"He is like some sort of tracking dog, caught on a scent," Orli marveled as Zach turned and made a beeline for a small hill nearby.

"Tracking," said the Seer in a musing voice.

"He does seem to know where to go on an instinctual level," Maxt reluctantly admitted. "He must be an incredible hunter in the World."

"He is an actor," the Seer said, puffing slightly from all the hiking, but rather proud of herself for keeping up with the men.

"An actor?" Orli and Maxt exclaimed, staring at Zach, who was standing on top of the hill, staring into the distance.

"Yep," the Seer replied.

The men exchanged a dubious look. The Seer laughed at them, for they had the disdain of men who were accustomed to a lot of physical activity and thought actors sat around all day doing nothing. They had no idea the amount of physical training that Zach would have to go through for movie roles, and if what Ben had told her about Zach's recent movie was true, the actor was probably in as good of shape, possibly better, than the two warriors from the Land.

The Seer eyed the men critically. Zach was easily as broad as Maxt through the shoulders, and probably stood barely an inch taller. Orli may have him in the shoulder region, but his overall build was much more willowy and lithe than the actor. Zach was muscles from head to toe, or so it appeared. Solidly built like her Maxt, and almost as handsome, in her decidedly biased opinion.

Zach turned suddenly and gave the Seer a blinding smile. She blushed, realizing she was gawking at him like a crush-stricken schoolgirl. He winked at her as she climbed to stand beside him.

"Quit comparing us," he scolded her lightly, making the Seer laugh.

"How did you know?"

"Ah, I'm an actor. We're used to being assessed like a side of beef, but I think Orli and Maxt might take offense," he replied easily, his eyes on the horizon, but the Seer could tell that kind of measurement bothered him. She laid a gentle hand on his arm.

"You are much more than the sum of your body parts," she informed him softly. "More than the pleasing planes of your face or the cut of your muscles or the charm of your smile. I value you for yourself, Zachary, as you should value yourself above all."

He tilted his head down to look at her, a contemplative look etched on his face. "That was…profound, and insightful. Value myself above all. It's a nice motto, actually."

"I'm not a Seer for nothin'," she joked in reply, then gave him a surprisingly coyish glance. "Just do not blame me for looking when the package is just so…nicely presented."

Zach roared with laughter, his amusement genuine. "All righty, then," he replied with glee. "Look away. Just don't let Maxt see, ok?" he said in a stage whisper.

"See what?" came the deep rumble of Maxt's voice. Zach gave an exaggerated wince, clutching at his heart dramatically as he staggered back a step or two.

"It was nice knowing you," he said spectacularly to the Seer. "I think I'm about to be killed."

The Seer actually snickered, then turned to Maxt. "Zach caught me admiring all of you," she admitted to him as Orli watched with something akin to horror. "All my fine men, so handsome and strong. Who can blame a girl for looking?" she fluttered her lashes at Maxt, who narrowed his green eyes in response.

Orli looked decidedly uncomfortable and shifted from foot to foot, which was very unlike his usual stoic and solid presence. Zach just watched the proceedings with amusement clearly written on his face.

Maxt growled low in his throat and advanced on the Seer. She threw up her hands in front of her in a gesture to ward him off. Orli started forward, concerned, but Zach held him back by the arm.

"Just watch," he advised Orli, who eased back, his hands still fingering his bow nervously. "And learn."

Maxt moved very quickly, scooping up the Seer and tossing her over one shoulder. She was laughing and protesting, smacking him on the back and butt as he turned to face the younger men.

"Any questions?" he said to them.

"None," Orli assured him, smiling and relaxing as he realized that the Seer and Maxt were simply goofing around.

"How fast are you going to run when you finally set her down?" Zach asked, "Because she is going to whale on you but good when she gets the chance." The Seer twisted her face around Maxt's side and gave him a grin.

"That's my boy," she crowed, earning her a rather hard smack on her rump from Maxt.

As Maxt turned and started down the hill, still carrying her over his shoulder, Zach could have sworn he heard the Seer mutter, "Promises, promises."

-13-
Campfires and Seduction

As they made camp that night, Zach became increasingly agitated. He was exhausted from the day's hike but worried that he might have a disturbing dream like the night before. He was therefore much more quiet than he normally would have been, a fact the Seer remarked on with no small concern. He shrugged it off to being tired, but she gave him a searching look that indicated he'd not fooled her.

After a quick meal, they lounged around their campfire talking and laughing easily together. Maxt was surprisingly amusing, especially in the way he and the Seer interacted. Zach could tell that not only were the two were deeply devoted to each other, but they also enjoyed one another's company. They had an easy rapport that was both light and loving, and to Zach, used to his high-powered parents and their business-like marriage, it was a marvel. Before long, however, it was time to unroll the sleeping pallets and bed down for the night.

Zach had agreed to take the first watch, more to delay going to sleep than anything else. He moved a few yards away from the campfire and settled down; his back against a tree. From this vantage point he could see a great deal of the surrounding area, and his watch would necessitate only a few walks around the camp to make sure no one was approaching.

The stars were impossibly bright overhead, the configurations unfamiliar to his eyes. A shooting star appeared on the horizon, and he made a wistful little wish, feeling strangely comforted by the action.

"What did you wish for?"

Zach was on his feet in an instant, his sword out and in front of him. Heart racing, he looked around, but could not find the source of the comment.

"Up here."

Zach craned his neck up. Sitting in the crook of the tree was Liz. She was wearing the same dress she'd had on the night of the party, the Grecian lines of it flowing over her bare toes, her hair still bound into the intricate knot that allowed some tendrils to flutter in the breeze. The tip of Zach's sword lowered to the earth as he stared at her, dumbfounded.

"What are you doing here?" he asked rather hoarsely.

"I'm not sure," she looked confused. "I was meditating on the back porch and suddenly, I was here. Well, not really here, per say, but…"

"I don't understand."

"I'm astral projecting, Zachary. My physical body is back on the porch in a rather comfortable lotus position, but I carried myself out of my body and somehow managed to navigate the Interdimensional Void and boom! I found you. Although I'm at a loss to understand why I'm sitting in a tree. I hated climbing trees as a child."

Zach sheathed his sword and reached up to her. "Come here, then. I'll help you get down."

She shook her head at him, smiling. "I'm not really here, Zachary. It's nice of you to offer help, but not necessary." She then leapt from the tree, landing lightly beside him. He could see that the lines of her body and dress were slightly blurred, as if ever so subtly out of focus. Then he noticed another odd thing and bent over, peering at her right shoulder.

Her gown bared the shoulder. Back home, it had been a smooth, unblemished slope that Zach had ached to press kisses against, but here in the Land, it was adorned with a glittery tattoo. How odd, for Liz did not seem to be a tattoo chick, even in her subconscious.

But there was a certain beauty to the swirling pattern of silvery glow. There was not a discernable design to the tattoo, rather it was an organic, flowing set of lines that graced her shoulder. Wait. Hadn't there been something in her quest…

"Seer Sign," Liz supplied softly. "When I'm in the Land physically, it would only show on the full moon. The Seer told me that hers has always shown up when she astral projects as well."

"Didn't Katie see the Seer when she astral projected?" Zach asked, trying to recall. "I don't remember her mentioning a silver tattoo when she wrote about the experience."

"The Seer's Sign is in a rather…inaccessible place," Liz said, her nose wrinkling with amusement. "Mine, as you can tell, is much more easily seen."

"It's beautiful," Zach declared, then gave her a wary look. "Wait a second. How do I know that you aren't Evil, trying to infiltrate the mission?"

"Good point," said Liz. "I'm proud of you for already assuming things can be different than they appear. So, how do you propose to tell the difference?"

Zach clicked his fingers. "I know! I sent you a letter with Ben. What did it say?"

Liz looked down at her hands. She plucked at her dress absently as she said, without looking at him, "You said that you'd do whatever you could to make sure I could make my own destiny and not have to do what was dictated to me."

Zach smiled, because that was indeed what he had written in the letter, but the grin faded at the somewhat disenchanted look on her face. "Why do I get the feeling that you're not happy with me for saying that?"

"I have to go now," Liz said abruptly, moving away from Zach.

Instinctively, he made to grab her arm, but his hand passed right through her form. Cursing, he ran to put himself in front of her.

"Wait. What did I say wrong?" When she was stubbornly silent, staring off to the side, he pressed, "Liz, you have to tell me so I don't make the same kind of mistake again."

Liz sighed and rubbed her forehead with one slender hand. Then her eyes pierced his, and he was surprised to read a deep seeded anger residing in the amber depths. "Don't think I'm some princess waiting in a tower for you to save, Zachary," she said hotly. "I can take care of my own destiny. I don't need you to be my champion, or my savior. I know I may look fragile but I'm much stronger than you could ever know."

Zach groaned. He'd really put his foot in it good, he thought. "I've read the accounting of your quest," he told Liz quietly. "I don't find you fragile or helpless. Honestly," he stressed as she snorted her disbelief. "I find that you're incredibly giving, friendly, and dedicated. You'd come to the Land if they called for you in a heartbeat. But I can't stand the fact that you don't get to call the shots for your own future."

"It is the way it is," Liz said simply, raising her hands. "I've come to grips with that fact."

"I know, but you have to understand something," Zach ran a hand through his hair. "When I was a kid, I was told what to do, what to read, what job to take. I was instructed on how to speak, what to like, even who my friends were going to be. I couldn't stand the fact that I didn't have a choice in the matter. So my entire adult life, short as it's been, has been about me making my own choices and decisions. When I see you being forced to wait, unsure what world you'll live in, putting your entire life on hold, well, it just makes me antsy and makes me want to give you freedom. That's all I meant."

Liz looked at him, understanding a little better what his life must have been like. "It must be making you insane, knowing that the Land is making choices and decisions for you," she whispered. "You aren't in control of your own destiny at the moment, just like when you were a child."

Zach shrugged. "It bothers me. I'm not going to front about it. But…when you've lived this way your entire life, you learn to go with the flow. Until it becomes unbearable, that is. Besides, seems like this is going to be an easy gig. Find this fortress and then Maxt and his people will do what they need to do about it. I should be home within a week."

Liz graced him with a smile and Zach felt immense relief, knowing they were back on stable ground. "I really do have to go."

"Thank you for visiting me," Zach said. "It helped."

"Good," she said, her outline blurring even more and fading into the night. "Sleep well, Zachary."

Zach stood still for a long moment, watching where Liz's form had stood. Then he sighed and quickly walked the perimeter of the camp before settling with this back against the tree. When he was relieved by Orli several hours later, Zach spread out his blankets and laid down on his back, cushioning his head on his hands as he looked up at the night sky.

Zach drifted to sleep, his eyes closing slowly. As he fell into slumber, his dreams started up. He was jogging on the beach with Tracy, who was hugely pregnant.

Then, he was sitting on his porch talking with Katie, who was glowing from head to toe in a light pink fuzzy color. She pointed over his shoulder and he turned to see Sasha in her wedding gown, sitting on the beach and staring out to sea.

"What's going on?" he asked Katie, who smiled at him and then split into a million pink pieces. In her place was the woman from his dream the night before. The black curly hair, green eyes and curved red smile were familiar to him, niggling the back of his mind.

"What do you want to have going on?" she asked him in a clearly seductive voice.

"Who are you?"

"Well, if I have to tell you, then what is the fun in the game?" she said, standing up to showcase a rather spectacular body in a skintight cat suit of black vinyl. She noted his perusal of her and smiled slowly. "Oh yes, Zach, I think you and I will get along nicely."

"What if I don't want to play the game?" he said lightly, but his heart was pounding. Damn the male body for its often involuntary reactions.

"Then I'll have to kill them," she said, gesturing. Zach looked over to see his companions sleeping by the fire, the Seer's face reflected in the fire, Maxt's form a black shadow behind her. In the distance, he could see Orli standing, staring away from the fire, scanning the horizon.

"No you won't," Zach vowed hotly, reaching for a sword that wasn't there, since he was still dreaming. "I won't let that happen."

She simply smiled at him, confidence oozing from her every pore. "We'll talk again, Zach," she promised, leaning over him and brushing his lips with her ruby red ones. He tried to twist his head to one side to avoid the kiss, but was somehow held immobile in the dream. "See? This is my realm, Zach. I control the action here. I control all your dreams and desires. I know what you desire, Zach. Believe me, I do." She trailed a long, sharp fingernail down his chest, then splayed her hand low on his belly. "Oh yes, we will talk again, Zach." She gave him a wicked smile and winked out of sight.

For the second night in a row, Zach sat bolt upright in his blankets, bathed in sweat. He was shaking, but whether it was rage or his physical reaction, he could not really tell. Those dream experiences were exhausting, he realized as he lay back down, weak and slightly feverish. Again, it took a long time for him to fall back asleep.

Morning came all too soon. Maxt woke everyone up as the sun touched the horizon and handed out a kind of jerky for their breakfast. Zach was tired, but again refrained from telling anyone about his night time wanderings and visitations. He also didn't tell the Seer about Liz's visit. That was private.

After they broke camp, Maxt turned to Zach. "Which way?" he asked gruffly. Zach nodded to the west and Maxt did not hesitate and started off in that direction.

Two nights of broken sleep had left Zach a little punchy. Halfway through the morning, he started humming songs. Soon he and the Seer were belting out Bruce Springsteen classics, and teaching Orli and Maxt their favorites. Maxt was particularly drawn to the oldies, which Zach found ridiculously hysterical for some reason.

"Why don't we sing more?" asked Maxt, his face full of boyish delight. "We used to sing all the time in the Land. Why don't we sing anymore? Where did all the music go?"

"I don't know," answered the Seer. "I've wondered about it periodically, but it seems that with our darker times fighting Evil, music has gone by the wayside. I don't believe I have been able to sing any of the songs from the World since I came back."

"Then why can you now?" asked Zach.

The Seer turned and looked at him with a questioning flare in her eyes. "I think it is because of you, Zachary. You are a Worlder, steeped in the traditions of your dimension. Music is intrinsic to your world so you are able to retain that part of you, even here."

"It is a shame that we have lost our music," said Orli.

"The shame is that your voice is like a seagull rasping," said Maxt with a laugh.

The Seer and Zach launched into more songs. They were finishing up the last chorus of an old Billy Joel song when they hit the first fence.

It was invisible, so one second they were walking along, singing at the top of their lungs, and the next, the Seer was thrown sideways into Zach, and then the two of them went tumbling backwards into Maxt and Orli. It was as if a force field had lifted them off their feet and tossed them back like leaves.

Maxt, who had been watching carefully, noticed that when the Seer had hit the fence, something had flashed into view. He caught a brief glimpse of criss-crossed wires that were set at regular intervals with small round balls before it faded back from view. Automatically, he called out what he was seeing, even as his companions sprawled back from the fence.

Zach and the Seer got up from the ground, Orli helping them. Maxt was staring intently at the fence, trying to see it again.

"Thanks for the concern," the Seer told him sarcastically, wiping leaves and grass off her leather pants.

"I hope to see more," Maxt informed her, his eyes still sweeping the area.

Zach joined him. "I thought I saw it too," he admitted. "Just as the Seer hit the fence, there was a brief impression of some sort of grid." He narrowed his eyes, trying to see if he could detect anything. Orli and the Seer joined the men staring at the space.

Slowly, as if by the force of those watching, the fence materialized in front of Zach's eyes. Zach didn't dare blink. He could see the black wires, crossing over each other, and at every intersection was a brown, round ball. It looked like a sophisticated form of tinker blocks, in his opinion. Worse, the fence was easily ten feet tall.

"I can see it," he said to the others.

"Can you?" Maxt asked Orli, who was well known for his excellent eyesight. The mountain villager swept the area in front of them several times, then finally shook his head in defeat.

"Well, the Worlder can see what the Land folk cannot," the Seer commented, dusting the last of the dirt off her hands. "That could mean several things."

"But mostly, it means that the fence was not made by someone in the Land," Maxt guessed.

"Yes," she confirmed, then frowned, adding softly, "but that begs the question…who did make it? That is the more confounding and disturbing question."

"I would think 'why' would be more worrisome," Orli commented.

"Oh, the why is obvious to me," Zach replied easily as he started to walk down the fence line, looking for a possible break in the fence. "It's to keep us out, which means we're on track to finding the hidden fortress."

"That makes sense," Maxt agreed, following Zach. "Do you see any weaknesses in the fence?"

"Not yet…wait!" Zach rushed ahead to where a boulder was lodged against the fence. He dropped to the ground, laying prone, peering across the grass. He reached out carefully, keeping his hand close to the ground, until his arm was sticking straight out from his body.

"Is it loose there?" Maxt asked.

"Nope," said Zach as he carefully rose, keeping his arm outstretched, the fingers curled as if holding an invisible bar. When he was on his knees, he turned carefully towards the fence, bringing his other hand up to join the first. He stood up, the muscles in his neck and arms bulging as he pulled on something that could not be seen.

"Are you yanking the fence up?" the Seer asked, incredulous.

Zach nodded, sweat breaking out on his temple. "It's limbo time. Go under," he instructed the Seer tightly. "Stay between my body and the boulder. I've got the bottom of the fence about three feet off the ground, so go under it belly first. Hurry."

The Seer immediately dropped and crawled under the fence. Maxt and Orli followed suit, after passing the large packs underneath the fence. Then Zach let the fence fall, his arms tingling with fatigue.

"Damn, Zach, you are on the opposite side of the fence," Maxt pointed out.

"Not to worry," he said, then simply walked through the fence with ease. The others goggled at him, not believing what they had just seen.

"How did you do that?" the Seer finally asked.

"Well, when you hit the fence, you were knocked into me. I never hit the fence, I only fell because of you," Zach pointed out, grinning.

"I figured I could go through the fence, and the more important thing was to get you three through first, then me."

"Why was it more important that we go through first?" Orli asked quietly, sensing there was more to this than Zach was letting on.

"I think I'm supposed to be getting through the fences," Zach observed. He'd no idea where this certainty came from, but he knew he was right. Knew it to the core of his very being. "But you guys aren't. If I went through the fence first, I'm willing to bet that a whole different defense system would kick in to keep you guys apart from me."

"That is an interesting theory," Maxt commented, his hands on his hips. "But if you were able to go through it, how did you pull it up from the bottom like that?"

"The top and bottom of the fence were made of thicker bars," Zach said, "but they were pliant, that much I could see how it molded to the Meadow's floor. So I found a place I could put my fingers under and started to lift it. Simple as that."

"Simple," Maxt said with a grunt, shaking his shaggy head. "Well, we know now there are defenses. We have to keep a sharp eye out. Especially you, Zach, since you might be able to see it first."

"I'd better not lead," Zach pointed out. "If I miss a sign, I could go through a fence and then we are separated."

"Agreed," Maxt said. "I shall take the point first, then."

-14-
Hidden Danger

Katie stepped out onto the deck, shivering slightly as the cool breeze struck her body. A cold front was moving through the Carolinas, bringing temperatures that were unseasonably chilly. Despite the brisk drop in the thermometer, Liz was sitting at the end of the dock, wrapped in a warm fleece sweatshirt, her hair pulled back into a long ponytail. Katie walked towards her, settling down next to the woman.

"You keep growing your hair and soon it will be impossible to tell you and Tracy apart from the back," Katie observed.

"My hair is more curls than waves," Liz said absently, plucking at a loose thread on her shoe. "And Tracy has darker streaks running through hers."

"Ah, true. So how are things going, Liz?"

She didn't even try to pretend she didn't understand the Oracle's question. "I'm so-so."

"It's tough," Katie agreed. "You don't want to get your hopes up, but you don't want to not support Zach in his quest. I'm guessing there's a little more than just a casual interest in how our current Protector is doing in the Land."

Liz shot her a wry glance. "Can't put much by you, can I?"

"Well, it helps that half of us were training binoculars on you and Zach when you were in the clench on the balcony," Katie admitted, then burst into laughter at Liz's horrified look. "Oh, honestly, did you think we were oblivious to the attraction the man has for you? And then, he sends you a note, a note you don't share with the rest of us, from the Land."

"It's so stupid," Liz said fiercely. "It's just because of his quest, that's all. He feels he needs to save me. When he comes back, it'll all be different."

"Why do you say that?" Katie asked with a puzzled frown. "Zach doesn't strike me as the type to play with someone's emotions."

"He's a movie star," Liz said flatly. "I'm a librarian. Figure the chances of that working out."

"He's a man, you're a woman," Katie corrected, gently but firmly. "Perhaps on some level, more importantly, you're a Seer and he's a Protector. The Land is a bond that precious few people share."

"He wants to save me, and I *hate* that. I don't need to be saved. I can do that myself. He needs to concentrate on his quest, not me."

"He is doing his quest," Katie pointed out. "The whys don't really matter, as long as the job gets done, right?"

Liz shrugged one shoulder. Katie tried another tact. "What do your instincts say about the matter?"

Liz closed her eyes, but Katie knew it wasn't to cast a thought forward. When she opened her amazing topaz eyes, they were full of tears. "I don't trust my instincts when it comes to these kinds of matters."

"Because of Valdeen?"

"Because of Valdeen," agreed Liz. "I trusted him with my entire soul. He was one of Evil's own and I didn't recognize it until it was almost too late. Because of my foolish infatuation, the Land was very nearly destroyed."

"No one holds that against you," Katie pointed out. "Valdeen fooled us all. Even Maxt. Hell, even the Prince of the freaking Land didn't realize he was a double agent. How could you be expected to discern it?"

"Because I'm a Seer, and I'm supposed to be able to ferret out Evil," Liz's voice was bitter.

"Evil is, by its very nature, a deceptive being. You were fooled by the master of deceit, and we all recognize that. I just wish you would give yourself a break."

"Well, it's useless to wonder about what will happen when Zach returns. What will be, will be." Liz stood up, holding a hand out to Katie. "I'm not going to waste my time wondering. I'll help him out however I can, but as for the rest… I think I will reserve the right to take it with a grain of salt."

"Help him out?" Katie queried, taking Liz's hand and allowing herself to be pulled to her feet. "How are you helping him out?"

Liz made a show of brushing off her pants, even though they were sand free. She shrugged and said in a nonchalant way, "The same way we all do, by being here if he needs us."

"Uh-huh," Katie was unconvinced. You didn't need to be a Seer to see the stain of a bright flush on Liz's cheeks. Something else was going on, she would bet her pink power on it.

As they walked up the long sea walk to the house, Katie started to ask Liz about dinner when the Seer suddenly bent over, clutching her middle. Katie wheeled towards her, her hands flaming pink. Whenever Liz did this, Evil was nearby. And it was generally bad. Very bad.

"What is it?" she barked, all business. "Is it Tracy? The baby?"

"No," Liz gasped, her whiskey colored eyes stark in her pale face. "It's Sasha."

Within seconds, Katie, Liz and Ben were in the car, heading towards Sasha's office. The woman was finishing up some final projects before her wedding day. They'd successfully managed to dodge Tracy, who was resting. Sarat and Owen were on a day trip to the local aquarium.

"What did you sense?" Katie interrogated Liz from the passenger seat while Ben zipped down the coastal road at a fast clip.

"It's bad," Liz said dully, although that seemed to be a complete understatement, forming the words with difficulty. "I'm not sure what's going on, but it ranks right up there with what I felt when Valdeen was finally unmasked." She dug her fingertips into her eyes. "Maybe I'm just having a flashback or something," she guessed desperately. "What could happen to Sasha at her work, for goodness sake?"

"I trust your powers," Ben said simply, his greenish blue eyes looking at Liz in the rearview mirror. "If you say Sasha is in trouble, we go. Katie, call William on his cell. Tell him to get over to Sasha's office. He's out getting some stuff done for the wedding. He may be closer, for all we know."

Liz settled back into the seat of the car, hoping that her hunch was wrong and they'd find Sasha sitting at her desk, happily finishing up some project.

Sasha was indeed sitting at her desk, having just put the final touches on a graphic for a local gift shop. She was closing up her desk, humming happily, when the door to her office opened, causing the cheery bell to give a jingle. Her part time worker was out to lunch, so Sasha called out to the customer that she would be out in a minute.

A second later, a shadow appeared in her door, which she caught out of the corner of her eye. Irritated that the customer had skirted the counter out front and barged into the back office, she turned stood and turned towards the doorway. As she saw who was standing there, her blood ran cold and her breath hitched noticeably.

"Hello Sasha," the tall, thin man said with a congenial smile on his narrow but handsome face.

"What are you doing here, Father?" Sasha managed. Her throat was tight but the words came out clear. Sasha was glad for that, because if there was one thing her father thrived on, it was the slightest evidence of fear.

The elder Vanden walked into the room, trailing one hand over the glossy cherry desk that Sasha had placed in the space. "Oh, I read about your engagement in the paper. Quite a fancy party you had the other night. Seems improper that I, as father of the bride, was not invited."

Sasha gave him an incredulous look. "You can cut the concerned father routine," she spat out. "I'm done with my family. You have no part in my life, and even less in my office. I'd like you to leave now."

Her father settled down in a chair, his fingers plucking at a crease in his pant leg. "Oh, how that crushes me to hear you say that your family is no longer welcome in your life. Your sister is devastated to not be in the bridal party. Who will walk you down the aisle?" he wondered, his hands steepled and resting against his chin.

Sasha just stared at him. No way was she going to tell him that Ben was walking her down the aisle. He'd lost all rights to question her a long time ago.

He sighed. "Still stubborn. It was always your biggest fault, Sasha. How I prayed for you, night after night, for that sinful pride of yours to be cast from your body."

"What do you want?" Sasha said in measured, clipped tones. "And don't give me that shit about wanting to be a jolly, happy family."

"Still cursing as well, I see," he gave another sigh. Sasha merely raised an eyebrow at him. He waved a hand. "All right, then. I've come to deliver a message, Sasha."

"From who?"

"From the Reverend, of course."

Sasha laughed sardonically. "Why should I care about a message from that cult crackpot? You may listen to his doomsday lines of bullshit, but I don't subscribe to the whacked sense of religion that you and my sister have embraced. Thank goodness Sean escaped that crap, for all the good it did him to get sucked into the skin trade."

"You'll want to hear this," her father promised.

"Right. Well, go ahead. What does Preacher Doom and Gloom have to say about me now?" Sasha shook her head and started to gather some papers from her desk, fully intending to only give her father half her ear while she finished clearing up the work space.

"He wants you to stop interfering with the Land."

The papers fell from Sasha's fingers, cascading to the desk and floor like a fluttering rain. Her heart dropped to her stomach. "What did you say?" she whispered, her fingers clutching the edge of the desk for support.

"I thought that would get your attention," her father grinned smugly. "I said, the Reverend wants you and your little group of friends to stop interfering with the Land."

"What do you know of the matter?" Sasha spat as terror made her pulse spike.

Her father frowned. "Not much, actually. Just that you and this group you are aligned with are helping this place, and mucking up the proper way of things. Sacrilege, really, to interfere with the cosmic plan. All things happen for a reason, Sasha. You are unable to glean that your meddling is going to cause terrible ramifications."

Sasha felt on more even ground. If her father was spouting off that she should stop helping the Land, then of course she would do the exact opposite. "I'm old enough to make my own decisions, Father. I think I know a lot more about the situation than you do, so you can just trot on back to the good reverend and tell him to shove his concern and his true master up his considerable ass."

Her father was on his feet in an instant, his face taking on a beatific look. "I told the Reverend that you would be unresponsive to reason. And that with a willful child such as yourself, more stringent methods had to be employed."

His face held such a look of joy that Sasha stepped back, repulsed. "What makes you think that I'm going to stand by and let you beat me? I'm no longer a child, and you no longer have control over me." She fell into a combatant stance. No way was she going to be a victim again. And little did her father know the skills she'd gained since leaving his compound.

"You are insignificant," her father maintained as he pulled off his belt, "but the message must be made clear to those within your group."

"I would hardly call my fiancé insignificant." William's voice came from the doorway. Despite her firm belief that she'd be able to take her father down and hardly break a sweat, Sasha had never been so happy to see another person in her life. It was just further proof that she was no longer alone in the world. She relaxed her stance. Her father would not try and force her to do anything when there were witnesses. He was an alley rat, preferring darkness and secrecy to cover his vile behavior.

William walked over to her and pressed a light kiss on her forehead. "Sorry I'm late, dear. I got caught at the tailor's. Fittings for the wedding and such."

"William, this is my father," said Sasha. "He was just leaving."

"This is not over," her father warned.

"Oh, but I think it is," Katie said, appearing in the door that William had just walked through. She and Ben slid into the room, their stances poised for a fight.

Sasha felt the support and love from William and her friends washing over her like a comforting blanket. She gave her father a brilliant smile. "Goodbye, Father." she told him with assurance.

"Oh, this is your dad?" Ben said with deceptive pleasantness. "I've waited a long time to meet you, sir."

Sasha's father turned, instinctively, holding out his hand in response to Ben's outstretched hand. Ben suddenly drew his hand back and without warning, cold cocked the man, clipping him in the chin with enough force to drive the man back into the wall.

"Darn, I was hoping I'd get to do that," William observed wryly.

"Nicely done, Ben," Katie said with a grin.

Sasha's father peeled himself away from the wall, dabbing at his lip, which was bleeding. Sasha tossed him a box of tissues from her desk. "Looks like you could use these," she said, stifling a laugh.

"You'll need a lawyer when I'm done with you, you arrogant whelp," the older man spat at Ben.

"Oh, I don't think so," William put in. "Otherwise, Sasha might be forced to explain how she was branded by you and your insane followers when she was a child. That wouldn't look too good in the church newsletter, now would it?"

Liz slumped against the doorway, her hand on the wall as if to steady herself. "He's evil," she gasped, pointing at Sasha's father. "Can't you feel it? It's all around him, like a cloud. It's difficult to breathe…"

"You people are the insane ones," Sasha's father gathered himself, knowing he was outnumbered. He tried for wounded dignity, and failed, probably because of the wad of white tissue that was clinging to his bottom lip, waving as he spoke. "Perhaps we can continue this discussion at another time, Sasha."

"Perhaps not," she replied easily. "Come back and try and see me again, and I guarantee you a stink so big you won't know which way is up."

"I think a nice big restraining order is in your future," William said to Sasha, who nodded thoughtfully.

"Yes, that will be the ticket," she agreed. "Goodbye, Father. And good riddance."

Her father stalked from the room. Sasha would have collapsed into the chair if not for William's hold around her waist. He gently lowered her, crooning into her ear. Now that her father was gone, the implications of what he'd said were roiling over her like acid. She couldn't get the words out, couldn't make her friends understand. She could only gulp air like a person held underwater for far too long.

Katie was again congratulating Ben, commiserating over his bruised knuckles. Liz was taking deep breaths, as if to regulate her inner and outer self, striving for balance. William simply hovered, unsure about why Sasha was still looking so distressed.

"He knows about the Land," Sasha gasped. All movement around her stopped. She quickly recounted what her father had told her. Katie, her face grim, spoke first.

"We need to get the others together. Talk about this. A message will need to be sent to the Land as well. Let's head back to the house. I'll text Sarat. Ben, warn Tracy we are coming home, and what just happened."

-15-
Obstacle Course

Maxt and Orli took turns leading the group, with Zach right behind them. Periodically they would stop, allowing Zach to scan the way in front of them carefully. Gone was the playful atmosphere of the morning as they all kept their guard up in the event that the next barricade was more overt.

The rest of the day passed in relative peace. At dinner that night, Zach again volunteered for the first shift of the watch. They didn't joke or laugh much around the campfire and prepared to retire early. The strain of knowing that someone or something had placed a deliberate barricade, one that was undetectable by the Land inhabitants, made the proximity of a hidden fortress that much more plausible.

As Zach scouted for a good place to sit during his watch, the Seer came up to stand near him.

"Is there something you would like to talk with me about?" she asked him softly, so the others by the fire could not hear her words.

"Why do you think that?" Zach hedged, scanning the horizon to avoid having to look the Seer in the eyes.

"I sense that something is troubling you," the Seer said calmly, "and it occurs to me that perhaps I could help you, if you would like me to. Your biorhythms are all out of whack."

Zach kept his breathing steady and risked looking at the Seer, keeping his face open and guileless. Thank God for acting classes. "I'm fine," he lied deliberately. "Just a little tired, that's all."

"If you are sure," the Seer said slowly. She clearly didn't believe him one bit, but Zach was betting she wouldn't breach his confidence by delving into his mind without permission.

"I'm sure," Zach said firmly.

He wasn't sure why, but he did not want to let the Seer know about his troubling dreams. Not yet. It was rather embarrassing; the way that strange woman was able to manipulate him in his subconscious. Until he could get control of his own mind, he wasn't going to admit to the Seer that he was having fantasies about some dark haired woman. As for the night time visit from Liz, that was still too personal. He would not tell the Seer until or unless he had a chance to discuss that action with Liz first. It didn't seem right to do otherwise.

"All right then," the Seer said, turning to go. Her pale ivory shirt was a gleam in the gathering darkness when she turned back to him, adding, "I am always here, Zachary. If you change your mind, I will listen."

"I know," was all Zach would say.

As the others around the campfire stilled, drifting into sleep, Zach prowled the edges of the camp, too restless to sit for any length of time. It seemed like his body was coursing with adrenaline, making his skin tingly and over sensitive to the cool night air.

When it came time for Orli to relieve him, there had been no visit from Liz. Zach was slightly disappointed by that fact, but figured astral projecting was not going to be a nightly occurrence.

Zach settled into his blankets, wary. He forced his mind to shut down, a trick he'd used to his benefit while filming the Phoenix, a shoot that required him to work late nights many times, and to grab sleep where and when he could.

It might have been the fact that he consciously willed himself to sleep, but Zach did not have a well-defined dream featuring the woman with the black hair and green eyes. He did have a series of jumbled up images that haunted him, highly sexual in nature, impressions of bare skin and forbidden kisses. A woman latched onto his neck, biting and licking him like his skin was coated in sugar. It wasn't really a dream, per se, but it was disturbing enough to have him wake up early in the morning, unable to sleep any more, his body a tight mass of sexual tension.

Zach nodded to Maxt and walked to the top of a nearby hill, where he put himself through the entire set of T'ai-Chi, needing the sense of balance that the routine would bestow upon him. When he came back down, shirtless and sweaty, the Seer handed him a plate of hot food, then peered at his neck, frowning.

"If I didn't know better, I'd swear that was a hickey on your neck, Zachary," she teased him.

Zach raised his hand to his neck. Sure enough, there was a slightly bruised spot there. He picked up his kit, pulling out the small mirror he had used for shaving. It did indeed look like a hickey. A sudden flash from his dreams the night before had him blushing.

Good God, if the hickey part were true, what of the rest? He shook his head, bewildered at how a dream could seem so real.

"Must be a bug bite," Maxt observed, shoveling in another mouthful of food.

"Right," Zach agreed firmly, pulling on his shirt. But he avoided the Seer's eyes as he sat down to eat.

"What's a hickey?" Orli asked the Seer, who gave Zach a rather helpless, 'how did I get myself into this conversation' glance.

"Don't look at me," he advised the Seer, pointing his fork at her. "You started it."

The Seer looked flustered, opening and closing her mouth several times. "Ask Tracy," she finally advised. Orli nodded good-naturedly.

"Chicken," Zach said with a smile.

"You bet your ass I am," she replied cheerfully; obviously glad to have dodged that particular bullet.

They broke camp and headed in the direction Zach indicated. Like the day before, Orli and Maxt took turns in the lead, with Zach trailing behind. Late in the morning, a glimmer ahead caught Zach's attention.

"Hold up," he called to Maxt, who was the leader at the moment. The guardsman halted immediately, glancing over his shoulder questioningly.

"Can I have some water?" Zach blurted as way of an excuse to join him. Maxt nodded, holding out his canteen.

Zach drew abreast with Maxt, squinting as he took a long drink of water. There, about two hundred yards ahead, was a shimmering wall.

It was as if someone had taken rippled glass and formed a barrier that undulated and moved.

"What do you see?" Maxt whispered to Zach, making it look like he was busy securing his canteen.

"A glass wall, about fifteen feet high," Zach replied without moving his lips. It was handy way for him to supply a clueless co-worker their lines on set.

"Any way to get around it?"

"Not that I can see right off the bat," Zach said.

The implications set in for Maxt immediately. Zach glanced over at Orli, who gave an almost imperceptible nod, indicating his excellent hearing had caught the conversation. His eyes were roaming around, seeing nothing but a large hawk in a nearby tree.

"I'm tired," the Seer complained suddenly. "I want to take a rest." Her voice was somewhat petulant, and quite unlike the norm for the Seer.

Maxt, recognizing the ploy immediately, and fell into the play. If anyone was watching them, it would not immediately appear like they had seen the barrier. "We need to keep moving," he said in a commanding voice.

"I am the Seer, and I say we take a break," she replied in a frosty voice, one that had Orli arching an eyebrow and Zach grinning into his pack.

"Can't hurt to take a rest," Zach put in. "I'm not used to this kind of hiking, you know."

With obvious ill humor, Maxt tossed his backpack down. "Fine," he growled. "But don't blame me if we fail to reach this mystical fortress. With the pace you are keeping we'll be lucky to reach the Beaches in a fortnight."

And here I thought I was the actor, Zach chuckled to himself, then said in a loud voice, "I'm going to go and scout out the area."

Leaving Maxt, Orli and the Seer behind, Zach followed along the fence line, wandering off now and again so it did not look like he was onto the barrier. He could not see any way for the fence to be breeched. Circling around, he came back to the group, coming up behind them.

"I see no way to get over or under the bastard," he informed Maxt with frustration. "Solid wall; goes deep into the earth. Too tall to climb over. Someone figured out that I was able to lift the last one and fixed it so I couldn't do the same here."

"Let me try something," the Seer suggested. "That tree over there," she nodded ever so slightly, "is it near the fence?"

"Yes," said Zach. "About four feet in from the wall."

"Good enough," she replied then walked over to it. She leaned over the two-foot tall sapling and spoke softly to it. The little tree started to sway back and forth, as if it were a snake to her charmer. The Seer stepped back and waited expectantly.

Suddenly, the tree erupted, growing taller and wider by the second. Maxt, Orli and Zach gaped at the sight. It finally stopped growing at about twenty-five feet. The Seer reached up and grabbed the bottom limb, swinging up into the tree's branches easily.

"Zach, you take our packs and walk through the fence. We can't risk you touching this Tree. You other two, get climbing. Let's see how much you remember from your childhood." She challenged them, moving higher into the Tree.

Zach scooped up the packs and walked through the fence. It gave off a slight tingling sensation as he passed through the wall. Setting the packs down, he looked over to see the progress made by his companions.

Orli had quickly passed the Seer and was almost to the top of the fence. Zach cupped his hands to his mouth. "A few more feet up, Orli, then you can climb over!"

"He's winning!" the Seer laughed, pulling herself up more rapidly.

Maxt, with his bulk and size, was having a difficult time maneuvering in and through the branches. "Could you not make this tree a little more roomy?" he groused as his bootlace got caught on a small branch.

Orli leaped from the tree, rolling as he hit the ground and coming up to his feet gracefully. The Seer was now inching her way over the fence top, her face screwed up in concentration. Once she was clear of hitting the fence, Zach called out to her to jump.

"Don't worry, I'll catch you," he promised, readjusting the baseball cap he wore so he could see her better.

The Seer launched herself from the tree. Zach planted his feet and caught the woman, the force of her fall knocking them both to the ground.

The Seer laughed as she lifted her head from Zach's chest. "Wow, I'm horizontal with Zach Neol." She giggled like a young girl.

"Get off my woman," Maxt bellowed from somewhere inside the tree.

"She's the one on top of me," Zach protested with a laugh as Orli assisted the Seer to stand. They turned to watch Maxt. A large branch, some two feet above the fence, was bouncing as Maxt moved along the branch, his legs wrapped around it.

"Lift your legs, Maxt," Zach called out as his feet came dangerously close to top of the glassy wall. Maxt nodded, his face screwed up in concentration.

"He has a fear of heights," the Seer confided, her eyes glued to Maxt.

"Look at the branch," Orli pointed. The farther out on the limb Maxt crawled, the more bent the branch became.

"Uh-oh," Zach said, seeing that it was only a matter of time before gravity took effect and sent the branch crashing down. He was opening his mouth to warn Maxt when the inevitable happened.

"Get out of the way," Zach yelled as the branch bent with a mighty creak and crack. He and the others scrambled in different directions as Maxt came tumbling down from the Tree, landing with a thud.

"Her, you catch," Maxt said as he rolled painfully to his hands and knees. "Me, you let fall like a…"

"Tree?" Orli supplied, grinning.

"That was a nifty trick," Zach said to the Seer. "The tree growing, I mean, not Maxt's impersonation of a flat footed squirrel."

The Seer smiled and turned to the tree and spoke to it softly. The branches, trunk and leaves grew smaller until it was once again a sapling some four feet on the other side of the fence. Only now, the little tree had a decidedly bent branch hanging from it.

Past the fence, the air was noticeably different. It was denser, more ominous. It took several steps for the feeling to sink in. It was a cloying feeling that plucked at their skin and wrapped around their brains. *You could literally taste the foulness in your mouth*, Zach realized with disdain.

"What is this?" Orli was sniffing the air. "I do not like this at all."

"Evil," the Seer shivered, wrapping her arms around her middle. "You can feel it in the wind."

Zach felt a sense of foreboding that permeated his entire being. The hike was becoming difficult, not that there was a difference in the terrain, more that it was as if they were pushing their way through a thick morass of negativity. The presence of Evil was also taxing them psychologically as the day wore on, lowering their spirits.

Zach, conscious of his natural tendency to fall into the doldrums, was especially affected by this ominous change. He was aware on one level that the sense of doom was coming from an external and unnatural force, yet it was still weighing on him heavily. He was beginning to think that this whole quest was hopeless.

The group trudged on, their heads bowed, silence reigning over them. Each was struggling with their own negative thoughts and images, unaware that the others were equally affected. Finally the Seer stopped, shaking her head.

"I have to stop this," she said aloud. "I'm doing fine with this quest. I am helping, I am making a difference in the Land. I have not failed." Her words grew more and more firm as she spoke.

The others stared at her, almost not comprehending her words due to the doubts swirling in their own minds. The Seer faced them, her face impatient. "Fight it," she demanded. "Fight the negative energy. Don't give into it. Allowing yourself to question your worth is one of Evil's most basic tricks. They want us to be discouraged and turn back."

"You are correct," Orli said, straightening his shoulders with effort. "They want us to feel unworthy and incapable. But we are not without talents to get through this."

"We have fought Evil at every juncture and won," Maxt declared, his hand going to his sword hilt. "We cannot let our own thoughts cloud out judgment."

They looked at Zach, who opened his mouth helplessly. He knew he needed to fight, but wasn't sure what for. What in his life was worthwhile and good anyway? Movie premieres and money and cars and other material goods were all he had to count. His family only cared about what he could do for them; his friends were few and far between. The Seer, Maxt and Orli were all fighting for the Land as much as for their loved ones, but what could Zach do for the Land? He hardly knew it, really.

Then the image of the Protectors as they sat on their sun-drenched deck swam to his mind. He could go on for them, he realized with wonder. Because whether he succeeded or failed, he knew, deep in his soul, that the Protectors would always be there for him. They would accept him regardless of his material wealth or his looks or his charm. They would accept him for him. The most important thing in their world was the Land. He would do this for them. And Liz. Yes, he could do this for Liz and the Protectors.

It was as if a weight lifted from his shoulders as he thought it through. He felt lighter, more positive, more energized. "We can do this," he said decisively. "I can do this. For the Protectors. For Liz."

They moved forward with more vigor, grimly determined to fight through the jungle of antagonism that permeated the area. Whenever one of them would falter, the others would immediately stop and bolster that person's spirits.

During their lunch break, when they were all sitting in a tight circle, eating bread and cheese, the Seer suddenly dropped her meal and stared straight ahead, her greenish eyes unfocused, her head tilted to one side as if she were listening to something. Zach, immediately concerned, reached for the woman.

"No!" roared Maxt, knocking Zach's hand away. "She is seeing something. Leave her."

The next few minutes were agonizing for Zach. The Seer was very still, those remarkable eyes staring sightlessly. Periodically her body would twitch as if her skin was being pricked and prodded. Her breathing shortened until she was almost panting, her muscles tight as though everything within her was physically clenched. Sweat broke out on her brow. When tears started to stream down her face, the actor could no longer stand it.

"Are her visions always this intense?" asked Zach helplessly.

Maxt, worry creeping into his forest green eyes, shook his head. "I have never seen it this bad. Whatever this foresight is, it is big, and affecting my Lady emotionally, physically and mentally."

The Seer came to life, breath exploding from her as her body convulsed to the side, going limp. Maxt barely caught her before she crashed into the ground, narrowly missing a large rock. The Seer curled into Maxt's warmth, weeping uncontrollably. Without missing a beat, Maxt hauled his woman into his large lap, cuddling her against him, patting her back and speaking low, nonsensical words to her while the woman tried to regain control. Zach and Orli exchanged worried glances.

Finally, the Seer calmed down, her body ceasing its relentless shaking. With one hand, she wiped away the tears, pushing at Maxt so that he allowed her to sit upright, although his arms were still around the woman. Still panting, the Seer stared at Zach.

"You…you."

"What about me?" asked Zach gently, moving in to put his hand on her skin, which was clammy and cold to the touch.

"Need…you…"

"Need me to what?" the actor prodded when she fell silent.

"We need you." The Seer leaned forward, her hands clutching Zach's wrists. Her eyes closed, the lids moving as if in REM.

"She is still in the throes of the sight. We must proceed carefully so as not to disturb what she is forecasting." Maxt said softly, then addressed his lady. "Who is we, love?"

"We. The Seers. Those that protect the Land. We. Liz, me, her."

"Her?" asked Maxt, shaking his head at Zach to keep the man silent. "Who is that, darling mine?"

"The child."

"What child?"

"The one that is hidden."

Understanding was starting to dawn on Zach. He knew. He knew what was happening, even as Maxt asked the next question.

"Who is hidden? Where?"

"Her. The child of potential, the child unknown to us. The child in the temple. The one they are hiding from me. From us. She is of my line, and yet masked from me until now. She cries. She seeks. She needs to be found. She needs to be rescued." The Seer paused then opened her eyes and stared at Zach. The stare was open, forthright, clear of anything other than the pain and anguish lingering in their depths.

"You are to rescue her, Zachary. She seeks you."

Zach closed his eyes, as if needing to block out the Seer's words, even though they rang so true deep in his soul. It was like a bell was sounding, a true chime that echoed his inner compass, guiding him along the path he'd trod since coming here. Odd that the path was still absolute, even if the goal had changed dramatically.

He'd been so certain that Liz needed to be rescued. It had fueled his actions, this sense of needing to save, to protect. Now, Zach realized that those emotions had likely been directed at the wrong person. He was here to save this child. The one hidden in the temple. One hand went up to his neck, where the love bite was still tender. He had a sneaking feeling he knew who was behind the child's kidnapping.

"Zach…"

"It's ok, Maxt," said the actor. "Just…give me a minute to recalibrate."

"We all need a minute," said Orli softly. "I shall go keep watch while you three do so."

Zach disentangled his hands from the Seer and stood up, walking several paces away before turning and coming back. He repeated the motion several times, swinging his arms, careful to walk in the direction they'd come before turning back so as not to trigger any alarms on the temple side of their trek. After doing this pace several times, he stood and took several deep, calming breaths, hoping to center himself. By the time he rejoined the Seer and Maxt, the woman was looking much better, the color back in her cheeks, all traces of pain and tears gone. She was sitting next to Maxt, looking wiped out but alert. Zach settled on the ground in front of her, cross legged, and enveloped her still chilled hands in his.

"Tell me everything."

"There's not much to tell," admitted the Seer. "I could sense this child, barely out of her toddler years. She has an incredible presence to her. How they've managed to mask her for this long…anyway. She's in that temple, all alone. Kept hostage. Says there is a mean lady there, and she's waiting for her hero."

"And you think that hero is me."

"Well, her specific thoughts on the matter were, and I quote, 'the pretty birdie man.' I think it's safe to assume she was referring to you, Zachary."

Maxt grunted. "Makes sense, Worlder."

Zach brought the Seer's hands to his lips, holding them there while he struggled with internal demons. Ignoring Maxt's warning grumble at the inherent intimacy of the gesture, Zach held the pose for a long time. The Seer seemed to understand the internal battle the man was going through, sorting through his deep seeded issues of being used, and his need to protect those around him. Reconciling those diverse emotions had to come before the man could accept this task.

The Seer knew Zach had made his decision when he released her hands and rose to his feet in a lithe lunge, one that was pure warrior and masculine grace. He adjusted his sword and tugged down on the baseball cap he was wearing.

"Let's go get her."

The Seer gave him a soft smile, laying one hand along his stubbled cheek. "Thank you."

Zach grimaced more than smiled. "I think you all could have found a better person than me for the task."

"The Land chose you, Zachary. That's all I need to know."

Late in the afternoon, a sudden, vicious wind tugged at the baseball cap Zach was wearing, ripping it from his head and sending it tumbling away. Zach chased after it—the hat had been a gift from the crew on the Phoenix movie and was a personal favorite—catching up with it several yards away. He resettled the hat and turned back to the others. The half smile on his face froze.

"Don't move," he yelled at them, holding his hands out in front of him as if to ward them off.

They halted, uncertain. Zach could see the Seer's mouth moving, then Orli and Maxt's, but no sound was penetrating the huge, pulsing barrier that was suddenly between Zach and them. Unknowingly, he had crossed yet another fence and was now on the opposite side.

Zach sighed and started towards the others. When he was on the same side, he would look for a way for all of them to cross, although this fence seemed to rise into the sky as far as he could see.

"I wouldn't cross that barrier if I were you." A cool and calm voice came from behind Zach.

-16-
Bargain Hunting

Zach turned slowly around, angling his body so he could still see his comrades, but also so he could keep this newcomer in sight. He knew that voice. It had literally haunted his dreams over the past few days. There she stood, in an emerald green gown that flowed over her sinuous body like liquid. Her black ringlets were cascading down her back and green eyes flashed with amusement.

"Mr. Neol, so nice of you to visit little ole me," she purred, one hip cocked out, her hand on her waist.

"Really bad Mae West impersonation you have there," he replied easily.

"Darling, I'm no impersonation. I am the real thing."

Zach stared at her, his mouth screwing up with consternation. "Nah, I don't think so."

She flicked a hand at him. Zach felt as if every bone in his body was frozen in place. Try as he could, he was unable to move a muscle.

"That's better," the woman said with satisfaction. "You're certainly delicious eye candy, but that mouth of yours could be put to better use. Now, be a good boy and listen to me, or I will be forced to put a bind on those beautiful lips you have." She patted his cheek fondly. Nodding towards the others, the woman said simply, "If they come through that fence, I will kill them."

"Somehow I doubt that," Zach said, each word coming with great difficulty.

She tapped a crimson tipped nail against her cheek. "Well, the Seer would be difficult, I grant you that. But those men? In a heartbeat, sugar. Just like that," she snapped her fingers briskly. "But it would be such a shame. They really are fine specimens. I wouldn't mind a sample of them, let me tell you. I just don't have time to indulge at the moment, I'm afraid."

"Why allow me through and not them?" Zach asked, curious.

"You…intrigue me," she said after a long pause. "I've been very bored lately. A little diversion is welcome. They, however, are not." She nodded in the direction of the three on the other side of the fence.

Zach opened his mouth to speak, but she pressed a finger to his lips. "Hold that thought, sugar," she whispered, then narrowed her jade eyes at the Seer, who was standing slightly before Orli and Maxt, her eyes narrowed in concentration. "Back off, old lady," the woman sneered, leaning forward slightly, her hands clenched in tight fists.

Out of the corner of his eye, Zach saw the Seer fly backwards into Orli and Maxt, who caught her as she tumbled to the ground. He strained against the invisible bonds, which only made it more difficult to move. With sudden inspiration, Zach made his body go totally limp. He should have fallen to the ground, but the woman's spell—or whatever it was—kept him upright.

However, it also, Zach discovered, allowed him to move within the constraints. His fingers were able to flex slightly. Encouraged, Zach concentrated on keeping his body limp, but then slowly trying to move his arm.

"So, do we have an accord?" the woman said briskly.

"I don't make agreements with people that I don't even know," Zach replied. It was easier to talk as well, he realized with a kind of grim glee.

"You haven't figured that out?" she pouted prettily. "I'm crushed. I would have hoped my reputation would have preceded me. After all, you are hardly the first Protector I have met. Surely they have told you of me?"

Comprehension dawned. "Of course. You're Zella," Zach guessed. "From Ben Harm's quest. And Sarat. You met Sarat in New York City."

"What do you know? There are some brains in that incredible body of yours," she laughed, tossing her hair over her shoulder. "The fence?" she arched a black eyebrow at him questioningly.

"What do I get in return?"

"You presume to bargain with me?" Thunderclouds rolled over that perfect face of hers. "I come here, in good faith, to give you a chance to save those people and you seek to push me?"

"I presume a lot. You never know if you don't ask," Zach replied. His right hand—the one facing the group still watching on the other side of the fence—was almost able to move freely. He started to work on his elbow next.

A slow, sensual smile spread over her. "Well, it does take a lot of guts to ask for more when you have so little to offer that I couldn't just take if I really wanted to," she said slowly, eying him like a piece of fine art. It annoyed Zach. That was the look that directors and producers and starlets all gave him. He wasn't a piece of meat, Goddamn it.

"Oh, that angers you, doesn't it, sugar?" Zella correctly read the emotions that must have flared in his amber flecked blue eyes. She sighed mightily. "It is what you are, Zach. You should accept it and revel in it, instead of trying to strive for more than you can be." She pursed her lips considering. "I'll tell you what, Zach. If, and this is still a very big 'if' in my book, you gain entrance to the fortress, then I'll take down this wall, and your little friends can come through. How does that sound?"

"Sounds like we have an accord," he replied, the anger still simmering underneath his very skin.

"You know, given the odds of this matter, I was rather expecting a female Protector," Zella said thoughtfully, circling around him, her hand trailing lightly on his waist. She laughed gaily. "Imagine my surprise and subsequent delight when you showed up, sugar."

Zach tensed involuntarily when her hand dipped indecently low on his butt, giving a firm squeeze. He forced himself to relax, but it was too late. His hand had gone immobile again. He groaned internally. It was back to square one, damn it all. Zella smiled wickedly and reached for his belt, unhooking his sword from his waist. Then she stepped back, hefting the object in her hands.

"I see no need for you to have this, Zach. Now, now sugar, don't be angry with me. I think you and I can come to an arrangement that is mutually agreeable," Zella continued in a companionable voice. "One that will suit your particular talents nicely. See you in your dreams, Zach." She kissed him on the lips, a move he was unable to avoid due to the body bind, then winked at him.

Zach felt rage boil over inside him as he saw his sword in her hands, despite his best attempts to ignore the way she was baiting him. She gave a deep, throaty laugh and disappeared. Just as instantly, the invisible binding dissipated. Zach, who was trying to keep as loose and relaxed as possible, was unprepared for the move and fell to his knees heavily.

***

"What is going on?" Maxt asked on the other side of the fence. "What is happening to him?" One second Zach was chasing his hat and the next, he was waving at them to stop. They were unable to hear a word he was saying and assumed there was another fence in front of them. Then, Zach was simply standing rigidly, half turned away from them.

"He's talking to something," Orli said, seeing Zach's lips moving.

"There's definitely something there," the Seer said, her eyes closed as she stretched out her mind. "A presence. But I can't seem to penetrate this wall to get a clearer picture of what it is."

"He seems to be immobilized," Maxt observed. "Look how his neck is straining, the muscles in his arms corded. He's trying to break free of something."

"Uh-oh," the Seer said suddenly, taking several steps forward. "I think we found our lost minion of Evil." She tilted her head slightly, concentrating hard on the presence.

"Be careful," Maxt warned her urgently.

The Seer nodded and continued to press. Suddenly, it was as if a hand had shoved her in the chest, pushing her backward until she fell. Orli and Maxt were at her side in a heartbeat, lifting her to her feet.

The Seer was seething with frustration. "That bitch!"

"Who?" Orli and Maxt asked at the same time.

"It's Zella," the Seer said grimly, "and she is toying with Zach. She's been tormenting him at night, from what little I could see when I finally got through to her warped mind."

"That is why he has not been sleeping well," Maxt reasoned, rubbing his chin thoughtfully.

"You noticed too?" Orli said, surprised.

"Hard to miss, when he is tossing and turning all night," Maxt pointed out. "Hey, his sword just disappeared."

"Did Zella take it?" Orli asked.

"She's gone," the Seer announced just as Zach fell heavily to his knees on the other side of the still invisible wall. They waited anxiously for the man to move.

***

Zach recovered slowly, pushing himself to his feet. He felt slightly ill from the brush with Evil, definitely off kilter from the contact. He blew out his breath and turned to face the others. He held up a hand, indicating the need to wait.

Then Zach opened his pack and withdrew a spiral notebook and pen that someone had so thoughtfully included in with his clothes. He wrote a message in large letters on the paper then walked as close as he could to the fence.

This near, he could feel the electrical vibrations of the wall. He gestured for the Seer to move forward, giving her a signal when to stop.

"It was Zella, all right," she said to the others. "She told Zach that if he helps us get across this wall, she will kill us all. Silly boy, why does he believe her?" The Seer shook her head, then continued to read. "He goes on to say that when he gains access to the fortress, this wall will collapse, and we can then get across. He's going on alone."

Immediately, Orli and Maxt started shaking their heads vigorously. The Seer also looked rather mutinous. Zach sighed and motioned for the Seer to step back. When she was even with the men again, Zach picked up a tree branch from the ground and flung it at the wall with all of his might.

The second the branch hit the wall, it was burned to a cinder. In the moment of contact, the full size and scale of the fence became evident to those still on the far side.

As the last sooty ash fell to the ground, Zach looked at the other three, his eyebrow raised sardonically, as if to say "See what I mean?"

"You win," the Seer said grimly, tossing up her hands. She pantomimed them staying where they were and making camp, then blew him a kiss.

Zach grinned at her, starting to turn so he could begin the rest of his solitary trek. Pausing, he carefully set his pack down and faced the three. Then he bowed deeply, his hand over his heart. Instead of feeling foolish like he expected, the gesture, especially when it was repeated by the three on the other side of the wall, made him feel better somehow.

Zach re-shouldered his pack and headed farther inland. He made a decision to not look back and stuck to his guns as he continued on his way. His instincts told him he was on track, and he hoped he would find this fortress of Zella's before too much time had passed.

"Safe journey, Zachary," the Seer said, her brow furrowed with worry. She wished he had told her about Zella's night time visits. She could have helped him block the Evil, the Seer was sure of it. To make matters worse, he didn't even have his weapon anymore. Now, he was continuing on alone and unprotected. Maxt put his arm around the Seer, knowing the woman he loved was concerned about Zach.

Together, they watched as he crested the next hill and disappeared from site. Orli eased back from the couple to give them some privacy, going to search out some wood for their campfire. It might be a long wait ahead, for all they knew.

As he pressed forward with as much speed as he could muster, Zach thought about the encounter with Zella. One thing was certain, Zach thought grimly, he was not stopping for the night. He'd push on until he was so exhausted he would not be able to dream. There was no way he was letting that woman into his psyche again to perform some new form of dream rape. Not if he could help it.

He paused as the sun set to eat some of the provisions in his pack and to fashion a kind of torch for the night portion of his trip. He was loath to keep hiking if he had no light, and although the moon was slowly but surely getting fuller, it was still casting a rather dim light over the nightly landscape.

Long after night fell Zach continued to roam further into the depths of the Meadows Region. There was an absence of sound, he realized, the usual crickets and other insect life having been still since he breached the last wall. Nor did Zach see any animals. Not a single animal or bird was evident as he continued to walk at a fast clip. The sooner he got to the fortress, the better, he rationalized.

Zach was getting ready to stop and light his torch, his eyes finally becoming too weary to see in the semi-darkness, when his glance fell on a strangely glowing object off to his right. Curious, he veered towards it.

The object was hanging from the lowest branch of a fairly tall tree, one of the tallest Zach had seen in the region. As he got closer, he could see that it was in fact several small round balls that were grouped together, almost like a massive, three-foot long bunch of grapes. The balls were giving off a soft white light.

Zach was reaching out to touch one of the balls when suddenly he perceived that something was moving inside them. He jerked his hand back quickly. Leaning in closer, Zach tried to see what was inside the grape like objects.

He could see a glimpse of movement, a fluttering of wings perhaps. The colors were deep and rich, he could tell that. As he watched, a great shudder seemed to race through the cluster of orbs. One of them fell to the ground, rolling to Zach's feet. Almost instinctively, Zach picked it up.

"I probably shouldn't have done that," he muttered to himself, staring at the ball lying in the palm of his hand. "Not the brightest bulb in the box today, are you Neol?"

The orb was strangely warm, and seemed to pulse with life. But the longer Zach held the object, the more he realized that, unlike Zella, it didn't feel inherently Evil. In fact, it felt rather miraculous, vibrant and full of positive energy. The ball started moving in his hand, and Zach brought it up as close to his eyes as he could.

In the depths of the ball was a teeny, tiny fairy. She had citrine and jade wings and a shock of black hair. Her face was scrunched up in either pain or anger. She was beating her hands against the inside wall of the ball as if trying to break out. Exhausted, she slumped to the bottom of the ball, wrapping her arms around her legs and burying her face in her knees. Her little shoulders and wings shuddered as she sobbed.

Zach peered at the rest of the orbs. Now that he knew what he was looking at, he could see that the other balls were occupied by a fairy as well, each one trying to break out of their encasement without success.

Zach looked back at the orb in his hand. The small fairy was now looking at him with a hopeful look on her tear-stained face.

"Do you need to get out of there?" Zach asked softly. He could only imagine how terrifyingly large he must look to the little gem-studded creature.

She nodded vigorously, scrubbing the back of her hand across her nose.

"Ok, then," Zach said. He was going to trust his instincts, he decided. This little creature was not Evil in any way, shape or form. He'd stake his life on it.

Zach reached for his sword, intending on getting the small knife concealed in the hilt to see if he could pry open the shell like covering. When his hand closed on nothing but air, he cursed.

"Damn, she took my sword," he remembered. Pulling off his pack, he opened up his shaving kit. Carefully, he took out a spare razor. "Stand back," he told the little fairy, who immediately crowded up against the far wall of her enclosure. Zach pressed down with the razor, applying pressure until the orb shattered in his hand.

The small fairy was left sitting amongst the ruins of her globe, her face looking as startled as Zach's. She was barely the size of his pinkie finger, perfectly formed, including a little diaphanous dress and hourglass figure that most women he knew would die for.

Then she stood up on his palm and blew him a kiss, zooming over to the rest of the globes. She started tugging on another orb, frantically trying to break into it. The whole colony was now moving as the other fairies, seeing the first one freed, renewed their efforts to get out.

"Hang on," Zach called to them. "Settle down, ladies. One at a time." He was afraid that they were going to hurt themselves in their efforts to escape. "If you all just calm down, I will make sure you are all released, all right?"

The first little fairy looked at him solemnly, then turned and seemed to address the rest of the fairies. The cluster stilled as they listened to her.

Zach reached out and plucked another orb. He had the fairy out in just a few seconds. As he did, that fairy and the first one flew up to the nest and detached another orb, bringing it down to Zach.

Soon, they had a system down pat. As more and more fairies were released, a chain grew between Zach and the nest. Fairy eggs were passed from fairy to fairy until they were deposited by Zach, who diligently continued to open the shells.

His razor gave out after the first fifty, and he switched to a pair of tweezers he found—probably left in his bag by someone he had vacationed with—and a rock. It took only a few taps with the rock on the end of the tweezers and the egg would open, spilling a new fairy to the ground.

Some fairies dedicated themselves to helping the new comers, walking them a short distance away from where Zach was kneeling.

He lost all track of time. All he knew was that the ground around him was becoming littered with the broken shells. A few fairies would zoom between eggs to help clean up the mess, but it was still beginning to pile up considerably. More unopened eggs were on the ground next to him, the fairies waiting patiently to be freed.

The first fairy continued to flit about the entire operation, obviously giving orders and in charge. Zach had to smile at her, she was simply too adorable for words. When not overseeing the birth of the colony, she would stand on Zach's shoulder, clapping enthusiastically as each fairy was freed from her egg.

Zach opened the last egg, releasing a fairy with sapphire and diamond wings. She was helped off to the recovery area by two other fairies, waving and giggling in Zach's direction as she was led away. Zach leaned back on his heels. His shoulders were aching, his eyes were blurring from exhaustion. The first fairy he'd freed from the eggs flew in front of his face and blew her breath at him.

Zach keeled over in a heartbeat, dead asleep. He never realized how the fairies, all working together, laid him out on the sweet meadows grass, converging around him so his entire body was outlined by their softly flapping wings. When Zella's presence gleaned by seeking Zach, they masked the human with all of their might. After all, the minion of Evil thought they were still trapped in their eggs, unable to hatch due to the oppressive maliciousness that permeated this part of the region. They saw no reason to enlighten her to the fact that they were free. To

Zella, it appeared that they were still clustered together in their eggs, helpless.

Fairy giggles are hard to suppress, however. The head fairy had to shush them several times so as not to wake the man who had worked so diligently to save them. He needed sleep, she scolded them. Dreamless sleep.

And that, they were able to give to him.

-17-
Fairy Lust & Fairy Dust

When Zach woke the next morning, the sun was far over the horizon. He sat up abruptly, dislodging several fairies that had taken up residence on his chest. He apologized to them, then paused when he realized that he could hear their chittering laughter and talk.

Looking around, Zach was amazed. The little fairies had been very busy. One group was working over something in the grass, their little hands flying as they appeared to be weaving some reeds. Another group was working near the tree where the nest was located, pulling on some sticks. Yet more were cleaning the nest area, carting off the shattered remains of the eggs and carefully burying them. Several other fairies were flying around the different groups, apparently overseeing the operations. Overnight, the glen had been transformed into a hive of industry.

A large contingent of fairies appeared to be simply watching Zach. He could see them, sitting cross legged on the grass or leaning against small rocks, all their intent eyes glued to him.

A blur of citrine and jade fluttered over to him, hovering near his nose. It was the first fairy he had helped release from the egg. She gave him a wink, her hands clenching a clipboard. "Good morning, Zachary," she chirped.

"You can speak," he said dumbly.

"Of course I can. I could last night, but you couldn't hear me," she said impatiently. "I'm all grown up now."

It was true she was much bigger. The night before she had been the size of a pinky. Now she was as big as his hand. The wings were so delicate and now he could see all the different gems flashing on them. Her eyes were a clear, deep purple.

"I'm Scarlet," she said with an impish grin.

"Hello, I'm Zach Neol," he replied stupidly.

She waved a hand. "Oh posh, I knew that already," Scarlet said flippantly. "You are an actor in the World Dimension and the newest Protector of the Land. You are also so much, much more. But I don't know if I am supposed to tell you all that. Anyway, you are very close to the fortress now, you know."

"How do you know all that? You were just born," he protested.

He started to get up but a group of fairies flew to him, carrying a flat stone piled high with fruit and other delicious looking food. Zach glanced to the side and saw that a group of fairies had built a kind of outdoor kitchen near a small campfire. He took the plate of food from the little ones, thanking them. Starved, he took a large bite of the food. It was delicious. Better than anything served in the best five star hotel.

"I'm an Interdimensional Fairy," Scarlet scolded. "I was born knowing everything I need to know. Weren't you?" She tilted her head to one side.

"Darlin', I'm still learning everything I need to know," Zach commented wryly. He set the rock down to stretch his arms high over his head for a moment. There was an appreciative sigh from the watching fairies. He picked up his make shift plate again, shaking his head. Strange creatures, these fairies.

"How very sad for you," Scarlet said seriously. "Well, we have decided to be with you until the Calling. You're pretty."

"What is the Calling?" Zach asked, polishing off the food on his plate. What he wouldn't give for some coffee, he thought wistfully.

"When we are Called," she said impatiently.

Zach quirked his eyebrows and set the empty rock aside. Scarlet called out and another group of fairies skimmed in to whisk the plate away. Another fairy gave Scarlet a small cup, the size of a thimble. She handed it to Zach. "Drink."

"What is it?" Zach asked, sniffing it suspiciously. It smelled, he thought with whimsy, like spring.

"Fairy wine," came the pert reply.

Zach shrugged and downed it in one gulp. A round of cheers welled from the fairies. The wine spread like a curious fire through down his throat and to his stomach. From there, he could feel the wine racing through his entire system like electricity.

"Whoa!" he said softly. He felt energized, as if his entire body had been given an electric shock. "That stuff is good."

Scarlet winked at him. "Just don't let on that I gave a minor the wine," she told him.

"Minor? I'm older than you by a couple of decades," Zach laughed.

Scarlet sighed, soul deep. "Pumpkin, I age a lot faster than you. Trust me on this. You are but an infant to a fairy like myself."

Zach stood up, towering over the little creatures. "Wow, I slept incredibly well," he said, stretching again, then scratching his head, bemused.

"We let you sleep deeply, and whenever she tried to find you, we hid you well." Scarlet's lip curled. With her shock of black hair and unusual eyes, she was a dead ringer for the early Elvis with that look.

"She? You mean Zella?" Zach asked. Scarlet nodded, the look of disgust still on her pixie face.

"We don't like her. She is rude and bad for the soul," the fairy said decisively. The watching fairies nodded fiercely in agreement. "And you needed sleep."

"Thanks, Scarlet."

"Glad to help. We have other things for you, if you are ready to go find the fortress," Scarlet said, her violet eyes hopeful. She clutched the clipboard to her chest expectantly.

"Just let me get cleaned up and changed, then I'll be ready to go," Zach said.

The fairy wine was still tingling in his veins, making him feel rather giddy and happy. He glanced down at his t-shirt, frowning. It was covered in grass stains, fairy egg gunk, and other unidentifiable matter. In addition, the climb through the Tree the day before had left him with several rips in the material. "I'm thinking this shirt is toast," he muttered, pulling it over his head.

A wail of fairy screams had him wheeling, expecting some sort of predator. Instead, all the fairies had stopped working and were gaping at Zach. A few had actually keeled over in a dead faint and were being fanned by their neighbors.

Even Scarlet was eyeing Zach with a sense of hunger that was rather disconcerting.

"Er, sorry," Zach said finally, "I'll just go behind those rocks…"

There was a well of protests from the fairies assembled.

"You're pretty," Scarlet said as she landed lightly on his shoulder, her bare feet warm against his skin. "We like looking at pretty things."

"Right, well, I don't particularly care to be ogled by a bunch of horny fairies," Zach retorted, snatching a fresh t-shirt—his last one he thought with disgust—and striding off to the stream he heard nearby.

Scarlet followed, her wings a blur. "Please don't be offended," she pleaded. "It's just that when we see such a pure soul, it touches us."

"Pure soul?" Zach paused in his motions of tossing the cool water in his face.

"Yes," Scarlet looked puzzled then started to laugh with glee. She literally had to sit on a rock and hold her sides, she was laughing so hard. "Oh, Zach! You thought we were staring at your body, didn't you?"

Now he was feeling slightly pissed off. "Well what else am I supposed to think when half the fairies in the glen faint when I take my Goddamn shirt off?"

"We don't look at the outer wrapping very closely," Scarlet admitted, and then gave him a coy glance. "Although yours does seem to be particularly nice. We are more interested in what is inside the heart. And when you take off your shirt, well, your pretty heart is just easier for us to see, that's all. You are pretty, and you are special. We like that."

"So all those fairies," Zach gestured, half turning. He caught sight of several fairies who had crept after them and were once again absorbed in watching him from various perches in the rocks, grass and foliage. "They are looking at my heart? Why?"

"We like pretty things," Scarlet repeated. "Your heart has remained remarkably pure, Zach. Despite everything, you are still capable of incredible acts of goodness. That takes a strong heart, a pure heart." Scarlet flew very close and put her tiny hand on the warm skin over his beating heart. She closed her eyes in near ecstasy. Taking a deep breath, she rolled her head to one side and smiled brilliantly. "Oh, that just feels so good. You have no idea…"

Zach was a little disconcerted. He'd never had anyone wax poetic about his heart before. And the little fairy appeared to be close to an orgasm from his heartbeat alone. Weird. Scarlet gave a sigh and backed up slightly.

"We need to get going if we are going to get you anywhere near the fortress before the Calling," she said sadly.

Zach nodded and pulled on his t-shirt. After rinsing off his socks and pulling on a fresh pair, he brushed his jeans off the best he could and started back to camp. When he got there, he found the fairies all waiting for him, expectantly.

Scarlet was in front of the group. She bowed deeply to Zach, the other fairies following her lead. "Zach Neol. Protector. Guardian of the Fairy Clutch. Potential…well. That will come later. We are indebted to you for your help. Without you, our entire clutch would have been lost. To thank you, we would like to make you our champion, and give you the honors thus due to you."

"Er, ok," Zach said. What could it hurt, he imagined, to be considered a champion of the fairies?

"A champion must have a weapon," she continued. Scarlet clapped her hands. A large group of fairies marched forward, carrying something above their heads. As they got closer, Zach could see it was a pair of sticks that had been lashed together in a crude approximation of a sword. The 'sword' had been placed in a sheath woven of meadows grass. The entire piece had been decorated with several flowers from the area, including the blossoms that Zach had seen in his shared vision with Liz. God, that seemed like eons ago.

Zach picked up the object with great care, expecting it to fall apart in his hands. The fairies were all beaming at him. Zach had a momentary image of him fighting his way through a maze with a wooden sword and had to work to suppress a chuckle. The fairies meant well, and he supposed the sword was symbolic, for the most part.

"Thank you," he said solemnly, giving the fairies a bow.

Scarlet gave a long suffering sigh. "You have to withdraw the sword from its sheath," she instructed him in a voice that sounded like an adult talking to a child. "Otherwise it won't work."

"Oh, ok," Zach said, gingerly shifting the woven sheath in his hand so he could gab the crossed wooden hilt. He started to withdraw it from the sheath, hoping he didn't look as ridiculous as he felt. As he did, a familiar ringing sound emanated from the object. To his amazement, as the wood cleared the fiber sheath, it changed to a gleaming, pure gold color. The sheath mutated as well, becoming fine leather tooled with golden markings.

Zach looked at the hilt of the sword. It was set with jade, citrine and diamonds. It was, Zach realized, a hilt he'd seen before. During the first vision he'd had, the one Liz had inadvertently shared with him back in the World Dimension.

"This is the sword I take into the fortress," he whispered. Giving it an experimental swing, he was pleased at the way it cut through the air. Perfectly balanced and extremely light, Zach knew that this sword was far superior to any he had ever seen. He sheathed it back in the scabbard, and then buckled it around his waist.

"Thank you, Scarlet. And to all the fairies of the glen," he added, bowing deeply.

The fairies accompanied Zach as he walked through the Meadows Region, zooming in and around his head, darting ahead like a group of mad butterflies. They sang wordless songs and danced along the ground, dropped flower pedals on Zach whenever possible. He took it all in good naturedly until they tried to drop a daisy chain around his head like a crown.

"No way. Knock it off," he said laughing, dodging the fairies.

Suddenly all the fairies simply stopped, turning their faces to the sky. The look of expectancy was so intense that Zach also glanced up to see what was happening.

He couldn't see a thing, but Scarlet flew up to him, her face smiling brightly. "The Calling!" she said happily. "Oh, Zach, it's the Calling!"

"Ok, then," he couldn't help but laugh at her exuberance. "What's the Calling?"

"Watch," she advised, then her little pixie face sobered. "Not many humans have seen this event. You are being allowed because you saved us, Zach. We are indebted to you. We'll never forget you." She flew up and gave him a kiss on the cheek. Then she held out a small vial tied to a chain. "Fairy wine," she whispered. "Just don't tell them where you got it from, ok?"

"All right," he replied, clipping the chain to his canteen. "I'll just sit here and watch, then." Zach settled down on the hillside.

The fairies were forming concentric rings on the ground, dancing in circles. Their jeweled wings were flashing in the sunshine, their faces alight with joy, the sound of their voices rising in a glorious song.

Overhead, a shaft of bright light suddenly shone down. Zach shaded his eyes. It was as if someone had opened a door in the clouds, letting in a pure white light. Fairies came pouring out of the door from above, spiraling down to the earth below. The fairies that Zach had freed started to rise, flying up to meet their brethren. When the two fairy trails met, suddenly a rainbow formed.

Zach was breathless. He could see the little fairies dancing along the rainbow, which led to the trapdoor high in the sky. Zach stood up and watched the procession, the fairies from above and below mingling and dancing and singing together. In the doorway, a face appeared. It was a man, with a bearded jaw and kind brown eyes. Zach was actually surprised he could see the man that clearly, since he was so far up in the sky.

"Daniel," Zach breathed.

The bright white light must be the Interdimensional Void. Amazing, really. The fairies continued on their way up the rainbow, the Grid Manager waving and clapping. When the last fairy was through the trap door, Daniel leaned down to grab some unseen handle. With one hand, he gave Zach a cocky salute and swung the door shut.

The rainbow fell away like a shower of gemstones, leaving Zach alone on the hillside of the meadows.

"Now that was the coolest thing I've ever seen," Zach said, his hands on his hips. The fairy wine he had consumed that morning was still coursing through his body, giving him energy and motivation to keep moving, despite the fact that with the fairies gone, the Evil tainting the air was thicker and more oppressive than ever. He picked up his pack and headed in the direction he knew the fortress was located.

It was lonely hiking without company. Zach missed the companionship of the Seer, Maxt and Orli. Even the fairies and their incessant need to bathe him with flowers would have been a welcome diversion from the never ending grassy hills.

Late in the afternoon, Zach was busy humming to himself as he trudged along. He wasn't really paying attention to where he was going, knowing that he was going in the right direction.

"Is that Beethoven or Mozart?"

Zach stopped, his sword cleared from the belt around his waist in one swift beat. It took a full, heart stopping moment for him to realize it was Liz in her Grecian dress walking beside him.

"Do not, I repeat, do not sneak up on me like that!" he ordered bluntly, sheathing the sword again.

"Sorry," she replied easily. "But I can't really stomp over to make my presence known. So why you are alone?"

Zach told her about the Seer's vision and the child trapped within the fortress. How he was the one to find her and rescue her. Liz took it all in well.

"I thought there might be more to this situation. Your propensity for the Seers seems to fall into place now."

"I have one Seer in mind more often than the others, although that poor child is my priority right now.

Liz ignored the first statement. "As she should be. Poor mite. Hey, isn't that a new sword?"

"Yes," Zach said, pulling it out again to show her. He told Liz all about the fairies, helping them get out of the eggs, and their remarkable gift to him.

"That is wicked cool, Zachary. What happened to your other sword, though?" Liz asked. Zach wanted to smack himself.

"Um," was about all he could say. Liz eyed him coolly.

"You might as well fess up," she told him. "I'll just hang out here until you tell me."

"Zella took it," Zach blurted.

"Zella?" Liz stopped and Zach followed, facing her. "You mean to tell me that Ben's Zella is here?"

"Why isn't she Sarat's Zella? Never mind. She's the one who built the fortress, apparently," Zach admitted. "She wants me and only me to get to it."

Liz's arms were crossed as she eyed Zach. "It's probably more that she cannot keep you out, so she's making it seem like a challenge."

"Perhaps," Zach said slowly. "But she's been very persistent while I've been here."

"Persistent? How?" Liz's dress was flowing in the wind, he realized absently.

"She was been able to freeze me in place. I think I can get away if I can keep relaxed but that is pretty damn difficult when she keeps fondling me."

"Fondling you?" Liz's voice was like ice.

Zach winced. Damn. Hadn't meant to tell her that. He sighed and rubbed his hand over his eyes. Best to come clean, then.

"She's been invading my dreams. Touching me, taunting me. Nothing I can't handle," he assured Liz, who was getting more and more rigid by the second. "But it doesn't make for restful nights. Then yesterday, she froze me when I was awake, which was the first time she'd ever done that. I think as I get closer to the fortress, she's growing stronger."

"Ok, let me get past the part where I'm pissed off as hell that she's touching you against your will. Deep breathing here. Ok. So what did the Seer say when you told her about Zella doing all that in your dreams?" Liz asked. When Zach wouldn't look at her, Liz narrowed her eyes. "Wait a minute. You did tell the Seer, didn't you, Zachary?"

"Erm, well, no."

-18-
Fortress Sighting

"You mean to tell me that you have been hiking with the Seer, the most knowledgeable woman in the Land when it comes to mind control and defenses, and you didn't tell her you were being invaded in your dreams?" Liz's voice rose several octaves. "I swear to you, Zachary Neol, if I was corporeal, I would beat you senseless!"

Zach groaned, tilting his head to one side. "Well, when you put it that way," he admitted, "I was being pretty stupid. But Liz, look at it from my perspective. It was intensely personal, and very embarrassing to discuss."

"You were being psychologically raped," Liz said adamantly, her voice softening as she backed off the heated tone. "Zella had no right to do that to you."

"On that, we agree," Zach replied readily. "But I don't see how to stop something that happens when I'm asleep and vulnerable. No one has defenses against that kind of attack."

"Well, you can put up blocks if you so choose, to make it more difficult for her to get into that thick but vulnerable head of yours. I can try to teach you, if you'd like."

"God, that'd be great, Liz," Zach said, feeling it was an inadequate thing to say when compared with the sense of relief he would have knowing he could have an uninterrupted night's sleep.

"No problem," she replied easily, then looked around at the terrain. "This will go easier the first time if you're lying down."

Zach shrugged out of his pack and set it to one side, then lay down on the fragrant grass, looking up at the impossibly blue sky. When he shifted, his sword belt dug into his side, so he unbuckled that as well, laying it to one side.

"Close your eyes," Liz said, settling on the ground cross-legged next to him. Well, actually, he realized, she was floating a few inches above the grass. It was pretty nifty looking. When his eyes were shut, she continued speaking in her soft, even voice, "Now I want to think of something that makes you really happy, or really content. It needs to be positive feeling, Zach. Don't try and cheat on this."

"If I think my happy thought will I fly to Never-Never Land?" Zach joked, keeping his eyes shut. "Hunt pirates and play with the mermaids?"

"I'd poke you in the arm for that if I could, Zachary, I swear I would. Why does everything have to be a joke with you?" Liz said with frustration, but humor laced her words as well. "Do you have your thoughts in place?"

"Yes," Zach replied with absolute seriousness, settling down and lacing his fingers, his hands on his waist. "I'm ready now, honest I am."

"I'm going to try and enter your mind. You may feel a tingling sensation at the base of your neck. Just don't drop the guard, keep thinking of positive things. Like a continuous loop." Liz arrowed in on Zach's mind. He had a good block in place, she realized with a grin. He was doing well. She pressed a little harder, then shot out of his head like an arrow.

"What the hell!" she exclaimed, scrambling to her feet and backpedaling several feet. Since her feet never touched the ground, it looked rather ghostlike.

"What?" Zach sat up and looked at her, confused.

"Your positive thoughts," Liz replied nervously, her hand reaching up to fiddle with her necklace, making the silvery tattoo flash in the afternoon sun. "They were about me."

"Well, yeah," Zach said, still confused. "You said to think of something that made me feel happy or content. That's you."

"You can't use me," Liz said slowly. "When someone is trying to push past your defenses, they will glean a little bit of what you are thinking. If Zella knows you have any sort of…attachment to me, she'll use that against you. I should have made that clear before."

"Oh, right," Zach had the distinct feeling he had offended Liz in some way, but for the life of him he could not figure out why she would be upset with him for being happy when he thought about her.

"Was there another memory you could use? Something recent, something that made you feel happy?" Liz sat back down again, her heart racing. She firmly pushed aside the implications of Zach's previous thoughts. Now was not the time to ponder that unexpected discovery.

"I should avoid thinking about the fairies."

"I agree. It needs to be something focused on you, as selfish as that sounds. Something you felt, something that made you happy that sprang from your abilities. It's hard to explain."

He snapped his fingers after thinking for several moments. "How about when I kicked Maxt's ass in a sword match?" Zach asked her with a rakish grin. "I felt pretty damn happy with myself, with my abilities. It was…all about me!"

"I heard about that. I was quite impressed," she replied with a laugh. "We all were, when Ben described what had happened. Tracy can't wait to get you back in the practice gym. That memory should work. Now, I'm going to try and get inside, and I mean *really* try. As soon as you think you feel me invading, push back and push back hard. Don't worry, you can't hurt me. I'm fully shielded, I promise."

Zach remembered the feelings that had surged through him during the bout with Maxt. The sheer joy at the feeling of the blades crossing, the mental agility needed to keep one step ahead of the guardsman. He felt a tiny tickling at the base of his neck, like an insect landing. Zach ignored it, concentrating on the fight, going through the memory step by step. He bided his time, then when he felt the incessant tickling growing stronger he gave it a mental push.

Liz was impressed. Zach possessed an incredible amount of control over his mind, she realized. Once he learned to focus a little better, she doubted she'd be able to get this far inside. She pressed harder but the block he had placed was keeping her at bay and only giving her minute glimpses of a swordfight. Better. This was much better.

Now, if he could manage to put up the same resistance for Zella, perhaps he'd be able to get some sleep, and she told him so quietly, still keeping the tentative contact with his mind. Zach smiled, his eyes still closed.

"I feel really relaxed right now, even though you're still in my mind," he said with contentment.

"Oh, sorry," Liz said, starting to pull away from him mentally.

"No, don't go, stay," he muttered, his mind softening as Liz stayed within his consciousness, like a gentle balm. "I feel very close to you right now, closer than I have since we were on the balcony. God, I wanted to kiss your bare shoulder then. I'm warning you now that I won't let another opportunity pass me by."

"Stop it, Zachary," she said, shifting uncomfortably.

He could sense her withdrawal, both her spirit form and in his mind, although he was surprised to realize she was still maintaining the slightest level of contact with his thoughts. "Why do you keep pulling away from me whenever I say something slightly personal in nature?"

"I don't trust sweet words," Liz said with a slight frost in her voice. "I've heard them before."

Zach sat up suddenly, looking at her with the gold in his blue eyes blazing. "I'm not Valdeen and I'm getting damn sick of you trying to make me into him."

"I made a huge mistake once," Liz said evenly, "one that had almost disastrous results for everyone involved. I'm not going to do that again. I can't risk it."

"Why would being with me qualify as a mistake?" Zach was having a hard time overcoming how incredibly affronted he was to be placed in the same category as Valdeen.

"Because you're different than me, Zach. You exist in an entirely different realm. Your world and mine don't mix, they never could." Liz tried to reason with him, sensing his anger over the issue but wanting to have this ridiculous infatuation out in the open and dismissed as soon as possible.

Zach could feel anger welling up inside him. It was a familiar feeling of frustration that stole over him whenever people assumed the public persona that his parents and agent had so carefully crafted was reality.

"I'm as human as you are. In fact, I would say that with your skills you're the one who is more different than me." Zach pointed out.

"That is precisely one of the reasons that you and I just make no sense at all," Liz blurted out, desperate for him to understand. "I can't handle a casual affair like you would be able to, Zach, it just isn't in me."

"Casual affair? Who the hell said anything about this being casual? It seems pretty deadly serious to me," Zach ground out between clenched teeth.

"It's just ridiculous for us to even be arguing about this," Liz said stubbornly. "You don't know anything about the real me, and I hardly know you at all."

"Do you really want to know me?" Zach challenged. "Then hang on, darlin'." He suddenly dropped his mental guards and Liz was flooded with his memories.

Images of working on a hot, confusing set, with directors calling instructions at him and a gut wrenching feeling that he was sinking into failure for not remembering his lines. His father yelling at him that he was an idiot for flubbing a take and berating him for not getting a desired part in a film. His mother telling him what to wear, say, and do at a party full of adults who in turn clucked or patted him. Her image, the face contorted into a sneer as she told him he had better learn to rely on his looks and charm to succeed in the field.

His first sexual encounter at an indecently young age, courtesy of an older guest star on his television show; his parents in a vicious argument over money where they nearly came to blows; Zach holed up in his bedroom playing video games while his friends snorted cocaine; the feel of his arm breaking beneath his father's angry grip.

Not all the memories had negative connotations, Liz was glad to note. There were times of joy as he laughed with his co-stars, the dizzying whirlwind of events, premieres, and openings. The overwhelming sense of rightness the first time he held the sword for *The Phoenix* shoot, the feeing of homecoming as he crossed the threshold into his beach house. The first time he watched Liz from his bedroom aerie, talking with the other Protectors on the sundeck. Fairies spiraling up a rainbow in the sky.

Yet these memories were shaded with a sense of frustration over his work, the feeling that he was simply a product to be placed before a camera and not a real, living person. The loneliness despite the vast number of people that surrounded him, taking from him, constantly taking. The feeling of not belonging, not caring, not wanting anything in life but to be appreciated for himself. Then there was the peace of coming to the Land and beginning to grasp that this place, this realm, this world, was his destiny.

Liz found herself staring at Zach's eyes, those amazing, cerulean eyes shot through with topaz glints. She broke the mental contact, easing from his mind gently so as not to leave him with a headache.

"You didn't have to do that," she admonished him, feeling oddly breathless, despite the fact that she was not really able to breath in her spirit form.

"I wanted you to see," Zach stated firmly and with no regrets. "You have to know that my life has not been perfect. I'm a deeply flawed man, Liz. I've seen too much and done too little."

"You've experienced things a person should never have to know," Liz replied gently, aching to put her arms around him, console him. What a lost child he had been. "It has made you a better person for it. That doesn't mean you're flawed, it means you have strength of character."

"I don't want to make the same mistakes my parents made. Always regretting the path not taken, the road not traveled. I never want my children to feel that they're worth only what they can give me, rather than what I can give them. If that makes my character strong, then so be it." Zach replied, his voice even.

"You walked away from your career just when you hit the pinnacle of success. Not many people could do that, and do it with your sense of conviction."

"I wanted enough money in the bank so that I never had to work again," Zach admitted. "I had made that choice a long time ago, Liz. I'll never work as an actor again. I know that now with more certainty than ever before."

Liz felt her spirit beginning to ebb. The prolonged contact with Zach's mind had weakened her. "I have to go, Zachary."

"I'm falling in love with you." He wanted it said before much more time had passed. She needed to know, and he needed to say it before he went into the fortress that lay ahead of him with all its darkness and shadows.

Liz's hand flew up to the chain around her neck. "Too soon."

"When you know, you know," he replied with a deceptively easy shrug. Yet Liz knew with absolute certainty that Zach was being completely honest with her, and that frightened her to no end.

"Someone once told me that when the right person comes along, they speak to your heart and soul and every fiber of their being," she whispered.

"Smart person," Zach replied, then stared straight into her topaz eyes. "You speak to me, to my heart and soul and every fiber of my being," he vowed. "Practically from the moment I almost landed on you." Her eyes widened with the implications, even as she started to float away from him.

"And you speak to mine," she admitted before disappearing into the air.

Zach sat very still for a moment, a foolish grin on his face. Finally he snagged up his new sword and stood, belting it back on his waist. "What do you know," he said out loud. "I guess she does like me."

Whistling, he set off in the direction of the fortress. Despite the still overwhelming sense of foreboding that was settling over the area, he was happier than he had been in a long while. Even as storm clouds formed over his head, hanging low and ominous, Zach found it was impossible to be upset about much of anything at the moment.

It was just getting dark when Zach crested a rise to find the fortress nestled in the hills before him, just as his mind's eye had recorded it during the vision shared with Liz. The stepped slopes of the pyramid rising up at least seven levels, vines covering the outside the terra cotta structure. Even in the gathering gloom, Zach could discern that the vines were teeming with the movement of all the creatures within the foliage.

The earth around the fortress had all gone black, as if the grass could not sustain contact with the structure. A grayish black fog was emanating from the base of the pyramid, making it look as though it were resting on lake of pitch black ice.

Zach sat on the hillside and watched the fortress for what remained of the day. As much as he wanted to head straight for the place, he knew he needed to learn more about it before charging forward. For the sake of the child trapped within, he needed to be thorough in his reconnaissance. There was also no way he was going to enter the fortress at the end of the day when his strength wasn't optimum. Now was the time for watching, then resting, then he'd go in full steam in the morning. He saw no one enter or leave the structure. There were no chimneys or other exhaust pipes that he could see, and there were no exterior windows, which was as he had expected.

The creatures crawling in and out of the foliage looked like large ferrets. About two feet in length, with sinuous bodies covered in black fur, a white mask like mark on their faces. A few times, the ferret creatures would cross another's path and a vicious fight would break out. The animals apparently had no compunction about killing their kin. After seeing one particularly cruel battle, ending with one ferret being ripped in two, Zach had witnessed enough.

"I think I'll just back track a hill or two and camp there," Zach said to himself, not wanting to take his rest beneath the shadow of the fortress just in case those animals were nocturnal and left the structure to hunt at night.

Since it was a good bet that Zella already knew he was nearby, Zach didn't bother trying to hide his presence. He built himself a good, big fire and hunkered down next to it.

Although Liz had taught him the skills needed to help kick Zella out of his mind, he was still a little leery of the technique. He'd proven he could do it when he was wide-awake, and with Liz, whom he trusted implicitly. But asleep was another thing, and adding Zella to that mix made it an even less appetizing situation.

When he felt his eyes begin to droop, Zach forced himself to think about the bout with Maxt. The feeling of happiness and power that had surged through him as he faced off with such a worthy opponent. With that image foremost in his mind, Zach drifted to sleep.

He could sense, in his slumber, a slight prickling at the base of his neck. He pushed back on it, hard, not willing to let Zella into his cranium in any way. The presence withdrew. Then it came back again, more persistent and forceful, the tingling becoming a rather sharp pain.

Zach was now dozing, grinning as he continued to block the attempts by Zella to penetrate his mind. When the sensation ceased once again, leaving behind a lingering feeling of frustration and anger at its failure, Zach crossed his arms over his sword and drifted further into sleep. He felt safer than he had in a long time.

-19-
Breaking & Entering

The next morning, Zach woke up slowly. He was confused and wet. He was confused because he was sleeping on top of his sword, which was rather painful. He was wet because the gloomy storm clouds of the night before had let loose their bounty. All on top of his head, it seemed.

With a groan, Zach pushed himself up and with great effort, stood. His fire had died out, much to his dismay, and his gear was now soaking wet.

"Great. Fabulous. Abso-freaking-lutely wonderful," Zach groused as he gathered his things. A flash followed by a roll of thunder greeted his assessment. "This is just how I want to be breaking into a seemingly impenetrable fortress," he said, slinging the wet pack over his shoulder with a grimace.

He chewed a piece of really bad jerky as he walked towards the fortress, feeling very out of sorts and grouchy. "Some hero," he said finally, giving himself a mental shake. "It's show time, Zachary Neol. Get your ass in gear and get that kid. Then you can go home and soak up the sun on your back deck, and hopefully convince a very fine looking Protector to rub oil all over you."

Zach trudged over the final hill to find the fortress much the same as how he had left it the day before, only now rain was falling all around it. Odd, though, the rain didn't seem to be falling on the structure itself. Naturally or magically water repellent, he wondered? Regardless,

185

water was not dripping off the vines, nor were the creatures covering it wet.

The closer Zach got to the fortress, the louder the sound of the animals was to his ears. They had noticed him, Zach realized, and were watching him with beady black eyes, their sharp weasel teeth clicking ominously. There had to be several hundred of the creatures clambering all over the structure's walls. The bloodlust that oozed from them was palpable.

Zach paused several yards away from the building. Withdrawing the sword from the scabbard, Zach faced the fortress, looking out from under hooded eyes at the structure. If he had been looking in a mirror, Zach might have been aware that his entire posture was changing as he morphed into a warrior stance, his eyes becoming steely and firm.

The rain was grinding to a halt, he noticed thankfully. Zach prowled the length of the fortress, ignoring the ferret like animals that followed him with their growls and hisses. When he and Liz had flown over the top of the fortress, they had seen the hidden doorway, located on the second stepped level. It had looked like a trapdoor that opened from the top of the first step.

That meant he had to get up the first tier, which was about ten feet off the ground. It also meant getting past the animals that were becoming increasingly agitated by his presence.

The area around the base of the fortress was barren of any sort of tree, rock, or other item he could use to stack up so that he could gain access to the second level. He had a coil of rope in his pack, and wondered if the vines attached to the side of the fortress were strong enough for him to somehow lasso and use as leverage.

Then Zach narrowed his eyes. The vines. They could be a natural rope, he realized thoughtfully. If they were strong enough, that was. Zach did not doubt his upper body strength—he knew he could pull himself up the stone face of the wall like a mountain climber—but he wondered if he could do it fast enough to avoid being ripped to shreds by the animals or by the sharp spike-like thorns that protruded from the foliage. Somehow, Zach doubted that he would be able to get to the next level without being detected by the animals. That meant he needed to get rid of those furry beasts, or distract them long enough for him to gain access to the building.

"What I wouldn't give for a little Oracle power right about now," Zach muttered as he continued to pace back and forth, thinking. "A little flash, a little flame, a big mess of fried ferret."

A sudden thought had him stopping in his tracks, a wicked smile on his face. "That'll work," he said to himself, then continued out loud, "I think I'll just sit here a spell," If Zella was watching, Zach was content to let her wonder what he was up to. He hunkered down, his pack in his lap before him. With stealth, he started to rummage in the pack for the items he needed, wanting to make sure they were dry and ready to go.

Then he waited. And waited. And waited some more. Time crept by slowly. The ferrets continued to prowl over the walls of the fortress. Zach simply closed his eyes. He had plans for the little furry bastards. He could wait.

The sun came out, chasing the last of the rain clouds away. Zach judged it to be midmorning, by the angle of the sun. *Plenty of time*, he thought to himself. *You've got plenty of time.* He was banking on the quick moving, quick drying rain. Hopefully, the entire area would be dry soon enough.

Within minutes, the area was sweltering as if it were a tropical rain forest. The puddles around the fortress dissipated. Even the ground around Zach went from a muddy mess to solid, dry ground in a matter of minutes.

"Gotta love the Land," Zach said to himself.

Zach decided to wait a little longer. He felt dull, listless. That was not a good thing. He got up and quickly put himself through an entire T'ai Chi set, hoping that the familiar moves and routine would calm and center him. By the time he was done, it looked like there had never been a rainstorm in the area.

Another postcard-perfect day in the Land; except, of course, for the ugly monstrosity of Zella's vacation home rising in front of him.

Finally, he deemed the time was right. Zach dug through his pack, pulling out what he would need. He made sure that the items were hidden inside his t-shirt or jeans pockets, or under the pack, so that Zella could not glean what he was getting ready to do. All the while he kept the loop of winning the sword match going in the back of his brain. It was becoming second nature.

He checked his pack, making sure that his gear was all securely fastened. Then he slung it over both shoulders, tightening the straps so that he could move quickly without it getting in the way of his range of motion. The high pack would also provide him with some protection for the back of his neck, which he knew would be a vulnerable spot. It seemed the ferrets liked to bite one another in that area, so Zach did not want to take any chances.

Zach approached the side of Zella's stronghold, his hands full. It was discomforting to realize he was not going to be able to have his sword drawn as he walked forward, but he simply did not have enough hands for the task.

Stooping, he picked up several rocks from the ground, wrapping them in material he had ripped from the dirty t-shirt he'd worn for the fairy birthing. Setting the rocks on the ground, Zach knelt next to them, working quickly. He reached inside his shirt and pulled out a bottle of cologne that had been in his shaving kit, a gift from a long forgotten girlfriend. Zach hated using cologne, but had simply left it in his kit for years. Now, he doused the five cloth covered rocks, the sweet smell of the cologne making his eyes water. From his jeans pocket, he fished out his lighter—another gift from a girlfriend who smoked and thought Zach needed a lighter, even though he never touched cigarettes or other smoked products—and then picked up one of the cologne soaked rocks.

"Let's play ball," he said with a wicked grin to the weasel-covered fortress.

With a swift move, he touched the lighter to the ball. As the material gushed into flames, courtesy of the alcohol in the cologne, Zach hefted the ball into the vines on the fortress. Within seconds, the vines had caught fire. Zach breathed a word of thanks, he'd been half afraid the foliage might be too damp to catch fire.

Quickly, Zach lit the rest of his makeshift Molotov cocktails and lobbed them into the vines. The ferrets were scrambling to get higher into the fortress, kicking and biting and screeching in their haste to escape the fire. Some were not fast enough to escape the flames and plummeted to the ground, screaming shrilly as they burned alive. None of the animals tried to flee the fortress, which surprised Zach. He'd figured he would have to fight some of the creatures on the ground as they fled the burning structure. Perhaps they were not allowed or capable of leaving the stone fortress, he thought. Well, that certainly was fine with him, as it made the beginning of his adventure easier.

The flames continued to spread. Soon the outside of the structure was ablaze over much of the first three levels.

Yet oddly, the top four steps of the pyramid did not burn, Zach noticed.

Zella, Zach thought, was onto him. There was no time to waste.

He picked his way end of the fortress where the trap door was located. This end of the building was not ablaze just yet; Zach had carefully set the fire at the opposite end. He still needed some vines to ascend to the second level and time in which to make the climb before the flames overtook this area of the structure.

Hoisting himself up, using his feet along the wall of the first level, Zach climbed to the top of the first step. It was rather difficult going, as he had to constantly work around the lethal three-inch spikes that the vine was studded with. Despite his care, Zach was bleeding from several long scratches before he reached the top.

Swinging up onto the first level, Zach found himself face to face with at least two dozen of the ferrets, that were all standing their ground over the trap door he'd seen from far above. They seemed to be guarding the door, Zach realized, and weren't concerned about the fire that was blazing over the structure. He wondered if they were under some sort of spell or compulsion to stay their ground. Certainly most wild animals would be doing everything they could to escape the fire.

"Bring it on," Zach said, his sword swiping from the scabbard in an instant.

The ferrets snarled and leapt. *These bastards are agile, and fast,* Zach thought frantically, trying to wade through them as quickly as possible. He was slicing left and right, hacking through the beasts. They were vicious creatures, and determined to get to him.

One industrious creature leapt from half way up the next level wall, landing on Zach's shoulders, its claws digging into his flesh, trying to rip and rend the skin. It was somewhat thwarted in its efforts by the pack Zach wore. It did knock him into the wall of the fortress, causing several spikes to sink into his arm and side.

Zach roared with pain and reached behind his neck, pulling the thing off him and flinging it directly into the fire, which was creeping closer and closer on this level. Instantly aflame, the ferret raced from the fire, inadvertently setting several of its colleagues ablaze as it passed.

Zach sank his blade into the nearest ferret, trying to get a better look at the trap door. If he didn't figure out a way to get down that door quickly, the flames that were rapidly heading his way would engulf him.

Zach could not tell—due to the ferrets and vines—if the door was locked, but he had to assume it would be. He was down to less than a dozen ferrets and worked diligently to dispatch them so he could see the trapdoor more clearly.

When the last ferret in his immediate area was killed, Zach stalked to the door, kicking aside the limp body of one of the creatures. The wooden door was indeed locked, a chain wrapped around the handle and attached to a bolt in the fortress wall.

"Nothing's going to be easy, is it, Zella?" Zach muttered with exasperation, and then tried pulling with all his might on the chain. As expected, it did not budge.

"All righty then," Zach said, reaching into his shirt for the last cologne soaked stone. Lighting it on fire he threw it with all his might at the wooden door.

This wood did not burn as easily as the vines. Zach frowned as the flames sputtered and died out, not even leaving a scorch mark on the wood. Yet the boards had splintered slightly due to the force of his throw. Eying the encroaching flames with unease, Zach started to batter the door with his feet hoping to break the door open.

Quickly, he realized that he was not going to be able to break the door down before the flames reached him. He knelt and looked at the padlock, trying to see if there was some way he could jimmy the lock. But he had no skill in that area, Zach told himself with disgust. What did he think he was doing, playing some part in a weekly adventure drama? He wasn't the McGyver type.

Desperate, Zach slid the end of the sword underneath the chain, hoping he could pry the bolt out of the floor. Likely all he would end up doing was snapping the sword in two, Zach thought with dismay. The heat of the flames had reached him, causing him break out in a sweat, the sound of the fire like a freight train headed his way.

Intent on prying out the bolt that held the chain to the wall, Zach stood up to give the sword better leverage. To his amazement, the sword cut through the chain like it was made of paper and not steel. Zach leaned down and touched the severed links thoughtfully. The chain was heavy, solid metal, and the edges of the cuts diamond sharp.

Zach looked at his sword thoughtfully. "Fairy magic," he said softly. "Excellent." Hefting the door open, Zach looked down. He could not see anything below him, not a light, not a shape, nothing.

He did not want to drop into the fortress without having some idea what was below. Searching around, Zach used his sword to hack off a piece of vine, which he then stuck into the flames that were by now only a few yards away. The heat was intense.

Zach dropped the burning vine down the trap door. It illuminated a drop of some fifteen feet, indicating that the fortress was sunk lower than the surrounding area. The corridor looked clear, and Zach was glad to see that there was an old fashioned torch sitting in a metal bracket, unlit.

Judging the drop carefully, Zach gripped the trap door by the inside handle. He'd have to jump down into the fortress and somehow still manage to get the trap door closed behind him, or the flames could creep down into the corridor below. Of course, that could still happen if the wooden door didn't hold against the flames, but Zach had a feeling that Zella would not allow the inside of her lair to be breached by the fire. Taking a deep breath, Zach dropped through the trap door, managing to swing the trap door closed behind him.

He hit the ground hard, automatically rolling to his feet, his heavy pack making the maneuver somewhat tricky. The area around him was lit by the feeble light of the burning vine, which was quickly going out. Otherwise, the corridor was pitch black.

***

Several miles away, Maxt, Orli and the Seer stared as the wall in front of them shimmered into sight, then vanished.

"Zach must have gotten into the fortress," Orli exclaimed, taking a step forward. Maxt put his arm on the villager's shoulder.

"Let us test it first," he advised, hefting a large stick. "It could be some sort of trick."

Orli nodded and Maxt hefted the stick at the wall. It landed far on the other side of it. The men exchanged grins and pulled on their packs, eager to head for the fortress.

The Seer, however, was holding back. "What is it, love?" Maxt asked her gently. "I thought you would be glad that Zach was able to find his way inside."

"I can't feel him anymore," the Seer worried, her eyes frowning. "It's like he dropped off my radar completely."

"Do you think he is hurt?" Orli asked with concern.

"No," she replied, thoughtful. "I think he did get inside the fortress. But this means that Zella, or whoever built the structure, has imbued it with shields against my powers."

"And that worries you?" Maxt said. "I took that as a given. You are having difficulty feeling the little girl, so to me it makes perfect sense that the fortress is shielded."

"I suppose you are right," the Seer conceded. "It was just so disorienting to have him simply disappear from my consciousness, that's all."

"So let us go to this fortress. Maybe if we are closer, you will be able to read him again," Maxt said, holding his hand out to the woman. The Seer nodded, and the trio crossed the place where the fence had been located, heading for the fortress with great haste.

***

Inside the fortress, Zach reached for the vine, hoping to use it to light the torch he had seen on the wall. The darkness was unnerving. He was not sure if it was his imagination or the fire blazing above, but he thought he could hear a faint whispering sound.

The sooner he had the torch lit the better. The vine was barely giving off any light, so he worked quickly, finding the torch and then lighting it. As the torch flared, Zach found that he was at the dead end of a corridor. Above him, the trap door was visible, set into the thick ceiling.

The walls around him were large terra cotta bricks, roughly three feet long and two feet tall. They gave the impression of mass and size, weight and stability. The corridor itself was about seven feet wide and fifteen feet tall. The floor was flagstone, with ribbons of the same reddish hue running through them.

The bricks were unadorned, with no etchings or markings. Although the Seer and Maxt had indicated that the structure was new, there was a remarkable sense of oldness to the building, as if it had been there for eons, the stones slowly wearing away.

Opposite the dead end, the corridor made an abrupt right turn. Zach was unable to see around the corner, but the slight whispering sound continued, and it seemed to be coming from that way. With his sword drawn, Zach headed for the turn.

When he came around the corner, Zach pulled up short. In front of him, the corridor was blocked. Growing out of the walls and ceiling were the same vines that had covered the outside of the structure. The spikes looked as lethal and strong by the flicker of his torch as they did along the outside of the fortress.

And as dry.

If he tried to get through the vines with the torch lit, he risked setting the whole mess on fire. Zach had no desire to be in the path of the flames.

Remembering the chain on the door above, Zach reached out with his sword and severed a branch of the vines. It fell to the floor, harmlessly. Zach hesitated for several seconds. Part of him expected the whole mass of vines to start moving on their own accord, like a living creature, but nothing else happened.

Zach shook his head. "This isn't a Saturday morning matinee," he told himself harshly. "Get it together, Neol."

He scanned the wall and found an empty sconce on the wall. The torch slid into the hole perfectly and was far enough from the vines to not be a hazard. Zach made a mental note to keep looking for other torches along the way, and to stash them in his pack for future use.

Using the sword like a machete, Zach started hacking through the vines. Mindful of the fact that at some future time he might have to be coming back this way, and in a hurry, Zach took the time to stack the severed vines along the walls, trying to leave somewhat of a cleared path through the jungle like mess.

It was hard going. Many of the vines were as thick as his thigh, and took several, heavy two-handed strokes to sever. Apparently Zella had figured out the ease with which he'd sliced the chain and made the vines more difficult to hack. To compound matters the atmosphere in the corridor was hot and humid, quite unlike the cool, clean fresh air of the Land. And the vines were dirty. Despite being careful, Zach was soon sporting several new nicks and cuts. Most of his injuries came from the vines that fell from the ceiling when he sliced through ones that were intertwined with them.

Zach kept a close eye on the torch as well, moving it along the corridor whenever he could do so safely. He could no longer see where the vines had started, as the beginning faded into darkness, but he was extremely satisfied to be making steady progress.

Finally, he stumbled out of the other side of the vine tunnel. He looked down at himself, shaking his head ruefully. He was a freaking mess. His jeans were shredded and covered in ferret blood; his shirt was a wreck. To top it off, he reeked of the cologne he had used as a fire accelerant.

Zach paused and gave a mental inventory of his clothes. With a sigh, he reached into the pack and pulled out his tuxedo pants and shirt. They were the last clothing items he had with him.

"Sorry, Giorgio," he muttered as he pulled off his ruined jeans and t-shirt. Standing in the middle of the corridor with his boxers and socks on, Zach was reaching for the shirt when a mocking voice came out of the shadows.

"What kind of guest comes into someone's residence and proceeds to make such a horrible mess?"

-20-
Waiting Games

"Well, let's call this meeting into order," Katie said, clapping her hands briskly. The rest of the group quieted, some taking seats, others, like Liz, leaning against the railing of the sun deck of the beach house.

"Am I supposed to be here?" Owen asked, raising his hand. "I notice that the other Significant Others are missing. I can leave if you all need your privacy." He started to rise.

Katie waved him back down. "No, no, sit. Steven and William called, they are going to be a little bit late. No need to wait for them, we can get started with the discussion. First things first…how is our little mother doing?"

Tracy beamed and patted her belly. "Chugging along nicely," she replied brightly. "William gave me a clean bill of health, and everything seems to be progressing nicely."

"We'll keep a close eye on the blood work," Amber added, "just to make sure the Too'ki virus doesn't mutate or anything with the pregnancy."

"How far along are you at this point?" Owen asked.

"About six weeks. William says that if it keeps progressing at this rate, I may have a seven month pregnancy as opposed to the usual nine," Tracy told them.

"Still no word on whether you can go to the Land?" Ben asked, turning towards Amber. The woman shook her head ruefully, setting her sparkly earrings dancing with the movement.

"I wish I had better news," she admitted. "But Daniel is as stumped as I am. We've never had much Interdimensional Travel before, and certainly no one who was done so with a trans-dimensional child in-utero. It is our belief that Traveling at this stage could be dangerous to both mother and child."

Tracy was sitting back, her arms crossed, toe tapping. Amber sighed and rubbed her eyes. "You don't know the fight I put up about this, Tracy," the fairy said crossly. "The favors I tried to pull in, the arguments, the research. I have literally exhausted all avenues. It's not my fault that everything seems to point to the fact that to try and Travel would be dangerous."

Tracy took a deep breath, "You're right, Amber," she apologized. "It's just so hard, being pregnant and knowing my husband will never…" she trailed off and sighed. "Well, you know the deal. I won't bore you with the details. I'm just having a really difficult time getting over this. But, we have other things to discuss."

"Onward, then," Katie agreed, although she knew how much Tracy was hurting over the fact that Orli could not be with her. "The wedding plans seem to be moving along nicely as well. Ten days and counting."

Sasha gave a wan smile. "Everything is on track," was all she would say, her fingers worrying the engagement ring on her left hand.

"Thinking about your father?" Katie asked gently, reaching out to cover her hands.

Sasha nodded, her eyes filling with tears even as her jaw jutted out with determination. "I'm not going to let him ruin my wedding," she stated firmly, then seemed to deflate before them. "But then I think about the fact that he knows about the Land, and it almost kills me."

"The Seer doesn't think that the cult knows all that much about anything," Katie reminded her.

"I can tell you with certainty that your father was rather clueless about the Land. He was just mouthing what someone else told him to do." Liz said.

"You read him?" Sasha asked.

Liz nodded. "Without reservation or hesitation. He knows that the mention of the Land makes you tense, and he likes that power to hold over you. But as for real knowledge of the Land and the big picture? He knows absolutely *nada*." She bit her lip, then risked saying the rest. "I should say that his mind was incredibly disorganized. He's been brainwashed for so many years, or something along those lines, and he is barely able to form his own, independent thoughts."

"But what about the Brethren leader, what was his name? Oh yeah, the Reverend Tranquility Mind. What the hell kind of name is that, anyway?" Ben said, running his hand through his spiked hair. "He could know more."

They all looked at Liz, how held up her hands in warning. "Don't look at me. I'm limited, you know. I've never met this man. I tend to be able to connect with touch or familiarity. If I were to stand outside the complex, I wouldn't be able to tell you if I'm reading the Reverend or the housekeeper. I'd have to be in the same room, or have touched him."

"So we still have no idea what they know, how they got their knowledge, and what kind of threat they could be to the Land," Sarat stated, ticking off the questions on one hand.

"Well, they are certainly much less of a threat now than they were yesterday," Steven said as he and William came out the sliding glass door, their faces wreathed in smiles.

"What have you done?" Katie asked her husband as he came up and slipped his arm around her waist. "You are grinning like you're a cat that just swallowed a canary."

"We've been busy, busy, busy," Steven said with a laugh. He turned to William, who was dropping a kiss onto Sasha's blond head. "You tell them, good doctor."

"I think I will," William said with good-natured ease. "Well, for the past three months, I've been working on a little project. As an emergency room doctor, I have, on occasion, treated some children from the cult complex. And it occurred to me that, given what we know happened to Sasha, other children could be in danger. So I started doing some research. I called other regional medical centers, hospitals, urgent care, any doc in the box I could find."

"You were trying to find a pattern of abuse in the children from the complex," Tracy said, a grin spreading over her face. "That's brilliant."

William nodded his head regally. "Why thank you. What came out was that not only were there several suspicious patterns in accidents, but a decided lack of ongoing, preventative care for those poor children."

"So then William came to me and we got in contact with the Child Protective Services. We simply presented our findings, our fears, and as good members of the community, suggested it would be wise for someone to look into the Church of the Brethren," added Steven.

"There was a raid on the complex today," William finished up, "based on the CPS investigation. They took all the kids into custody."

Over the resounding applause from the other Protectors and their loved ones, Steven held up his hands. "Wait! It gets better," he vowed. "When they were in the process of getting the kids, the sheriff's office stumbled onto a warehouse full of heroin and cocaine."

"Apparently, it's how the Reverend Tranquility has been funding his little exercise in religious freedom," William sneered. "So now, pretty much everyone is in jail."

Sasha stood up and faced William, her face incredibly serious and intense. "He's in jail?"

"Yes," William replied, "Your father is in jail."

"Will he be there a long time?"

"As long as humanly possible," Steven replied. "Susan is working for the county. You know that's gotta be good, having our own Interdimensional lawyer on the case."

"Consider it an early wedding gift," William said softly, his crystal blue eyes locked on Sasha's. "He won't ever hurt you, or another little girl again."

She leaned into his warm, solid bulk. "Thank you," she breathed, feeling a decade of hurt and pain washing away.

"I love a happy ending," Sarat said happily, leaning back in her chair.

"What about our other matter?" Ben asked, leaning forward. "What news of Zach and his quest?"

"Why don't we ask Liz?" Katie said with a wicked little grin, turning in the woman's direction.

Liz chewed on her bottom lip as everyone swung to look at her. "What?" she asked as innocently as possible.

"The Seer tells me that you have been sneaking into the Land to visit Zach," Katie told her. "Astral projection across the Void. Very tricky from what I'm told."

"Very tricky indeed," said Amber, clearly surprised.

Again, all the faces swung towards Liz, who felt her back straighten. "Is that not allowed?"

"Darlin', you're a Seer," Amber said emphatically. "You can do whatever you want in that regard. I'm just pretty danged impressed with your abilities."

"What is curious to me," Sarat said with narrowed eyes, "is why you didn't feel you could tell us about these little excursions."

Liz shifted uncomfortably. How could she explain that she felt that her discussions and visits with Zach were intensely private? That would imply an intimate level to their relationship that Liz did not feel existed. Yet she couldn't ignore the fact that she had purposely withheld information from the Protectors about Zach.

After opening and closing her mouth several times, Liz finally blurted, "I went twice. Saw Zach two times. He was on the way to the fortress."

She fell silent for such a long time that Katie felt obligated to prompt her. "And?"

Liz sighed and told them about the fairies, the sword, the fact that Zella was trying to torment him, the fences and the fact that he was forging on alone. Then she dropped the bombshell about the child Seer that might be hidden within the fortress walls. When she finished, the others simply stared at her.

"Well, that's all," she said, somewhat defensively.

"You've been hanging out with Zach and you never told us," Tracy said slowly. "I think I should be mad at you, but I find I can't be."

"I feel the same way," Ben admitted. "I should be furious, but I think it's rather…"

"Sweet," Sasha stated.

"As in, he's sweet on you," Sarat said with satisfaction.

"It's not like that at all!" Liz was well aware that she was blushing wildly. "Well, he may think there's more to it than there is, but that's just because of the situation."

"Uh-huh," Katie said, her arms crossed. "Just what *does* he think, Liz?"

She dropped her eyes to the deck floor. "He says he loves me," she mumbled miserably, refusing to meet their eyes. "But it's silly. He's just reacting to the Land, and to the fact that his quest is tied up with me, and all. It's his over active protective instincts coming into play, that's all."

"Zachary Neol said he loves you," Sarat repeated slowly, as if savoring every word.

"He doesn't strike me as the type to toss those words out without some thought and reason going into it," said Katie thoughtfully.

"He's not," Tracy agreed. "He's the eternal bachelor, and all his girlfriends said he would never but never say the 'L' word."

"It's just because of the situation," Liz said stubbornly. "Besides, I haven't been able to make contact with him for several hours."

That got their attention. "You were in constant contact with him? Mentally?" Amber asked, coming to her feet.

"Well, yes," Liz replied, confused. "It wasn't like I can constantly read his mind or anything, I just had, well, an awareness of his consciousness. Isn't that normal?"

"Um, no! It's rather amazing," said Amber, taking Liz's hands in hers. "It's beyond amazing. To be able to reach across the Void and have that kind of awareness…" she trailed off, speechless. Which for Amber, was a rare occurrence indeed.

"Well, it's gone now," Liz said finally, pulling her hands from Amber's grip. "He's gone into the fortress, I think. And that means Zella is in there too."

"Can you try and get into the fortress?" Katie asked Liz, then turned to Amber before the woman could answer, "*Should* she try to go into the fortress?"

Amber shrugged, her eyes pensive. "I don't think it could hurt," she said finally. "I mean, we know that Zella is willing to bend the rules, and be particularly nasty. I think that Zach could benefit from seeing Liz."

"Could benefit from seeing…you make it sound so clinical," Liz muttered.

"Oh, no, honey, it's anything but clinical," Katie assured her. "The man is in love with you. He said it himself."

"When he's back home, and the real world here is surrounding him, he'll realize it was all a mirage, a product of his experiences in the Land," Liz recited, as if it was a mantra that she had told herself over and over again.

"You keep telling yourself that, if it helps," Katie said, holding up a hand when others would have interrupted to belabor the point. "And then when he comes back home, see what happens, and then you'll know for sure."

"You'll see," Liz said, her jaw line firm, but Ben noticed she was playing with her Protector pendant, as she normally did when nervous. "It's just a phase, that's all."

"But if it isn't," Sarat said with sexy giggle, "I want to know all the details, Liz. Each and every delicious one!"

-21-
Zella Returns

"Good afternoon, Zella," Zach said politely, deliberately continuing his movement and snatching up his shirt. Donning it, he turned slowly in her direction, buttoning the front. Damn his luck, Evil incarnate shows up and he was caught wearing Amber's favorite black silk boxers with red hearts. Real action hero stuff.

Zach tried to redeem his macho image by giving her a mocking gaze. "If you wanted someone to feel like a welcome guest, then you should've put a doorbell outside. Or, at the very least, left a clear path to your sitting room."

Zella sauntered out of the shadows. She was in her *Matrix* mode today, Zach noticed, shiny vinyl from head to toe, skintight and black as her rotting heart. Her hair was pulled back from her face, spilling over one shoulder in a riot of pitch colored curls. The green eyes were amused and smiling, her hand on her hip, the lethally long crimson tipped nails tapping the leather.

"Nice tattoo you have there, sweetie. Shame you had to go and cover it all up. I have to say, Zachy, I'm highly impressed with your innovativeness," Zella commented, sauntering towards him, all hips and rolls of oozing sexuality. Emphasis on oozing. Yet, this close, he could sense the Evil roiling off her like heat waves in the desert.

"Well, I'm a highly impressive guy," Zach said, finishing his last button. He eyed his fairy sword, which was half hidden by his pack.

He hoped that Zella would not see the weapon and confiscate it like she had his Phoenix sword.

"With a highly impressive ass to boot," she said, eying the aforementioned anatomy with a clinical eye. "All that martial arts you partake in have certainly paid off." She pouted when he pulled on his tuxedo pants.

"Oh, now that's just not fair," she complained lightly, one finger reaching up to tap on her cheek. "I think that your previous look was much more, shall we say, delectable?"

"Consider me removed from the smorgasbord," Zach said as cheerfully as possible. He had a part to play, after all. He clapped his hands together and gave her his most wicked and lethal grin. "So what happens next, sweetheart? What other little joys await me in your fortress?"

"Hmmmm," she said, leaning in very close and whispering into his ear, "wouldn't you like to know…"

"Well, you could certainly save us both a heap of trouble and hand over the little girl now. I'll take her out of here and be on my way, and we can just both call it a day," Zach negotiated easily, spreading his hands.

"So you know about the child?" A black eyebrow arched. "I wonder how."

Zach fell silent. Zella flinched first.

"No matter," Zella purred, walking around him in a tight circle. It made Zach extremely uncomfortable, especially when she was behind him, but he forced himself to not move. She hadn't pulled the old freeze and squeeze routine yet, so he wasn't about to push it with her. "Zachy, you know I can't let the girl go. Not yet, anyway."

"What are you waiting for?" Zach blurted, then could have cursed himself.

"We don't wait. We act. And this is part of the process," Zella said with a light laugh. She inclined her head, almost regally. "I suppose there is no harm in telling you the truth. Otherwise you'll never figure it out and that would be, frankly, boring. We are awaiting the final confirmation that the child is, in fact, a Seer."

"Waiting for the full moon?"

"You have done your homework. We have kept the child out of

the Land until this cycle, this is true. Now we simply need to wait and see if the connection is made. I see no reason not to tell you that, since there's no way you will be able to reach her before that is definitively determined."

"And if it is determined?" Zach asked.

"She will be removed from the Land again. Then, an accelerated growth potion, so that she will reach her maturity in a matter of months. Then, well, I'm sure you know of the plans we had for that so-called Worlder Seer. What was her name?" Zella's mouth made a moue of a frown. "Oh yes, Liz. The librarian." The exotic woman shuddered.

"You'll breed the girl like a show dog," Zach supplied grimly. "Hoping to raise your own little stable of Evil Seers."

"Smart *and* sexy," Zella purred, running her hand up his arm, laughing when he pulled away from her touch. "I was actually hoping they'd send Liz to save the child. I'd like to get a piece of her for killing Valdeen. He was such a pretty boy, and quite an amazing man. Oh, I miss having him in my bed. So…energetic. If one appreciates primitive species, that is. And I do, Zachy. I really do. Valdeen was…special. I shall have to hurt that librarian bitch personally for taking him away from me."

Zach started to count to one hundred, forcing himself to breathe easily. He didn't want to let Zella know he was easing into a slow burn over their treatment of Liz or the little girl. Better if she thought him a stupid actor, playing a part. Little did she know just how much he was pretending.

Zella paused, looking Zach up and down thoughtfully. "You know, I think you could make up for his loss," she observed, her tongue darting out to touch her lips.

"I don't think that's a likely scenario," Zach said truthfully. "I'd have to say with confidence that there is slim chance of your getting any piece of the Z-unit."

"I'd say my chances are better than that," Zella purred.

"Nah, I don't care to share my bed with Evil," Zach said with a distasteful grimace.

"Oh, but darling, you have in the past, so why stop yourself now?" Zella said, watching his dawning, horrified reaction with great relish. "You aren't so far from me, Zach. We are of the same ilk. You know that, deep down inside. And you aren't all that different from Valdeen. Bred for certain functions, and good at them, too."

Zach's nostrils flared, his temper starting to rise, as it did whenever he was reminded of Valdeen. "I was actually glad to hear that Liz killed the bastard," he said, his even tone belying the turmoil churning underneath. "Proves that you Evil folk aren't as strong as you like to think you are."

"Valdeen was a mere child when compared to me," Zella said, her eyes flashing. "He was limited in his scope and abilities because of his Lander roots. It weakened him greatly, and inhibited his true potential. I, on the other hand, am a fully functional partner in the realm of Evil. I won't make the same mistakes that Valdeen did, Zachy. You can't win. Not against me."

Zach smiled, rocking back and forth on the balls of his feet. He was glad to see the woman was getting riled by his behavior. It was her weakness, that ego of hers. "That remains to be seen, Zella. You didn't think I would get into your little fortress here either. And I did. So perhaps you'd better rethink your position on the issue."

Zella's eyes narrowed dangerously, then she regained her balance with some effort. Turning to the corridor that Zach had just cut through, she waved her hands.

Zach groaned. The vines were restored, the mass once again impenetrable to pass through without hacking your way in. All that work, the careful stacking, the slicing of the vines, it had all been for nothing.

"That's better," Zella said with satisfaction, then peered closer at the discarded vines stacked along the wall. "But how on earth did you get through there in the first place?"

Zach tried to distract her from the cut vines. It wouldn't take an expert to see that they had been sliced by some sort of knife or sword.

"I think that it's telling that whenever we Worlders go up against Evil, we managed to kick your asses without the fancy tricks, Zella. We play fair, and we always win. So why don't you get the hell out of my way and be done with it?"

Zella flashed her hands at him in a sudden snaking movement. He was frozen in place, cursing. "Well, as long as you don't think I'm playing fair, I think I'll just give myself a little more leverage then," she said, reaching for his pack. "I don't think you'll be needing this, Zachy," she said, hefting it up and then making it disappear in a flash of ocher light.

Zach mentally groaned, thinking about all his equipment that had been in that bag. He was no McGyver but he'd managed to improvise his way into the temple. Now, all that potential was gone. But that was the least of his worries at the moment as Zella's eyes widened dramatically.

"What have we here? A new sword? No wonder you were able to get through my vines so easily." She turned to him, her voice full of mocking reproach. "Now, we can't have you running about my home with a sword, can we?"

"Seems to me you don't want a fair fight," Zach pointed out as she reached for the sword and scabbard, lying on the stone floor, the stones gleaming in the torchlight. "You having all the resources while I'm left with nothing is just not very sportsmanlike of you."

She paused mid-bend, sending him a sly smile. "Good sportsmanship was made up by folks who don't understand the true power of using their darker tendencies."

Her hand closed around the sword. Instantly, she yelped and shot back several feet, cradling her one hand with the other. She looked up at Zach, horrified.

"Where did you get that sword?"

Zach smiled, eyeing the blistered and red hand that she was nursing. It looked really painful. "It's not a sword," he replied with pleasure, "it's just two sticks lashed together and put in a sheath of woven grass."

Zella's eyes narrowed dangerously. "Fairy magic," she spat with real heat and disgust, looking at the sword with distaste evident in their green depths. "Those damned IDF bitches have helped you. How? When?"

It was Zach's turn to raise his eyebrows. "In my dreams?"

Zella gave something that sounded dangerously like a growl. "This isn't over," she snarled at him.

"It won't be over until I walk out of here with the child," Zach agreed easily.

"Your arrogance will be your downfall," Zella predicted in an ominous voice before disappearing in a flash of white light.

Zach collapsed to his knees, her spell over his body receding as she left. "And your temper will be yours," he said quietly into the empty corridor.

Looking down at the ground, Zach sighed, taking a brief inventory of what remained of his belongings. He had his sword and belt, which had a canteen strapped to it, along with the small jug of fairy wine. He had his destroyed jeans and t-shirt, the former still housing the cigarette lighter in the front pocket. She hadn't stolen his tennis shoes, for which he was eternally grateful. He also still had the torch, which Zella had not thought to take with her.

"Well that was dumb of her," Zach said. He picked up his clothes and rolled them into a small ball, tying them to his sword belt. He wasn't leaving anything behind.

After strapping on the belt, Zach stood, taking the torch out of the socket. "Let's rock and roll," he muttered, heading down the corridor at a fast pace.

The strange whispering was still echoing down the hall, barely to be heard. It was annoying, a constant, incessant undertone of words that could not be understood. Zach rounded the next corner, half expecting to see a crowd of people gathered, speaking in hushed voices.

The corridor was empty. That automatically made Zach nervous. Something was going to happen, and soon. Waiting for the next trick in Zella's bag was nerve wracking, to say the very least. He drew his sword, feeling infinitely more comfortable with its weight in his hand. Zach moved forward, step by cautious step.

He was a mere five or six steps down the corridor when it hit. A maelstrom of wind, howling around his body. Dust and particles blinded his eyes, the vicious wind clawing at him like a wild animal. The wind passed after a few minutes, leaving him rather breathless but otherwise unharmed.

He felt a sense of wild hope. Was this the best Zella could do? Hope to knock him over, bash him into the stone walls? Ridiculous. He'd just get over to the wall, hug the rock as he made his way down the corridor.

As if on cue from some unseen and diabolical director, the walls in front and behind him simply melted away. Beneath him, the corridor floor narrowed into the size of a footstep, spanning a chasm so deep,

Zach could not see the bottom. The walls spread until they were at least fifty feet apart, leaving Zach teetering on the narrow rocky span.

"Whoa," Zach said, clutching the sword in one hand and the torch in the other, balancing desperately on the narrow ledge. If he dropped the sword, he'd have no weapon. If he dropped the torch, he'd have no light. Neither option seemed ideal.

Zach sheathed the sword, holding the torch close to his body. He started to make his way across the narrow bridge, concentrating as hard as he could on reaching the other side, which was roughly a football field length away from him. Ok. He could do this. He considered himself to have good balance, given his extensive martial arts work. He was also not generally afraid of heights, so the distance didn't overly bother him. Zach figured he would just get across the span and be done with it.

Zach had forgotten about the wind, however. And when it came howling out of nowhere to buffet him, he was completely unprepared. For a precious few seconds, Zach was convinced he was going over the edge of the bridge. He was actually teetering on one leg, his arms and other leg pin wheeling desperately.

Somehow, he managed to keep a hold of the torch, but barely. As the storm continued to rage around him, Zach tried crouching down as low as possible against the bridge, wrapping his legs around the rocky span for added leverage. The wind continued to buffet him one way, then the other, a ferocious beast intent upon getting him off the precarious perch of stone.

Back in the World Dimension, Zach had stood outside in a hurricane once, and that kind of wind was nothing compared to what he was experiencing now. At least with a hurricane, the wind generally came in one steady direction. On the bridge, Zach felt that this was what being in the center of a tornado must be like, except this funnel cloud didn't pass by, it kept coming back again and again to torment and thrash at him like a cat batting a toy on a string. He finally just hunched over as low as possible, to give the wind the least amount of resistance. The torch fluttered and went out, plunging him into inky blackness, making it even more difficult to hold onto the stone ledge that was his only salvation.

"Crap," Zach yelled into the wind. This was the last thing he needed. Stuck on a narrow, rock bridge with no light, and no way of knowing how long the storm was going to last. This definitely sucked. Big time.

The wind finally stopped with a suddenness that almost had him falling off the bridge when it ceased. "Ok, then," Zach said, struggling to his feet. His legs were shaking from the exertion of holding onto the bridge. "Just get across the bridge, Neol. Just get across the bridge."

He paused, wondering if he should try and relight the torch while on the bridge. He decided against it, not knowing if he was going to be hit with another mini-tornado anytime soon. Zach stuck the torch into the belt, hoping it would stay put for the duration.

In the pitch black of the corridor, Zach started edging forward, slowly and steadily. He had no idea how much farther he had to go, how soon his feet would slide onto the solid floor of the corridor. For all he knew, Zella could make him walk this bridge forever, extending it until kingdom come.

"No negative thoughts, Neol," Zach thought to himself, stretching his arms out to the side like a circus performer on the high wire. Yet he tried to keep hunched over slightly, so to be closer to the bridge should that wicked ass wind kick up again.

When it did blow in, it knocked Zach to one side. For one split second, heart-lurching moment, he lost contact with the stone beneath his feet. Arms flailing as he fell, Zach barely caught the bridge with one arm, his rib cage smacking into the rocks with a painful thud. He gripped the span tightly, his legs swinging in the empty space.

The one good thing was that by dangling from the bridge, he was out of the worst of the wind. Concentrating, Zach was able to pull his legs up and wrap them around the bridge. Slowly but surely he climbed to the top of the expanse, the rough stone digging into his chest and legs as he lay down on the span. Zach pressed his cheek to the rough surface, patiently waiting out the tornado.

When the last of the wind howled off into the ravine, Zach sat up, straddling the bridge. He scooted forward, deciding it would be better for him to be closer to the floor. It was slower going, but he felt safer, especially since he could not see a foot in front of his face.

When his legs, moving beneath the bridge, hit against the far wall of the chasm, Zach breathed a sigh of relief and literally crawled off the span. He sprawled on the ledge, rolling onto his back. Wincing, he reached behind and pulled the torch from the small of his back.

"Get up, get up, get up," he chanted to himself, then willed himself to his feet. His legs, albeit shaky, were planted on firm rock, for which he was eternally grateful.

Zach reached into his pocket, breathing a sigh of relief when he closed his hand around the lighter. A moment later he had the torch lit and swung it around to see the gaping chasm he'd just crossed.

The way behind him looked no different than the way before him; a stretch of corridor lined with stonewalls. Zach shook his head and turned the opposite direction. He rounded two more corners without incident, gathering a few more unlit torches as he went.

Zach's eyes were gritty with dust from the wind, but he didn't dare waste water washing them out. He came around another corner and drew up short.

He'd entered a large room, with stone walls that rose up at least a dozen feet. The ceiling overhead was glowing gently. Zach peered at it, realizing that some sort of luminous moss was covering the entire space. He debated dousing the torch, but finally decided that he'd rather have the fire close at hand, available to use as an alternative weapon. The strange whispering sound was still evident, the words hovering just under his detection. At least while he'd been in the storm, he couldn't hear the stupid whispering. It was getting frustrating, that incessant noise.

The way into the room, immediately in front of Zach, started twisting and turning upon itself. A few times he had to make a choice as to which way to turn. It was when he hit a dead end that the realization of what he was in finally hit Zach.

"A maze," he whispered. "This is a huge maze. Ok. Time to think it through, Neol."

Zach prided himself on his sense of direction, and had been great at mazes his whole life. He backtracked to the next juncture then oriented himself, taking another direction. He got further in before the way was once again blocked.

Patiently, Zach backtracked and then started in another direction. Suddenly, a whirring noise had him whirling, sword and torch at the ready. What greeted his eyes made him curse fluently.

-22-
Tricks and Treats

A large section of the maze wall was slowly closing behind Zach, blocking the way he had just traveled. If Zach hadn't witnessed it, he would not have known it was happening. He wondered how many wrong turns he had made due to the walls changing.

"This just got a whole lot more difficult," Zach realized aloud. It didn't help matters that he wasn't really sure where the exit of the maze was located. It could be in the middle of the room, or at the far side. There was really no way of knowing.

All Zach could do, in the end, was press forward. Since the corridors were linear, he was going to assume that this maze was simply an extension of a corridor. Therefore, he decided to simply head for the opposite side of the room, hoping the exit lay there.

Periodically, Zach looked up at the ceiling, marking certain patterns within the growth, orienting himself slightly. It became a touchstone for him, indicating his progress, which was disgustingly slow.

To add to the worries, Zach was getting tired. He had no way of knowing how long he'd been inside the fortress. Time had ceased to exist for him. It could be mid afternoon, it could be the middle of the night. All he knew for sure was that he was slowly sinking into a pit of exhaustion. He was stumbling slightly on his feet, and his eyes were increasingly burning from exhaustion as well as from the debris flung at him during the windstorms.

Finally, he stopped. "This is stupid." If he didn't get some rest, and

Zella came along, there would be hell to pay. The woman was too sharp for him to go up against her in his current state and wandering the stone maze was making him duller by the millisecond.

Zach hunkered down against a wall, leaning his back against the rough exterior. Sitting cross-legged, he laid the unsheathed sword across his lap. Closing his eyes, he prepared to drift and get whatever kind of sleep he could. When the wall behind him gave a faint rumble, Zach jumped away quickly, but not before the t-shirt and jeans that were tied to his belt became caught underneath the moving stone. It was a flashback to every biblical motion picture he'd seen growing up, and the very real threat of being trapped by the moving stone made his heart race.

Frantically, Zach pulled on the bundle, which was still tied to his waist. The wall was forcing him relentlessly back, and he was in danger of getting crushed between the moving wall and its new location if he did not get free.

Moving awkwardly, Zach managed to get the sword between his body and the wall, severing the rope tie. He stumbled out of the way of the closing rock, his shoulder connecting painfully with the edge as he barely cleared it.

"Goddamn bitch can't let me even sleep in peace," he grumbled, rubbing the spot irritably.

He could have sworn he heard a chuckle wafting through the air at his words. Sighing, Zach moved forward until he found a fairly large junction where four tunnels intersected. He settled smack in the middle of it, knowing that if the walls near him started to move, he'd hear them in enough time to get out of the way. Or, at least he hoped that would be the case.

Zach spent a moment fortifying his mental blocks and ensuring they were in place. He certainly did not want Zella wandering through his cerebrum. Finally, he felt like he could try and get some rest without fear of the woman breaking into his brain and messing with him.

Zach's head dropped, his arms resting lightly on his legs, over which the sword was laid. Again, his long days on set came in handy. He could fall asleep in virtually any position, a technique that would certainly be useful in Zella's fortress.

Zach dozed fitfully, never falling under long enough to achieve a dream-like state. Idly he wished that Liz would come visit him, however, he figured that it would not be a good idea for the Seer to try and enter the fortress. Zach was aware of the maze continuing to move around him, the sound now becoming commonplace to him. He also felt like he was drifting along the current of the whispering voices, their constant murmur becoming like a familiar song.

Several times, Zach was jerked into full consciousness when one of the walls adjacent to his location would begin to move. Wearily, he would get to his feet and move to another four-way juncture where he would settle back down for another doze. It was certainly not the ideal way to get some rest, but Zach felt strongly that he needed to give his body and mind a break before moving on.

After several hours and tries, however, Zach came to the conclusion that it was hopeless to try and sleep in the maze room. All the moving parts, and the resulting need to keep mobile, along with the need to be constantly aware of what was going on around him was just not conducive to rest.

Wearily, Zach got to his feet. He looked at the ceiling to try and orient himself then started forward again.

The walls, it seemed to him, were moving more rapidly than ever before. Zach wondered if he had made a huge miscalculation—it seemed the longer he was in the room, the faster it was going to change. Zach rounded a corner and stopped short, the blood draining from his face as he recognized what he was facing.

In front of him was the entrance to the maze. He'd worked for hours, and had gotten nowhere.

"Real men don't cry, Neol," he muttered to himself. Zach hung his head, discouraged, then glanced up at the ceiling. Something about the sight had him staring. An idea formed in his mind as he noted the gap between the top of the rock wall and the ceiling of the cavern. The idea sparked a sense of hope; an emotion that was in small supply currently.

"That might work." He started for the center of the maze again, this time ignoring the moving walls. He wasn't interested in getting to the other side at the moment, but kept scanning the stone walls, seeking the right opportunity.

Finally he found the kind of wall he was looking for. The gaps seemed to be a tad wider between the bricks on this part of the wall. Securing his sword to his thigh with a piece of material torn from his tuxedo shirt, Zach took a deep breath and ran towards the wall, leaping at the last second. The walls were about fifteen feet high at this point, and made up of the same kind of blocks that lined the corridors. He hoped to be able to latch onto the top of the wall and pull himself up, helping the process by wedging his toes between the cracks.

Zach was, apparently, overly optimistic about his ability to leap tall buildings in a single bound.

He missed the top of the wall by several inches, his body slamming full force into the rocky wall. Sliding back down, painfully, he tried the next option. Reaching up as high as he could, Zach wedged his toes and fingers into the cracks between the bricks in the wall and, using his fingertips, started to pull himself up the side of the maze.

He had worked with some of the best mountain climbers when training for *The Phoenix*. One of the key scenes in the movie entailed his character scaling a sheer rock wall to escape the prison his arch nemesis had placed him in. This wasn't much different than scaling a natural rock ascent, Zach realized with some grim satisfaction. He was able to concentrate and quickly gain the top of the wall.

As he had anticipated, Zach was able to stretch out on the top of the wall, and there was roughly a three-foot gap between the walls and ceiling. From this vantage point, Zach was able to see across the room. There appeared to be an opening, possibly the other corridor leading away from the maze.

"Excellent," Zach whispered then started the torturous crawl over the top of the walls. They were only about a foot wide, and Zach found himself inching along on his belly, bumping and scraping himself on the rough surface.

Yet he was definitely making better progress on top of the walls than he had down below. A few times, he was forced to hold on for dear life when the walls shifted while he was crossing them, and once he was actually forced to jump off the top of the structure or risk being squashed between two walls.

Zach waited until the walls stopped moving but then climbed right back to the top of the wall again, stretching out and continuing his trek across the expanse of the room. He kept an eye on the shifting walls, and after some time, he was able to see a kind of pattern forming in the way the movement occurred. That helped him anticipate where and when the walls would start to swing and to position himself accordingly.

The ceiling above also gave him some grief. It was rough-hewn rock, and at times would dip so low that he could not pass under it. When that occurred, he was forced to move over several walls and try again.

In addition, the growth on the ceiling that pulsated with luminous light kept getting scraped off onto him, dusting his body. Soon his back was covered with the stuff, which was irritating when it touched his bare skin, like a mild form of sub terrain poison ivy.

After what seemed like an eternity, Zach finally reached the opposite side of the cavern. He lowered himself to the floor, taking a deep breath of relief as he stepped into the corridor beyond. As had happened before with the bridge, the corridor behind him morphed from a room full of shifting, moving rock walls to a simple corridor.

Zach pulled one of the torches from his belt, and lit it with his lighter. During his crawl, he had only lost one of the torches he had managed to collect, and considered himself lucky that he hadn't dropped more.

"Onward," he said aloud.

The whispering voices continued to swirl around him, tugging at his mind and leading him forward. Part of him wondered if it could be the Seer child, reaching out to him. But he didn't dare lower his mental guards to find out for sure, since that would be like waving a red flag at Zella to come over and play. He'd like to avoid that at all costs for while, Zach realized with a grim smile.

He trudged along, the corridors seeming to stretch on forever. Zach was aware that he seemed to be continually climbing, which to him was a good sign. His gut was telling him that the child was at the apex of the fortress.

Zach noticed some other changes as well. The air seemed to be growing more humid, the stone actually dripping with moisture, their red tone deepening until they were the color of old, dried blood. Moss started springing from the cracks between the bricks and the sound of water dripping from the ceiling was a constant background noise. Zach wiped the sweat off his face, blowing out a quick breath.

Up ahead, Zach could discern a glimmer on the walls, like the reflection of water. Soon the reason became evident, as he stood at the edge of a huge sub terrain lake. The black waters stretched out before him, the rocky, uneven walls of the cave meeting up with the softly lapping water of the lake. There was no bridge, no footpath, and no easily discernable way to get across the water at all.

Weird. From the outside, the temple did not seem to be big enough to house this kind of expanse. Then again, the maze and the stone bridge had appeared, in retrospect, to be nothing more than part of the basic tunnel. This, too, could be some elaborate hoax, a mirage.

Zach eyed the water, warily. It was dark in the cave, and he was unable to see how deep the water reached. It could be ankle deep; it could plunge down several thousand feet. One could not be sure what kind of fun Zella had thought up for this particular obstacle. The ceiling above was lined with the same kind of luminous growth as in the maze, the eerie light bouncing off the water and casting reflections against the walls of the cave.

If this was an illusion, could he simply walk into the lake and it would disappear? Or were there some other rules at play? Those stone walls had been real, for one. He easily could have been crushed by them. If Zella was able to warp reality into her own little horror house way, then this was most likely a very real lake, and he'd do well to treat it with caution, no matter how impossible it seemed to be that such a huge expanse was housed in the upper regions of the stone temple.

Zach squatted next to the edge of the lake, running his hand over his stubbled chin, thinking. He grabbed for one of the unlit torches and leaned out over the water. Holding the torch by one end, he lowered it into the water to see if he could gauge the depth.

A flash of something pale white gleamed into view. Zach had barely enough time to snatch his hand back as a white fish, about the size of his palm, jumped out of the water, aiming for his flesh. Zach had an impression of teeth—lots of them—set in a circular mouth. The teeth looked razor sharp and deadly. He fell back on his butt, scrambling to get back from the edge of the water, the torch dropping into the water with a splash. It sank quickly, the ripples moving outward in its wake.

"What the hell was that?" Zach asked out loud, his voice echoing across the chamber. Cautiously, he looked into the water.

Just below the surface, he could discern a swarm of the pale fish, hundreds of them. He could see no evidence that they had eyes, as if they had bred or mutated within a dimly lit environment. Each did possess the same gaping mouth and sharp triple row of teeth that had so startled Zach a moment earlier. Upon closer inspection, the creatures looked like a cross between an eel and a fish.

They resembled, Zach realized, the lampreys he had seen back home, a tube of a fish with a mouth set in the end, the tail a tapered fin like protrusion. Hadn't Ben encountered something like this down in the depths of the ocean by the Barrier? *Yeah. Sea eels.* They generated electricity, too. He watched for a while longer, noting that yes, there seemed to be sparks flying off the fish whenever they touched tails, and the flash of electricity appeared painful judging by the flinching motion of the ones that were stung.

"Swimming is officially out of the question," Zach muttered. No way was he going to get one of those suckers attached to his legs. As there was no boat available, naturally, he was going to have to find another way to gain the opposite shore.

The walls of the cavern were rough, he noted, speculating. If he could propel himself across the walls, much like rock climbing, he could make it to the other side. Zach blew out his breath. That kind of horizontal work was extremely difficult, especially given the fact that the walls looked slick with moisture. He'd have to rely on brute strength to get across. But what other option did he really have at the moment?

After taking a few moments to secure his gear to his body, Zach reached out and tried to find a good starting handhold to work across the lake. Luckily, the rock wall was very uneven, so Zach was confident that he would be able to find enough nooks and crannies to utilize in the climb.

Instantly, the water below him started to churn as the eyeless fish attempted to jump out of the lake and snap onto him. Zach quickly worked his way up the wall, so that he was some five or six feet above the surface. He doubted the fish could leap that high.

Traversing the space horizontally turned out to be much more difficult than Zach had anticipated. The rock wall was slippery beneath his feet and hands, which made finding a firm grip virtually impossible.

He was using an entirely different set of muscles than he'd expected and soon his shoulders and calves were screaming from the extended time supporting his not-inconsiderable bulk. Sweat dripped into his face, making his eyes burn and vision blur, but he had to content himself with occasionally wiping his face against his shoulder, which was pretty inefficient and generally succeeded in getting the luminous crap from the maze room into his eyes, making them burn.

To make matters worse, the eyeless fish were jumping higher and further, as if motivated to taste his flesh. The splashing of their bodies hitting the water was both an impediment and an impetus. He was motivated to keep moving because there was no way he was going to fall into the lake with those freaky creatures. Yet the constant fear of doing just that was also draining his strength. The fact that he flinched every time some water splashed onto his skin from the feeding frenzy below did not add to his sense of comfort or secure grip on the wall, either.

About half way across, Zach reached for a rather prominent handhold. His fingers closed around it and he shifted to move his foot to the left. His right foot slipped, and Zach found himself swinging above the lake, holding onto the wall with one hand.

As he swung out, away from the wall, Zach could see the small fish swarming around underneath him. He could also see, to his absolute horror, what else lay beneath the lake's surface.

The smaller fish were apparently the babies. Mommy was reclining along the bottom of the lake, her huge body coiled much like a snake. As Zach swung over her, the creature followed his path with her head moving like a pendulum. A large mouth was gaping and easily some twenty feet across, the triple row of teeth showing in her gaping mouth. Zach knew instantly that if this creature so desired, it could easily reach him where he was perched on the wall.

Zach turned back to the wall, his feet scrambling to find a foothold as his heart beat a wild tattoo. When he finally got his toes firmly wedged into a crevice on the wall, he worked his way as high up the wall as his aching muscles would allow, all the time continuing to move inexorably to the other side of the lake, foot by agonizing foot.

Every ten feet or so, Zach risked a glance over his shoulder. So far, the mammoth creature at the bottom of the lake had not moved, other than her mouth turning to follow his progress. Realistically, Zach wasn't sure how long his luck would last in that factor.

He could see the other side of the corridor, the terra cotta brick walls looking infinitely welcome to him. The last few feet would be the trickiest of the trek, Zach realized. He'd have to get closer to the surface than he cared to be, especially now that the mama eel was aware of his presence.

He was about six feet from the end of the rock wall, trying to figure out the best way for him to get to the corridor. As he plotted his handholds an absence of splashing caught his attention. Warily, he realized the little fish had stopped agitating the surface of the water. Now he could only hear a dripping sound.

Swallowing hard, Zach looked over his shoulder. The site that met eyes made him start scrambling for the far shore, stealth be damned.

The large lamprey like creature was rearing out of the water, aiming its large circular mouth directly at Zach. He literally flung himself at the opening some three feet away as the fish eel lunged at him. The thing's mouth hit the wall where his body had been suspended but a moment before.

Zach's chest hit the edge of the tunnel wall, his legs submerged in the inky black water. Luckily for him, the small fish did not seem to want to compete with their mother and left him alone. Pulling and kicking frantically, he managed to pull himself into the corridor, crawling across the floor rapidly to get away from the opening.

The fish rammed the corridor opening and hung there, the circular teeth clicking frantically at nothing. Zach rolled to his feet and pulled his sword, taking a swipe at the vulnerable looking center of the thing's mouth.

With an unearthly shriek, the fish jerked loose and sank under the water, thrashing wildly.

Zach watched as the water stilled then the subterranean lake shrank, becoming a corridor with a small puddle in the middle of it. Cautiously, Zach looked into the splash of water. There was a thin, worm like creature in the depths of the puddle. Zach brought his sword down onto the worm, crushing it with grim satisfaction. A tinny-sounding scream came from the worm as it died.

Turning, Zach realized he was weaving with exhaustion, his equilibrium completely shot as adrenaline seeped from his body.

"Rest," he mumbled, the tip of his sword dragging the floor. "I need some rest." He walked forward several steps, eager to put some distance between him and the part of the corridor that housed the lake. Sinking to the stone floor, Zach put his head back against the wall and closed his eyes.

-23-
I'll Take Curtain Number Three, Please

He could have been dozing for a minute, it could have been an hour. The whole time continuum seemed out of whack for him inside the walls of Zella's little house of horrors. Regardless, it was not very long, before Zach was roused by the sound of someone whistling a merry tune. The cheerful noise was getting closer by the second.

Cracking one eye, Zach could see a shadow approaching. It was coming from the way he needed to travel, so it could literally be anything. He pushed himself up from his sitting position with a groan, all his muscles and tendons popping painfully as he stood up. Then, he squared his shoulders to face whatever was coming around the bend.

When Zella's form came into view, Zach suppressed another groan. Just what he needed when he was hungry and sleep deprived. She was dressed in low-rise jeans and an abbreviated red gingham checked top tied between her rather magnificent breasts. The midriff baring shirt also showcased her flat abs, complete with a green gem in her belly button. Her hair was loose and cascading down her back and in one hand she carried...a fishing pole?

Zach resisted the urge to shake his head, to clear the mental image from his cortex. But then he realized that the woman was, indeed, carrying a bamboo rod fishing pole and a bucket of bait. A straw hat was jammed on top of her head, and her slender feet were barefoot, a toe ring glinting in the torch's light.

"Hey there, Zachy," Zella chirped cheerfully as she passed by him standing in the corridor. He might have been an acquaintance she was greeting on her way to the local watering hole.

Zella came to a halt by the puddle, frowning at the mangled worm that was floating in the water. She turned hard green eyes towards Zach. "That wasn't very nice," she scolded, waggling a finger at him. "You ruined my fishing hole."

"You know, I'm really not interested in what you say or what you think," Zach pointed out, not willing to play the game just yet. "I was just trying to catch some Z's."

"Oh, I don't think I can let you sleep, Zachy," Zella said companionably, swinging the bait bucket back and forth slowly. "You're turning out to be a very resourceful young man. I have to say, that stamina bodes well for you, at least for when I get you in my bed. Which will happen in time. The best is yet come, as they say."

"Oh joy," Zach said. A muscle in his thigh was starting to shake and he willed it to be still, not wanting to show an ounce of weakness in front of the woman.

"Well, since my fishy is dead and gone," Zella gave a heartfelt sigh, "and there isn't much to be done with you that you won't do to yourself eventually, I guess I'll mosey along." She sauntered back by Zach, then snaked her arm out to fling it around his neck like a vise. Zella pulled Zach's lips down to hers.

Zach immediately pulled back, instinctively and quickly seeking to break the contact. Zella clung to him like ivy, dropping the pole so that her other arm twined around his neck as well, her lips working his greedily.

A faint buzzing started in the back of Zach's brain, seeping through him like wildfire. It swamped his reasoning, stilled his conscious, willed his emotions into a dark tempest of desire and hunger. As if in a dream, one of Zach's hands delved into her black curls, his lips angling on hers to match the intensity of the kiss, his eyes closing in lustful bliss. It was as if he were drugged and had no control over his actions, nor did he care about the consequences of what he was doing. He just wanted to lose himself in the intoxicating kiss.

Dimly, in one part of his still functioning brain, Zach heard the clatter of his sword falling to the ground. The sound of that clear, ringing noise cleaved through his mind like a trumpet. His eyes opened like a shot and he shoved Zella away from him as hard as he could.

The woman hit the opposite wall pushing herself off with a sly, slow grin. "That, my friend, was highly promising," Zella purred, bending to pick up her fishing pole, her other hand touching her lips, which were tinged with blood welling from the intensity of the kiss.

"No," Zach said as he scooped up his sword from the floor. "That was nothing. An aberration, a slip, the result of exhaustion and mental meddling. I don't want you, Zella. I don't desire you. I could never want someone like you." His voice was thick with self disgust. Even though he knew that the kiss had something to do with Zella, with some sort of spell she had cast, it still galled him that he had responded in any way.

"Ah, but for a moment in time, no matter how brief, you *did* want me," Zella said, tapping her cheek with one finger. "Think about that, Zach, as you continue on your way. Think about the fact that you are no different than me, despite your rather pathetic attempts to be some sort of do-gooder. We are of the same ilk, Zachy."

"No," Zach repeated, shaking his head stubbornly. "I'm not like you. I choose not to be like you. Ever."

Zella ignored him, blowing him a kiss. "See you around, Zachy," she said with a giggle, then left, whistling her merry tune as she skipped away.

"My name is Zach," he muttered, but she just waved her hand before turning the corner.

Zach stood stock still, every muscle shaking with rage and exhaustion. *She was wrong*, he told himself staunchly. He was not ruled by lust or desire or darker thoughts. He had strived to fight those tendencies his whole life. He would not give in to it now. He could not afford to fail this mission, this quest. Giving in to Zella's taunts, allowing her to goad him and get under his skin, figuratively or literally, was just foolish on his part.

Following in Zella's footsteps, Zach rounded the corner to find the passageway empty, stretching into the distance, the slope upward more pronounced.

The whispers were back and growing louder. He could hear snatches of words now.

"Home."

"…to work."

"…for the…"

"Need."

"…good of the family."

"Staying here…"

He strained, trying to catch the whole conversation, but the whispers still eluded him despite his best efforts.

Zach continued down the corridor, which was continuing to slope up steeply at this point. The angle impaired his vision somewhat, but he was confident that Zella was no longer ahead of him. She had probably gone back to whatever lair she kept in the fortress, ready to plot her next move. He was rather surprised that she hadn't tried to physically harm him back in the corridor, or simply have that large lamprey thing suck him off the wall. Or even why she tolerated his presence in her fortress in the first place. There seemed to be some sort of rules to his passage through the fortress, rules that he did not know or understand.

It seemed almost like she was toying with him, like a cat playing with a mouse before the final pounce. This mental game she was playing, trying to convince him he was like her, well that was just plain weird. Zach didn't know what to think of that behavior, frankly.

A faint sound reached his ears. Zach stopped and bent down, trying to see as far ahead of him as possible. He crept forward and turned yet another corner.

The main corridor continued on, straight ahead. Now, however, side corridors had appeared. The doorways were arched and lead into pitch black tunnels. As Zach watched, a young child, barefoot with a mop of yellow curls, wearing a sleeveless, ivory knee length nightgown, ran from one door and across the tunnel, disappearing into another side door.

Zach's eyes widened, his heart pounding at the sight of the little girl.

Could he have found the child Seer? He moved to the door that she had disappeared through, but could see nothing but blackness and a cold breeze. Zach found himself reluctant to step through the doorway into that inky murkiness of another corridor. He heard an enchanting giggle and wheeled around quickly, catching a hint of the child's dress as she raced across the corridor and into another darkened doorway.

Zach raced across the corridor and looked in the doorway. Nothing, he realized, pounding his fist against the stone archway in frustration. He turned around, scanning the rest of the tunnel. A little face peeked at him from around the doorway at the far end, a golden mop of ringlets bouncing over bright blue eyes.

Zach crouched down so that he was less threatening, wishing he wasn't so tall and broad. Hell, the sword strapped to his waist probably didn't help things either. "Hey there, sweetie," he said softly, trying not to seem so, well, large and male. "Come on over here."

The little girl shook her head, her cherubic face frowning at him. Zach inched forward, trying to get closer. The little girl dodged back around the corner, disappearing into the blackness.

Zach strode forward, cursing under his breath. Then a sound behind him had him whirling again, to find the little girl standing a few feet behind him, shyly staring up at him through her yellow curls.

Zach smiled down at her. "What's your name, sweetie?" he asked her gently.

She frowned, the expression giving her an adorable pout. One bare foot came out to wipe at the floor as if she were sweeping something. Finally, she shrugged.

"You don't know your name?" said Zach.

Again she shrugged, one shoulder moving up and down despondently.

"How long have you been here?"

She looked at him blankly. Zach figured that questions were getting him nowhere. He was no expert with kids, after all. He had no idea how to tell how old she was, or if she was hurt or even if she wasn't well fed. Time to try another tact.

"Do you want to get out of this place, sweetie?" he asked her. "Go and see a nice lady who can help you understand what you can do?"

The little girl stuck her thumb in her mouth and shook her head, her blue eyes wide.

"She lives in a pretty house," Zach tempted the little girl. "And she has a wonderful laugh. I think you'll like her lots."

The wide blue eyes filled with tears. "Oh, sweetie, don't cry," Zach said softly, easing forward again. He was almost in reach. "It'll be all right, I promise you that. I won't let anyone hurt you."

The little girl narrowed her eyes at Zach, obviously distrusting him. He inched up another step, holding his breath. One more step and then he'd be in reach. But if he grabbed her and she fought him, she could end up terrified of him, and that would make getting out of this stone mad house horribly difficult.

The little girl skipped back several paces, her face intensely distrustful. Zach had to work hard to suppress a growl of frustration. "Sweetie, my name is Zach," he tried again. "I'm here to rescue you. Have you ever heard a story about a prince coming to rescue his princess? Well, I'm your prince. So let's get out of this dungeon and back to the castle, ok?" He was grasping for straws and he knew it.

The little girl darted through one of the doorways. Zach made a desperate swipe for her dress and just missed, catching only the wind of her wake as she disappeared.

Zach hung his head, then waited. Sure enough, he could hear the pitter patter of her feet behind him. He didn't look in her direction.

"Welcome back, sweetie," he kept his voice low and even. "Want to play a game?"

"No." She had a small, lisping voice. Zach smiled. It was a big step, her actually speaking to him.

"Do you want to sing some songs?" he hoped he knew some that were appropriate for her age.

"No," came the adamant reply.

"What do you want to do?" he asked her, his eyes on the empty corridor ahead of him.

"Kill you," came her soft voice. It was close. Very close.

Zach wheeled around. The little girl was standing a mere two feet from him, a huge dagger in her hand and bloodlust clear in her blue eyes. She raised the dagger and lunged at him, a snarl on her face.

Zach stepped out of the way, and as the little girl went by, scooped her up from behind, one arm around her waist. He plucked the dagger out of her hand and flung it to one side. The little girl exploded into a frenzy, kicking, biting, and flailing her body.

Zach was astonished by her reaction. Just trying to get his arms around the girl was virtually impossible. She scratched him up good, her little nails digging into his flesh.

"Calm down, sweetie, calm down," Zach kept repeating. She was panting with her efforts to fight him off, furious words spewing from her lips. Zach was horrified when he realized that they were curse words he would expect to hear from the most rugged stage hand, not an innocent little girl.

Zach dropped the child and pushed her away from him. He swept up the knife and turned towards the little girl, who was sobbing pathetically in the middle of the corridor, her hands covering her eyes and shoulders heaving.

"You are not the child Seer," Zach stated with absolute conviction. Then he turned and walked away from her.

A few steps away, Zach paused and looked over his shoulder. The doorways had disappeared, and in the middle of the floor was a small doll, made of sticks, with a fluff of golden hair. Abandoned, like an eerie voodoo doll.

Zach blew out his breath. *Mirage,* he thought with satisfaction. Thank goodness he'd figured it out before trying to force the child to come along with him. The amount of sabotage the fake child could have done would have been astronomical. In fact, Zella should have made the doppelganger be more sweet and innocent, willing to join Zach. It would have caused more harm that way.

Regardless, Zach felt very lucky to have escaped another of Zella's little mind games. He wondered how many more he would have to face before he got to the top of the fortress. He glanced at the scratches along his chest and arms. No matter that she wasn't real, the child had caused him real physical damage. These mirages could hurt him if he allowed it.

Zach continued to walk down the corridor, his sword out. His stomach was rumbling and he was getting lightheaded from lack of sleep and food. Far up ahead, Zach could see a strange glow. He wondered if he was getting closer to the source of the whispering, since it was getting louder and louder.

The closer he got, the stronger the light, which was flickering with a reddish hue. The glow, it turned out, was from a wall of fire that bisected the corridor. He had no idea how deep the band of fire was, or if it was covering yet another trap, like a hole in the floor or something else equally fun and treacherous.

Zach paused in front of the wall of fire, feeling a ridiculous urge to start singing a Johnny Cash song. He laughed to himself, convinced that was the funniest thing he'd ever thought in his life.

"Get a grip, Neol," Zach said, shaking his head briskly. He sat down in the middle of the corridor, staring at the fire wall. He stared at the obstruction, letting his mind drift. Or, if he were honest with himself, he was pretty much incapable of concentrating at the moment. Zach was really sinking into a state of half consciousness, hoping a good idea would somehow stumble into his mind.

The whole place was bizarre. All of the obstacles had been somehow natural. He remembered that mechanical devices did not operate in the Land and wondered if Zella was bound by the same constraints. Of course, the rest of the obstacles had all turned out to be fake Zach realized with a snort. The vines may have been real, but the bridge was not. Nor was the maze, or the lake, or even the little girl. They were all fabrications, illusions, lies. Tricks. They could hurt him, only if he allowed it. All he had to do was get through the flames. That was it.

Zach opened his eyes and looked at the fire with steely resolve in their amber tinged blue depths.

Standing up, Zach faced off to the fire. "I'm willing to bet that you are as fake as that little girl was," he said. The flames roared in response, crackling merrily. He could feel the heat pouring off the surface of the wall, but disregarded it resolutely.

"You are not real," he repeated then rushed through the wall of flame.

He passed right through the fire, the intense heat of the blaze making his skin burn. At least the remaining evidence of the luminous crap that was irritating his skin burned away. When he broke through to the other side, Zach gasped for air, spinning around. Other than singed eyebrows and a little smoke coming off his shirt, he was fine.

As he expected, the flames were gone.

"Tricky little minx," he whispered.

-24-
Zella's Lair

Buoyed by the success with the fire wall, Zach continued forward with a much higher degree of cockiness. He was walking with more spring in his step as he rounded yet another corner.

Then he stopped short, staring.

The walls were no longer flat. He was in a circular room. He looked, but could not see the way out of the room. It looked like a dead end, but that did not fool Zach. This was the way forward, he was sure of it.

The walls were adorned with faces that had been carved out stone, the images were caricatures of people with various kinds of emotions. Set at various levels, the faces protruded from the walls, their blank eyes staring, mouths leering and smiling and crying and set in rage. The macabre scene made it appear that people had been cast in stone at various points in their lives, their faces stone medallions of emotion.

One thing became abundantly clear almost immediately. The stone people were the source of the whispering that had been hounding Zach the entire time he had been inside the fortress. The sound was louder here, and as he turned to take in the entire room, he could piece together the differing sounds from the figures.

Immediately, he was leery of what this room might represent.

"They're fake," he told himself firmly. "Fake, lies, not real." Resolutely, he started into the room, passing between the figures without even looking their way. His eyes scanned the room, trying to figure out how to make the exit appear. Behind him, the way he had come into the room sealed itself, leaving him trapped in the circular room.

"Zachary Neol," one of the figures said in a clear voice. "You're going to fail at this quest."

The use of his name startled Zach, his eyes jerking towards the stone figure. The face was set in a frown, the way the eyes were carved making it appear to have a blank stare. The nasal tones continued to emanate from the figure's sneering mouth.

"Yeah, I'm talking to you, Zachary. You think you're so smart, so clever. You're nothing but a small boy inside that man's body. And you aren't cunning enough to win."

"That's the voice of my first tutor, who came to the set to teach me," Zach whispered. "Mrs. Duranski. She hated me."

"For good reason," the voice harrumphed. "Caught you cheating, didn't I?"

"No, I wasn't," Zach said, his throat closing up at the memory, "and you screamed at me in front of the entire cast and crew on stage."

"You were a little snot then, and it hasn't changed," the stone figure taunted him.

"You aren't real," Zach said and continued to search for the way out, ignoring the words that the statue continued to hiss his way.

"Zach. Zach!" Another mask was calling out to him. It was a female voice, sultry and smooth as silk. "Zach, do you remember me? We had such a wonderful time together."

"You took advantage of a twelve year old child," Zach said tightly, his breath hitching. "You thought it would be amusing to have sex with a child when you had a guest role on the sitcom I was in."

"Ah, but you were already so mature," the voice purred. "Look at it this way, Zachy, I gave you the basics you'll use throughout your life."

"I was scared, confused, and afraid." Zach said steadily.

"You were hard, ready, and horny," the voice retorted.

"Taking advantage of a young man's natural reactions doesn't make it right," Zach said firmly. "You are not real."

As he continue to prowl the room, seeking the exit. Figure after figure, face after face, mask after mask continued to speak to him, reminding him of his foibles of youth, his insecurities, his fears. When yet another stone figure started to speak, Zach tried to interrupt it right off the bat.

"You are not real," he snapped, but the stone figure continued to speak.

"You do not interrupt me." The voice was a dead ringer of his mother's most irritated tone.

"Oh Christ, I don't need this," Zach said, shaking his head. The voice continued to harangue him.

"You need to focus, Zach. You never could focus on what you were doing. All those people are depending on you, and what are you doing? Wasting time as usual. Wasteful, Zach, wasteful. And when you're wasteful you are being irresponsible. I don't understand what you're doing here. This place is not for you, you are no hero. How could you possibly be a hero when you cannot focus?"

"Man, you have her stream of consciousness down pat," Zach marveled as his eyes scanned the ceiling, desperate for a way out. "The babbling and circling and then harping on the same topics over and over. A real master of babble, that's my mom. But I still say that you aren't real."

"Do not speak to your mother that way!" This voice was roared from the opposite side of the room.

Zach groaned. Great, he thought, the gang's all here. "And here comes the dad routine," he said under his breath.

"What did you say? What are you saying? I will teach you to respect your elders, Zach Neol. You need to learn from us, gain wisdom. We have given up everything for you and you return that with the gratitude of a flea. You will listen and do what we tell you, Zach. And you cannot do this task. You will fail. Because you aren't capable of being a hero, Zach."

"I'm not interested in being a hero," Zach replied absently, pushing on a wall that remained solid. "I am interested in getting you all to shut up, however."

"I will have respect!" his father's voice yelled. "If I have to beat it into you with every fiber of my being, I will not tolerate you being less than one hundred percent responsive to your parent's wishes."

"That stopped working a long time ago," Zach said stubbornly. "I don't think a stone mask can do much whomping, so that's just a plain ole' baseless threat."

"All you are is a pretty face and a hard ass," came another voice, this one of his agent. "I've tried and tried to get you to realize that you gotta play to your strengths, but you wanna keep doin' cerebral stuff that your fans won't appreciate. I never told you this before, but it's my firm belief that Zach Neol could never be anything more than eye candy."

"That's what we try to tell him," his mother screeched. "We keep telling him and telling him and telling him that he needs to work to his looks, but what does he do? Goes off and play a cartoon character." She sniffed.

"Well, it did showcase his body," his father's voice mused. "But covering his face in the critical scenes with that stupid mask was sheer folly. Zach will never be more than the sum of his parts."

The voices began to build and build all around him, each one rising in volume and intensity, trying to out speak the other.

Zach stood in the center of the room, eyes closed, breathing heavily. The words, the weight of the combined vitriol spewing from the rock mouths pushed down upon him, dragging him to his knees like a rabid dog pack attacking its prey. The sword, still clutched in his hand, clattered against the cobblestone floor as he bent over, his forehead resting against the stone. Gasping for breath, he tried to push away the voices, the sensations, the emotions. All his life, all his failures, all the pressure of being who he was expected to be rather than who he felt he should be…it all coalesced in that chamber. His back was breaking under the combined weight of their wants and his own self-loathing. Gleeful, the voices increased in volume, sensing victory.

In the midst of the turmoil swarming around him Zach sensed a soft touch on his mind, a glimmer of sensation. It wasn't Zella; the brush was innocent and sweet. It wasn't Liz, whose presence was like a warm bath of love. It wasn't the Seer, her power and motherly concern always evident when he sensed her nearby. No. This was something entirely different.

It was the child. She was reaching out to him in his time of need. She was trying to soothe him, comfort him, bring him a measure of peace.

That gentle touch, that infinite contact with such pureness, was all Zach needed. Like a grounding wire, he was pulled away from the disastrous voices and plugged back into his own skin. Clutching the child's sensory pat to his soul, Zach cradled the feeling to his battered skin and forced himself to his feet. Despite the weaving of his physical body, the need for food and sleep overwhelming, Zach felt strong.

He let out a roar of rage that had all the voices stilling.

His sword in his hand, Zach slowly turned in a circle. "You are not real," he said firmly, "but the words you're speaking are real. I've heard them all my life. I've been told to be a certain person, act a certain way, feel a certain emotion, live a certain lifestyle. Well, I didn't do that, did I? You all tried to make me the man you thought I *should* be, either through intimidation, threats, undermining, physical pain or emotional blackmail. You kept me isolated and away from people who could give me the love and support I craved…well no longer. I'm not going to listen to any of you any more because you failed.

"Despite your best efforts, you failed. I became the man I am because of the choices I made. And while that doesn't make your words any less real, it makes them irrelevant. They simply don't matter. Not any more.

"You do not matter. All that I care about is living my life my way, and doing what I feel is the right thing. You don't matter. None of you. I'm through trying to live up to your expectations, and I'm through listening to them, too. We are done."

It was, obviously, the right thing to say. The walls melted away, leaving Zach in a corridor with a large doorway at the end. It looked like an entrance to a medieval room, the huge brass hinges and planked wood giving it a solid and substantial feel.

Zach walked towards the door, determined to get this over with as soon as possible. There had never been a door before, and this one seemed very significant. Somehow more permanent to the structure, instead of a roadblock. Zach assumed this meant that he had reached the pinnacle of the fortress.

When he got within a few feet of the door, the back of his head exploded in pain. He teetered on his feet, going to his knees and then to the ground in slow motion as the world closed in around him, fading into black.

***

When Zach woke up, his head was pounding. Bleary eyed, he looked around him.

He was obviously in the top room of the fortress. It was roughly thirty feet by thirty feet, the ceiling soaring about twenty feet above his head.

The room was decked out like a luxurious penthouse, sofas and chairs abounding. There was even a large fireplace at one end, where flames curled and flickered. A wet bar, complete with bottles and glasses, graced one wall, while an immense media system crawled along the other. Zach shook his head at that. He knew that none of it could possibly work, not in the Land. It was all show and pretension.

Zach shifted his feet and several things registered. The first was a clinking sound; the second was a weight around his ankles and wrists. Looking down, he discovered that his feet were shackled to the floor. His hands, he realized, were tethered to opposite sides of the wall, and it appeared a complicated pulley system was in place.

Experimentally, Zach tugged on one wrist. Immediately, there was a whirring noise and the chain attached to that hand became noticeably shorter.

"Ah, the simplicity of the device is absolutely diabolical."

Zella's now familiar purr filled the room. She was walking up stairs that were set into the floor of the room, her hips swaying as she ascended. Wearing the emerald green dress that hugged her curves, she sauntered towards Zach. In one hand, she carried a leash that was tethered to the collar of a huge ferret. The beast was the largest he'd seen yet, easily four feet long. The thing snarled at Zach, lunging towards him in a flurry of claws and teeth. Zella chided the animal like it was a Pomeranian with an attitude issue and fastened the leash to an iron circle that was set in the wall.

Zach wasn't liking this situation one bit. The fact that he was shirtless added to the vulnerability of the situation, and not knowing where his belt and equipment were located majorly sucked. Involuntarily, he moved a step back, which had the corresponding effect of making the chains on his arms even tighter. He cursed to himself at his stupidity. His arms were now stretched out from his sides at roughly a forty-five degree angle. Ok, so every time he moved, he was going to be stretched out on the rack.

Note to self: No more moving.

Once that thought was firmly lodged, he went on to the next issue. His physical condition. "What did you hit me with?" he asked, the back of his head in agony.

"A baseball bat," Zella replied absently, petting the ferret. "A simple, effective method of subduing one's enemies, I have found."

"You can say that again," Zach replied sarcastically.

"I'll be with you in a second, Zachy," she said to him, crossing to the wet bar.

Opening a bag, Zella made a production of extracting a hypodermic needle and vial of medicine. She measured out a precise amount and flicked the end of the needle expertly.

Zach was now feeling tendrils of panic floating along his skin. Who knew what was in that vial, and what it would do to him. Instead of crossing over to him, however, Zella turned to a large sofa by the fireplace. Zach squinted. He could barely see a small mound of fabric on the sofa. Zella knelt on the floor next to the sofa and Zach realized with horror that the fabric was actually the dress of the child he had been seeking. The potential Seer. Zella pulled up one thin arm and sank the needle into the child's vein. Since there was no movement from the child or verbal protest, Zach had to assume the little girl was unconscious.

The sight of that tiny hand, dangling limply as Zella pumped her full of who-knew-what, filled Zach with a rage that was unlike any he had ever felt before. He felt the conviction, deep in his belly, that he was going to get that child out of this hellhole, and if he died trying, it would be fine by him. He was confident that if he went down, Zella was going with him for the ride, and with the maximum amount of pain.

Zella was now strolling towards Zach, her eyes full of amusement as she saw the expression etched across his face. She laughed at him. "Now, Zachy, there's no need to be irritated with me. She's a possible Seer. I couldn't very well let her run around the fortress, now could I? She came close to reaching you a moment ago. I couldn't let a full connection be formed."

"She's a child, not an experiment," Zach said tightly. No need to enlighten the bitch that an emotional connection had indeed been made. But he couldn't let her callous treatment of the child go unchallenged. "Who knows what the junk you are giving her is doing to her system. Even I know you can't give a Land person Worlder medications. They have different physiologies."

"I'm not stupid, Zachy," Zella retorted sharply. "The sedative we've been giving her is a derivative of a native Land plant. That the idiots here have not figured out its sedation properties is not my concern. And if she dies? Who cares? We'll find another candidate for the breeding program. We've several we're watching in the World as we speak."

Zach's eyes were glued on the little girl's still form. Drugged. Bred. Dead. The words rolled around in his brain like fire. "I will kill you for this," he told Zella with absolute seriousness.

"Oh pooh," Zella knocked the sentiment aside with her hand. "We'll get along just fine, Zach. When this little episode is over, and you're away from the Land, in your own element, you will come to appreciate the plan and its execution. I cannot wait to get you to my home dimension. It's such a delicious place, so steeped in evil and debauchery. You'll fit right in."

"I could never appreciate kidnapping and drugging a child," Zach informed her. Odd, but until now, the concept of the child had been just that, a concept, an idea, a goal. Now, she was very real and it was killing him slowly that he could not simply scoop her up and carry her out of this horrible place.

Zella ducked under the chains, and trailed a finger over his back, tracing his Phoenix tattoo. Zach's resulting spontaneous shiver and corresponding tightening of the chains made her laugh deep in her throat. "It was always meant to be this way, you know," she whispered into his ear, her sharp pointed tongue darting out. "You were ordained to be mine."

"I've got other plans, thanks," Zach said lightly.

Zella chuckled. "You have a destiny, Zachy. Stop denying it. This failure only makes the conclusion that much more defined."

"What makes you think I will fail?" Zach replied.

"You have failed, Zachy," she said, ducking back under his arms and standing in front of him, her green eyes confident.

"No," he said, equally cocky.

"No?" One black eyebrow winged up, her arms crossing. "Given the fact that you are tethered up like the pet you were meant to be, that tonight the full moon will show this child to be a Seer, and that she will be taken from the Land immediately thereafter indicates to me that you have, indeed, failed." She enunciated the word carefully.

Zach said nothing and stared at her, unwilling to allow her to goad him any further.

"We'll have such fun together," Zella cooed, stepping close to him. "You were made for Evil, Zachy. Just give over to the pleasures that await and forget all about the Land, the World, all of it. You don't ever need to worry about the mundane things."

"I like the mundane world."

"You'll like me better," Zella promised. "The other alternative is to stay here, in this fortress, and wait for it to blow up. Because that's what will happen when I leave the Land. This structure and everything around it? Bye-bye!" She waggled her fingers at him, those full red lips still curved in a sarcastic smile.

Zach froze, thinking of the Seer, Maxt, and Orli, who were probably camping on the fortress' very doorstep.

Zella laughed at his dismay and twined her arms around his neck, her perfume clogging his nostrils. When Zach would have jerked back, she warned softly, "The chains, Zachy."

She pulled his head down and took her time working over his lips. Zach held resolutely still, not giving her an inch or a response. By keeping his eyes open and focused on the little girl, he was able to withstand the fogging of his brain that had happened before. Zella bit his bottom lip as she withdrew, and none too gently, making him wince.

"Don't disappoint me," Zella said to him softly. "I don't take kindly to being disappointed. Especially when it comes to my fun and toys." The ferret hissed its agreement at the assessment.

"I am not now, nor will I ever be, your toy," Zach replied evenly.

"But you already are," Zella told him, obviously enjoying his discomfort. "The sooner you realize it, the better it will go for you."

Zella meandered back to the bar, shutting the medical bag and tidying up the mess. Then she returned to him, caressing his chest with her long fingers, her nails lightly raking over his skin with predatory satisfaction. "I have to go and prepare for tonight," she told him. "I'll be back when the moon is out."

"Kinda hard to see the moonlight in the middle of this fortress," Zach pointed out wryly.

"Oh, I've thought of that," Zella replied easily, casting her eyes upward. "In fact, I should open the skylight, so that we can tell when the moon is directly overhead." She went to another crank and turned it, a grinding sound coming from overhead. Far overhead, a small crack appeared, a mere square foot in total.

"Aren't you afraid your little furry buddies out there will swarm through the hole?" asked Zach.

"They left after you entered the temple. They weren't needed any longer."

After bracing the mechanism, Zella smiled at Zach, approaching him yet again. Her hand trailed down his belly to toy with the waist of his tuxedo pants, which by now were hanging in shreds around his calves. When the questing fingers dipped even lower, the muscle in Zach's cheek clenched and he kept his gaze on the child, anger pumping through him at the way they were both being used by Evil.

Zella chuckled. "Nice," she noted. "Very nice." Her hand withdrew and she ambled down the stairs, leaving the ferret with Zach and the child.

-25-
Escapism

Zach waited until all sound of Zella's passing had ceased. Then he leaned forward to see if the child had moved at all. Unfortunately, this only made the chains tighten again, stretching his arms out completely to the sides. Any more movement and Zach would no longer have to wonder if the medieval rack was an effective way to torture a body.

Zach hung his head and closed his eyes, trying to clear his mind of the ever-present panic associated with being held against his will. He needed to think, needed to plan. He took several deep breaths, trying to clear his mind of all distractions, including the metal cuffs chafing his wrists and ankles with increasing irritation. Empty his mind, get it clear…it was a common habit of his during the filming of *The Phoenix* to ensure he got into character. Well, now he needed to get into his own mindset, one free of panic and pain.

Slowly, Zach's mind cleared, becoming an empty slate. As he continued to go through the breathing exercises, he felt a slight niggling at the base of his neck. Immediately wary of Zella and her penchant for messing with him, Zach cautiously probed the entity that was a knocking at his mental door.

It wasn't Zella, Zach realized immediately. There wasn't the lingering mental stench of Evil he associated with the woman. And it wasn't Liz, either. Her touch was now so familiar and comforting to him that he couldn't mistake this tentative probing for her cool and calm mental touch. No, this seemed more like the gentle stroke he'd felt in the stone face room. Zach's eyes opened and he sought out the little girl on the sofa. Could it be the child? Could she be trying to reach out to him even in her unconscious state?

He didn't dare drop his mental shields, however, for fear that Zella would be able to tell and take advantage of the situation. No way was he letting that bitch back into his noggin, not if he could help it. But if it was the little girl…

"Sweetie, are you awake?" Zach called out, keeping his voice calm and even. "Can you open your eyes for me?"

There was no movement from the couch, but the mental touch, as faint as a butterfly, stilled. The ferret still chained to the far wall growled deep in its throat, menacingly. Zach shot it a quelling look.

"It's ok, sweetie," Zach continued to speak. "I'm here to rescue you, but I could use a little help myself. If you wake up, maybe you can help me."

The contact withdrew, but he could tell it was just beyond him, as if wary. Even though he could fully understand her point of view on the situation, Zach wanted to growl in frustration, like the ferret, but refrained with great restraint. No need to give the little girl any more reason to fear the situation, after all.

Zach continued to talk, beseeching the little girl to respond, but it was to no avail. Zach then tried craning his neck to look behind him, trying to see the pulley system that was holding him captive. If he could get a good look at it, perhaps an idea might spark in his mind.

He was also keeping an eye on the skylight. At the moment, sunshine was pouring into the opening, yet he could tell that the shadows were lengthening steadily. Time was running out, and he still had no idea of what to do.

Perhaps Zella was right. Maybe it was time to realize that he had failed in his quest. That he was the first Protector to ever let the Land down, and with devastating consequences. She could be right in that his destiny lay in some other direction. He'd tried to be noble and good and honorable and all he had to show for it was a pair of iron bracelets. He had committed the cardinal sin in acting and had worked against his character.

Zach sighed, closing his eyes. *No,* he thought with determination. *I'm more than the sum of my body parts, I'm more than just eye candy,*

I'm more than the bone structure of my face or my physical body. I am a Protector of the Land, and I got here using my brain and my brawn and my sheer willpower. I have people who trust me, who want me to succeed, but who will support me even if I don't.

But I haven't failed, Zach thought with renewed energy. *I just haven't figured out the solution yet.*

A shimmer caught his attention. Cascading from the skylight was a stream of greenish gold sparks. They coalesced and suddenly, Liz was standing in front of him, smiling broadly. Her grin faded when she took in his condition and his imprisonment.

"Oh, Zachary," she cried, started forward.

"I'm fine," he said, never so glad to see a living soul in his life, even if she was non-corporeal. "Listen, Liz, the little girl is over on the sofa. Zella drugged her with something, but I swear she was trying to get into my mind a few moments ago. Can you try and communicate with her? Being another Seer, and a woman, she might be more receptive to you than me."

"I can try," Liz said. She hurried over, her face growing compassionate as she looked down at the girl. "Poor little munchkin," she murmured, and then knelt by the sofa, concentrating.

The ferret seemed unaware of Liz's presence, but was watching Zach as he appeared to talk to nothing, its black, beady eyes reflecting red from the fire. Zach was actually comforted by the beast's lack of awareness, figuring that if the ferret didn't know Liz was there, then neither would Zella.

While Liz tried to communicate with the child, he was dealing with another issue. Zach was finding it harder to hold still, to keep his arms outstretched without an involuntary tug or movement. He couldn't rest his arms against the chain, or it would tighten. Standing with his arms held out, the weights on the wrists becoming heavier by the second, was costing him precious strength. He found himself swaying slightly. His back was aching and his chest burned as the chains ratcheted up another notch. He stifled the groan that rose in his throat, not wanting to distract Liz.

She finally stood back up and came over to Zach, her face troubled. "She's there, but deeply sedated."

"Can you cleanse her system somehow?" Zach asked, desperate.

"Because if we can rouse her, maybe she can help me out of this contraption. I have a feeling there's a simple pin mechanism that releases the tension. I saw a device like this in a movie once."

Liz passed through him, a not altogether unpleasant feeling. "Yes, that's what it is." Her voice came from behind him. "She should be able to work the latch. Zach, your sword is here as well."

"Good. I was hoping Zella wouldn't be able to take it. So can you try and get the medicine out of the little girl?"

Liz sighed. "I personally don't know how," she admitted, but hastened to add when Zach's shoulders slumped, "but the Seer is outside. She's being prevented from entering the fortress through astral projection. I guess my being from the World allowed me past the enchantments. I'll go ask her if she has any ideas."

"Hurry," Zach said grimly.

Liz nodded and dissolved, heading for the skylight. Zach waited impatiently for her return. He marked off at least ten minutes before Liz was before him again.

"She walked me through what to do," said Liz, rolling her shoulders as if to prepare for battle. "If I seem unresponsive, don't worry about me. I'll have to go deep into her systems to start the process rolling."

Zach endured another agonizing half hour while Liz worked to clean out the girl's system. The shadows were lengthening even more, clearly signaling that the sun had begun its final descent. Zach worried that Zella might sense Liz's presence and return at any second. At least the worry kept his mind off of his own physical predicament, which was quickly becoming dire. He wasn't sure how much longer he'd be able to keep his arms in the precarious position.

Finally, Liz's head rose up. The little girl on the sofa started to move, slowly but surely. Zach smiled. It was working. They had a chance.

"Wake up, Sweetie," Liz said to her gently.

"That's what I called her," Zach told the Seer.

"I know," Liz was watching the girl as she sat up, rubbing her eyes as if she were waking from a long nap. "She told me about the nice man who was calling to her. She said he gave her a new name."

"A Seer named Sweetie?" Zach chuckled, despite the growing pain in his shoulders. "That's a good one."

The little girl opened her wide blue eyes, staring at Zach. With the mop of golden curls and ivory dress, she looked exactly like the mirage in the corridor. Only this child, Zach knew, was the real thing.

"Sweetie, remember what I asked you to do when you were sleeping?" Liz asked her quietly. "About helping to get the nice man out of the chains?" The little girl nodded her expression still rather confused and solemn.

"I need you to really concentrate," Liz told her. "You need to get up and go behind the man. See the long metal pin that is sticking out of the chains? I need you to tug that loose. Can you do that? Can you, Sweetie?"

The little girl clambered off the sofa. On unsteady feet, still obviously experiencing some effects of the drugging, she toddled across the floor. A hiss from the ferret had her stopping instantly, her entire body shaking, but Liz hastened to point out that the creature was tethered. When the little girl got near Zach, she stopped, staring at him with apprehension, one finger hooked inside her lip.

"It's ok, Sweetie," Zach said, purposely pitching his voice in a low, reassuring manner. "I want to help you get out of here. But I need to be free to do that, and I know you can help me."

The wet finger popped out and pointed in his direction. "Stay!" she ordered in a lisping voice.

"All right, Sweetie. I'll stay," Zach replied, casting an amused look in Liz's direction. She smiled back, but her eyes remained worried.

The little girl continued on her way, Liz following. "That's right, Sweetie," he heard Liz coaching. "Just pull that one out. Brace yourself, Zach."

When the tension on his arms suddenly snapped and released, Zach fell to his knees in relief. The little girl skipped over and patted him on the cheek with one damp hand. "Better," she pronounced.

"Definitely better," he told her gratefully, wanting to scream as the blood returned to his battered and stretched arms. "Now if we could just get these chains off me, I think we might have a fighting chance."

"There's a key over here, hanging on the wall," Liz observed. "But it's high enough that she won't be able to reach it without some help. Damn this astral projecting! I wish I were corporeal so I could really help out."

"There's a poker by the fire," Zach noted, simply resting his currently useless arms on his legs. "Maybe she can use that to knock it off or something."

The poker proved to be too heavy for the little girl, but she was able to handle the hearth broom from the same set. Within minutes, the little girl was handing Zach the key.

"Thank you Sweetie," he said. "I want to give you a big hug when I get these nasty things off, ok?"

She nodded, sticking her finger back in her mouth and watching him with adoring blue eyes.

"Another Zachary Neol conquest," Liz observed.

Zach mustered a wink for the little girl and gave Liz what he hoped was a smoldering look. He was too tired to know if it really worked or not.

"Since you seem so resistant to the idea of my loving you, I just might have to look at other alternatives," he said lightly, releasing one of the shackles.

"It's—"

"I know, I know, I bloody well know," he said with a touch of heat as he attacked another set of manacles. "It's too soon. It's too intense. It's too out of the norm. Bullshit. I know it's for real. I just want to know when you're going to get it through your head that I mean what I say. Always. I need you to remember it. Always."

"Let's not get into this right now," Liz said, eyeing the child who was watching the byplay with interest.

"Agreed. Sweetie's what important right now," said Zach, unlocking the other wrist with great relish, kicking the chains out of the way and turning towards the little girl. "Now that I'm officially free, where's my hug?"

Liz watched the little girl fling herself into Zach's arms, feeling a funny ache and tug at her insides. Zach was soothing the girl, running his hand down her head and back, rocking slightly. His movements were instinctual and innocently sweet, the bond forming between the two brought a tear to her eye. It was just…beautiful.

"Ok, Sweetie. I'm going to put you down and then, let's see about getting the heck out of here, ok?"

"What's your plan?" Liz asked him, striding across the floor with him. He'd retrieved his sword belt and was fastening it around his waist as they talked. She noticed his arms were shaking, whether from the strain of being chained or exhaustion, she couldn't tell. Either way, it was worrisome.

"The sofa is about ten feet long," Zach pointed out. "I'm going to stand it on one end underneath the skylight. I'm six foot four, and I can lift her over my head, so let's be conservative and say I get 18 feet out of the combination. That'll still be short." He gazed around, rubbing his chin with his hand.

"When is the last time you slept?" Liz asked him shortly, seeing the weave and sway of his movements.

He stared at her blankly for a moment, blinking several times as he tried to think it through. "The night before I entered the fortress."

"That was days ago, Zachary. Days."

"Huh. Well. Time sure does move differently in here."

"And food?" Liz persisted. "When was the last time you had something to eat, Zachary?"

Zach turned to her, hands splayed in defeat. "It was the same time frame, ok? Look, Zella took my pack first thing, and that's where all my food was. She's been just relentless with her tricks and her mind games and her…well, let's just say sleep wasn't possible and leave it at that." His eyes lit on the ottoman and he snapped his fingers. "That'll work! I'll put that on top of the sofa, and that should give me the two or three feet I'll need to reach the skylight. She's skinny enough to fit through it."

Liz watched as Zach muscled the sofa into place, frustrated yet again at her inability to help with the process. She wasn't sure he was going to be able to achieve the leverage needed to get the sofa on its end, but finally, with all his muscles bulging, he was able to get the massive piece on its end. The size of the sofa made it a pretty stable tower, which surprised them both.

Standing on a chair, Zach lifted the leather ottoman over his head and capped the sofa. Stepping back, he nodded with satisfaction as sweat streamed down his back.

"Ok, then. Now to get some things stacked up so we can climb up there," he said. "Liz, you need to go out and tell Maxt and Orli that I'm going to be pushing Sweetie through the skylight. They need to get her and then get the hell out of this place."

"What about you?" she asked urgently. "They have to stay to help you get out of this place."

Zach stared at her evenly. "They need to get Sweetie as far from this temple as possible, as quickly as possible."

"Why? What aren't you telling me, Zachary?"

The silence was thick. The child Seer came over to Zach and leaned against his legs. He patted her riot of curls before turning to Liz.

"Zella has this place rigged to explode when she leaves the Land."

"That doesn't mean that Orli and Maxt should desert you," Liz said stubbornly.

Zach put his hands on his hips, facing her squarely. No shirking, no way to hide it. So he went with honesty, as he always tried to do. "I can't fit out the skylight, Liz, and I've been through this place once. I don't think I have it in me to get back out, not in enough time before it blows up. Maxt, Orli and the Seer need to get as much distance between this place and them. For their sakes, for the child's sake, and for the Land."

"Zachary..." she trailed off, helpless.

He was merciless, cutting across her attempts to reason with him. "Listen to me, Liz. If I succeed, and kill Zella, this place is going to explode before I can escape. If she succeeds, and kills me, then she's going to go after the child again. Either way, I'm dead. Either way, those three out there and this little precious child," he scooped her up in his arms and the child flung her spindly limbs around his neck, "need to be as far away as possible. You know it and I know it."

"You just want me to leave you here to die?" Her words were rising with shock. Zach nodded his head toward the little girl.

"This isn't about me. It can't be about us. It has to be about her, and what she means to the Land. She's my quest. I have to succeed."

"But I can't just walk away. You can't possibly want to be left here to face that bitch alone...not after all you've been through."

"What I want and what is reasonably going to happen are two completely different things," Zach told her with real regret, scrubbing at his bristly chin once more. "I wanted to dance with you again, Liz. I really did. I wanted to kiss your shoulder...and so much more."

Tears were streaming down her cheeks. "Zachary," she choked out, helpless.

Zach glanced at the skylight. "It's getting dark," he said, "and Zella will be back soon. Go and tell the others that I'm sending the child out. And Liz, don't come back in here. It's too dangerous."

"You can't make me stay away," she replied, stubborn.

"Damn it, you'll be more of a distraction than a help, don't you get it?" Zach roared, his brain still feeling like mush from lack of sleep and food, not to mention the raging headache courtesy of the kiss from a baseball bat. "If there's the slightest chance of me getting out alive, it depends on killing Zella before she can kill me. I can't be worrying about your aura and concentrating on that job at the same time. If you want that slim chance, you have to promise me you won't come back in here."

Silence stretched out between them, a gossamer thread of pain and hope mingling together like a spider web.

"I promise," she finally whispered with great reluctance.

Zach tilted his cheek so it rested against the child's golden curls, keeping his amber flecked eyes firmly locking onto Liz's. He wanted her to remember this moment. He needed her to remember his words. "Never doubt this, Liz. I love you."

Liz nodded. "I…believe you."

Her form coalesced into the shower of sparks and fog as Liz rushed out the skylight to alert the others. Zach leaned back to look at the child in his arms. She was watching him with solemn expectation.

"Do you like to climb, Sweetie?" he asked her. She nodded, her blue eyes lighting up with joy. "Good. Because we are going to climb way up there." She clapped her hands behind his neck and bounced, making Zach bite his tongue from the spasm of pain that her movement rippled through him. He smiled at her again. First priority…get her up and out. Then he could rest his weary muscles for a brief few moments.

Together, Zach and the child climbed onto the table. Zach stepped on the back of the chair, lifting her up to the ottoman. His gaining the top of their makeshift tower was a slightly more hairy proposition, but finally he was standing on the ottoman, the child in his arms. As he looked down at the room, something gave him pause. He smiled with wicked delight at the sight of his Phoenix sword hung by the fireplace like a trophy. *Why, that stupid bitch*, he thought with derision. Perhaps this was the first of many mistakes the woman would make.

Forcing himself to look back up, Zach could see that the skylight was very near, and with great hope, Zach turned to the little girl.

"When I lift you up, I want you to try and pull yourself out of the hole up there, ok? There will be one or two really nice men waiting for you. They'll take you to a wonderful woman who will teach you all about how to be a Seer." The little girl eyed the hole in the ceiling then clung to Zach's neck tightly. "I know it looks scary, Sweetie. But honest, the men are probably climbing the side of the tower right now, ready to meet you. It'll be fine, I promise. Now give me a kiss and I'll lift you up."

She complied, smacking him wetly on the cheek. Zach smiled and lifted her straight up towards the skylight. He could tell the sun was close to setting, a kind of twilight having fallen. The little girl scrambled and grabbed for the top of the tower, pulling herself up. Zach pushed on her feet, standing up as high as he could on his tip toes to give her enough height. Thank God for all the strength training he'd done on his last film.

The child managed to hook her arms over the top of the roof and pulled herself out of the fortress. When her little feet disappeared, Zach gave a huge sigh of satisfaction. Orli's face came into view over the skylight.

"We have her," he said softly. Zach knew from the expression on his face that the villager knew that Zach was going to go on his own little suicide mission.

"Do me a favor," he told Orli, who nodded, waiting expectantly. "Tell the others to watch over Liz. This is going to hit her hard. Two losses in less than a year. Damn. I hate doing this to her."

"The Seer is having a hard time keeping her from coming in the fortress with you," Orli admitted. "Liz was not able to get in until a few hours ago and her aura has just been prowling around the outside."

"I'm going to close the skylight," Zach decided. "I think that when Zella opened it, that gave Liz the access in. If it's shut again, the way will be closed and she'll be forced to stay outside."

"Do you need anything?" Orli asked. "Weapons? Water? Food?"

"Water and food," Zach said immediately. Yet when Orli tried to pass them down, the containers and food disintegrated as they passed into the fortress. "Well, that settles that," Zach said with regret.

"Thanks anyway, Orli. Take care of yourself, and Tracy. Don't forget what I asked you to do."

"It will be done," Orli said with great seriousness. "Zach...I know not what to say to you."

"Then the best bet is to not say anything, my friend."

Zach gave him a cocky salute, forcing a grin on his face, then jumped off the sofa. With a quick twist of his hand, the skylight clanged shut.

-26-

The Art of Confrontation

In the darkness of the room, lit only by the flames in the large fireplace, Zach crossed to the Phoenix sword on the wall. He took it down, smiling at the sight and familiar weight. Unsheathing it, he could see that it was still intact, the blade sharp as sin. He belted the sword to his waist, the blade lying along his left side, the fairy sword along his right. Now, all that was left to do was wait for Zella, he thought adjusting the two belts so that he could use them both during the inevitable fight. As he made the adjustments to the belts so that they lay flat against his body, Zach's hand glanced over the small jug of fairy wine that Scarlet had given him. It seemed so long ago, that time in the meadows with the Interdimensional fairy eggs.

Zach picked up the small jug, carved and etched in beautiful patterns. The container held a sparkly liquid. As Zach looked at it thoughtfully, he recalled the surge of energy and strength that had flowed through him when he had drunk the wine back in the meadows. With a smile, he opened the vial, downing the contents in one gulp.

Instantly, Zach felt veins of magic spiking through his entire body. The tingling sensation, the feeling that he could do anything, everything, and that the word failure was a distant memory. He felt more alert and strong than he had in days. As the fluid spread to every cell in his body, he gave an all over body shake of appreciation.

"Nothing like a shot of fairyade to perk up a soul," he said with jovial satisfaction.

Along with the physical rejuvenation, Zach felt more mentally optimistic and ready to engage in the final battle of wills and strength with Zella. Yet he had no illusions. The woman was stronger than she appeared, for she was a minion of Evil. He could not be swayed by the feminine packaging. It was the inner spirit that he had to concern himself with, after all. And her inner spirit was packing with nothing lacking, that was for sure. It was going to be one hell of a fight.

Zach was certain of one thing. One of them was going down, and Zach was going to do all he could to ensure it wasn't him, even though he knew that killing the minion would lead to his death by explosion. He was honest enough to know that, yeah, that was going to seriously suck, but there was nothing he could do about it. That the child was free, and the Land and Liz safe…that was going to be his legacy, and he was surprisingly satisfied with the outcome of his choices.

Zach took several moments to set all the furniture back in its rightful place. He figured if it looked the way Zella had left it, she would surely not know how the child had escaped. That might give the others outside the temple more time to get away. Perhaps even the Griffins could be persuaded to come and sweep the child away.

Finally, Zach settled down in a chair by the fire, allowing the fairy wine to continue to sing and dance throughout his body bringing strength to his muscles. He was content to wait, actually. Every minute was furthering the escape of the others. He figured at least an hour or two had passed since he'd pushed the little girl out the skylight to freedom. Let Zella take her sweet time. It would certainly work out better for him in the long run.

Finally, Zach heard Zella walking up the steps. When she came into the room, the first thing she saw was the empty set of chains. Then her horrified green eyes flew to the sofa where the child was no longer sleeping.

Zach spoke from the shadows where he was sitting. "Nice of you to stop by."

"How did you get out?" she said, truly bewildered. It was the first time he had seen her flummoxed, and he reveled in her confusion.

"I'm the Phoenix, baby," Zach replied smoothly, rising from the chair, a sword in either hand. "I always rise from the ashes."

"Where is the child?" Zella screeched, wildly looking around. "Where have you hidden the girl?"

"I'm sorry, the party you are seeking is no longer available," Zach mimicked, the swords gleaming in the firelight as he continued to stalk Zella.

Zella stopped, her hands loosely fisted by her sides. "She's outside the fortress," she said, in a faraway voice, then her tone hardened as she looked back at Zach. "I'll simply go and snatch her away from those idiots once again." Her voice was supremely confident.

"It's hard to snatch something when you are dead," Zach commented. "While you may be able to appear at will, if you go after her now, I'll still be here, in your lair. And I'll wreak such havoc on this place, Zella, such havoc that you'll be speechless by my audacity. Besides, something tells me that at the bottom of those stairs lies the way in which you and your kind travel between dimensions."

The woman's eyes widened slightly, and Zach knew that he was onto something. "You weren't just gone preparing for tonight, you were at your master's feet, gloating about it."

Zella went white with rage and Zach continued to press her, irritating her and making her focus on him, not the child or the others. "So I think I'll just be moseying down those stairs to see just how you people are traveling between the dimensions. Wouldn't that be a sight to see? Or even use? I could just get out of here, and you'll have to explain that to your boss as well as your inability to keep the child Seer."

Zella morphed out of the green dress and into her black vinyl outfit, a sword in either hand, hair pulled back into a high ponytail. "On second thought, I think I'll just kill you first, then get the child," Zella commented coolly, swinging her blades loosely. "It turns out that you Hollywood types are simply too high maintenance to keep around."

"Let's go then," Zach replied with his most devastating grin, slightly crouching, his eyes focusing on her feet. They'd tell what her first line of attack would be.

Zella charged right in, swinging a tri-bladed sword in his direction. Zach parried it neatly, barely meeting her second sword with the Phoenix blade as she hacked it at him from a side angle. He pushed her away effortlessly.

"I've got the better reach, and the stronger arm," Zach told her grimly. "Give it up now, Zella darlin'."

"I'm faster and more nimble," she replied easily, proving her point with a rapid fire volley of slashes and stabs. "So why don't you just give it up, Neol?" she slashed at his wrist, leaving a shallow scratch.

"We seem to be at a stalemate, then," Zach replied easily, frowning slightly at the scrape as they circled around one another. Zach kicked a chair out of the way and Zella used that moment to lunge at him. Zach narrowly missed the thrust and knocked the blade to one side, pivoting and pushing her away from him yet again. He took a wide swipe at her midsection that had her sucking in her breath deeply to avoid being sliced. She growled and started a vicious counter attack.

Zach was moving his feet fluidly, the fairy wine giving him added dexterity that made the rapid pace bearable. He knew if he had engaged Zella while in his previous weakened state, he never would have gotten this far. She was fast, good, and pure Evil with the blades. He had several nicks on his arms and ribs, but took satisfaction in knowing he had given her as many as she'd given him. He'd actually been worried that he wouldn't be able to attack or harm a woman, but strangely her gender didn't matter to him in the heat of the battle. She was Evil, and that was the only label that mattered to him.

Zach danced out of the way of a particularly rapid series of thrusts, and suddenly felt the rapid sting of claws and teeth at his back. Without his realizing it, Zella had backed him directly into the path of the giant ferret that was still chained to the wall. Zella was grinning at him with satisfaction, watching her pet attack him with animal vengeance.

Quickly, Zach reversed the one blade in his hand, stabbing the ferret that was trying to claw its way up his back to his vulnerable neck. The beast went limp behind him. The other blade, Zach brought up high over his head to forestall Zella's next blow.

The steel rang like a bell. It was the fairy sword, Zach realized, that was keeping his head intact and attached to his body. Using his superior upper body strength, he pushed Zella from him and rolled to one side, coming up on his feet gracefully.

The ferret was dead. Zach spared it but a glance before returning his attention to Zella. She was staring at the beast with a strange expression on her face. It was almost like...grief.

"He was my brother," she whispered.

"Excuse me?" Zach strained his ears, certain he had heard her wrong.

Her response was a roar of feminine anguish. Then she was advancing on him again, a Fury in black vinyl, metal blades and snarls. Zach found himself slipping into a purely mechanical mode, parrying and shoving, swiping and thrusting as they worked their way across the floor. All his training and experience during the filming seemed to flow from him without effort, and it was what he needed while trying to figure out a way to regain the upper hand.

Zella reached up and snagged one of the chains that had been holding Zach, swinging it at his head with a surprising amount of power and velocity. Zach ducked the chain, which left him vulnerable for a split second. Realizing the weakness in his stance, he twisted his blade up and over his shoulder, just in time. Her sword came down, and if not for the blade he'd positioned, his neck would have been severed. As it was, her sword still nicked his shoulder.

Zach levered her sword up and away, rolling backwards and coming up with both swords crossed. She prowled in front of him, swinging her swords in circles by the wrist, eying him with speculation.

"You're quite good," Zella acknowledged. She wasn't even breathing heavy from the exertion.

"You're quite good," he repeated, adding with a cocky grin and a waggle of his eyebrows, "but I'm better."

"I drew first blood," she reminded him, cocking one eyebrow in his direction.

"Doesn't matter who draws first blood," Zach retorted with feeling. "What matters is who draws the last."

"Do you really think you can kill a woman?" she mocked. "Your misguided honor won't allow that at all."

"You aren't a woman," Zach replied evenly. "You could be a Hollywood agent with your appetites but you aren't a woman. I'm really not sure what you are, but I'm beginning to get a good idea."

Zella pouted, the red slick of her lips pursing, the green of her eyes flashing in the dim light. "I'm beyond your reckoning, Zach. Me, and my kind, we are going to dance on the bones of your race and civilization. We are all that you cannot be, and we will not fail in our mission."

Enough chit-chat, Zach thought. Time to get this over and done with. Hopefully the others were far enough away that they'd escape harm from the fortress explosion. He squared off against Zella, steeling mind and body for the coming attack. "Actually, I find you rather boring," he replied, knowing it would incite the woman. An angry opponent was often one who would let their guard down. "I find I want this farce over with, once and for all." Then he launched his offensive, one sword arching to the head, the other to the belly.

Everything seemed to coalesce into this moment…all his anger and frustration at his prettified life, all the angst and fear that he was going to be alone forever, all the panic and protectiveness over Liz and the others fleeing the temple. He was but one purpose, and that was to beat Zella down. She was the epitome of all that he feared and hated and despised. She represented the biggest threat to his loved ones… his family. His real family, the family of his heart. It was as though the past was siphoning out of him, leaving him filled with the purpose of a Protector of the Land…and all those who came with it. Despite knowing them for a short period of time, Zach felt a sense of homecoming the likes of which he'd never experienced in all his years and travels. No matter what, those people at the adjacent beach house would care for him, look out for him, help him. He was certain of it. The warmth of their love spread through him like the fairy wine and he was buoyed by their unspoken, unseen presence. It centered in his chest and radiated throughout his system, giving him strength and resolve to get this job done.

They had his back. All the Protectors who'd come before, and those that would come after. It was more than a group, it was…a community. One that he belonged to with all his formidable heart and soul, even if his time in that group was destined to be limited.

"It ends now."

He engaged Zella with a ferocity that seemed to shock the woman… something Zach had a feeling she'd never encountered before. Being Zella, however, she recovered quickly and met him midway.

Zella countered his aggressive attack with both of her swords, her arms straining with the effort. The steel of the blades sang as they rippled up and down one another. Zach continued to press inward on his swords, feeling her give ever so slightly in response.

Quickly, he released the pressure on the swords. Zella, caught unawares, stumbled slightly. Zach hesitated only a heartbeat, then, remembering the limp hand of the little girl, plunged the fairy's sword deep into her chest. A fountain of blackish red blood gushed forth. When droplets of it touched Zach's skin it burned like acid.

Zella gave an unearthly scream, buckling off the sword, her blades dropping to the ground with a clatter.

Zach kicked her swords to one side, well out of the way, and stepped back, watching her dispassionately, his own swords still held in either hand.

Zella sank to the floor, her hands coming to her chest. They pulled away, covered in a blackish red liquid. Snarling, she launched herself at Zach, her hands curled like claws.

He sidestepped easily, and Zella sprawled to the floor, face down. The lines of her body blurred, becoming fuzzy. In the blink of an eye, she morphed into a ferret, large and black and very much dead.

"I thought so," Zach said with satisfaction, sheathing his swords. He felt dizzy and lightheaded. The fairy wine, he figured, was loosing its potency. Then the floor beneath him began to quake and shake.

"Well Neol," Zach said to himself. "I guess this is it."

The floor buckled as a roar seemed to build up from several stories below. The ceiling overhead cracked, stone raining down into the room. Zach sidestepped one particularly large piece, then felt the explosion in the very soles of his feet.

The next instant he was being flung into the air, flying higher and higher into the impossibly deep blue sky of the Land. The force of the explosion was incredible, the heat chasing him into the sky.

He was certainly going a long way up, Zach thought idly. That would make the descent rather, well, interesting. As he continued to ascend, a thought surfaced to his mind, a memory really. Dancing the tango with Liz in the basement of the beach house.

Ah. It was a good memory. One he'd take with him. He just wished he'd had a chance to dance with her one more time.

His body finished the final arch, achieving the highest point in the curve and started the inevitable descent.

Suddenly there was a tremendous jerking on his arm. The force of the grab was enough to have his already strained muscles screeching in protest, the bone in his shoulder popping with a wrenching rip of pain.

Zach looked up in astonishment. There was an open trapdoor in the sky. Framed in the door was a bearded man wearing a flannel shirt over a white t-shirt, a baseball cap placed backwards on his shoulder length dark brown hair. The man was holding onto Zach's wrist with a grip of steel.

"Hey there," the man said in a congenial voice.

-27-
Into the Void

"Hey," Zach replied automatically.

He looked down, seeing the smoking ruin of the fortress far below him, the green meadows stretching out on either side. He was literally hanging in the sky, held by the man in the trapdoor.

"Let's get you up and out before all hell breaks loose," the man said, pulling Zach up by one arm as easily as if he were a child.

As Zach cleared the doorway, he found himself in an alien environment, where the floor, walls and ceiling were a pure, soft white. "There you go," the man said, setting Zach on the ground, then reaching out to steady him as Zach swayed slightly. "Easy there, bucko." He sniffed. "Hey, you've had some fairy wine. Well. I guess that explains a lot."

Zach watched as the man lowered the trapdoor, which closed seamlessly, not a hint of a handle remaining. Brushing his hands off briskly, the man turned to Zach.

"I'm Daniel," he said politely, holding out his hand. "Grid Manager around these parts."

Zach shook it as the walls behind Daniel shimmered and thousands of fairies came into view, their jeweled wings glittering in the light. Daniel jerked his thumb over his shoulder at them. "And those are the ten thousand fairies that would have killed me if I allowed your ass to go splat all over the Meadows Region."

Daniel leaned in towards Zach, lowering his voice to a conspirator level. "You've got to watch the charisma thing you've got going," he confided to Zach, "they're impossible whenever you're around."

"They like my pretty heart," Zach said dumbly, still feeling massively confused. Was he dead?

"Ah, well, that's what they say," Daniel replied with a grin, "but I've got the purest soul around and you don't see them pining over my sorry corporeal form." He clapped Zach on the back, making the larger man stumble. "Whoops, sorry, forgot about the fact that you are pert near spent." Daniel apologized while again steadying Zach. The fairies tittered and flew around the Void, dipping close to the men.

"What is happening?" Zach asked finally. One fairy, Scarlet it turned out to be, settled herself on Zach's shoulder, sighing happily.

"A moment," Daniel held up his hand. Then he put his fingers in his mouth and gave a sharp whistle. A pair of fairies separated from the pack. "Tell Amber she'll have an incoming in Sector 9B," he told them. The fairies zoomed off.

"Well, it's like this," Daniel said, using his hands as he spoke. "Evil keeps bending the rules. They are not supposed to take up permanent residency in a dimension unless the dimension is a certain percentage Evil. Obviously the Land is not at that kind of ratio. So technically, we could argue that Zella's fortress was a violation of those rules. Now, Evil will argue that the structure was a temporary residence, for the express purpose of kidnapping the child Seer. The way I see it, that's just semantics. You killed Zella—huge thumbs up for that, by the way—and therefore you should live. But she rigged her fortress to blow and that, my friend, is just not fair."

"Uh-huh," Zach said dully. "I think I got that."

"So I'm going to drop you back into the World Dimension," Daniel informed Zach easily. "I have to warn you, it's not going to be an easy ride. You'll have to free fall a long way before you reach the ground."

"And no parachute, I'm guessing," replied Zach.

"Nah. No can do. But I can drop you over water, where there is a slim chance you could survive. I'll do all I can to make sure you get to the water alive. It's the best I can offer." Daniel conceded. "So here's the choice. I can let you back into the Land, where you will undoubtedly splatter over a good quarter acre of the Meadows, or I can drop you into the water of the World dimension and we can all hope that the

Protectors find you before you sink. Your choice." He finished with a quick nod of his head.

Zach snorted. "Duh. Water."

"Thought so. This way, then."

They started to walk across the white space, the fairies trailing behind, their conversation a constant rain of noise chiming musically in his ears. With each step, Zach felt the fairy wine effects fading. He was feeling every ache, every pain, every cut and every strain. In addition, the lack of sleep and food was definitely getting him, making his brain fuzzy and confused. He knew he should be asking Daniel questions, pumping him for information in case he should survive the coming fall, but just didn't have it in him to be coherent. He had no idea how long they had been walking, when finally Daniel paused.

"Ok, then." The man said, bending down and pulling up a section of the floor. Zach leaned out and saw, far below, a grayish blue expanse of ocean. It was a long, long way down, Zach realized, swallowing heavily. This was gonna hurt like a sonofabitch.

"I hope I gave the Protectors enough time," Daniel commented as he also looked down at the sea far below, then smacked his forehead. "That reminds me, you need to have this." He pulled out a necklace from his jeans pocket. It looked like a white plastic chain, from which dangled a round white pendant, completely smooth and clear, save for a small red stone impeded deep within the material. Daniel slipped it over Zach's head. "I know you guys usually get this from the Prince, but since you aren't going back to the Land—smart choice, by the way—I figured I should give it to you. I know I could have Ben do it, but what the hell. When do I get a chance like this, to give one of you guys the necklace?"

"This is a Protector necklace?" Zach said dubiously, fingering the smooth plastic pendant.

"Of course it is. Looks different depending on where you are located. And hey, I don't think you dudes understand how important these necklaces are." The Grid Manager tapped the pendant. "These are your most important protection in the World Dimension. Make sure that you and the others never, and I mean never, lose them. Capice?"

"Yes," Zach replied, fisting the pendant in his hand. It was warm, or his fingers were growing cold. He couldn't tell which. "Don't lose the pendants. Got it."

"All righty then. Off you go," Daniel said, then snapped his fingers. "Oh, and tell Amber when she comes to visit to bring more pulled barbecue pork." He smacked his lips appreciatively. "Can't get enough of that stuff, ya know what I mean? Oh, and hush puppies, too. Love me some hush puppies."

As Zach looked at Daniel incredulously, the man gave him a sharp shove, sending him through the door and tumbling to the ocean below.

Zach felt himself falling through the sky. The water below was rushing up towards him frighteningly fast. He'd parachuted before and had enjoyed the experience. This, not so much. When he hit the water, the salt in his open wounds made him yelp in pain and shock. He flailed his arms, trying to keep afloat. The gentle swells of waves were washing over him, pushing him about like a cork.

Zach tried to float on his back, but kept slipping beneath the surface as his strength failed him again and again. He would fight his way to the air above only to have the ocean pull him back under repeatedly.

He was drowning, Zach realized with some surprise but no real shock. He was simply too tired to keep swimming. He wondered if it wouldn't be easier to just give in to the temptation to sink, but then found himself thrashing and kicking, trying to reach the surface one last time.

A hand closed around his waist, propelling him up. Zach turned his face to see Ben Harm swimming beside him, dressed in a wetsuit and wearing an expression of grim determination. They broke the surface together, Zach gasping and Ben breathing as easily above the waves as he had below. Zach tried to flounder and keep himself afloat.

"Lay back and relax," Ben shouted to Zach over the sound of the ocean. "You hit the water pretty hard. We have Jet Skis. Sasha and Steven will bring them over and we'll get you on board. Until then, I'll keep you above the surface. Relax, buddy. I got you."

Zach nodded wearily. He'd never been so glad to see someone in his entire life. It was a relief to surrender his well being to someone he trusted. Trust. What an amazing thing.

The sound of a motor reached his ears. Sasha was on her jet ski, while Steven on another one was maneuvering closer to Zach.

"He's bleeding pretty badly," Zach heard Ben say to Steven. "We need to get him out of the water before he attracts every shark between here and Key West."

Steven nodded and reached down. It took both men, but finally Zach was on the back of the Jet Ski, holding onto Steven for dear life. He rolled his head to look at Sasha, who was waiting patiently for Ben to climb on board behind her.

"Damn, you do amazing things to that wetsuit," Zach croaked at her, giving her a grin.

Sasha shook her head in dismay. "Half dead and you're still flirting."

"Yeah," he agreed. "Some things never change."

She smiled back at him. "Glad you're home, Zach," she said, gunning the engine of the Jet Ski and heading towards the shore, which was still a long way away.

"Hang on," Steven advised Zach, secretly worried that the man was too weak to maintain a grip over the breakers.

In the distance a huge spear of swirling black and white rose into the sky. Lighthouse, Zach realized. Daniel appeared to have dropped Zach in the rather isolated stretch of the Hatteras National Park, a narrow spit of land that was rarely visited this time of day or year. Thank goodness for small favors.

Zach was not ashamed to admit that he was leaning onto Steven's bulk gratefully, half unconscious. The ride to the shallows was mercifully short, but incredibly rough. Every bounce, every jostle had him groaning. Finally, Steven cut the engine.

"We can't go through the breakers up ahead on these," he explained to Zach. "Owen's coming out to take our Jet Ski, then he and Sasha will get them to the marina. You, Ben, and I are going to head into shore. We'll help you, so don't worry. William's waiting for you with his medical kit, so hang on. We're almost home free."

"Liz?" Zach said, the one word wrenching from deep within him.

"She's on the beach." It was Ben talking now. He was again in the water, treading next to the Jet Ski. The waves were continually lifting them, making Zach's stomach roil unpleasantly. Owen's dark head was bobbing alongside the Jet Ski, ready to take over for Steven. "Along with the others. Come on. Let's get you home, Zach."

Home. Zach slipped into the water, and although it should have been a blow to his ego, he felt no shame acknowledging that it was only with Ben and Steven's help that he managed to get past the breakers. Finally, his feet were on the sand beneath the surf, the stuff slipping and sliding with the ebb and flow of the salty water. He was being supported between the two men, his arms around their shoulders, slogging through the long stretch of surf that extended to the shore. The water was up to their waists, and the waves continued to crash into them in regular pulses.

William met them half way to the beach, ripping off the cap of a syringe with his mouth and sinking it into Zach's bicep.

"Well, hello to you, too," Zach managed to say as a second shot hit home.

"Tetanus and antibiotics," William explained, running critical eyes over Zach. "I think the rest can wait until you get ashore."

Over William's shoulder, Zach could see the group of Protectors clustered on the beach. A tall, slender form separated from the group, rushing down to the edge of the surf.

Just seeing her was as effective as chugging a mini shot of fairy wine. As adrenaline raced through his body, Zach pushed past William and half stumbled, half ran to Liz. She was wearing one of those filmy sundresses she favored, the hem of it wet from the foam of the sea at her ankles. Her hair was long and flowing, her face wreathed with smiles and tears.

Without a word, without a second of hesitation, Zach pulled her into his arms, crushing her against him, his lips on hers like a dying man slaking his thirst. Her arms wrapped around his waist, squeezing him equally tight. The kiss lasted an eternity, yet it was not nearly enough for him. It was, he knew in his heart, only the beginning.

His hand delved into her hair, pulling her closer to him. She laid her head on his shoulder, her tears mingling with the salt water that was covering him, one hand fingering the silvery chain around his neck. Zach blew out a deep breath, his eyes raising to the sky in silent benediction. Together, they turned and walked to the beach, the men helping whenever Zach threatened to pitch face first into the ocean.

As soon as his feet cleared the water, Zach found himself surrounded by the Protectors. A towel was thrown around his shoulders, a water bottle was pressed into his hand. Katie was passing her Oracle glowing hands over the knot on his head, possibly the worst lingering injury he had from the encounter with Zella. When the pain eased he groaned gratefully. Tracy unbelted the swords from about his waist, assuring Zach they would take good care of them. After the isolation of the past few days, having people pamper him was a welcome, yet overwhelming, relief.

Yet time and again, his eyes would seek out Liz's. She was always watching him steadily, her topaz eyes serious. Finally, she stepped forward.

"Zach needs to get home," she said decisively. "After a good, long, hot shower, William can give him a thorough examination."

"Liz is right," agreed Katie. "If we stay on the beach, we might garner attention. It would be hard to explain some of these injuries to the local state troopers." Her fingers hovered over a particularly rough patch on Zach's wrist where the shackle had rubbed the skin raw, her cornflower blue eyes hardening with anger at the thought of how those injuries must have come about.

Zach was grateful for Ben and Steven quietly taking up a place on either side of him. His muscles were close to total rebellion, and he knew he would need their support.

Zach was soon ensconced in the back seat of a large SUV. Liz climbed in next to him and shut the door. Then she reached over and guided him down so that he was lying across the seat, his head in her lap. He sighed with utter contentment. Odd how he'd never noticed how being in a safe place could be such a blessing.

"It will take about an hour to get home from here," Katie said as she started the car. "I'll keep it as steady as possible." William got into the front passenger seat, ready to help should Zach go into a delayed shock, his icy blue eyes raking over Zach's body with cool clinical detachment before turning back to speak with Katie quietly.

As the car moved forward, the rumble of the road and vehicle, combined with his position on the bench seat made Zach feel like he was cocooned somewhere alone with Liz, who was watching him with a tender expression. He sighed with contentment, allowing his muscles to fully relax. This was…heaven.

"Do you want to know something?" Liz asked him quietly, smoothing the hair from his forehead.

"What?" he asked drowsily, turning his face to nuzzle her hand when it paused a moment. The stroking continued and he sighed contentedly.

"When I was in the Land, the Seer gave me a reading. She said that I would find my peace and my place with the eternal bird. The Seer thought that meant my astral projection, but I never thought that was the case." Liz's fingers were soothing and Zach felt he was floating along on her words. "The first time I saw you, on the beach after you almost clocked me, I knew. I knew the reading meant you. And it scared me to death. I thought it was too big for me, too soon, too instinctive. I thought I'd found the person before, and it ended with disastrous results."

"That wasn't your fault." Zach said softly.

"I know. But now, when I think back, I realize that when I first heard about the Land, I thought that it was too big for me to handle. When I heard that I was a Seer, I thought that was too much for me to be expected to do. Then when Evil was brought into the mix, I figured that he was too overwhelming for little ole me." Liz tilted her head as she looked down at Zach, whose topaz flecked blue eyes were watching her with intensity.

"Now? What do you think now?"

"I know that it isn't a matter of these things being too big for me to handle. It's a matter of my being big enough to handle them. And I am. If I'm capable of handling the Land, being a Seer, and fighting Evil, well then, being in love with you shouldn't be so hard, after all." Liz smiled down at him. "Because I am in love with you, Zachary Neol."

Zach sighed happily. "About time you realized that," he said, turning his head to press his lips to her wrist.

"I might have to go back, Zach. I might have to go to the Land." She didn't dare tell him about the vision she'd had months ago, of her leaving the World Dimension, regardless of the wedding band she'd had on her finger. But now…maybe the rescue of the little Seer would change that possible future. Perhaps. Zach needed to know the possibilities.

"I'd be upset with you if you were called and didn't go. My love can handle you going to the Land, Liz. It can handle anything but you not giving it a try."

"That's enough for you?"

"Your love is enough."

He fell silent for several moments, simply relishing being alive. He had Daniel to thank for that fact, he knew. Then his eyes flew open.

"Oh, shit! Before I forget… Amber needs to take Daniel more barbeque and hush puppies."

"We'll make sure she knows," Liz said with a chuckle. And another thing," Liz leaned over and whispered into his ear, "You owe me a dance."

"Do me a favor," Zach murmured, closing his eyes in contentment. "Wake me up for Sasha and William's wedding, and we'll dance then."

"Sounds like a plan," Liz promised as in the front seat of the car, Katie and William exchanged smiles.

***

Dance they did, on the beach as the sun set behind the house. Close and slow, their bodies in tune with one another and with their love shining for all around them to see, Liz and Zach danced as if the world had winnowed down to just the two of them.

Chinese lanterns decorated the dance area, tables and chairs set right on the sand. The wedding had been performed, rings exchanged, the kiss bestowed. The Protectors and their loved ones engaged in the ancient ritual of toasting the bride and groom.

Sasha, radiant in her soft white dress with flowing sleeves and low, scooped neckline and William in his crisp blue suit, kicked off their shoes and in the groom's case, his jacket, to race into the shallows of the ocean. Laughing, William scooped up his bride and swung her in a circle, her dress flowing out as they moved. Then William tripped and they both went crashing down into the surf, still laughing hysterically. When William tried to stand back up, Sasha retaliated by yanking him back into the surf along with her, kissing him soundly.

The rest of the Protectors waded in after them, splashing and laughing along with them.

All Things Great and Small

From Entertainment Wow! Magazine:

"When I entered the hotel suite to interview the newly reclusive movie star Zach Neol, I wasn't sure what to expect. After all, the man has virtually disappeared from the radar of Hollywood. In fact, if not for the release of his mega block buster " *The Phoenix*" onto a special edition DVD, I doubt he would have deigned to do the interview at all.

"Entering the suite, I was greeted by the gorgeous Mr. Neol, who was dressed in a simple outfit of blue jeans and white button down shirt, the latter contrasting his deep tan. The blue eyes were as sharp and brilliant as ever, the smile easy going and devastatingly sexy. Zach shook hands with me and we settled by the windows of the hotel, which overlooked the town that Zach has, for all intense purposes, abandoned.

EW: So what have you been up to, Zach?

ZN: Not much.

EW: I'll say. We haven't heard much about you lately. Since your appearance at the Oscars last March, you have been pretty much incognito.

ZN: As much as I can be, I guess. (He adds a philosophical shrug)

EW: You must be thrilled with the pre-sales of *The Phoenix* DVD.

ZN: Well, it's always appreciated when the public likes your work. And I know that the unavoidable delay in getting the disc out was frustrating to many fans. I just appreciate their patience while we made sure that the extra scenes were executed with the kind of detail that the original film embodied.

EW: So what's next for Zachary Neol?

ZN: (laughs) Hanging out with my friends, enjoying life, being normal.

EW: It's hard to be normal when your face is plastered all over magazines and tabloids.

ZN: Well, I learned a long time ago that I have no control over what other people think or say about me. It just doesn't matter any longer.

EW: Your estrangement from your parents has provided a great deal of press fodder lately. Do you have any comment on that?

ZN: (frowns slightly, picking at the knee of his jeans as he thinks for a long moment about his answer) I really don't know what to say about that. They want to have a relationship with me based solely on my acting. I wanted to have a relationship that's about being a family. When you have such diametrically opposed viewpoints, it's difficult to find a common ground.

EW: What about your agent? You fired him pretty summarily, but there has been no word about who you are signing with to represent you in the future. What gives?

ZN: Again, I think it was a matter of divergent and polar opposite ideas of what I'm going to do with my life. I see no reason to have an agent, because I see no need for me to be an actor at the moment.

EW: You're retiring, then?

ZN: I don't consider it retiring. I'm just moving on to other work. Work that's not in the entertainment field. (Rubs his chin) It's intensely private and personal, so I choose not to say anything more than don't expect me to be in a movie or television anytime soon.

EW: Speaking of private and personal…

ZN: (interrupting) Oh boy, here we go.

EW: (laughing) Well, you brought it up, not me. What about your personal life? There were some interesting tabloid shots of you with a variety of women recently.

ZN: Those are some amazing friends that I've met recently. It rather amused them, and their husbands, to be linked romantically with me in the tabloids. We get a kick out of it. There's a tally going on, and I think they're competing to see who can be linked with me the most. It's kind of funny. As funny as that kind of intrusion can be, that is.

EW: So there's no one special is in your life?

ZN: (Flashes that famous Zach Attack smile) I didn't say that.

Almost on cue, the door to the suite opens. A tall, slender woman with long blondish brown hair and amazing whiskey colored eyes glided into the room. Possessing a Grace Kelly kind of beauty, made approachable by the liberal sprinkle of freckles across her nose, she should have been wearing a marabou trimmed gown instead of jeans and t-shirt with a wizard rock star band emblazoned across the front. She was startled to find this reporter ensconced with Zach. When she started to leave, Zach stopped her, gesturing her over to his side. Up close, her face was even more arresting and serene.

ZN: What's up, Sugar?

Mystery Guest: I was just going to remind you that we're meeting everyone for dinner soon. I didn't realize you were still working.

ZN: No worries. I'll be done here soon. Concert afterwards?

MG: If you want to go.

ZN: Wouldn't miss your favorite band for the world, sugar.

Zach kissed the woman's hand, their eyes meeting with a sense of intimacy and love that was palatable. After she glided from the room, Zach turned back to me, one eyebrow arching as I dramatically patted my heart.

EW: Wow. That seemed like the real deal.

ZN: It is.

EW: Does she have a name?

ZN: Sure she does. And if she ever wants to give it, fine. But it won't come from my lips. What we have is intensely private and personal, and I won't discuss it. Not now, not ever.

EW: When did you meet?

ZN: A few months ago at a friend's wedding. It was an instant thing for us.

EW: That's pretty quick.

ZN: (shrugs and opens his hands helplessly) When you know, you know. Why fight it?

EW: So you're in love, and walking away from a red hot career. Can you exist without the limelight that has been a part of your life for as long as you can remember?

ZN: (again the thoughtful look) There are more important things than the limelight. And in all honesty, I haven't been content with the entertainment field for years. The decision to leave was not based on my relationship; it is based on me and my need to have more in my life.

EW: So your life is full?

ZN: The mythical cup runneth over, darlin'. And I wouldn't have it any other way.

Zach ended the interview then, looking longingly at the door through which the woman had left, the love on his face transforming his rugged movie star looks into something much more profound and beautiful. It appears, dear readers, that Zachary Neol has found his place in life. And it seems to be, sadly for us, far away from the silver screen. I found as I shook hands with him after our interview, that I was wishing him the best of luck as if I would never see him in the public eye again.

I think I was right about that assessment.

-The End-